ROGER ZELAZNY

ISLE OF THE DEAD

EYE OF CAT

ROGER ZELAZNY authored many science fiction and fantasy classics, and won three Nebula awards and six Hugo awards over the course of his long and distinguished career. While he is best known for his ten-volume Chronicles of Amber series of novels (beginning with 1970's *Nine Princes in Amber*), Zelazny also wrote many other novels, short stories, and novellas, including *Psychoshop* (with Alfred Bester), *Damnation Alley*, the award-winning *The Doors of His Face, The Lamps of His Mouth* and *Lord of Light*, and the stories "24 Views of Mount Fuji, by Hokusai," "Permafrost," and "Home is the Hangman." Zelazny died in Santa Fe, New Mexico, in June 1995.

ISLE OF THE DEAD

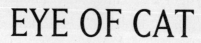

EYE OF CAT

ROGER ZELAZNY

ibooks
new york
www.ibooksinc.com

DISTRIBUTED BY SIMON & SCHUSTER

EYE OF CAT. 7

ISLE OF THE DEAD 257

EYE OF CAT

For Joe Leaphorn,
Jimmy Chee
and Tony Hillerman

At the door to the House of Darkness
   lies a pair of red coyotes with heads reversed.
Nayenezgani parts them with his dark staff
   and comes in search of me.
With lightning behind him,
   with lightning before him,
   he comes in search of me,
with a rock crystal and a talking ketahn.

Beyond, at the corners by the door
   of the House of Darkness,
lie two red bluejays with heads reversed.
With lightning behind him,
   with lightning before him,
he parts them with his dark staff
   and comes in search of me.

Farther, at the fire-pit of the Dark House,
   lie two red hoot-owls with heads reversed.
He parts these with his staff
   and comes in search of me,
   with rock crystal and talking ketahn.

At the center of the Darkness House
   where two red screech-owls lie with heads reversed,
Nayenezgani casts them aside
   coming in search of me,
   lightning behind him,
   lightning before him.
Bearing a rock crystal and a talking ketahn,
   he comes for me.
From the center of the earth he comes.

Farther . . .

Evil-Chasing Prayer

PART I

Night, near the eastern edge of the walled, sloping grounds of the estate, within these walls, perhaps a quarter-mile from the house itself, at the small stand of trees, under a moonless sky, listening, he stands, absolutely silent.

Beneath his boots, the ground is moist. A cold wind tells him that winter yields but grudgingly to spring in upstate New York. He reaches out and touches the dark line of a slender branch to his right, gently. He feels the buds of the fresh year's green, dreaming of summer beneath his wide, dark hand.

He wears a blue velveteen shirt hanging out over his jeans, a wide concha belt securing it at his waist. A heavy squash blossom necklace—a very old one—hangs down upon his breast. High about his neck is a slender strand of turquoise *heiche*. He has a silver bracelet on his left wrist, studded with random chunks of turquoise and coral. The buttons of his shirt are hammered dimes from the early twentieth century. His long hair is bound with a strip of red cloth.

Tall, out of place, out of time, he listens for that which may or may not become audible: indication of the strange struggle at the dark house. No matter how the encounter goes, he, William Blackhorse Singer, will be the loser. But this is his own thing to bear, from a force he set into motion long ago, a *chindi* which has dogged his heels across the years.

He hears a brief noise from the direction of the house, followed immediately by a loud crashing. This does not end it, however. The sounds continue. From somewhere out over the walls, a coyote howls.

He almost laughs. A dog, certainly. Though it sounds more like the other, to which he has again become accustomed. None of them around here, of course.

William Blackhorse Singer. He has other names, but the remembering machines know him by this one. It was by this one that they summoned him.

The sounds cease abruptly, and after a short while begin again. He estimates that it must be near midnight in this part of the world. He looks to the skies, but Christ's blood does not stream in the firmament. Only Ini, the bird of thunder among the southwestern stars, ready with his lightning, clouds and rain, extending his headplume to tickle the nose of Sas, the bear, telling him it is time to bring new life to the earth, there by the Milky Way.

Silence. Sudden, and stretching pulsebeat by pulse-beat to fill his world. Is it over? Is it really over?

Again, short barks followed by the howling. Once he had known many things to do, still knew some of them. All are closed to him now, but for the waiting.

No. There is yet a thing with which to fill it.

Softly, but with growing force, he begins the song.

First man was not exactly jumping with joy over the dark underworld in which he was created. He shared it with eight other humans, and the ants and the beetles and later the locusts whom they encountered as they explored, and Coyote—the First Angry One, He-who-was-formed-in-the-water, Scrawny Wanderer. Everyone multiplied; and the dragonflies, the wasps and the bat people later joined them; and Spider Man and Spider Woman. The place grew crowded and was full of bugs. Strife ensued.

"Let's get out of here," a number of them suggested.

First Man, who was wise and powerful, fetched his treasures of White Shell, Turquoise, Abalone, Jet and the Red-White Stone.

He placed the White Shell in the east and breathed upon it. Up from it rose a white tower of cloud. He placed the Turquoise to the south and breathed upon it. From it there rose a blue cloud tower. To the west he set the Abalone, and when he had breathed upon it a yellow cloud tower rose up in that place. To the north he set the Jet, and touched by his breath it sent up a black tower of cloud. The white and the yellow grew, met overhead and crossed, as did the blue and the black. These became the Night and the Day.

Then he placed the Red-White Stone at the center and breathed upon it. From it there rose a many-colored tower.

The tower to the east was called Folding Dawn; that to the south was called Folding Blue Sky; to the west, Folding Twilight; that to the north, Folding Darkness. One by one, Coyote visited each of them, changing his color to match their own. For this reason, he is known as Child of the Dawn, as Child of the Blue Sky, Child of the Twilight and Child of Darkness, along with all his other names. At each of these places, his power was increased.

While the towers of the four cardinal points were holy, giving birth to the prayer rites, the central one bore all pains, evils and diseases. And it was this tower up which First Man and Coyote led the People, bringing them into the second world; and, of course, along with them, the evils.

There they explored and they met with others, and First Man fought with many, defeating them all and taking their songs of power.

But this also was a place of suffering, of misery, a thing Coyote discovered as he went to and fro in the world and up and down it. And so to First Man he took the pleas that they depart.

First Man made a white smoke and blew it to the east, then swallowed it again—and the same in every direction. This removed all the evils from the world and brought them back to the People from whence they had come. Then he laid Lightning, both jagged and straight, to the east, and Rainbow and Sunlight, but nothing occurred. He moved them to the south, the west and the north. The world trembled but brought forth no power to bear them upward. He made then a wand of Jet, Turquoise, Abalone and White Shell. Atop this, he set the Red-White Stone. It rose and bore them upward into the next world.

Here they met the many snakes, and Salt Man and Woman and Fire God. Nor should Spider Ant be forgotten. And light and darkness came up from the towers of the four colors, as in the other worlds.

But then First Man set a streak of yellow and another of red and yellow in the east, and these halted the movement of the white light.

And the People were afraid. Salt Man counseled them to explore in the east, but the streaks retreated as they advanced. Then they heard a voice summoning them to the south. There they found the old man Dontso, called Messenger Fly, who told them what First Man had done. The yellow streak, he said, represented the emergence of the People; the other, vegetation and pollen, with the red part indicating all diseases.

Then Owl and Kit Fox and Wolf and Wildcat came, and with them Horned Rattlesnake, who offered First Man the shell he carried on his head—and promises of offerings of White Shell, Turquoise, Abalone and Jet in the future. First Man accepted the shell and its magic and removed the streaks from the sky.

The People then realized that First Man was evil. Coyote spied upon their counsels and reported to First Man that they knew he had stopped the light in the east to gain a treasure.

When later they confronted him with it, First Man replied, "Yes. It is true, grandchildren. Very true. I am evil. Yet I have employed my evil on your behalf. For these offerings shall benefit all of us. And I do know when to withhold my evil from those about me."

And he proceeded to prove this thing by building the first medicine hogan, where he shared with them his knowledge of things good and evil.

He remembered the party the night before he had found the coyote.

Garbed in the rented splendor of a shimmering synthetic-fibered foursquare and blackrib Pleat & Ruffle evegarb, he had tripped through to the mansion in Arlington. Notables past and present filled the sparkling, high-ceilinged rooms. He was decidedly Past, but he had gone anyway, to see a few old friends, to touch that other life again.

A middle-aged woman of professional charm greeted him, approached him, embraced him and spoke with him for half a minute in the enthusiastic voice of a newscaster, until a fresh arrival at his back produced a reflex pressure from her hand upon his arm, directing him to the side.

Grateful, he moved off; accepting a drink from a tray, glancing at faces, nodding to some, pausing to exchange a few words, working his way to a small room he recalled from previous visits.

He sighed when he entered. He liked the wood and iron, stone and rough plaster, books and quiet pictures, the single window with its uninterrupted view of the river, the fireplace burning softly.

"I knew you'd find me here," she said, from her chair near the hearth.

He smiled.

"So did I—in the only room built during a lapse in taste-lessness."

He drew up a chair, seating himself near her but facing slightly past her toward the fire. Her heavy, lined face, the bright blue eyes beneath white hair, her short stocky figure, had not changed recently. In some ways she was the older, in others she was not. Time had played its favorite game—irony—with them both. He thought of the century-old

Fontenelle and Mme. Grimaud, almost as old as he. Yet there was a gulf here of a different sort.

"Will you go collecting again soon?" she asked him.

"They've all the beasties they need for a while. I'm retired."

"Do you like it?"

"As well as anything."

Her brows tightened in a small wince.

"I can never tell whether it's native fatalism, world-weariness or a pose with you."

"I can't either, anymore," he said.

"Perhaps you're suffering from leisure."

"That's about as exclusive as rain these days. I exist in a private culture."

"Really. It can't be as bad as all that," she said.

"Bad? Good and evil are always mixed up. It provides order."

"Nothing else?"

"It is easy to love what is present and desire what is absent."

She reached out and squeezed his hand.

"You crazy Indian. Do you exist when I'm not here?"

"I'm not sure," he said. "I was a privileged traveler. Maybe I died and no one had the heart to tell me. How've you been, Margaret?"

After a time, she said, "Still living in an age of timidity, I suppose. And ideas."

He raised his drink and took a big swallow.

". . . Stale, flat and unprofitable," she said.

He raised the glass higher, holding it to the light, staring through it.

"Not that bad," he stated. "They got the vermouth right this time."

She chuckled.

"Philosophy doesn't change people, does it?" she asked.

"I don't think so."

"What are you going to do now?"

"Go and talk with some of the others, I guess, have a few more drinks. Maybe dance a little."

"I don't mean tonight."

"I know. Nothing special, I guess. I don't need to."

"A man like you should be doing something."

"What?"

"That's for you to say. When the gods are silent someone must choose."

"The gods are silent," he said, finally looking into her bright ancient eyes, "and my choices are all used up."

"That's not true."

He looked away again.

"Let it be," he said, "as you did before."

"Don't "

"I'm sorry."

She removed her hand from his. He finished his drink.

"Your character is your fate," she said at last, "and you are a creature of change."

"I live strategically."

"Maybe too much so."

"Let it be, lady. It's not on my worry-list. I've changed enough and I'm tired."

"Will even that last?"

"Sounds like a trick question to me. You had your chance. If I've an appointment with folly I'll keep it. Don't try to heal my wounds until you're sure they're there."

"I'm sure. You have to find something."

"I don't do requests."

". . . And I hope it's soon."

"I've got to take a little walk," he said. "I'll be back."

She nodded and he left quickly. She would too, shortly.

Later that evening his eyes suddenly traced a red strand in the rug and he followed it, to find himself near the trip-box.

"What the hell," he said.

He sought his hostess, thanked her and moved back to the transport unit. He pushed the coordinates, and as he entered he stumbled.

Freeze frame on man falling.

There was a time when the day light was night light.
Black-god rode upon my right shoulder.
Time spun moebius about me, as I sailed
up Darkness Mountain in the sky.
And the beasts, the beasts I hunted.
When I called them they would come to me,
out of Darkness Mountain.

It had snowed the previous night, dry and powdery, but the day had been unseasonably warm and much of it had melted. The sky was still clear as the sun retreated behind a dark rocky crest, and already the cold was coming back into the world, riding the wind that sighed among the pine trees.

Silvery strings of sunlight marked the higher sinews of a mesa far to the right, its foot already aswirl with gray in the first tides of evening. At least there would be no snow tonight, he knew, and he could watch the stars before he closed his eyes.

As he made his camp, the coyote limped after him, its left foreleg still bound. Tonight was the night to take care of that, too.

He built his fire and prepared his meal, the piñon smoke redolent in his nostrils. By the time that it was ready the day was gone, and the mesa and the ridge were but lumps of greater darkness against the night.

"Your last free meal," he said, tossing a portion of the food to the beast at his feet.

As they ate, he remembered other nights and other camps, a long trail of them stretching back over a century. Only this time there was nothing to hunt, and in a way this pleased him.

Drinking his coffee, he thought of the hundred-seventy years of his existence: how it had begun in this place, of the fairylands and hells through which he had taken it and how he had come—back. "Home," under the circumstances, would be more than an irony. He sipped the scalding brew from the metal cup, peopling the night with demons, most of whom now resided in San Diego.

Later, with his hunting knife, he removed the dressing from the animal's leg. It remained perfectly still as he did this, watching. As he cut away at the stiff material, he recalled the day some weeks before when he had come upon it, leg broken, in a trap. There had been a time when he would have acted differently. But he had released it, taken it home with him, treated it. And even this, this long trek into the Carrizos, was for the purpose of turning it free at a sufficient distance from his home, with a full night ahead to tempt it into wandering back to its own world, rather than prolonging an unnatural association.

He slapped its flank.

"Go on. Run!"

It rose, its movements still stiff, leg still held at an awkward angle. Only gradually did it lower the limb as it moved about the campsite. After a time, it passed into and out of the circle of firelight, remaining away for longer and longer periods.

As he prepared his bedroll, he was startled by a buzzing noise. Simultaneously, a red light began winking on the small plastic case which hung from his belt. He switched off the buzzer, but the light continued to blink. He shrugged and put it aside, face down. It indicated an incoming call at his distant home. He had gotten into the habit of wearing the unit when he was near the place and had forgotten to remove it. He never wore the more elaborate version, however, and so was not equipped to answer the call from here. This did not seem important. It had been several years since he had received anything which might be considered an important call.

Still, it troubled him as he lay regarding the stars. It had been a long while since he had received any calls at all. He wished now that he had either carried along the unit's other component or had not brought anything. But he was retired, his newsworthiness long vanished. It could not really be important. . . .

. . . He was traversing an orange plain beneath a yellow sky in which a massive white sun blazed. He was approaching an orange, pyramidal structure covered with a webwork of minute fractures. He drew near and halted, hurriedly setting up the projector. Then he commenced waiting, occasionally moving to tend another machine which produced a continuous record as the cracks grew. Time meant very little to him. The sun drifted slowly. Abruptly, one of the jagged lines widened and the structure opened. A wide-shouldered form covered with pink stubble rose up suddenly out of it, swaying, a raw, bristle-edged opening facing him forward of the bulbous projection at its top, beneath a dazzling red band of jewel-like knobs. He triggered the projector and a gleaming net was cast upon it. It struggled within it but could not come free. Its movements came to correspond with a faint drumming sound which might be his heartbeat. Now the entire world crashed and fell away and he was running, running into the east, younger self of his self, beneath a blue sky, past saltbush and sagebrush, clumps of scrub grass and chamisa, the sheep barely noting his passage, save for one which suddenly rose up, assuming all the colors of the dawn, swaying. . . . And then everything swam away on dark currents to the places where dreams dwell when they are not being used. . . .

Birdnotes and predawn stasis: he was cast up onto the shoals of sleep, into a world where time hung flexed at the edge of light. Frozen. His emerging awareness moved slowly over preverbal landscapes of thought he had quitted long ago. Or was it yesterday?

He awoke knowing that the call was important. He tended to his morning and removed all signs of his camp before the sun was fully risen. The coyote was nowhere in sight. He began walking. It had been a long time, too long for him to go further into the portent. His feelings, however, were another matter. He scrutinized them occasionally, but seldom examined them closely.

As he hiked across the morning, he considered his world. It was small again, as in the beginning, though this was a relative matter—relative to all the worlds he had traveled in. He moved now in the foothills of the Carrizo Mountains in Dinetah, the land of the Navajos, over twenty-five thousand square miles, much of it still grazing land, over a million and a half acres still wildland, bounded by the four sacred mountains—Debentsa in the north, Mount Taylor in the south, San Francisco Peaks in the west and Blanco Peak in the east, each with its stories and sacred meanings. Unlike many things he had known, Dinetah had changed only slowly, was still recognizable in this, the twenty-second century, as the place it had been in his boyhood. Returning to this land after so many years had been like traveling backward in time.

Yet there were differences between this day and that other. For one, his clan had always been a small one, and now he found himself its last survivor. While it was true that one is born a member of one's mother's clan but in a sense is also born for one's father's clan, his father had been a Taoseño and there had been very little contact with the pueblo. His father—a tall, sinewy man, an unusually gifted tracker, with more than a little Plains blood—had come to live in Dinetah, as was proper, tending his wife's flocks and hoeing her corn, until the day a certain restlessness overtook him.

Even so, it was not the lack of clan affiliation which had altered his life. A Navajo has great potential for personal contacts through the complex network of tribal interrelationships, so that even though all of the people he had known in his youth were likely dead, he might still find ready acceptance elsewhere. But he had returned with an Anglo wife and had not done this. He felt a momentary pang at the thought, though more than three years had passed since Dora's death.

It was more than that. A Navajo alone, on his own, away from the People, is said to be no longer a Navajo—and he felt that in a way this was true, though his mother, his grandmother and his great-grandmother were buried somewhere near the place where he now lived. He knew that he had changed, changed considerably, during the years away. Yet so had the People. While the land was little altered, they had lost many of the small things he remembered, small things adding up to something large. Paradoxically, then, he was on the one hand of an earlier era than his contemporaries, and on the other . . . He had walked beneath alien suns. He had tracked strange beasts, worthy of Monster-Slayer himself. He had learned the ways of the *bellicanos* and was not uncomfortable among them. There were degrees after his name, some of them earned. There was a library in his head, held firmly in the trained memory of one who had studied the chants of *yataalii*. More traditional yet more alien he found himself. He wanted to be alone, whatever he was.

He broke into an easy jog, telling himself that its purpose was to get the cold out of his bones. He ran past walls and outcrops of granite and sandstone, hillsides of piñon and juniper. Dead yuccas, their leaves touched with ice, lay like burned out stars nailed to the ground along his trail. The snow glinted on distant mountain peaks beneath a perfectly clear sky. Even after the cold had left him, he maintained his pace, deriving a kind of joy from the exertion.

The day wore on. He did not break his stride, however, until midmorning, when he halted for a brief meal upon a hillside commanding a long view down a narrow canyon where sheep grazed on dry grasses. In the distance, smoke rose from a conical, dirt-insulated hogan, its Pendleton-hung door facing him, there in the east.

An old man with a stick came out from behind a cluster of rocks, where he might have been resting while watching the sheep. Limping, he took a circuitous path which eventually brought him near.

"*Yá'át'ééh*," the man said, looking past him.

"*Yá'át'ééh*."

He asked the man to share his food, and they ate in silence for a time.

After a while, he asked the man's clan—it would have been impolite to ask his name—and learned that he was of the Rabbit Redwater People. He always found it easier to talk with the older people than the younger ones, those who lived far out rather than near the cities.

Eventually the man asked him his own clan. When he

told him, the other grew silent. It is not good to talk of the dead.

"I am the last," he finally said, wanting the other to understand. "I've been away a long time."

"I know, I know the story of Star Tracker." He pushed down upon the crown of his wide-brimmed black hat as a gust of wind struck them. He looked back along the trail to the north. "Something follows you."

Still smiling at the way the old man had named him without naming him, he turned his head and looked in that direction. A large ball of tumbleweed bounced and rolled along the foot of the hill.

"Russian thistle," he said.

"No," the other replied. "Something more dangerous."

Despite his years, the fear of the *chindi* rose for a moment out of his youth. He shuddered beneath the touch of the wind.

"I see nothing else," he said.

"You have been gone for many years. Have you had an Enemyway?"

"No."

"Perhaps you should."

"Perhaps I will. You know a good Enemyway singer?"

"I am a singer."

"Perhaps I will see you again on this before long."

"I have heard that Star Tracker was a singer. Long ago."

"Yes."

"When you come by again we will talk more of these things."

"Yes."

The man looked back once more, along the trail.

"In the meantime," he said, "follow a twisted path."

"I will do that."

Later, as he passed along the streaky blue shale and frozen crimson clay of a dry riverbed, naked cottonwoods flanking it like fracture lines against the cold blue of the sky, he thought of the old man's words and the things of which they reminded him—of the sky creatures and water creatures, of the beings of cloud, mist, rain, pollen and corn which had figured so prominently in his childhood imagination—here in the season when the snakes and the thunder still slept.

It had been a long while since he had considered his problems in the old terms. A *chindi* . . . Real or of the mind—what difference? Something malicious at his back. Yes, another way of looking at things . . .

The day wore on to noon and past it before the butte near his home came into view, a high-standing wind-sculpture reminiscent of something he had once seen in a seaweed-fringed valley beneath the waters of an alien ocean. He halted again at this point to eat the rest of his rations. Nature had long moods in the Southwest, he reflected, as he looked off in that direction. While it was true that the land was little altered, there had been some change between the then and the now. He could just make out stands of blue spruce near the monolith's base, a tree he had not seen in this area a century and a half ago. But then the climate had also altered somewhat during the span, the winters becoming a trifle more clement, coming later, ending a bit sooner than they once had.

He filled his pipe and lit it. Shadows like multitudes of fingers stretched slowly out of the west. To run all this way, then sit and rest when the end was in sight—it seemed the thing to do. Was he afraid? he wondered. Afraid of that damned call? Maybe that was it. Or did he want a last slow-moving view of this piece of his life before something happened to change it? There had been a song. . . . He could not remember it.

When he felt that the time was proper he rose and began walking through the coolness and shadow toward the large, distant, six-sided house with the door to the east, his hogan that was not exactly a hogan.

The sky was darker by the time he reached the neighborhood of his dwelling, and the trees curtained off even more of the light, casting an as yet starless evening over the raised log-and-stucco structure. He wandered about it for several minutes before approaching from the east and mounting the rough-cut decking with which he had surrounded the place. He entered then and turned on the light. He had his own power supply, rooftop and below-ground.

Moving to the central *fogon*, he arranged some kindling and struck it to fire. He disrobed then, tossing his Levi's and red-and-white flannel shirt into a hamper along with the rest of his clothing. Crossing to a tall, narrow stall, he entered and set the timer for a three-minute UHF shower. Water was not a thing to be expended lightly in this region. When he emerged, he drew on a buckskin shirt, khaki bush pants and a pair of soft moccasins.

Activating his news recorder and display screen and adjusting it to some of his general interests, he passed to the small, open kitchen area to the right and prepared a meal, amid hanging *ristras* of chilis and onions.

He ate in a low, fur-covered chair and the walls about him were hung with rugs from Two Gray Hills and Ganado, interspersed with framed photographs of alien landscapes. A rack of weapons hung on the far wall; a meter-square metal platform enclosed by shining vertical bars of varying heights stood nearby, a large console with a display screen to its right. Its message light was still blinking.

When he finished eating, he toyed with his belt unit and put it aside. He went to the kitchen and got a beer.

DISK 1

CHILEAN QUAKES ABORTED

TAXTONIES ARRESTED

and three demonstrators were apprehended after reportedly setting fire to the car belonging to the official responsible for the ruling

PETROCEL DENIES PATENT INFRINGEMENT
CLAIMS "GREW OUR OWN," DIRECTOR OF
RESEARCH INSISTS

A MILD SPRING FOR MUCH OF THE NATION
EARLY FLOOD WATCHES IN MISSISSIPPI VALLEY

CHIMPANZEE COMPLAINS OF ART THEFT

References to a drugged banana figured prominently in the bizarre statement taken today by Los Angeles detectives

KILLED THEM "BECAUSE THEY WERE THERE,"
MOTHER OF THREE EXPLAINS

It's been a long time since you left me.
Don't know what I'm gonna do.

I look up at the sky and wonder—
Earthlight always makes me think of you.

COLUMBIA STUDENTS SKYDIVE FROM ORBIT
TO SET NEW RECORD

"Naturally the university is proud," Dean Schlobin remarked, "but

STRAGEAN AMBASSADOR CLOSETED WITH
SECRETARY-GENERAL

Stragean Ambassador Daltmar Stango and Consul Orar Bogarthy continue a second day of talks with Secretary-General Walford. Speculation on a breakthrough in trade-agreement negotiations runs high, but so far the news community

W. COAST DOLPHINS PRESS CLAIMS
A-1 CANNING BELIEVED READY TO SETTLE

BAKIN M'BAWA PREDICTS END OF WORLD AGAIN

I sip the beer and hear the music,
Watch the ships as they arrive.
You packed your bag and went away,
love I feel like H-E-L-L5.

CHURCH OF NATURAL LIFE RADICALS SUSPECTED
IN SPERMOVA BANK BOMBING

MAN SUES TO RECOVER FORMER PERSONALITY

Relying on a district court order, Menninger officials performed

BANK OF NOVA SCOTIA COMPUTER
CHARGED WITH FELONY IN BONDS
MANIPULATION SCANDAL

Oh, I'm sittin' here and hurtin'
In this slowly turnin' dive.
If you ever want to reach me
Just dial H-E-L-L5.

hate   somewhere he still exists and there is no force great enough to keep me from him forever   it has taken a long while to learn the ways but soon i will be ready   i am ready   eight days and had i known then what i know now he would be gone   i would be gone   burned?   burned they say?   nevermore amid the slagheaps to chase the crawling tubes and crunch them for their juiciness?   but this air too i breathe and only the jagged and the straight lightnings hold me here   i know the way beyond them now and the trees outside the walls   visions of cities the lesser ones bear   i know the ways i know the forms   wait   the lesser ones' twisted minds tell me what i need   one will come one day who will know of the one who is not like the others who still exists   i will leave for that somewhere he exists   eight days   i died a little he will die wholly   nothing can keep me from him forever   i will talk first now i know of it   words like the crawling things   crunch them taste their juiciness

strike now and see the lesser ones draw   back   now i
know them i will use them   words   to tell him the why of
it   now i will be a sphere and roll about   ha! lesser
ones!   hate   i will talk it that when   tell it then   eight
days   burned   hate

Back when Nayenezgani and his brother were in the process of disposing of the monsters the People had found
in the new world, there were some—such as the Endless Ser-
pent—who were, for various reasons, spared. Yet even these
were tamed to a degree in their acknowledgement as necessary evils. The world was indeed becoming a safer place,
though some few yet remained.

There was, for instance, Tse'Naga'Hai, the Traveling
Rock, which rolled after its victims to crush and devour
them. Nayenezgani traveled on a rainbow and the crooked
lightning in search of it. His brother having counseled him to
take the magic knives with him, he had all eight of them
about his person.

When he came to the place called Betchil gai, he took out
his two black knives, crossed them and planted them. Beyond, he planted the two blue knives, crosswise. Farther
along, he crossed the two yellow knives and planted them.
Farther yet, he planted the two knives with the serrated
edges, also crosswise.

He moved then in sight of the giant Rock.

"What are you waiting for, Tse'Naga'Hai?" he asked it.
"Do you not pursue my kind?"

With a crunching, grinding noise, the mossless boulder
he had just addressed stirred. It moved slowly in his direc-

tion, gaining momentum noticeably after but a few moments. It almost took him by surprise with the speed with which it approached.

But he whirled and raced away. It came on rapidly at his back, gaining upon him.

When he reached the place of the serrated knives, Nayenezgani leaped over them. The Rock rolled across them and a big piece broke away.

He continued to flee, jumping over the yellow knives. Tse'Naga'Hai rolled over them also, and another fracture occurred; more pieces fell away.

By now, the Rock was bouncing from side to side and rolling in an irregular pattern. And when Nayenezgani leaped over the blue knives and the Rock crashed into them and bounced over, more pieces fell away. By now, its size was considerably reduced though its velocity was increasing.

Nayenezgani sprang over the black knives. When he heard the Rock grating and cracking itself upon them, he turned.

All that remained was a relatively small stone. He halted, then moved toward it.

Immediately it swerved, altering its course to bound away from him. Now he pursued it into the west, beyond the San Juan River. Finally, there he caught it, and much of the life and wit seemed gone out of it.

"Now, Tse'Naga'Hai," he said, "the power to harm me is gone from you, but you are not without a certain virtue I noted earlier. In the future you will serve to light the fires of the Dineh."

He raised what remained of the Rock and bore it off with him to show to First Woman, who otherwise would not have believed what he had done.

Finally he sighed and rose. He crossed to the console beside the area enclosed by the shining bars. He pushed the "Messages" button and the display screen came alive.

EDWIN TEDDERS CALLED, it read, followed by the previous day's date and the time—the time when his unit had signaled in the wilderness. Below, it listed six other attempts by Edwin Tedders to reach him, the most recent only a few hours ago. There was an eastern code and a number, and a request that he return the call as soon as possible, prefaced by the word URGENT.

He tried to recall whether he had ever known an Edwin Tedders. He decided that he had not.

He punched out the digits and waited.

The buzzing which followed was broken, but the screen remained dark.

"Yes?" came a crisp male voice.

"William Blackhorse Singer," he said, "returning Edwin Tedders's call."

"Just a moment, please." The words hurried and rose in pitch. "I'll get him."

He tugged at a turquoise earring and regarded the blank screen. A minute shuffled its numbers on a nearby clock-display. Another . . . The screen suddenly glowed, and the heavily lined face of a dark-haired man with pale eyes appeared before him. His smile seemed one of relief rather than pleasure.

"I'm Edwin Tedders," he said. "I'm glad we finally got

hold of you, Mr. Singer. Can you come through right now?"

"Maybe." He glanced at the gleaming cage to his left. "But what's this all about?"

"I'll have to tell you in person. Please reverse the transfer charges. It is important, Mr. Singer."

"All right. I'll come."

He moved to his trip-box and began its activation. It whined faintly for an instant. Zones of color moved upward within the shafts.

"Ready," he said, stepping into the unit.

Looking down, he saw that his feet were growing dim.

For a moment, the world was disarrayed. Then his thoughts fell back into place again. He was standing within a unit similar to his own. When he raised his head he looked out across a large room done up in an old-fashioned manner—dark paneled walls, heavy leather chairs, a Chinese rug, bookshelves filled with leatherbound volumes, drapes, a fireplace burning real logs. Two men stood facing him—Tedders, and a slight, blond man whose voice identified him as the one with whom he had first spoken.

"This is Mark Brandes, my secretary," Tedders stated as he watched him step down.

He inadvertently pressed his palm rather than clasping hands, in the old way of the People. Brandes looked puzzled but Tedders was already gesturing toward the chairs.

"Have a seat, Mr. Singer."

"Call me Billy."

"All right, Billy. Would you care for a drink?"

"Sure."

"I have some excellent brandy."

ROGER ZELAZNY

"That'll be fine."

Tedders looked at Brandes, who immediately moved to a sideboard and poured a pair of drinks.

"Early spring," Tedders said.

Billy nodded, accepted his glass.

"You've had a fascinating career. Both freezing and time-dilation effects kept you around till you could benefit from medical advances. A real old-timer, but you don't look it."

Billy took a sip of his brandy.

"This is very good stuff," he said.

"Yes. Real vintage. How many trackers are there around these days?"

"I don't know."

"There are others, but you're the best. Old school."

Billy chuckled.

"What do you want?" he asked.

Tedders chuckled also.

"The best," he said.

"What do you want tracked?"

"It isn't exactly that."

"What, then?"

"It's hard to know where to begin. . . ."

Billy looked out the window, across the moon-flooded lawn. In the distance, the prospect was broken by a high wall.

"I am a special assistant to Secretary-General Walford," Tedders finally stated. "He is here—upstairs—and so are the Stragean ambassador and consul—Stango and Bogarthy. Do you know much about the Strageans?"

"I've met a few, here and there."

"How did they strike you?"

He shrugged.

"Tall, strong, intelligent . . . What do you mean?"

"Would you want one for an enemy?"

"No."

"Why not?"

"They could be very dangerous."

"In what ways?"

"They'd be hard to stop. They're shapeshifters. They have a kind of mental control over their bodies. They can move their organs around. They can—"

"Walk through walls?"

Billy shook his head. "I don't know about that. I've heard it said, but I've never—"

"It's true. They have a training regimen which will produce this ability in some of them. Semireligious, quite arduous, takes years, doesn't always work. But they can produce some peculiar adepts."

"Then you know more about it than I do."

"Yes."

"So why ask me?"

"One of them is on her way here."

Billy shrugged.

"There are a few thousand around. Have been for years."

Tedders sipped his drink.

"They're all normals. I mean one of those with that special training."

"So?"

"She's coming to kill the Secretary-General."

Billy sniffed his brandy.

"Good that you got word," he finally said, "and can turn it over to the security people."

"Not good enough."

Throughout the conversation, Tedders had been struggling to obtain eye-contact. At last Billy was staring at him, and he felt some small sense of triumph, not realizing that this meant the man doubted what he was saying.

"Why not?"

"They're not equipped to deal with Stragean adepts," he said. "She could well be too much for them."

Billy shook his head.

"I don't understand why you're telling me about it."

"The computer came up with your name."

"In response to what?"

"We'd asked it for someone who might be able to stop her."

Billy finished his drink and set the glass aside.

"Then you need a new programmer or something. There must be a lot of people who know more about Stragean adepts than I do."

"You are an expert on the pursuit and capture of exotic life forms. You spent most of your life doing it. You practically stocked the Interstellar Life Institute single-handed. You—"

Billy waved his hand.

"Enough," he said. "The alien you are talking about is an intelligent being. I spent much of my life tracking animals—exotic ones, to be sure, some very crafty and with tricky behavior patterns—but animals nevertheless, not creatures capable of elaborate planning."

Cat . . .

". . . So I don't see that my experience is really applicable in this situation," he concluded.

Tedders nodded. "Perhaps, and perhaps not," he said at last. "But in a matter like this we should really be certain. Will you talk with the Stragean representatives who are visiting here? They can probably give you a clearer picture than I can."

"Sure. I'll talk to anybody."

Tedders finished his drink and rose.

"May I get you another of those?"

"All right."

He replenished the snifter. Then, "I'll be back in a few minutes," he said, and he moved off to the right and departed the room.

Billy set down the glass and rose. He paced the room, regarded the titles on the bookshelves, felt the volumes' spines, sniffed the air. Mingled with the smell of old leather, a faint, almost acrid aroma he had not been able to place earlier came to him again, a scent he had experienced upon meeting Strageans in the past, in another place. They must have been about this building for some time, he decided, or have been in this room very recently, to mark it so with their presence. He remembered them as humanoid, over two meters in height, dark-skinned save for silvery faces, necks and breasts; flat-headed, narrow-waisted beings with wide shoulders, collarlike outgrowths of spiny material which served as sound-sensors and small, feral eyes, slitted, usually yellow but sometimes cinnamon or amber in color; hairless, graceful in a many-jointed, insectlike way, they moved quietly and spoke a language that reminded him vaguely of Greek, which he did not understand either.

It is language, he decided, that sets the sentients apart from the animals. Isn't it?

Cat. . . ?

He moved to the window, stared out across the lawn. Difficult to cross there without being detected, he concluded, with even the simplest security devices in operation. And this place must have plenty. But she could assume almost any guise, could penetrate the place in an innocuous form. . . .

Why be furtive, though? That is what they would be expecting. While the defenders were concentrating on the sophisticated, why not hijack a heavy vehicle, come barreling across the lawn, crash through a wall, jump down from the cab and start shooting everything that moves?

He shook himself and turned away. This was not his problem. There must be plenty of people more qualified than himself to second-guess the alien, no matter what the computer said.

He returned to his chair and took up his drink. Footsteps were approaching now from the direction in which Tedders had departed. Footsteps, and the soft sound of voices, accompanied by a faint ringing in his ears. The language of the Strageans ranged into the ultrasonic on the human scale, and though they narrowed their focus when speaking Terran tongues there were always some overtones. Too long a conversation with a Stragean normally resulted in a headache.

He took another drink and lowered the glass as they rounded the corner.

The two Strageans wore dark blue kilts and belts which crossed their breasts like bandoliers. Ornamental pins or badges of office were affixed to these latter. Between Tedders and the aliens walked another man, short, heavy, with just a fringe of dark hair; his eyes were jadelike under heavy brows; he wore a green robe and slippers. Billy recognized him as UN Secretary-General Milton Walford.

Tedders introduced him to Daltmar Stango and Orar Bogarthy as well as to Walford. Everyone was seated then, and Tedders said, "They will tell you more about this."

Billy nodded.

The Stragean known as Daltmar Stango, staring at nothing directly before him, recited: "It has to do with the coming of your people to stay on our world. There is already a sizable enclave of them there, just as there is of our kind here on Earth. There has been very little trouble on either world because of this. But now, with my present mission to negotiate political and trade agreements, it appears that the settlements will become permanent diplomatic posts."

He paused but a moment, as if to refocus his thoughts, and then continued: "Now, there is a small religious group on Strage which believes that when Terrans die there, their life essences foul the place of the afterlife. Permanent posts will guarantee that this group's fears will be realized with increasing frequency as time goes on. Hence, they are against any agreements with your people, and they would like all of them off our world."

"How large a group are they?" Billy asked.

"Small. Fifty to a hundred thousand members, at most. It is not their size which is important, though. They are an austere sect, and many of them undertake a severe course of training which sometimes produces spectacular effects in the individual."

"So I've heard."

"One such individual has taken it upon herself to correct matters. She commandeered a vessel and set a course for Earth. She feels that an assassination at this level will disrupt our negotiations to the point where there will be no treaty—and that this will lead to the withdrawal of Terrans from our world."

"How close is she to the truth?"

"It is always difficult to speculate in these matters, but it would certainly slow things down."

"And she's due to arrive in a few days?"

"Yes. We received the information from other members of her sect, and they could not be more precise. They did not learn the story in its entirety until after her departure, when they informed the authorities. They were anxious that it be known she was acting on her own initiative and not under orders."

Billy smiled.

"Who can say?" he said.

"Yes. At any rate, since a message can travel faster than a ship, the warning was sent."

"You must know best how to stop one of your own people."

"The problem seldom occurs," Daltmar said. "But the customary method is to set a team of similarly endowed adepts after a wrongdoer. Unfortunately . . ."

"Oh."

"So we must make do with what is at hand," the alien went on. "Your people will try to intercept her in space, but projections only give them a twenty-seven percent chance of success. Have you any ideas?"

Cat?

"No," Billy replied. "If it were a dangerous animal, I'd want to study it in its habitat for a time."

"There is no way and no time."

"Then I don't know what to tell you."

Walford produced a small parcel from the pocket of his robe.

"There is a chip in here that I want you to take back with you and run through your machine," he said. "It will tell you everything we know about this individual and about others of that sort. It is the closest thing we can give you to a life study."

Billy rose and accepted the package.

"All right," he said. "I'll take it home and run it. Maybe something will suggest itself."

Walford and the others rose to their feet. As Billy turned toward the transporter, the Stragean called Orar Bogarthy spoke.

"Yours is one of the aboriginal peoples of this continent?" he said.

"Yes," Billy replied, halting but not turning.

"Have the jewels in your earlobes a special significance? Religious, perhaps?"

Billy laughed.

"I like them. That's all."

"And the one in your hair?"

Billy touched it as he turned slowly.

"That one? Well . . . it is believed to protect one from being struck by lightning."

"Does it work?"

"This one has. So far."

"I am curious. Being struck by lightning is not the most common occurrence in life. Why do you wear it?"

"We Navajos have a thing about lightning. It destroys taboos. It twists reality. Not a thing to fool around with."

He turned away, moved ahead, punched a series of numbers, stepped up into the unit. He glanced up at the expressionless humans and aliens as the delay factor passed and his body began to melt.

Traveling the distance from hill to hill,
passing from place to place as the wind passes,
trackless. There should be a song for it,
but I have never learned the words.
So I sing this one of my own making:
I am become a rainbow, beginning there
and ending here. I leave no mark
upon the land between as I arc
from there to here. May I go in beauty.
May it lie before, behind, above and below,
to the right and the left of me.
I pass cleanly through the gates of the sky.

*　　　*　　　*

We call it the Enemyway, the old man said, but the white people came along and started calling it a squaw dance—probably because they saw the women dancing for it. You get a special name if you're the one they're going to sing over, a warrior's name. It's a sacred name you're just supposed to use in ceremonials, not the kind you go around telling everybody or just letting people call you by.

It all started, he said, back when Nayenezgani was protecting the People. He killed off a whole bunch of monsters that were giving us a hard time. There was the Horned Monster and Big God and the Rock Monster Eagle and the Traveling Rock and a lot of others. That was why he got to be called Monster-Slayer. His fourth monster, though, was called Tracking Bear. It was a bear, but it looked more like a lion the size of a floatcar. Once it came across your tracks, it would start following them and it wouldn't stop until it had found you and had you for dinner on the spot.

Nayenezgani went out and tracked the tracker and then let it track him. But when it finally found him, he was ready. He wasn't called Monster-Slayer for nothing. When it was all over, the world was that much safer.

But at about that time, it started to get to him. He suffered for it because of all those enemies he killed, and the bear just added another one to their band. Their spirits followed him around and made him pretty miserable. This is where the word *Anaa'jí*, for the Enemyway, comes from. *Naayéé'* means an enemy, or something really bad that's bothering you. Now, *neezghání* means "he has gotten rid of it," and *ana'í* means an enemy that's been gotten rid of. So

Anaa'jí is probably really the best word to call it by. It's a ceremony for getting rid of really bad troubles.

He paced. the screen still glowed. He had not turned off the unit after viewing the chip. The walls seemed to lean toward him, to press in upon him. The wind was singing a changing song he almost understood. He paused at various times, to inspect an old basket, an ancient flaked spear point, the photograph of a wild landscape beneath an indigo sky. He touched the barrel of a high-powered rifle, took the weapon into his hands, checked it, replaced it on its pegs. Finally he turned on his heel and stepped outside into the night.

He stood upon the decking which surrounded the hogan. He peered into the shadows. He looked up at the sky.

"I have no words . . ." he began, and a part of his mind mocked the other part. He was, as always, conscious of this division. When it had first occurred he could no longer say.

". . . But you require an answer."

He was not even certain what it was that he addressed. The Navajo language has no word for "religion." Nor was he even certain that that was the category into which his feelings fell. Category? The reason there was no word was that in the old days such things had been inextricably bound to everything in one's life. There was no special category for certain sentiments. Most of those around him even now did not find this strange. But they had changed. He had also, though he knew that his alteration was of a different order. "He behaves as if he had no relatives"—this was the worst thing one Navajo might say of another, and he knew that it applied to him. The gulf was deeper than his absence, his marriage, anything he had done. Others had gone away for long times, had married outside the clans, and had still come back. But for him it was part of a temporal experience, literally as well as spiritually true. He had no relatives. A part of him wanted it that way. The other part . . .

"I may have done a great wrong," he continued. "If I took him from his land, as the People were taken to Fort Sumner. If I took him from his own kind, who are no more. If I left him alone in a strange place, like a captive among the Utes. Then I have done a wrong. But only if he is a real person." He scanned the skies. "May he not be," he said then. "May it all be a dream of possibility, a nothingness—that which has troubled me across the years." He circled the hogan, staring off into the trees. "I had thought that not knowing was best—which may make me a coward. Yet I would have gone on this way for the rest of my days. Now—"

An owl fled past him, making a soft whooing noise.

An evil omen, a part of his mind decided, *for the owl is the bird of death and ill things.*

An owl, the other part affirmed. *They hunt at night. It is nothing more.*

"We have heard one another," he called after the bird. "I will find out what I have done and know what I must do."

He went back inside and reached up among cobwebs to where a key hung from a *viga*. He took it into his hand and rubbed it. He ran his finger along it as if it were as unusual an item as the spear point. Then, abruptly, he dropped it into his pocket. He crossed the room and switched off the glowing screen.

Turning, he then stepped among the bars of the trip-box, activated the control unit and punched a code. He focused his eyes upon the red Ganado rug and watched it turn pink and go away.

Darkness amid the tiny streetlights, and the sound of crickets outside the booth . . .

He stepped out of the shelter and sniffed the damp air. Large, shadow-decked trees; enviable quantities of grass furring hillsides; heavy, squat, monolithic buildings, dark now, save for little entranceway lights providing tiny grottoes which only accentuated the blackness elsewhere; no people in sight.

He moved along the sidewalk, crossed the street, cut up a hillside. There were guards about, but he avoided them without difficulty. Balboa Park was quiet now, its spectacles closed to the public until morning. The lights of San Diego and the traffic along its trailways were visible from various high points he crossed, but these seemed distant, part of another world. He moved soundlessly from shadow to shadow. He had chosen a public booth he had sometimes liked to use long ago, when he had come on normal, daytime business, enjoying the walk rather than tripping directly into the place with which he was associated. That place, of course, was now closed for the night, its trip-box also shut down.

For fifteen minutes he continued his trek, climbing and hiking toward the vast, sprawling complex that was the Interstellar Life Institute. He avoided sidewalks, parking lots and roads as much as possible. Mixed animal smells from the San Diego Zoo were occasionally borne to him in open areas by vagrant currents of wind. Rich and jungley, the smells of some of the zoo foliage also came to him. These sensations stirred memories of other exotic creatures in other places. He recalled the capture of the wire-furred wullabree in a pen of ultrasonics, the twilpa in an ice pit, four outan in a vortex of odors. . . .

The ILI complex came into sight and he slowed. For a long while he stood halted, simply watching the place. Then, slowly, he circled it, pausing often to watch again.

Finally he stood at the rear of the building near a small parking lot containing but a single car. He crossed and used his key in the door of the employees' entrance which adjoined it.

Inside, he moved without the need for light, traversing a series of corridors, then mounting a small stair. He came to a watchman's station he remembered, then used his passkey to let himself into a nearby maintenance supply closet. There he waited for twenty minutes until a uniformed old man shuffled by, halted, inserted a key into the alarm unit and moved on.

Shortly thereafter, he emerged and entered the first hall. Some of the life units at either hand were eerily illuminated, simulating the natural lighting cycles of their inhabitants' homes, tinged by odd atmospheric compounds or reflecting meteorological peculiarities necessary for the creatures' well-being. He passed drifting gas balloons, crawling coral branches, slimy Maltese crosses, pulsating liver-colored logs, spiny wave-snakes, a Belgarde simoplex gruttling in its tangle-hole, a striped mertz, a pair of divectos, a compacted tendron in a pool of ammonia. The stalked eyes of a wormsa marakye followed his passage as they had that day on the wind barrens when it had almost collected him. He did not pause to return this regard, nor to inspect any of those others he knew so well.

He traversed the entire hall, departed it, entered another. The faint hum of generators was with him always. Despite the hermetic quality of the life units, unusual odors reached him from somewhere. He ignored all of the signs, knowing what they said. The specimens in this second hall were larger, fiercer-looking than those in the one through which he had just passed. Here he glanced at several with something almost like affection, muttering quietly in the language of the People. He began humming very softly as he entered the third hall.

After only a few paces, he began to slow.

Rocks on a plain of fused silicates . . . No visible partition between that place and the rest of the hall, as in a few others he had passed. Atmospheric equivalence . . .

He continued to slow. He halted.

A weak, pointless light suffused that plain. He seemed to hear a sighing sound.

His humming ceased and his mouth grew dry.

"I have come," he whispered, and then he approached the exhibit placarded TORGLIND METAMORPH.

Sand and rock. Yellow and glassy and orange. Streaks of black. Nothing stirred.

"Cat. . . ?" he said.

He drew nearer and continued to stare. It was no use. Even his eyes could not tell for certain. It was not just the lighting.

"Cat?"

He searched his memory of the manner in which the display had originally been set up. Yes. That rock, to the left . . .

The rock moved, even as he recalled the disposition of the environment. It rolled toward the center. It changed shape, growing more spherical as it negotiated a dip.

"There is a thing I must say, a thing I must try to do. . . ."

It elongated, unfolded a pair of appendages, propped itself upon them.

"I have wondered, wondered whether you might really understand me, if I tried—hard enough."

It grew another pair of appendages toward its rearward extremity, formulated a massive head, a fat, triangular tail.

"If you know anyone, you know me. I brought you here. The scars of our battle have been erased from my body, but none gave me a greater fight than yourself."

Its outline flowed. It became sleek and glistening, a thing of rippling cords beneath a glassy surface. Its head developed a single faceted eye at its center.

"I have come to you. I must know whether you have understanding. For a time I thought that you might. But you have never shown it since. Now I must know. Is there sense in that brute head of yours?"

The creature stretched and turned away from him. "If you can communicate with anyone, in any fashion, let it be me, now. It is very important."

It paced across the area toward his right.

"It is not just idle curiosity that brings me here. Give me some sign of intelligence, if you possess it."

It looked at him for a moment through that cold, unblinking gem at its head's center. Then it turned away once again, its color darkening until it could go no further. Coal, inky, absolute blackness filled its outline.

The shadow slid away toward the rear of the area and vanished.

"In a way, you have pleased me," he said then. "Goodbye, great enemy."

He turned, headed back through the hall.

Billy Blackhorse Singer. Man of the People. Last warrior of your kind. You have taken your time in coming.

He halted. He stood absolutely still.

Yes. The words come into your head. I can formulate some likeness of a human tongue and utter them if I choose, but we may as well be more intimate, who are closer than friends, farther than affection.

Cat?

That is right. Just think it. I will know. Cat serves well to name me—a lithe and independent creature, alien in sentiments. I read only the thoughts you choose to surface, not your entire mind. You must tell me all of the things you wish for me to know. Why have you come?

To see whether you are what I now see you to be.

That is all?

It has bothered me that you might be so. Why did you not communicate sooner?

At first I could not. My kind transmitted only images—of the hunt—to others like ourselves. But the power slowly grew as I regarded the thoughts of those who came to view me this half-century past. Now I know much of your world and your kind. You, though—you are different from the others.

In what way?

Like me, a predator.

Cat! Why did you not tell someone, once you knew how, that you are a sentient, intelligent being?

I have learned many things. And I have been waiting.

For what?

I have learned hate. I have been waiting for the chance to escape, to track you as you once tracked me, to destroy you.

It need not have gone this far. I am sorry for the pain I have caused you. Now that we know what you are, amends can be made.

The sun of my world has since gone nova. The world and all others of my kind are no more. I have seen this in the minds of my attendants. How can you restore it to me?

I cannot.

I have learned hate. I did not know hate before I came to this place. The predator does not hate the prey. The wolf actually loves the sheep, in its way. But I hate you, Billy Blackhorse Singer, for what you have done to me, for having turned me into a thing. This sophistication I learned from your own kind. Since then I have lived only for the day when I might tell you this and act upon it.

I am sorry. I will speak with the people who run this place.

I will not respond to them. They will think you demented in your allegations.

Why?

That is not my wish. I have told you my wish.

He turned back toward the area, moving to the place where force fields contained the dark, larger-than-man-sized creature which now sat nearby, studying him.

I do not see how your wishes will be realized, but I am willing to try to help you in any other way.

I see something.

What do you mean?

I see that you want something of me.

It is nothing, I now realize, that you would care to give.

Try me.

I came to learn whether I had wronged you.

You have.

To see whether you are truly intelligent.

I am.

To ask your assistance, then, in preventing a political assassination.

There followed something like laughter—hollow, without humor.

Tell me about it.

He described the situation. There was a long silence when he had finished.

Then, *Supposing I were to locate this being and thwart her? What then?*

Your freedom would of course be restored to you. There would be reparations, probably a reward, a new home. Some equivalent world might be found. . . .

The dark form rose, changing shape again, becoming bearlike, bipedal. It extended a forelimb until it came into contact with the field. A rush of sparks cascaded about the area.

ROGER ZELAZNY

That, Cat told him, *is all that stands between you and death.*

That is all you have to say—that now that we can communicate we have nothing to talk about?

Do you not recall that long week you stalked me?

Yes.

It was only by a fluke that you captured me.

Perhaps.

Perhaps? You know it is so. I almost had you there at the end.

You came close.

I have relived that hunt for fifty long years. I should have won!

He slammed against the field and sparks outlined his entire figure. Billy did not move. After a time, Cat drew back, shaking himself. He seemed smaller now, and his body coiled around and around upon itself, sinking to the ground.

Finally, *You have already offered me my liberty, without conditions,* Cat said.

Yes.

The reward and reparations of which you spoke mean nothing to me.

I see.

No, you do not.

I see that you will not help in this. Very well. Good night to you.

He turned away again.

I did not say that I would not help.

When he looked back it was a swaying, hooded, horned thing which regarded him.

What is it that you do say, Cat?

I will help you—for a price.

And what is that price?

Your life.

Preposterous.

I have waited this long. It is the only thing that I want.

It is an insane offer.

It is my only offer. Accept it or not, as you choose.

Do you really think you can stop a Stragean adept?

If I fail and she destroys me, then you are free and no worse off than before. But I will not fail.

It is unacceptable.

Again the laugh.

Billy Singer turned and walked from the hall. The laughter followed him. Its range was approximately a quarter of a mile.

DISK II

BODY OF UNION LEADER FOUND IN ORBIT

Would have been incinerated upon reentry several days

EIGHTEEN INDICTED IN LUNAR DEALS

GULF HURRICANE ABORTED

he climbed Mount Taylor, birthplace of Changing Woman, sacred peak of the turquoise south. The clouds were heavy in the north, but the sun shone to his left. A cold wind sang a fragile song. He cast a pinch of pollen to each of the world's four quarters. As his existential mood deepened a *yei* came to him in the form of a drifting black feather

GENEFIX—REVLON MERGER HINTED

EUTHANASIA VICTIM TELLS ALL

CALL FOR PARANORMALS

The UN Secretary-General's office early this morning

. . . I feel like H-E-L-L5!

CHURCH OF CHRISTIAN RELATIVITY TAKES STAND

Her sensors held as the ship banked. Running the defense system would not be so difficult after all, her instruments informed her. She meditated for half a minute upon the flame and the water, visible mutabilities symbolizing the change-flame. Flow, she imaged, into the ancient forms

FLOODING IN L.A.-PHOENIX TUNNEL
MAN CARRIED TWO MILES

"Your horses are yours again, grandchild," he says as he sits down beside me.

"Your sheep are yours again, grandchild," he says as he sits down beside me.

"All your possessions are yours again, grandchild," he says as he sits down beside me.

"Your country is yours again, grandchild," he says as he sits down beside me.

"Your springs that flow are yours again, grandchild," he says as he sits down beside me.

"Your mountain ranges are yours again, grandchild," he says as he sits down beside me.

*   *   *

Blessed again it has become, blessed again it has become!
Blessed again it has become, blessed again it has become!

He had crossed the dried lava flow, which in his day everyone had known to be the congealed blood of Yeitso, a monster slain by Nayenezgani. And then he had continued upward along the slopes of Mount Taylor, its heights hidden today by a great, rolling bank of fog. A nagging wind clutched at his garments with many hands, a black wind from out of the north. A holy place was necessary for the thoughts he wished to think on this bleak day. It had been over a century since he had visited Mount Taylor, but its nature was such that it had been left undisturbed through all these years.

Climbing . . .

Cat my chindi . . . *Ever at my back* . . .

Climbing, his hair gleaming from a recent shampoo with yucca roots . . .

. . . All things past come together in you.

Climbing, into the fog now, the wind abruptly dying, stones dark and slippery . . .

. . . And how shall I face you?

. . . Mountain held to the earth by a great stone knife, pierced through from top to bottom, female mountain, you have seen all things among the People. But do you know the stranger stars I have looked upon? Let me tell you of them. . . .

The climb was slow and the mists pressed upon him, dampening his garments until they clung. He sang as he ascended, pausing at several places, for this was the home of Turquoise Boy and Yellow Corn Girl, and in some versions of the story it was here that Changing Woman had been born.

. . . I have lost myself among bright stars.

He passed a group of stone people who seemed to nod behind their veil of mist. The fleecy whiteness which surrounded him made him think of his mother's sheep, which he had herded as a boy. His thoughts followed them from their old winter hogan, its forage exhausted, to the high summer camp, where meals were cooked and eaten outdoors and the women set up their looms between the trees. His uncle, the singer, would gather herbs and dry them in the sun. The old man held a medicine bundle for Female Shootingway, of the five-night chantway. He also did the five-night Blessingway chant and knew minor Shootingway ceremonies, as well as the five nights of Evilway. And he knew the Restorationway of every living thing.

When the word came that the government inspectors were waiting at the sheep-dips, a festive spirit danced among the settlements like a humpbacked piper. The camp was broken, and the sheep bells clunked as the animals were herded down from the mountains to the place of the dips. The dips themselves stank of sulphur, and the smell of sheep dung was everywhere, not least of all upon one's boots. It was a slow, dirty business, as the sheep were run through the dips one by one, counted, collected together, certified as free of ticks and disease for another season. The air was filled with dust from the moving animals. Soon flocks of them covered the hills like fallen clouds, barking dogs moving among them.

As the day progressed, a holiday atmosphere would spread among the stench and the noises. The smells of mutton stew, fry bread and coffee, mingled with the fragrance of piñon smoke, began to move through the air. Laughter would rise with greater frequency. Gambling would begin. Songs would be heard. Here or there, a horse race, a chicken-pull . . .

And the garments would improve as the work was done. The woman who might have worn a wool shawl and carried a sun umbrella while herding her sheep from the pen to the dip now had on her best bright three-tiered skirt, a satin shirt and velvet overblouse with silver collar points and silver buttons running down each shoulder seam to the wrist, silver bowknot buttons down the front, a heavy squash blossom necklace, several strands of turquoise within it. The men appeared in velveteen shirts with silver buttons, silver and turquoise bands about their black hats, green and blue bracelets, rings, necklaces—from Pilot Mountain, Morinci, Kingman, Royston. And there were jokes and dancing, though no stories of the supernatural variety, for the thunder and the serpents were awake. Re remembered his first squaw dance on such an occasion. He had had nothing with which to pay, and so he had danced and danced for most of the night, listening to the girls' laughter, moving finally like a man 'in a dream, until an opportunity—perhaps intentional?—presented itself, and he fled.

And now . . .

This past summer he had visited a contemporary sheep-dipping. The genetically tailored animals were immune to most of the old diseases. Still, a few parasites could cause annoyance. The sheep were run through a quickly assembled, lightweight, odorless aerosol tunnel, counted and sorted by computer and penned behind a series of UHF walls broadcast from tiny units dropped casually upon the ground. For the most part, meals were prepared in quick, efficient—if a bit old-fashioned —portable microwave units. The evening's music was chip-recorded or satellite-

broadcast. Most of the dancing that followed he did not recognize. There seemed to be fewer traditional garments in
sight, fewer people doing things in the right manner. Not too
many horses about. And a young man actually came up to
him and asked him his name. . . .

. . . *Mountain held to the earth by a great stone knife,
pierced through from top to bottom, blade decorated with
turquoise, color of the blue south, female mountain, upon
your summit a bowl of turquoise containing two bluebird
eggs covered with sacred buckskin, mountain dressed in turquoise, eagle plumes upon your head, you have seen all
things among the People. For a man, however, to see too
much of change may damage his spirit. I have seen much. . . .*

He climbed a lightening way, through the houses made
of dark cloud, rainbow and crystal. When he emerged onto
the high slopes, into brightness beneath an unscreened sun, it
was as if he stood upon an island in the midst of a frothing
sea. The land was covered over in every direction by a cot-
tony whiteness. He faced each of the world's corners and he
sang, making offerings of cornmeal and pollen. Then he
seated himself and opened his unwounded deerskin pouch,
removing certain items. For a long while he thought upon
the things that came to him then. . . .

That line of clouds . . . so like a curved dirt altar. A mushroom in its nest upon it. Night. He had eaten the bitter medicine and listened to the singing and the drumming. The rattle
and the feather fan were passed. Each person sang four
songs before handing on the regalia. A feeling of extreme
weariness had come over him even before it was his turn. He
understood that John Rave had once said that this was the

effect of the peyote struggling against a person's vices. His throat felt constricted and very dry. He wondered how much of this was spiritual and how much physiological.

He had been going through a very unusual period in his life. He had been away to school. The old ways no longer seemed right, but neither did the new ones. He understood that the Native American Church had appealed to many who felt themselves between worlds. But he had also, already, taken anthropology courses, and he felt a thin edge of estrangement—like a knifeblade—inserting itself between him and the experience even now, after only a few weeks of Peyoteway. The brilliantly colored hallucinations were often fascinating, yet he and his thirst had stood apart.

But this night was somehow different from other nights. . . . He felt this as he passed the rattle and the fan and, looking up, saw that a rainbow was forming. It did not seem at all out of place, and he watched it with interest. It seemed simultaneously distant and near, and as he stared there was movement upon it. Two figures—and he knew them—were passing along its crest as upon the arch of a great bridge. They halted and looked down at him. They were the Warrior Twins—Tobadzischini, Born-of-Water, and Nayenezgani, Monster-Slayer. For a long while they simply stared, and then he realized that it might not really be himself that they were regarding. From a sudden movement, he became aware of a great black bird, a raven, perched upon his left shoulder. Fleetingly, beneath the rainbow, a coyote passed. Nayenezgani strung his bow with lightning and raised it, but his brother placed his hand upon his arm and he lowered it.

When he looked again to his left, the raven had vanished. When he returned his gaze forward, the rainbow was smaller, fading. . . .

The next day he was weak, and he rested and drank liquids. His thought processes seemed sluggish. But the vision was somehow very important. The more he examined it the more puzzling it became. Was it the raven that Nayenezgani had been about to shoot, or was it himself? Was the bird protecting him against the Warrior Twins? Or were the brothers trying to protect him from the bird?

In the light of his recent anthropological studies, it became even more involved. Raven did figure in some of the People's stories—particularly around the Navajo Mountain, Rainbow Bridge, Piute Canyon area—as a demonic force. Yet this had not always been so, though the time when things were otherwise lay beyond the memory of anyone alive.

Raven was a principal deity among the Tlingit-Haida people of the Pacific Northwest, and these people spoke a language of the Athabascan group. The Navajo and their relatives, the Apache, also spoke an Athabascan tongue and were the only people to do so outside the Northwest. In ancient times there had been a migration which had finally led the People to the canyons and mesas of Arizona, Utah, Colorado, New Mexico. In the days of their wanderings they had followed hunters' deities, such as Raven, Mountain Lion and Wolf, who had accompanied them on the long trek southward. But the People had changed when they had settled, attaching themselves to a particular area, learning agriculture from the Zuni and the Pueblo, weaving from the Hopi and, later, sheepherding from the Spaniard. With the passing of a way of life, gods of the old days were eclipsed. Raven—or Black-god, as he was now known—had even fought an inconclusive duel with Nayenezgani between San Francisco Peaks and Navajo Mountain. So Raven was a figure out of the very distant past. He had been honored when the People had been hunters rather than herders, farmers, weavers, silversmiths.

The Peyoteway, he knew, was an even newer thing, learned from the Utes. And it was new, in many ways, also for those who were lost, though it might touch upon ancient chords. The crossed lines on the ground behind the altar were said to be the footprints of Christ. He chose to regard them as giant bird-tracks. He knew that he would never go back to the Peyote hogan, for this way was not his way, though it had served to bring him an important message. For good or ill, he saw that he was marked to be a hunter.

He would finish school and he would learn the songs his uncle wished to teach him. He knew without knowing how he knew that both of these things would be important in the hunting he must one day do. He would venerate the old ways yet learn the new —the very old ways, and the very new—and in this there was no contradiction, for a Navajo was one of the most adaptable creatures on Earth. The nearby Hopis danced and prayed for rain. His people did not. They sought to live with their environment rather than to control it. The Pueblos, the Zunis, the Hopis lived clustered together like *bellicanos* in condominiums. His people did not. They lived apart from one another and families took care of themselves. Other tribes incorporated *bellicano* words into their language to explain new things. Even in the twentieth century the Navajo language had evolved to cover the changing times, with over two hundred new words just to name the various parts of the internal combustion engine. They had learned from the Anglos, the Spaniards, the Pueblos, the Zunis, the Hopis. They had flowed, they had adapted, yet had remained themselves. Not for nothing did they consider themselves descendants of Changing Woman.

Yes. He would learn both the new and the old, he had told himself. And Black-god would accompany him on the hunt.

And this had come to pass. Yet he had not counted on so much change on the part of the People in the time-twisted times he had been away. They were still the People, different from all others. But their rate of change and his had been different.

Now, looking across the world from atop Mount Taylor, he saw that Black-god, who had chosen him, had kept his promise, making him into the mightiest hunter of his time. But now he was retired and those days were past. It seemed too much of an effort for an individual to adapt any further. The People as a whole were an organic thing and had had much time to adjust, slowly. Let it be. His design was drawn. Perhaps it was right to walk away from it now in beauty and die like the legend he had become.

He began the mountaintop song for this place. The staccato words rolled out across his world.

As the day wore on the clouds became colored smoke below him. Something passed overhead, uttering a single cawing note. Later he discovered a black feather which had fallen nearby. As he added it to his *jish* in the unwounded deerskin pouch, he wondered at its ambiguous character.

Black, the color of the north, the direction in which the spirits of the departed travel. Black north, from which the *chindi* returns, along with other evil things. Black for north, for death. Yet Raven might cast a black feather, send it to him. And what might that imply?

Whatever . . . Though he could not read its depths, he could see its surface. He drew circles in the dust with his forefinger, and then he rubbed them out. Yes. He knew.

But still he sat there, on his island in the sky, and the day drifted through noon. Finally the call he had been expecting came. He knew that it would be Edwin Tedders before he heard the voice.

"Billy, we are getting very nervous here. Have you gone over the data?"

"Yes."

"Did you come up with anything?"

"Yes."

"Can you trip through now?"

"No. There's no box anywhere near here."

"Well, get to one! We've got to know, and I don't want it on the phone."

"Can't do that," he said.

"Why not?"

"If the lady in question numbers among her other virtues the ability of knowing what people have on their minds, I don't want her getting this from you."

"Wait a minute. I'll call you back."

A little later, the second call came through.

"Okay. This is the tightest fit. Listen, Targetman will be a skip and a jump away from a box to no one here knows where. And it blows immediately after tripping."

"If she can kill its juice—"

"Maybe yes, maybe no. We're also calling in human psis."

"There aren't all that many and they aren't all predictable. Right?"

"A few are very good. And some are here already."

"They find you anything?"

"Nothing yet. Now, what do you have in mind? Can you state it in such a general fashion that we'll have an idea without details she can use?"

"No."

There was a pause. Then, "Christ! We've got to have *something*, Billy! We might be falling over each other."

"You won't even know I'm around."

"You *will* be in the area?"

"No details, remember? Your own psis might even get it from you—then she might get it from them if she misses you."

"If you're going to be in the neighborhood a psi might just as easily get it from you."

"I don't think so. Primitive people can sometimes go black on a telepath. I've seen it happen on other worlds. I've gone primitive again."

"Well, how soon will you be on the job?"

Billy regarded the sinking sun.

"Soon," he said.

"You can't just state simply what you're going to do?"

"We're going to stop her."

"You've become royalty or an editor? Or acquired a tapeworm? What's this 'we'? You have to let us know if you're bringing other people in on this."

"I'm not bringing other people in on it."

"Billy, I don't like this—"

"Neither do I, but it will be done. You won't be able to reach me after this."

"Well, goodbye. . . . That's it, then. Good luck."

"Goodbye."

He faced the white east, the blue south, the yellow west and the black north and bade them goodbye; also, the Holy People of the mountain. Then he climbed back from one world to the other.

> *The Iroquois called you*
> *the Being without a Face.*
> *I go to look and see if this is true,*
> *great Destroyer*
> *who goes about menacing*
> *with couched lance and raised hatchet.*
> *I put my feet down with pollen*
> *as I walk.*
> *I place my hands so,*
> *with pollen.*
> *I move my head with pollen.*
> *My feet, my hands, my body*
> *are become pollen,*
> *and my mind, even my voice.*
> *The trail is beautiful.*

My lands and my dwelling are beautiful.
Aqalàni, Dinetah.
My spirit wanders across you.
I go to see the Faceless One.
Impervious to pain may I walk.
With beauty all about me may I walk.
It closes in beauty.
I shall not return.
Be still.

Ann Axtell Morris and her archaeologist husband Earl told the story of the two Franciscans, Fathers Fintan and Anselm, who traveled in the place of the white reed, Lu-ka-chu-kai, in the year 1909. There, south of the Four Corners, in the roadless and wild mountains, they rested one afternoon while their Navajo guide took a walk. Later the guide returned with a large, decorated ceramic water jar. Father Fintan, who knew something of Indian pottery, recognized the uniqueness of the piece and asked where it was from. The guide did not give the location. He did say that it came from an abandoned city of the Anasazi, the Old Ones, a place of many large houses and a high tower—a place where many such jars, some still filled with corn, lay about, as well as blankets, sandals, tools. But he had simply borrowed the jar to show them and must replace it, for one day the owners might return. But where was this place? The Navajo shook his head. He walked off with the pot. After half an hour he was back, Later the priests described the pot to the Morrises, who felt it to be from the Pueblo III period, a high point in southwestern culture. And surely the place would be easy to locate, knowing that it lay within half an hour's walk from that campsite. They searched several times, without success. And Emil W. Haury spent half a summer there in 1927 but was not able to discover the lost city of Lukachukai. There is now a city in Arizona which has taken that name. Rugs are woven there. The story of a lost prehistoric city in those mountains somewhere to the northeast of Canyon de Chelly has since been dismissed as apocryphal.

It was the wind that gave them life. It is the wind that comes out of our mouths now that gives us life. When this ceases to blow we die. In the skin at the tips of our fingers we see the trail of the wind; it shows us where the wind blew when our ancestors were created.

Translated from the Navajo by
Washington Matthews, 1897

The box hummed and the outline occurred, quickly to be filled in and solidified as they watched.

A tall, well-dressed black man of middle years smiled, stepped down and moved forward.

"Good to have you here," Edwin Tedders said, shaking his hand and turning toward the others. "This is Charles Fisher, stage magician, mentalist."

He indicated a pale woman whose blue eyes were framed by an ultrafine net of wrinkles, her blond hair drawn back and bound.

"This is Elizabeth Brooke, the artist and writer," he said. "Perhaps you've read—"

"We've met," Fisher said. "How are you, Elizabeth?"

She smiled.

"Fine, for a change. And yourself?"

Her accent was British, her ring was expensive. She rose, crossed to Fisher and embraced him lightly.

"Good to see you again," she said. "We worked together several years ago," she told Tedders. "I'm glad you could get him."

"So am I," Tedders said. "And this is Mercy Spender. . . ."

Fisher moved to the heavyset woman with puffy features and watery eyes, a red spiderweb design beneath the skin of her nose. She wiped her hand before clasping his. Her eyes darted.

"Mercy . . ."

"Hello."

". . . And this is Alex Mancin. He works for the World Stock Exchange."

Alex was short and plump, with a boyish face beneath graying hair. His eyes were steady, though, and there was a look of depth to them.

"Glad to meet you, Mr. Fisher."

"Call me Charles."

"Glad to meet you, Charles."

". . . And this is James MacKenzie Ironbear, a satellite engineer," Tedders said, moving on.

"Jim."

"Dave."

James Ironbear was of middle height, solidly built, with long black hair, dark eyes and a dark complexion. His hands were large and strong-looking.

"We've worked together, too," he said. "How've you been, Charles?"

"Busy. I'll tell you all about it later."

"And this," Tedders gestured toward the large smiling man with narrow pale eyes who stood beside the bar, a drink in one hand, "this is Walter Sands. He plays cards, and things like that."

Fisher raised his eyebrows, then nodded.

"Mr. Sands . . ."

"Mr. Fisher."

". . . And so we are gathered," Tedders said. "Everyone else has reviewed the chips."

"I have, too," Fisher said.

"Well, everyone else has an opinion. Do *you* think you'll be able to detect the approach of the Stragean adept?"

"I'm not sure," Fisher replied, "when it comes to an alien with some sort of training."

"That's what everyone else said. May I offer you a drink?"

"Actually, I'd like some food. I came from a different time zone. Haven't had a chance at dinner yet."

"Surely."

Tedders moved to an intercom and pressed a button, ordered a tray.

"They'll serve it on the second floor," he said. "I suggest we all head upstairs and work things out there. It may be a bit more . . . removed . . . from any action that might occur. So if anyone wants to take a drink along, better get it now."

"I'll have a gin and tonic," Mercy said, rising.

"Wouldn't you rather have a cup of tea?" Elizabeth asked her. "It's very good."

"No. I'd rather have a gin and tonic."

She moved off to the bar and prepared herself a large drink. Elizabeth and Tedders exchanged glances. He shrugged.

"I know what you're thinking," Mercy said, her broad back still toward them, "but you're wrong."

Walter Sands, standing beside her, grinned and then turned away.

Tedders led them from the room, and they followed him up a wide staircase.

It was a front room to which he conducted them. There was a large table at its center, a small piece of equipment on it. A half-dozen comfortable-looking chairs were placed around the table; there was a couch to the left and four smaller tables near the walls, left and right. Three trip-boxes capable of accommodating a pair of people each had been installed along the rear wall. Tedders halted in the doorway and gestured along a cross-corridor.

"Charles," he said, "your bedroom is the second door to the left up that way."

He turned back.

"Make yourselves comfortable, everyone. This is where you will be working. We should have two people in here at all times, listening for the alien while the others rest. You can pair off as you wish and make up your own duty roster. That small unit on the table is an alarm. Slap the button and irritating buzzers will go off all over the place. If you are in your rooms and you hear it, wake up fast and get over here. You can use the trip-boxes to get out if all else fails—"

"Wait a minute," Alex Mancin said. "All of this is of course essential, but you've just raised a question that's been bothering me and probably the others, too. Namely, how far does our responsibility here extend? Say we detect the alien and give the alarm. What then? I'm a telepath, but I can also transmit thoughts to others—even nontelepaths. Perhaps I could broadcast confusing images and downbeat emotions to this creature. Maybe the others can do other things. I don't know. Are we supposed to try?"

"A good point," Walter Sands said. "I can influence the fall of dice. I might be able to affect someone's optic nerves. In fact, I know I can. I could leave a person temporarily blind. Should I try something like that—or do we just leave the defense to the tough guys once the enemy is in sight?"

"We can't ask you to jeopardize your lives," Tedders replied. "On the other hand, it would be a great help if you could manage something along those lines. I'm going to have to leave that part to your discretion. But the more you can do, the better, even if it is only a parting shot."

"Charles and I once combined the force of our thinking to pass a message under very trying circumstances," Elizabeth said. "I wonder what would happen if all of us attempted it and directed the results against the alien?"

"I guess that's for you to work out," Tedders said. "But if you're going to try it, don't just blast away at anything indiscriminately. We may have outside help."

"We will learn quickly to recognize the guards if we haven't already done so," Sands said.

"But you may occasionally pick up the thoughts of someone who is not one of the guards," Tedders stated. "I don't want you trying to fry his frontal lobes just because he seems a little different."

"What do you mean? Who is it?" Mercy inquired. "I think you'd better explain."

"His name is William Blackhorse Singer, and he's a Navajo Indian tracker," Tedders replied. "He's on our side."

"Is that the guy who practically filled that Interstellar zoo out in California?" James Ironbear asked.

"Yes."

"What, specifically, will he be up to?"

"I'm not certain. But he says he's going to help."

They all stared at Tedders.

"Why don't you know?" Fisher said.

"He thinks the alien might be a telepath, too. He doesn't want to risk her learning his plans from us. And he thinks he might be able to block a telepath, at least part of the time."

"How?" Sands asked.

"Something to do with thinking in a primitive fashion. I didn't understand it all."

"The Startracker," Ironbear said. "I read about him when I was a kid."

"He a relative or something?" Fisher asked, moving toward a chair and seating himself.

Ironbear shook his head.

"My father was a Sioux from Montana. He's a Navajo from Arizona or New Mexico. No way. I wonder how you think primitive?"

A man carrying a tray came up the hall. Tedders nodded toward Fisher as he brought it into the room. It was delivered and uncovered. Fisher began his meal. Ironbear seated himself across from him. Elizabeth drew out the chair to Fisher's right, Sands the one to his left. Mancin and Mercy Spender seated themselves with Ironbear.

"Thank you," Mancin said. "We are going to have to discuss this now."

"You will have no objections if I record your discussion?" Tedders said. "For later reference."

Sands smiled and an olive left Fisher's salad and drifted toward his hand.

"If you have a machine capable of recording our deliberations I would be very surprised," Mancin said.

"Oh. In that case, I guess there is no reason for me to remain here. When should I check back with you?"

"In about an hour," Mancin said.

"And could you send up a large pot of coffee and some cups?" Ironbear asked.

"And some tea," Elizabeth said.

"I'll do that."

"Thanks."

Tedders moved toward the door.

Mercy Spender looked at her empty glass, began to say something and changed her mind. Elizabeth sighed. Sands chewed the olive. Ironbear cracked his knuckles. No one spoke.

"It is said that you Papagos have songs of power which give you control over all things."

"So it is said."

"Is it not true?"

"We have no control over the minerals beneath our land."

"Why is this?"

"We are not Navajos."

"I do not understand."

"The Navajos have a treaty with the government which gives them these rights."

"And you do not?"

"To have a treaty with the government you must first have made war upon it. We never looked ahead to see its benefits and we remained at peace. A treaty beats a song of power."

"You make it sound like a card game."

"The Navajos cheat at cards, too."

*   *   *

"Coyote, you learned the secret of the floating-water place. You kidnapped the child of Water Monster whom you found there. As a result of your tampering with these forces you have unleashed floods, disasters, upheavals of nature. These have led to death, disorder and madness among the People. Why did you do it?"

"Just for laughs."

*   *   *

"I understand that Begochidi-woman, Begochidi, Talking-god and Black-god created the game animals, and so they have control over the hunt?"

"Yes. They can help a hunter if they wish."

"But you no longer hunt as much as you used to."

"This is true."

"Then they have less work these days."

"I imagine they find ways to keep busy."

"But, I mean, are these the full parameters of their functions as totemic beings within the context of your present tribal structure?"

"What do you mean?"

"Is that all they do?"

"No. They also revenge their people upon anthropologists who tell lies about us."

In the center of my house of yellow corn I stand,
     and I say this: I am Black-god who speaks to you.
I come and stand below the north. I say this:
Down from the top of Darkness Mountain which lies
     before me a crystal doe stands up and comes to me.
Hooftip to kneetip, body to face, followed by
     game of all kinds,
it walks into my hand. When I call to it, when I pray
     for it, it comes to me, followed by game of all kinds.
I am Black-god who speaks to you. I stand below
     the north.
They come to me out of Darkness Mountain.

Mercy Spender,

born at an illegal distillery in Tennessee,
orphaned at the age of 5,

raised by an eccentrically religious aunt on her mother's side
    & her deputy sheriff husband,
    who was taciturn & mustachioed,
    liked bowling & fishing
    & sang in a barbershop quartet.
along with two older girls
    & a boy who raped her at age 11, Jim,
    now a real estate appraiser,
lost any desire for further education at age 12,
sang in the church choir
& later in a bar called Trixie's,
had a series of tediously similar love affairs,
began drinking heavily at age 19,
discovered the joys of the Spiritualist Church at age 20,
    where her peculiar abilities blossomed
    shortly before her commitment
    to a drying-out sanatorium in South Carolina,
    where she found peace
    in the shelter of the therapeutic community, spent the
        following 12 years singing, playing the organ,
giving readings & comfort at the Church
& drinking & returning to the therapeutic community
for peace & shelter & drying out,
& singing & comforting & supporting & reading
& drying out &

            we understand, sister, rest with us,
                the same under skin, all

Alex Mancin,

born in New Bedford,
passed through a number of private schools,
doing well without trying hard,
mastering the complicated computer World
    Economy game model by age 11,
J.D., Yale, M.B.A., Harvard Business School,
passing through three marriages,
doing less well without trying any harder, by age 36
father of two sons (twins) & three daughters
    for whom he feels as much affection
    as he has ever felt for anyone,
aware of everyone's opinion about him
    because of his strange sensitivity to thoughts
    & not really caring a bit,
passionately devoted to a kennelful of Italian greyhounds,
    like Frederick the Great, whom he also admires,
    & far more concerned about canine thought-processes
    than those of people,
an absolute master of the money market,
rich as Croesus,
slow to anger & very slow to forgive,
greatly concerned about his appearance & dress,
wondering occasionally whether there is something he
    is missing,
seeking—every two or three years (unsatisfactorily)—
        for omitted fulfillments
        in orgies of high cultural immersion
        & passing love affairs

with very young women,
highly intelligent & partially numb

> *a piece of everyone,*
> *none of us complete, brother,*
> *save when together,*
> *like this*

Charles Dickens Fisher,

born in Toronto of a physician father & sociologist mother,
became fascinated by illusion at an early age,
put on magic shows for his sisters, Peg & Beth,
was a good student though not an outstanding
    one,
read the lives of the great illusionists,
    Houdin, Thurston, Blackstone,
      Dunninger, Houdini, Henning,
learned that he could cast illusions himself
    with no other equipment
    than strong thoughts,
left school & became an entertainer
against his parents' wishes, grew famous as an in-person
    showman
        (his illusions would not televise),
was later approached by the government
    on the basis of an uncanny mentalist act
    he subsequently tried,
has since done considerable security work
both in & out of government,
        never married, always maintaining

that the life he leads is too demanding
of his time & energy,
that he will not change
& that he will not be unfair
by subjecting another person
to confinement in a pigeonhole
in his schedule,
is actually afraid to commit himself
too strongly to another human being
or to give up the emotions
of audience attention he feeds upon,
possesses the compassion of a full empath,
has a few good friends & many acquaintances,
is aware of his deficiencies
& mocks himself often,
tends to grow maudlin around the holidays,
still dotes on his sisters & their children,
has never been fully reconciled with his parents,
sometimes hates himself for disappointing

but here we are
what we are,
& knowing it all,
there is shelter
& pain drains away

Walter Sands,

left home when he was 14,
    after blinding the stepfather who beat him,
knowing he had the power & could make his way,

big for his age,
won most fights
   (with a little help from the power)
& most games of chance
   (ditto),
seldom held a real job,
   save as a kind of cover,
enlisted in the Perimeter Patrol at age 18—
   the international Coast Guard-like space service—
   for a 4-year hitch
   because he wanted to see
   what was Out There,
was well-liked,
could have become an officer if he'd cared to stay,
didn't, though,
   because he'd seen what he'd joined to see
   & that was enough,
grew darkly handsome,
avoided close emotional involvements
   though he liked people,
   singly & in groups,
except once,
married at 28, divorced at 30,
   one daughter, now 16, Susannah,
   whose picture he carries,
   & that was enough,
likes spectator sports, travel & historical novels,
seldom overindulges in anything,
is totally irreligious,
   but prides himself on a personal code involving honor,

which he has only violated 6 or 7 times
and always felt bad about
afterwards,
is normally trustworthy but seldom trusts,
    having seen the insides
    of too many heads,
suffers, if anything,
    from a feeling that life is
    & always will be
too secure & bland a thing for him,
which is why he enjoys vicarious risks,
which usually turn into sure things,
leaving him vaguely dissatisfied

> *this one may prove*
> *more interesting,*
> *fortunate brother,*
> *if not peace*
> *then adrenalin*
> *to you*

Elizabeth Brooke,

daughter of Thomas C. Brooke, painter, sculptor,
    & Mary Manning, concert pianist, author,
younger of two daughters,
showed artistic & literary aptitudes in early childhood,
vacationed with her family every summer
    in France, Ireland
    or Luna City,
schooled in Switzerland & Peking,

married Arthur Brooke (first cousin) at age 24,
widowed at age 25,
no children,
lost herself in social work
   on Earth & off
   for the following 6 years
   where her unfolding talent
   was both her joy & her grief,
returned to writing & painting,
   exhibiting extraordinary perceptive powers,
   understanding of the human spirit
   & technical abilities,
has enjoyed a liaison with a high-ranking
   MP for the past 6 years,
has always felt partly responsible for Arthur's death
   because of a series
   of bitter confrontations
   following her discovery of his homosexuality

> *we hold you, sister,*
> *against the*
> *unchanging past*
> *in warmth*
> *& full understanding*

James MacKenzie Ironbear,

half Scot, half Oglala Sioux,
born on reservation land,
parents separated early,
raised by his mother in Bloomington, Indiana,

& Edinburgh, Scotland,
   where she worked for the universities'
   custodial staffs,
displayed high mechanical aptitudes
   & telepathic abilities
   before age 5,
seldom visited relatives on his father's side,
first-class baseball & soccer player,
could have gone professional
   but preferred the engineering
   he pursued
   on his athletic scholarship,
his best friend an Eskimo boy from Point Barrow,
   they spent their summers together in Alaska during
     their college careers
   as rangers in Gateway to the Arctic
   National Park,
fathered one son, now in his teens
   & living in Anchorage,
later served in Perimeter Patrol
   where his telepathic ability
   came to the attention
   of government authorities,
was recruited for occasional. work
   of the sort Charles Fisher
   did for them,
   which is where he met Fisher,
   becoming friends with him,
has since fulfilled 5 separate
   one-year contracts in space engineering,

working half of the year in orbit,
is on leave of absence from his sixth,
   pending divorce from Fisher's sister, Peg,
   who works for the same company
   & resides in the great tube
   of Port O'Neill
   with their daughter Pamela,
attended his father's funeral this past summer
   & was surprised to find himself deeply saddened
   that he had never known the man,
had suddenly decided to chuck everything
   & study music,
   an enterprise commenced
   when he sobered up a month later
   & followed diligently
   until this call came in,
finding himself thinking more & more
   of his shrunken father,
   lying there in a beaded leather jacket,
   & of the son
   he has not seen in years

> *come close, brother,*
> *where we who*
> *are greater than one*
> *hold greater understanding,*
> *absorb more hurt*

It is good that you wish to walk in beauty, with beauty all around you, my son. But a hunter should not speak prayers from the Blessingway during the hunt, for they all have the life blessing at the end and you require a prayer of death. To Talking-god must you speak, and to Black-god: Aya-na-ya-ya! Eh-eh-eh! Here is the time of the cutting of the throat! Na-eh-ya-ya! It happens in a holy place, the cutting of the throat! Ay-ah, na-ya-ya! The cutting of the throat is happening now in a holy place! Na-ya-ya! It is the time of the cutting of the throat! Ya-eh-ni-ya!

"It is not always life that must be blessed."

Night. He stands before the force wall. He watches the rock unfold itself.

There are clouds in your mind, hunter.

There are many things in my mind, Cat.

You have come. Have we a bargain?

Do as I asked you and I will do as you asked me.

We have a bargain. Release me.

It will take a minute or so.

The form rose to become a white pillar, the single, faceted eye drifting upward along it. Billy Singer moved to the area where the controls were housed. He opened the case and lowered the potential of the field.

The base of the pillar split and forelimbs disassociated themselves from the main mass higher up. A bulbous protuberance grew at the top, the eye coming to rest at its center. The forked segments became leglike. A tightening at the middle was suddenly a narrow waist. The head elongated, growing vaguely lupine. The shoulders widened, the arms and legs thickened. Excess mass was shifted behind, becoming a broad tail. The manlike thing was tall, over two meters, and it darkened as it moved forward, exhibiting a grace which suggested earlier rehearsal of the form.

Silent for all of its bulk, it removed itself from the enclosure and went to stand before the man.

I suggest you restore the force screen. That way it could be several days before they notice my absence. I have accustomed them to such a situation by assuming the appearance of portions of the habitat for days at a time.

I had already thought of that, Billy replied. *But first I wanted to watch you change.*

You were impressed?

Yes. You do it quickly, he said in his mind, turning the field on again. *Come. I'll take you to a trip-box now. You will have to charge it to my number without my card—which will require a confirmation by me from the other end, since I'll have to pass through first and—*

I know how they work. I have had little but the thoughts of your fellows to full me for a long while.

Come, then.

Billy turned away and moved across the hall.

You show me your back. Do you not fear that I will leap upon you and rend you? Or is your action calculated?

I feel you wish to encounter the Stragean. Kill me now and the opportunity will be lost to you.

A shadow as silent as himself—somewhat more manlike than moments earlier, and hence more alien—came abreast of him to the left. It matched his pace, the movements of his arms, all of his rhythms. He could feel its power as they glided through the hall. Inhabitants of the enclosures they passed shifted uneasily, whether in sleep or full wakefulness.

Billy felt a touch of amusement in the alien mind at his side—and then a broadcast *Farewell!* which roused the creatures to frantic activity.

He led the way outside, where he breathed deeply of the night air. The creature at his side dropped to all fours, then moved away, sliding into and out of shadows from unsuspected directions as they advanced.

From somewhere up ahead, a dog began to bark—a sound terminated in midnote to the accompaniment of a brief thrashing noise. Billy did not change his pace, knowing by senses other than sight that Cat was with him all the way to the trip-box.

All right, he said. *I'll key the thing. I will go through to a small public box a few miles from the place we will be guarding. If there is any reason at that end for you not to come through, I will use the communicator. Otherwise, be ready to follow me.*

A piece of shadow came loose nearby and drifted toward him. It was even more manlike in proportion now and had fabricated what could have been a long black cloak out of its own substance. The massive, faceted eye was deeply submerged within its head and masked by connective tissues in such a fashion as to give the impression of a pair of glittering, normally placed eyes.

On second thought, Billy said when he looked at him, *I believe you could pass even if there is someone there.*

I see the direction of your thoughts, if dimly. I will formulate something to resemble darkened glasses and muster something nearer to human skin-coloration. Why are your thoughts so clouded?

I am practicing to deceive our enemy, Billy replied, entering the box. *I will see you soon.*

Yes. I cannot be lost so easily, tracker.

He watched Billy manipulate the controls and fade within the enclosure. Then he entered there himself. Extending what had become his right hand, he covered the slot where Billy had briefly inserted his credit slip. A portion of that appendage flowed into the opening and explored there for a time. When the call came through, he withdrew it and allowed himself to be transported.

Strange, a singing in his mind. Was there something in the places between the places, to sing so of frost and iron, fire and darkness? In a moment, it and its memory were gone.

> *Between the worlds walking.*
> *Between the worlds walking.*
> *Between the worlds walking.*
> *Between the worlds walking.*
> *There is something*
> *Before me, behind me,*
> *to right and to left,*
> *above and below.*
> *What, on all sides,*
> *is it?*

Alex Mancin hit the button when he detected the presence, a moment before Walter Sands's hand jerked in the same direction. Buzzing sounds filled the house and light flooded the lawns about it.

Yes

Mercy Spender joined them a moment later,
sitting up in her bed
    I can feel them
        Them?

joined Fisher, putting down his book
      There is only one
  A man

Ironbear joined, from sleep
moving strangely
nearby
Singer
no doubt
  No man

joined Elizabeth, chasing dreams of dolphins
Something else
thing filled with hate
flowing
Together then

Sands joined
  let us explore this
      Yes

      together we move
  There is a man
    fading now
and something else
alien thing
  aware of us
    fading also
with the man

the thing is not the thing
we seek

it hunts
with the man

our common enemy

retreating now

it sensed us

we know its signature

Shall we follow?

turn off the alarm
the guards come
we must report

I will follow

went Mercy, departing

the beast
if I can

and I the man

moved Ironbear away

though the trail
I fear
is covered now

apart break we then

we will report

Mancin and Sands, dividing

The following day, within a stand of trees about forty
meters from the road, Billy Singer sat beside an icy stream,
his back against a large, warm rock. He was eating a roast
beef sandwich, watching the flight of birds, listening to the
wind and observing the behavior of a small squirrel in the

lower branches of a tree upstream, to his right.

Something hunts nearby, the other told him.

Yes, I know, he answered in thought.

Something large.

I know that, too.

It comes this way.

Yes. What is it?

I cannot tell. Come inside. We will observe.

Billy rose silently to his feet. The rock split down the middle vertically and opened like an upended clam. Even as he watched, the cavity within grew large, outside surfaces swelling proportionately. He entered, and it closed about him.

Darkness, pierced by a few small holes, forward . . .

He placed his eye against one. He was facing the stream. For a time, nothing happened. Several more apertures appeared before him, but the section he regarded remained unchanged.

Then he heard the splashing sounds. Something was approaching from beyond the shrub-lined bend. His stream of consciousness fell still. His was now the passive eye of the hunter, discerning everything before it without reflection. His breathing slowed even further. Time ceased to exist. Now . . .

First, a shadow. Then, slowly, the branched head appeared from beyond the bend. A deer, browsing along the stream bed . . .

Yet . . .

It moved again, forward, the rest of its body coming into view. There was something wrong with the way that it moved and held its head. The legs did not bend in quite the proper fashion. And the shape of the head was unusual. The cranium rose too high above the eyes. . . .

Deerlike . . . Yes. A good approximation, perhaps, for someone who had only studied tridees of the creature. No doubt close enough to deceive any casual observer. But to Billy it could only be deerlike. He wondered whether Cat realized this, too.

. . . *Yes* drifted through his mind.

Immediately, the creature before them froze, one less-than-delicate forelimb raised. Then the head turned, moving through unnatural angles to survey everything at hand.

Moments later, the creature exploded into movement, the entire body twisting, elongating, legs thickening, shortening, bunching.

And then it sprang off, back in the direction from which it had come.

Even as this occurred his shelter opened, regurgitating him with some force, and by the time Billy had regained his footing Cat was in the process of transformation back into the form of the hunting beast.

Not waiting for the metamorphosis to run its course, Billy ran in the direction the creature had taken, splashing into the stream and following it beyond the bend.

His eyes scanned both banks, but he discerned no signs that it had departed the water at either hand. He splashed onward, over gravel, sand and slick rocks, continuing his surveillance.

For a long while, he followed the twisting, watery route. But he heard no further sounds from ahead, nor could he detect any evidence of the creature's having departed the stream. He halted at a rocky shingle to study it with extra care. As he did, he heard sounds of approach from the rear.

Farther ahead! Farther ahead! Cat told him. *I've touched her mind. It slips away. But she betrays herself occasionally.*

He turned and raced ahead. Cat bounded past him.

Something is happening. She is shifting again. She is up high somewhere now. She—Lost her . . .

Billy continued his advance along the watery way. Cat hurried on ahead and was lost moments later beyond the screening brush. After perhaps five minutes, Billy found what he had been seeking.

There was sign of something having left the water. He followed it up and to the right. The first clear print he located, however, was a peculiar, triple-pronged thing. But it was sufficiently large, and its depth in soil of that consistency was indication of the sort of mass that he knew he followed. The spoor led him off toward higher ground, and the next clear print he came upon showed a further alteration of shape.

And he came across the even fresher signs of Cat, still on the trail. Cat's tracks were far apart and deeply sunk.

The way remained clear and he was able to increase his pace. Moving at a very fast walk, uphill, down, then up again, he felt the old tingling sensation as the quarry's track vanished, to reappear forty feet away, lighter, slightly reshaped, and then to vanish again. Pictures occurred within his mind, his natural ability to form them enhanced by his alien experiences. He read the sign correctly, and he looked upward in time to see a vast, dark shape glide overhead, moving in a southwesterly direction. And even as he hurried to climb a tree, he knew that, for the moment, the quarry had won.

He achieved a suitable vantage only in time to see the dark thing slip out of sight beyond a distant tree-line.

. . . *How clever!* Cat's thought came to him. *I wonder whether I could do that?*

At least it was not headed toward the mansion, Billy said. *We had best return to our post, though.*

You go, Cat replied. *I am going to try following her. I will meet you there later.*

Very well.

Before he climbed down he noted through an opening in the leaves an area above him that had been blackened and broken. It had not been a recent thing, but he shuddered at one of the old superstitions reaching out for him at this time. Of all the trees present, he had chosen a lightning-struck one to climb. Thing of ill-fortune. . . He sang a section from the Blessingway as he descended. The part of him which did not fear the lightning was standing far away now, clad in different garments.

How much had the Stragean learned of what it was that pursued her? Cat, keep your presence of mind, he thought. Do not betray yourself in the fury of the hunt. Or are your instincts proof even against one such as you follow?

He reached the ground and turned back. What would Nayenezgani have done?

He did not know.

*   *   *

Sun come down the sky from straight to slant again drifting waterwards gaze of Billy's mind with it to flow time undoing knots touch of cloud to dark the sky as hand with knowledge of own scoops among sands at shore blue gray white yellow no red no real black no matter bird above hunkered form of man on tree limb singing leaves shifting in wind fish in water decomposable soda bottle decomposing across the riverrun.

Without thought, dipping his hands. A pinch of sand in the right palm, beneath the second finger. Hand turning. A trickle from the index finger, thumb regulating its flow. Movement. The hand has not forgotten. The lines. The angles. Blue and white and yellow here. *Náa-tse-elit*, the Rainbow *yei* taking form, guarding the south, the west and the north, open to the east. Within, the body of Thunder, *Ikne'etso*, a bat guardian above his head, messenger of the Night, east, an arrow, *ash-tin*, west. A great power here. One of the unpredictable, dangerous gods. Holder of lightning. Humming to himself, pieces of the Mountain Chant, finishing, staring, Billy. For a long time, staring.

Slowly, the awareness. A peculiar thing to have done. Consciously or automatically. Of all things to call upon, why Thunder? For that matter, why call at all? However things fell out, he would be the loser. Yet he reached forward to touch *ikne'eka'a*, the lightning, to transfer the medicine and the power, since it was there before him.

And now . . . A day sandpainting must be erased before the sun sets. With a sacred feather staff it is to be erased. He recalled the black feather in the tchah and withdrew it and used it to this end, casting the sand away into the water.

> *Sun go down the sky rolling west*
> *Time undoing knots*
> *No real color*
> Ikne'etso *and* Naa-tse-elit *into the riverrun*

> *recirculation*

Singing now. Billy Blackhorse Singer. At the corner of the estate. Night. Spring constellations filling the heavens. Coyote cries faded.

They had located her again at evening, circling, circling at a great distance, probing, carefully advancing. They had waited.

She had come, slowly, in many guises. Skimming, burrowing, flowing. They had waited. And when the night was complete, she came on.

One moment Cat had been at his back, dark stony buttress to the wall itself. Then a huge shape had drifted overhead, blotting stars. The buttress had flowed upward, coalescing into a nightmare outline atop the wall. Then a second dark shape rode the air currents, sought altitude, circled, slid through the night toward the house.

He was never certain at what point the encounter occurred and the struggle commenced, whether it was in the air, on the ground, outside the house or within. But he heard a series of unearthly cries at about the same time that the lights came on all over the grounds. He remained unmoving in his shadowy corner, listening to the various sounds which ensued—crashes, buzzes, the breaking of glass, several small explosions. These continued for nearly a minute before all of the lights went out.

And he waited. He could think of nothing for which he might hope. He remembered things, and he sang the song softly.

Then the silence came again. He regarded the sky as the moment stretched. His words neither hurried nor slowed in their passage across the night.

A single loud crash occurred, followed by some lesser sounds. Then again the silence. A small light appeared behind a pair of upstairs windows.

Cat?

A large form emerged from the front of the house, dropped to all fours, moved slowly away. Nothing moved to interfere with it. The night remained quiet. Billy followed its progress with his eyes. He knew that it was time for the song to end. He carried a knife and a computer-targeting laser sidearm. If this were the Stragean, he felt obliged to attempt her destruction. He drew the weapon and placed his thumb on the set stud.

This is how you keep your promise, hunter?

Cat!

Yes. She fought well but she is dead. I have broken her. Shall we see now whether you can activate the weapon before I can reach you? Ten meters separate us and I am ready to spring. The weapon is faster than I am, but is your thumb? I will know the moment that you decide to move it. Go ahead. Any time now . . .

No.

Billy tossed the weapon into the shrubbery to his right.

I did not know which of you it was moving this way.

He detected a sense of puzzlement, underlined by a touch of pain.

You were injured?

It is nothing.

Both remained unmoving.

Finally, *As you said, any time now,* Billy stated.

You offer me no contest.

No.

Why not? You are a predator, like me.

We have a bargain.

What is that when it is your life? I expected resistance.

Cat detected something like puzzlement.

I made you a promise.

But I took it to mean that you would await my attack here and defend yourself when the time came.

I am sorry. That was not my understanding. But now I have no intention of giving you a token fight. You require my life. Take it.

Cat began a slow advance, his form dropping nearer and nearer to the ground. When he raised his head once more it bore an enormous, horned, fanged, semihuman face—a bestial parody of Billy's own. Suddenly then, Cat reared, to raise that head fully eight feet above the ground. He glared down.

Billy shuddered, but he held his place.

You are taking much of the pleasure from it, hunter.

Billy shrugged.

That cannot be helped.

Cat began to unfurl great membranous wings behind him. After a time, he folded them about himself and became a still, dark pillar.

Finally, *If you can make it over the wall before I reach you,* Cat said, *I will let you go.*

Billy did not move.

No, he said. *I know that I could not do it. I will not make the attempt just to provide you with sport.*

The pillar blossomed, an exotic flower opening to reveal a tigerlike head. It swayed toward him.

You pursued me for over a week, Cat said at last. *While I have dreamed of your death, I have dreamed, too, of hunting you. Your death alone should be sufficient, but I do not want it to be over with in an instant. It troubles me, too, that I do not know whether this desire springs from that which I know best—the hunt—or whether my long mental association with your own kind has taught me somewhat of the joys of prolonging an enemy's agony.*

Both are sufficiently primitive, Billy replied. *I wouldn't worry about it.*

I do not. But I desire the hunt, and I see now that only one thing will make you give it to me.

And what is that?

Your life. A chance to regain it.

Billy laughed.

I have already resigned myself to dying. Do you believe yourself the only misfit alien on this world, Cat? My people—my real people—are also dead. All of them. The world in which I now find myself is a strange place. The Dineh are not as I once knew them. Your offer only brought my condition into full focus. And I have prepared myself for this.

Cat drew back.

Years ago, he said, *I saw in your mind a great pride in your people's ability to adapt. Now you say that it is gone from you. I say this means that you have become a coward, seeing death as the easy way out.*

Billy stiffened.

That is not true!

Look within yourself. I have but given you an excuse to resign.

No!

Then fight me, Billy. Pit your skills against me one more time.

I—

You are afraid now, where you were not before. You are afraid to live.

That is not so.

Would you say it four times, man of the People?

Damn you, Cat! I was ready, ready for you! But you are not satisfied with just my life. You wish to fill me with uncertainty before you kill me!

If that is what it takes, yes. I see now that there would be small pleasure in slaying you like some brainless piece of meat that waits to be slaughtered. My full revenge requires the joy of the hunt. So I will make you an offer, and I will have you know that my promise will be as good as yours, Billy Singer—for I cannot let you beat me even in that thing. Go. Flee. Cover your trail, tracker. I will give you what I judge to be an hour —and I am fairly good at estimating time—and then I will pursue you. You tracked me for nearly eight days. Let us call it a week. Keep alive for that long and I will renounce my claim upon your life. We will go our ways, free of one another.

And what will be the rules? Billy asked.

Rules? If you can kill me before I kill you, by all means do so. In any manner. Go anywhere that you wish by any means that you choose. Anything is fair. There are no rules in the hunt. Live out the week and you will be rid of me. You will not make it, though.

Who can say?

What is your answer?

Billy turned, took several quick steps and leaped, catching hold of the top edge of the wall. He drew himself up in a single, swinging motion.

Start counting, he said, as he dropped down onto the other side and broke into a run.

Cat's laughter followed him for over a minute.

PART II

Things that flee and things that pursue
have their seasons.
Each of us hunts
and each of us is hunted.
We are all of us prey;
we are all predators.
Knowing this, the careful hunter
is wary. The prey, too, learns boldness
beyond its normal reach.
And then there is luck,
and then the gods.
The hunt is always uncertain.

We skinned the wolf
and in the morning
a human hide hung there.
At night, it became again
the pelt of a wolf.

There is no certainty,
there is no law
in the hunt.

Talking-god be with me.
Black-god be with me.
Luck and boldness
be with me, too.

The First Day

Without slowing, he illuminated the dial of his watch and checked the time. An hour. He smiled, because it seemed that Cat had overlooked the obvious. He could get far in that time, and all was fair. . . .

He maintained the steady pace which he could keep up for most of a day. To give in to fears and sprint now would be to leave himself exhausted in the face of possibly necessary exertions later.

The wind whipped by him, and deeper patches of shadows took on an ominous character, hiding eyes, fangs, movement. . . .

Dead. The Stragean was dead. A being able to cause fear in the highest circles. Dead. And Cat had slain her. Soon Cat would be bounding along, coming this same way. Cat's enormous, faceted eye could, he believed, see into the infrared, distinguish polarized light. He was still not certain as to all of the senses Cat possessed. He could see Cat now, like a giant *chindi*, not even slowing as he followed the trail.

Beads of perspiration formed on Billy's brow. A part of him saw the beast's powers from a completely rational standpoint. He had fought Cat before when Cat was much more naive. But Cat had had fifty years in which to become sophisticated in the ways of this world. Cat suddenly became phantomlike at another level, no longer the —beast that had been, but something returning, as from the north. . . .

He fought back a renewed desire to increase his pace. There was ample time, he told himself, a sufficiency in which to make good his getaway. And why should there be fear? Bare minutes ago he had been ready to die. Now at least there was a chance. He strove to contain himself within the present instant. The past was gone. He had some say in the making of the future, but this was contingent upon his behavior now. It was going to be all right. Long before the hour had run out, he would be totally safe. It was only a matter of minutes, really. . . .

He jogged on, his mind fixed upon his goal. At last it came into sight, the trip-box station which would place him beyond Cat's reach in the barest twinkling. He saw the lights of the small building at the crossroads beyond the field he was now entering. Something about it, though . . .

As he moved nearer, he realized that the front window of the place was broken. He slowed his approach. He could see no one about.

He halted and looked inside. There were three units, lined against the far wall. All of them were wrecked. It was as if a piece of runaway heavy equipment had passed through, snapping or twisting the gleaming standards, upsetting the control units. The power banks, he noted, were untouched.

Cat . . .

That last time Cat had gone out, ranging far to scout the area . . . Cat had foreseen a possible escape on his part with flight in this direction, had acted to remedy this means of retreat.

He looked about. The damage should have registered itself at the area control center. But the hour was late. No telling when a repair crew might be by.

A map. There would be a line map inside for the area. He moved to the doorway and entered.

Yes. On the wall to his right. He studied the disposition of the red dots representing boxes in the area, located his own position, looked for the next several.

Four miles to the nearest one.

Would Cat know its location? Would Cat have bothered to look at this thing on the wall, realizing it was a map? And even if this were the case, would Cat have gone to the trouble to wreck another? True, he might have wanted to cover all bets. . . .

But no. Cat's surprise at his failure to flee had seemed genuine. Cat had expected him to run. While it might be possible for him to elude the beast and make it this far, it seemed unlikely that he could reach the next one under these circumstances. So even if Cat did know about it, chances were that the next box remained unmolested.

Still, a map and the land itself were two different things. He was not exactly certain as to the disposition of that next red dot. Even with the grace period, he could be cutting things short.

He departed the wrecked station, took his bearings and recommenced his steady stride, cutting through a skeleton-limbed orchard that rattled about him as he passed. A rabbit sprang from behind a clump of grasses to veer across his path and vanish into the shadows to the left. The grasses were damp, and soon the lower portions of his trousers were soaked through. Somewhere a dog began barking. He suddenly felt as if he were being watched, from no particular direction. Again the fleeting shadows writhed images.

For a moment, he wondered what time it was, and then the desire to know this thing fell away. Abruptly, he found that he was happy. A part of his mind was almost cheering for Cat, hoping that even now the beast was on his trail. Let it be close. Let it be very close and clean, he felt. Or else what the joy in such a context? This was the most alive he had felt himself in years. There was a new song inside him now, accompanied by his drumbeat footfalls.

He did not try to analyze the shifting of his mood. The clutter of circumstance was far too dense for introspection, even had he felt so inclined. For the moment, it was sufficient to ride with the beat of his flight.

There were times when he felt certain that Cat was right at his back, and it did not seem to matter. Other times, he felt that he had already won, that he had far outdistanced his pursuer, that there was no chance of his ever being overtaken. All of his senses now seemed touched with an unusual acuity—the tiniest night movement was instantly identified, from the faintest rasp, thump or crackling; shadowy forms grew far more distinct, and even odors took on a new significance. It had all been this way once, yes, long ago. . . .

It was before everything that the world had been this way, that he had been this way. Running. Into the east. Vision as yet unclouded by veils life was later to drop upon him. He had been eight or nine years old before he had learned to speak English. . . .

But after all of this, he wondered, what traces really remained of his shift from a near-neolithic to a high-tech society? He had lived more years under the latter than under the former, if these things were to be measured solely in years. The shift had been made successfully, and both ends of his personal spectrum were available to him.

But it was the primitive which ruled as he ran. Yes. And this part preferred the day to the night. Yet the joy remained. It was not that there was an absence of fear. Instead, the fear was contributing something to that peculiar species of elation which had risen within him.

As he pounded along, he wondered what the situation was back at the mansion. What had Walford, Tedders, the defenders and the Strageans made of that sudden attack followed by the death of the adept —with no explanation as to what had occurred? Naturally they would suspect his part in it, but they must be puzzled by his absence. Even now they must be trying to reach him—though this time he was not even wearing the paging unit.

Would they ever learn? He wondered for the first time what Cat might do later—if things were all over and he, Billy Singer, had walked into the north. Would Cat retire to some wilderness area and spend his days passing as some garden variety predator? It seemed possible, but he could not be certain. He could not tell whether Cat's hatred was focused upon him solely or whether he might hold all of humanity responsible for his captivity. Images moved within Billy's mind—crouching in a cage day after day, year after year, being stared at by passing knots of people. If their situations had been reversed, he felt that he would hate all mankind.

A sense of irritation began to grow. Why shouldn't Cat consider him a sacrificial lamb and let it go at that?

He shook his head. No real reason for assuming that Cat would run amok later. He had given no such indication. What was he doing thinking these thoughts, anyway? Looking for trouble? It was him that Cat wanted, not him plus everybody else. And after he had gotten him, it would all be over with. .\. .

Sacrificial lamb . . . He thought again of the sheep he had herded as a boy. Long, slow days under skies hot and cool, big skies . . . Lying on a hillside. Whittling. Singing. Foot-races with other children. His first tumble with that girl from over the ridge. What was her name? And later with her sister. Hard breasts under his hands. The sheep about them unconcerned. Clouds like sheep on the horizon. Sheep. Lamb of God. Dora in the sky with turquoise. Running . . .

Cat. Running. How will you track me, Cat? Do you follow the same signs I would? Or does your alien eye trace different marks of passage? Either way, there is no time to mask this trail. Escape first. Hide afterwards. Speed now is all. Speed, opportunity. Chance. How near might you be, anyway? Or are you still waiting for the time to run?

Turquoise in the sky with Dora to the drumbeat footbeat here below. On the hillside, far ahead, lights. Night air comes in, goes out again. Stride is steady. Veer left, beyond the death-shaped boulder. Up then. Cat come. Into the black bag. Full entropy is all. But first.

Minutes melting, one to the other. In the distance, the hum of a super battery-powered vehicle above the cleared trail which had once been a roadway, lights raking tree trunks. Heading for the station perhaps. Ay-ah! We live. Unless Cat even now . . .

Drawing nearer, he slowed. This would be the place for an ambush. Why not check the time? Because Cat might have lied to gain this much of a chase. Once through the box and the beast would be baffled. Wouldn't he?

Walking now, he examined a new proposition. What had Cat said about understanding the boxes?

No. Even if he could black-fare his way, he would not know where to go. . . .

Cat is a telepath.

But of what sort? He had estimated Cat's ability as a hunting/locator thing, refined, to be sure, during his long confinement, but basically quarry-intensive, at about a quarter of a mile. Still, there were human telepaths he knew of who could send and receive around the world and through outer space. Yet, again, such sophisticated ones he felt he could block to some extent by slipping back to boyhood thought patterns. But Cat, too, was primitive. It might not serve to hide him from the beast. In which case.

The devil with you, Cat!—on all fours now, carefully clearing the way before him of anything which might give rise to the slightest sound, his jewelry wrapped in a handkerchief and stuffed into his pocket, hands moving deftly, knees and toes advancing into the cleared area in total silence. *Find me if you can. Fight me if you do.*

No response. And nothing between here and there that

he could conceive of as a transformation of his adversary. The car drew up before the building and hovered. No one departed it.

He was on his feet and sprinting across the final meters of the field, through a fringe of trees, over the road-bed trail. A glimpse through the station window: the units were intact.

Almost laughing, he thrust the door open and crossed the threshold. Empty. Safe. Breathe easily. He straightened from his half-crouch, removed his hand from the handle of his knife. Closed the door. All right. Five paces to liberty.

The unit to his far left was humming in preparation for a transfer. Curious, he watched it. It was an odd hour and a fairly isolated station; he wondered who might be coming through. Shortly, the outline began to form. It was that of a woman, somewhat stocky, with close-cropped brown hair. She wore a dark suit and carried a recording unit bearing the insignia of a major news service in her left hand. Her eyes fixed upon him as she took on solidity.

"Hello," she said, studying his garb.

She stepped out of the unit.

"Hello."

"Coming or going?" she said.

"Just going. I only waited to see if you were someone I knew."

"You're a real Indian, aren't you? Not just someone dressed that way."

"I am. If you called ahead for a car I just saw one pull up out front."

"I did. That must be it." She started forward, then hesitated. "Do you live in this area?" she asked him.

"No. Just visiting."

He moved toward the nearest unit.

"Just a second," she said. "I've come here on a story, or what could be a story. Maybe you'd know something about it."

He forced himself to smile as he took another step. "I doubt that. Haven't seen anything newsworthy."

"Well," she persisted, "there have been reports of peculiar security measures being taken at the Walford place for some time now. Then suddenly this evening there was apparently a power failure and some disturbance. Now they've gone completely incommunicado. Would you know anything about this?"

He shook his head, moved forward and stepped into the unit.

She followed him and took hold of his arm just as he inserted his strip into the slot, effectively blocking his transit.

"Wait. There's more," she said. "Then we learned that the trip-boxes nearest to the place had been damaged. Are you aware that the next station to the east is out of order?"

"Could it be a part of that power failure?"

"No, no. They have their own power packs —the same as Walford's place, for that matter."

He shrugged, hoping her hand would slip away.

"I'm afraid I don't know anything about it. Listen, I'm in a hurry—"

"You haven't seen or heard of anything unusual in this area?"

He noted that her recorder was switched on.

"No," he said. "I've got to be going now—"

"It's just a feeling," she said, "but I think you know something about this."

"Lady," he said, "your car is waiting. Go and see for yourself like a good reporter. I wouldn't hang around here, though."

"Why not?"

"Maybe something will happen to this one, too."

"Why should it?"

"How should I know? But if there's something dangerous going on, you want to be in its path?"

She smiled for the first time.

"If there's a story in it, yes."

He pushed coordinates. "Good luck."

"Not yet," she said, still holding his arm. "Have you been by that way at all?"

"Get out of here," he told her, "in the car, or by one of the other booths. Hurry! This place isn't safe. Don't hang around."

"I'll be damned if I'll let you go now!" she said, reaching toward a penlike device clipped behind her lapel.

"Sorry," he said, and he jerked his arm free and pushed her backward. "Do what I said!" he cried. "Get out!" and the fading began.

When he stepped from a unit in London's Victoria Station, pocketing his strip, he had to restrain himself from running. He drew the back of his hand across his brow and it came away wet.

He headed for the nearest exit. The light of a gray morning shone through it. He was arrested momentarily by the smell of food from a twenty-four-hour diner. Too near, he decided, and he moved on outside.

He passed a line of sightseeing hover-vehicles, another of taxis, their operators nowhere in sight. He continued along the way for a time, turned at random in a vaguely northward direction and left the sidewalk. He followed a footpath among trees leading down what had once been a wide thoroughfare. There were fewer streets now than there had been a hundred or even fifty years before, on the occasions of earlier visits he had made. Some main arteries were kept cropped for freighters and the occasional personal hovercraft, some had become malls, some had simply deteriorated, most had become inner-city wilderness areas, or parks, as he used to call them.

He followed the twisting ways for about half an hour, putting a good distance between himself and the station, as the day continued to lighten about him. Muffled by the trees, the sounds of the awakening city grew. He bore to his right, moving into the fringe area.

Above, beyond the walkway, he scanned the faces of opened and opening establishments. Farther ahead, beyond an archway, off a courtyard, he glimpsed a café's sign. He mounted a stair to the walk and headed in that direction. He was, he judged, somewhere near Piccadilly Circus.

Right at the archway, he froze, overwhelmed by a recurrence of the feeling that he was being observed. He looked about. There were a number of people on the walk and in the courtyard, several of them as distinctively dressed as himself for different parts of the world, but none of them seemed to be paying him particular heed, and none seemed large enough to represent the total mass of his adversary.

Of course, it could be something behind him in the woods. . . .

He did not feel like discarding any sort of warning, even a premonition. So he began walking again, passing the archway. In an alcove near the corner ahead, he could see a trip-box. Giving in to nervousness might be a sign of weakness as well as caution, but there was also much to be said for holding onto as much peace of mind as possible when one was running. He quickened his pace.

As he advanced, he saw that the alcove also contained a police callbox. A jerking of its alarm handle should result in the in-tripping of a bobby within seconds, a setup similar to that in use almost everywhere these days. Not that he could see this as helping him very much if he suddenly discovered Cat at his back. A delaying action, at best. And he would probably be condemning the cop to death by calling him. He moved a little more rapidly. He saw the head of a coyote —no, it was a small dog—appear around the corner of the alcove, looking in his direction. His sense of urgency grew. He fought but could not resist a desire to look back.

When he did, he felt a sudden wave of dizziness. A large man wearing a black cloak and glasses was just emerging from among the trees. Billy broke into a run.

He located and withdrew his credit strip as he raced ahead. He turned it to the proper position for immediate insertion into the machine's slot. A wave of fear washed over him, turning quickly to despair. He was suddenly certain that he could not make it in time. He felt a powerful impulse to halt and wait for his pursuer.

Instead, he plunged into the box, thrust the strip into the slot and rapped out a set of coordinates. Turning then, he saw that the man had dropped to all fours and was racing toward him, changing shape as he came. Someone screamed. Overhead, a dirigible was passing. The entire tableau grew two-dimensional and began to fade. Goodbye, Piccadilly. . . .

Run, hunter, he heard faintly amid his thoughts. *The next time . . .*

He stood in a booth at Victoria Station, shaking. But now it was reaction rather than fear. The fear, the despair, the certainty of doom had vanished at the instant of transport. It was then he realized that Cat must have been projecting these feelings onto him, a slightly more sophisticated version of his old prey-paralysis trick—a thing he had several times felt in its more blatant form years ago. He was startled at the extent to which Cat had developed it since then.

He keyed a chart onto the directory screen and took a new set of coordinates from it. His pursuer might have caught Victoria Station from his thoughts, and—

As he faded, he saw something beginning to take shape two booths up from him, something resembling a tall, cloaked, less-than-human figure still in the process of widening its shoulders and lengthening its forelimbs.

"Damn!"

Yes!

Coming through in Madrid . . . Bright sky through a dirty window. A crowd of commuters. No time . . .

He keyed the directory, hit more coordinates. He looked about as Madrid began to go away. No sign of an incoming torglind metamorph. He began to sigh. Finished sighing at the Gare du Nord box-section in Paris. He summoned the local directory and tripped again.

Walking. Day brighter yet. From the Tuileries Station. Safe now. No way for Cat to have followed this time.

Passing up the Champs-Élysées. Crossing from the fringes of the park over the cyclists' trail and onto the walkway, he smelled the aromas of food from the nearest sidewalk café. He passed several before he settled upon one with a vacant table, close to a trip-box, commanding good views in both directions. He seated himself there and ordered a large breakfast. When he had finished he lingered, drinking countless cups of coffee. Nothing threatening appeared and he felt the flickering beginning of a sense of security. After a time, a feeling of lethargy settled upon him.

Night. It was late morning here, but it was night in the place he had left. He had been a long while without sleep.

He got up and walked again. Should he jump to another city to obscure his trail further? Or had he covered his tracks sufficiently?

He compromised and tripped to the Left Bank. He walked again. He knew that his thinking was foggy. Filled first with the necessities of his flight, his mind was now reduced to slow-motion movement by reaction, by fatigue. It would be easy to obtain a stimulant to restore full alertness, by communication with his medical computer and a request for transmission of a prescription order to a local pharmacist. But he felt relatively safe now, and he would rather rest and restore his natural energies than proceed by artificial means at this stage of affairs. His body might ultimately

prove more important than his mind, his feelings and his re-
flexes surer guides than any elaborate plan. Hadn't he already decided that primitive was best against a dangerous
telepath? Sleep now, pay later, if need be.

He located a hotel called the St. Jacques near the
University. There were several trip-boxes in the neighborhood and one off the lobby. He took a third-floor room there
and stretched out on the bed, fully dressed.

For a long while he stared at the ceiling, unable to sleep.
Images of his recent flight came and went. Gradually,
however, other images intruded, none of them pieces of recent things. He drifted with them, his breathing slowing, and
finally they bore him off.

. . . Watching Dora before the video console, summoning
up swarms of equations, fingers moving across the keyboard
as his mother's had across the loom, introducing new variables, weaving the fresh patterns that resulted. He did not
understand. But it did not matter. Her hair long and blond,
her eyes very pale. He had met her on his return from a long
expedition, when the Institute had sent him back to school
for an update on astrophysical theory and improved naviga-
tional techniques. She had taught mathematics there. . . . The
equations turn to sandpaintings and finally to skulls, animal
as well as human. Dora is smiling. Dimly he remembers that
she is dead. Would she still be alive if she had never met him?
Probably. But . . . The screen has become a slot machine now,
and the skulls keep turning and stopping, coming up different colors. . . . The colors line the walls of the canyon
through which he walks. Long bands of strata in the rough-
ness to right and left. Strewn at his feet are the skulls and

other bones, some of them gray and gnawed, cracked and weathered, others ivory fresh, some of them inset with turquoise, coral and jet. There comes a sound at his back, but he turns and nothing is there. It comes again, and he turns again, and again there is nothing. The third time it comes, he thinks that he detects a fleeting shadow as he spins around. The fourth time, it is there, waiting. A coyote stands laughing beside a pile of bones. "Come," it says, and it turns away. He follows, and it leads him among the shadows. "Hurry," it says, loping now, and he increases his pace. A long time seems to pass as they move through hidden places. Dark places. Places of forgetfulness. Dora following. Firelight and dancers. Sounds of rattles and drums. Nightclub through a whiskey haze. The dusty surface of Woden IV; the tanklike beasts which dwell there. Bones underfoot, bones all about. Falling, falling . . . Sounds at his back. His shadow preceding him as he pursues the furry tail of the Trickster. "Where are we going?" he calls out. "Out and up, out and up," comes the reply. His shadow is suddenly enveloped by that of a larger one, from something just at his back. "Hurry! Out! Up! Hurry!"

Awakening to urgency: day grown dimmer beyond the window. And what was that sound on the stair?

Out and up? Too strong a thing to ignore. He could almost still hear the coyote beyond the window.

He rose and crossed the room, looked out. There was a fire escape. Had he noticed it on checking in? He did not recall.

He raised the window and stepped outside. He did not question the warning. He still seemed to be moving within the dream. It seemed perfectly reasonable that he continue on the course he had been following. The evening air was cool, trail lights illuminated the way below. That damp, pungent smell on the breeze . . . The Seine?

Up!

He climbed. With some difficulty, he was able to draw himself onto the slanting roof. People were moving along the Rue des Écoles trail, but no one looked upward. He began moving to his right, toes in a rain gutter, hands sliding along slate. The dreamlike quality persisted. He passed chimneys and a dish antenna. He saw a corner ahead. There came a faint, hollow, hammering sound, as of someone pounding on a door, below and to his left. He hurried.

The crashing, splintering sound which followed stirred his imagination but vaguely. There was a booth fairly near now, were he on the ground. . . .

He moved as if following a magic trail, leading toward another fire escape he now had sight of. Even the sounds of pursuit, as a large body passed through his hotel window, ringing upon the metal stair, and then reared to scrabble at the roof's edge, seemed but part of some drama of which he was not even an interested spectator, let alone a principal. He continued to move mechanically, barely aware that his pursuer was addressing him—not with words, but with feelings which he would normally, under the circumstances, have found disquieting.

He glanced back as he took a turn, in time to see the large, oddly shaped figure in black begin to draw itself upward onto the roof. Even when the guttering tore loose beneath its weight and the figure clawed unsuccessfully to gain purchase on the building, he felt no surge of adrenalin. As its downward plunge began, he heard it call: *Today luck is with you. Make the most of it! Tomorrow—*

Its words and movements ceased when it landed in a clump of shrubbery below. And it was only then that he felt as if he were suddenly awakening, realizing that the world actually existed, that his position had been precarious. He drew a deep breath of the night's cold air, swung onto the fire escape and began his descent.

When he reached the ground, the figure was still a dark mass within the *rue*'s trailside growth. It was making small movements and a wheezing noise, but it seemed unable to rise and continue the pursuit. It was only after he had hurried into the box, summoned forth new coordinates and encoded them that Billy began to wonder.

DISK III

COMPUTER FILES PATENT INFRINGEMENT SUIT

BRG-118, recipient of the 2128 Nobel Prize in Medicine, this morning filed suit in the district court in Los Angeles claiming that J & J Pharmaceuticals

SATELLITE THIEF STRIKES AGAIN

Valuable experimental components were removed from Berga-12 by a person or persons unknown during a power failure now believed to have been induced by

SOLAR REGATTA TO SAIL THURSDAY

REPORTER FOUND BRUTALLY SLAIN

In an out-of-the-way trip-box station in upstate New York, reporter Virginia Kalkoff's mangled

Don't know what I'm gonna do . . .

SPRING STORMS HIT SOUTHWEST

SERIES-12 ARTIFICIAL HEART RECALLED

Apologizing for the inconvenience

*   *   *

In the days before Nayenezgani, Old Man Coyote once came upon the Traveling Rock in his journeying about the land. It had spoken to him and he had answered. Amused that a huge pile of stone should possess sentience, he quickly set about mocking it.

First he painted a grotesque face upon its side.

"Old Man Stone, you are frowning," he said.

"I do not like this face you have given me," it replied.

"And you are bald," Coyote said. "I will fix that."

He climbed atop the stone and defecated.

"Brown curly locks suit you well."

"You annoy me, Cayote," it said.

"I will be back in a while to build a fire at your base and cook my dinner," Coyote said, "as soon as I have hunted."

"Perhaps I, too, should hunt," it said.

Coyote set off through the woods. He had not gone very far when he heard a rumbling noise behind him. When he looked back he saw that the stone, rolling slowly, had commenced following him.

"Holy shit!" said Coyote, and he began running.

As he ran along, he saw Mountain Lion resting in the shade.

"Mountain Lion!" he called out. "Someone is chasing me. Can you help me, brother?"

Mountain Lion rose, stretched and looked back.

"You've got to be kidding," Mountain Lion said when he saw Traveling Rock. "I've no desire to be a flat cat. Keep going."

Coyote ran on, and later he passed Bear just emerging from his den.

"Hey! Bear, old buddy!" he cried. "I've got someone after me. Will you help me?"

"Sure," said Bear. "There aren't many things I'm afraid of . . ."

Then Bear heard the noise of pursuit and looked back and saw Traveling Rock.

". . . But that's one of them," he said. "Sorry."

"What should I do?" Coyote yelled.

"Cultivate philosophy and run like hell," said Bear, returning to his den.

Coyote ran on, down to the plains, and Traveling Rock picked up speed behind him.

At length, Coyote saw Old Buffalo grazing amid long grasses.

"Buffalo! Save me! I'm being chased!" Coyote cried.

Old Buffalo turned his head slowly and regarded the oncoming boulder.

"You can have all the moral support I've got," Buffalo replied. "But I just remembered it's time to move the herd. We've about grazed this area out. See you around, kid. Hey, gang! Let's get our tails across the river!"

Coyote continued to run, gasping now, and finally he came to the place where the hawks were resting.

"Help me, lovely fliers, mighty hunters!" he called. "My enemy is gaining on me!"

"Hide in this hollow tree and leave the Rock to us," said the chief of the hawks.

The Hawk Chief gave a signal then and his entire tribe rose into the air, circled once and fell upon the Traveling Rock. With their beaks, they prized away all of its loose covering, and then they went to work along its fracture lines, opening, widening, removing more material. In a short time, the Rock was reduced to a trail of gravel.

"There," said the Hawk Chief to Coyote, "it is over. You can come out now."

Coyote emerged from the tree and regarded the remains of his enemy. Then he laughed.

"It was only a game," he said. "That's all it was. I was never in any real danger. And you dumb birds actually thought I was in trouble. That's funny. That's real funny. No wonder everyone laughs at you. Did you really think I was afraid of that old rock?"

Coyote walked away laughing, and the Hawk Chief gave another signal.

The hawks fell upon the stone chips, gathered them and began reassembling them, like pieces of a gigantic puzzle.

When the Traveling Rock found itself together again, it groaned and then, slowly at first, began rolling, off in the direction Coyote had taken upon his departure. It picked up speed as it moved and soon came in sight of Coyote once more.

"Oh, no!" Coyote cried when he saw it coming.

He began running once again. He came to a downhill slope and began its descent. Traveling Rock picked up speed behind him, narrowed the distance that separated them, rolled over him and crushed him to death.

A circling hawk saw this take place and went back to report it to the others.

"Old Man Coyote has done it again," he said. "He never learns."

The Second Day

Night, with mist banks drifting down rocky slopes, stars toward the center of the sky, moonrise phosphorescence at the edge of things. The floatcar followed the high, craggy trail, winding between rock wall and downward slope, piercing stone shoulders, turning, dipping and rising. Sheep wandered across the way, pausing to browse on spring grasses. There were no lights in the countryside; there was no other traffic. The windshield occasionally misted over, to be cleared by a single, automatic movement of its blade. The only sound above the low buzz of the engine was the occasional urgent note of a gust of wind invading some cranny of the vehicle.

Billy entered a curve bending to his right, a steep rise to his left. He felt more secure with every kilometer that passed. Cat had proved more formidable than he had anticipated when it came to using the trip-boxes and functioning within cities. He was still uncertain as to how the beast had been able to determine his whereabouts with such accuracy. A gimmicking of the boxes he could understand, but knowing where to go to find him . . . It almost smacked of witchcraft, despite the fact that Cat had had a long time in which to plan.

Still, a change of tactics now ought to provide him with the leeway he would need for a total escape. He had tripped back to the Gare du Nord after fleeing the stunned Cat on the Left Bank. From there he had transported himself to Dublin, a city he had visited a number of times during Irish excursions, consulted the directory and tripped to Bantry, from which he had once spent several weeks sailing and fishing. There, in that pleasant, quiet corner of West Cork, he had taken his dinner and known the beginning of this small security he felt. He had walked through the town there at the head of the bay, smelling the salt air and recalling a season that might have been happier, though he now saw it as one of his many periods of adjustment to yet another changed time. He remembered the boat and a girl named Lynn and the seafood; these, and the fact that it was a small, unhurried place, permitting him to slip gradually into a new decade. Could something like this be what he really most needed now? he wondered. He shook his head. His grip tightened on the wheel as he negotiated a twisting descent.

Time to think. He needed to get to a safe place where he could work things out. Something was very wrong. He was missing important things. Cat had come too damned close. He ought to be able to shake him. This was still his world, for all of the changes. An alien beast should not be able to outwit him here. Time. He needed some time in which to work on it.

Vary the pattern, he had decided. If he had left some trace behind him in the boxes, some means by which his destination choices might become known, this move on his part should cancel that effect. He had rented the vehicle in Bantry and begun the northward drive along the trail he remembered. Passing through Glengarriff, he had continued onto this way toward Kenmare, moving through a countryside devoid of trip-boxes. For the moment, he felt free. There was only the night and the wind and the rocky prospect. He had been caught off balance by Cat's releasing him the previous evening. He had done nothing but improvise since then. What he had to come up with now was a plan, a general defense to sustain him through this trial. A plan . . .

A light in the distance. A pair of them now. Three . . . He raised a container and took a sip of coffee. His first mistake, he decided, had probably been in not tripping enough. He should have continued his movements to really cloud the trail. Cat had obviously been close enough to pick his destination from his mind. Even when he had jumped more than once, Cat could have been coming in as he was tripping out, and so could have learned the next stop.

Four . . . Kenmare would still be some distance beyond the first scattered farms and rural residences. This night was crisp. He descended a long slope. Abruptly, the trees were larger along the trailside.

The next time he would really mix it up. He would jump back and forth among so many places that the trail would be completely muddled. Yes, that was what he should have done at first—

The next time?

He screamed. The mental presence of Cat suddenly hung like the aroma of charred flesh about him.

"No—" he said, fighting to regain control of the vehicle which he had let swerve at his outburst.

He bounced across a field at a height of perhaps two feet, heading toward a steepening rise. Too abrupt a change in attitude would overturn the car.

Pulling the wheel around, he succeeded in veering away from the slope. Moments later, he was headed back toward the trail. Although he peered in every direction his light traveled, he saw no sign of the hunting beast.

Back on the trail once more, he accelerated. Shadows fled past. Tree limbs were stirred by the wind. Bits of fog drifting across his way were momentarily illuminated by the vehicle's beams. But this was all that he saw.

"Cat. . . ?" he finally said.

There was no reply. Was he so on edge that he had imagined that single phrase? The strain . . .

"Cat?"

It had seemed so real. He struggled to reconstruct his state of mind at the time of its occurrence. He supposed that he could have triggered it himself; but he did not like what this implied about his mental equipment.

He spun through a number of S-shaped curves, his eyes continuing their search on both sides of the trail.

So quickly . . . His confidence had been destroyed in an instant. Would he be seeing Cat behind every rock, every bush, from now on?

Why not?

"Cat!"

Yes.

Where are you? What are you doing?

Amusing myself. The point of this game must be maximum enjoyment, I have decided. It is good that you cooperate so well for this end.

How did you find me?

More easily than you might think. As I said, your cooperation is appreciated.

I do not understand.

Of course not. You tend to hide things from yourself.

What do you mean?

I know now that I can destroy you at any time, but I wish to prolong the pleasure. Keep running. I will strike at the most appropriate moment.

This makes no sense at all.

No. Because you will not let it. You are mine, hunter, whenever I choose.

Why?

He came onto a long, tree-lined curve. There seemed to be more lights far ahead.

I will tell you, and it will still not save you. You have changed from what you once were. I see that within you which was not there in the old days. Do you know what you really want?

To beat you, Billy said. *And I will.*

No. Your greatest wish is to die.

That is not so!

You have given up on the thought of keeping up with your world. For a long while you have waited and wished for an appropriate way out of it. I have provided you with such an occasion. You think that you are running from me. Actually, you are rushing toward me. You make it easy for me, hunter.

Not true!

. . . And the lovely irony is that you do not admit it.

You have been in the minds of too many Californians.

They're full of pop psychology . . .

. . . And your denial of it makes it that much easier for me.

You are trying to wear me down mentally. That's all.

No need for it.

You're bluffing. If you can strike now, let's see you do it.

Soon. Soon. Keep running.

He had to slow the vehicle for a series of turns. He continued to scan both sides of the trail. Cat must be near in order to reach him, but of course he had the advantage of straight-line travel whereas the trail—

Exactly.

Overhead, s piece of the night came loose, dropping from the top of a high boulder which leaned from the right. He tried to brake and cut to the left simultaneously.

A massive, jaguarlike form with a single, gleaming eye landed on the vehicle's hood forward and to the front. It was visible for but an instant, and then it sprang away.

The car tipped, its air cushion awry, and it was already turning onto its side before he left the trail. He fought with the wheel and the attitude control, already knowing that it was too late. There came a strong shock accompanied by a crunching noise, and he felt himself thrown forward.

Deadly, deadly, deadly . . . Kaleidoscope turning . . . Shifting pattern within unalterable structure . . . Was it a mistake? There is pain with the power . . . Time's friction at the edges . . . Center loosens, forms again elsewhere . . . Unalterable? But— Turn outward. Here songs of self erode the will till actions lie stillborn upon night's counterpane. But—

Again the movement . . . Will it hold beyond a catch of moment? To fragment . . . Not kaleidoscope. No center. But again . . . To form it will. To will it form. Structure . . . Pain . . . Deadly, deadly . . . And lovely. Like a sleek, small dog . . . A plastic statue . . . The notes of an organ, the first slug of gin on an empty stomach . . . We settle again, farther than ever before . . . Center. The light! . . . It is difficult being a god. The pain. The beauty. The terror of selfless—Act! Yes. Center, center, center . . . Here'! Deadly . . .

necess yet again from bridge of brainbow oyotecraven stare decesis on landaway necessity timeslast the arnings ent and tided turn yet beastfall nor mindstorms neither in their canceling sarved cut the line that binds ecessity towarn and findaway twill open pandorapack wishdearth amen amenuensis opend the mand of min apend the pain of durthwursht vernichtung desiree tolight and eadly dth cessity sesame

We are the key.

He awoke to stillness and the damp. The right side of his forehead was throbbing. His shoulders ached and he became aware of the unnatural angle at which he lay. His right arm felt wet. He opened his eyes and saw that the night still lay upon the land. He stretched out his left hand and turned on the interior light. As he did, shards of glass fell from his sleeve.

He saw then that the windshield was uncracked, and that the wetness on his arm had been caused by the spilled remainder of his coffee. He placed his fingertips on his forehead and felt no break in the skin, but he could already detect a swelling in the sore area.

The vehicle lay on its right side, off the trail, its front end partly crumpled against a tree. There were other trees and shrubs in the vicinity, masking him somewhat from the trail. He looked upward and to his left, and he could discover no reason for the broken side window.

Then his gaze fell upon the headrest. There were four parallel slash marks in the covering material beside his head, as from a set of razor-sharp claws. He looked again at the broken side window. Yes . . .

Cat?

Silence.

What are you waiting for?

He swung his feet about, set them carefully against the far door and rose into the semblance of a standing position. Immediately he grew dizzy and clutched at the steering wheel. When the spell passed, he attempted to open the door. It yielded to his fourth effort with a grinding, scraping sound. He caught hold of the frame and drew himself upward, suddenly recalling having done something similar with an old blue pickup truck, coming home from a Saturday night in town an age ago.

There was a trail. Even in the dark he could read it. Cat had been there and gone. He felt the broken twigs, traced impressions in the earth with his fingertips. He followed it for perhaps twenty meters, heading off across the countryside. Then he rose and turned away.

What's your angle, Cat? What do you want now? he asked.

He heard only the wind. He walked slowly back to the roadway and continued along it. He was certain that only a few miles remained until he reached the town.

Perhaps ten minutes passed. No other traffic had come along, but he suspected that he was not alone. A large body seemed to be moving far off among the trees to his left, pacing him.

All right, Cat, he said. *There is no point to my taking evasive action now. If you are going to strike, strike. If not, enjoy the walk.*

There was no response, and he broke into a jog.

A feeling of nausea came over him before he had gone far. He ignored it and kept moving. He decided that it could be a reaction to the blow on his head.

But as he ran, his feelings came to include a fear that Cat was about to spring on him. He tried to thrust it away but it grew, and then he recognized its irrational roots.

I feel it, Cat. But I know what it is, he said. *What's the point of it? I'm still going on to Kenmare, unless you kill me. Are you just playing games?*

The intensity of the feelings increased. His breathing grew ragged. He felt a sudden urge to urinate. A sense of imminent doom was upon the trail for as far ahead as he could see.

Something like a small dog crossed his path. In that instant, his apprehensions vanished.

Was that the shadow I saw in the woods? he wondered. Is Cat long gone? Was my fear real, rather than induced?

Or is it all your doing, Cat? Is it your plan to make me doubt myself, to break me before you destroy me?

He jogged for a mile before a floatcar approached from the rear and drew abreast of him. Its driver offered him a ride into town.

As they moved forward, Billy felt within him the distant laughter of his pursuer.

*   *   *

To get out, to go away, to think. These were his preoccupations as he came into the town. He needed to escape for even a short while to someplace where Cat could not observe the workings of his mind. It was necessary that he continue his flight, try yet again to blur the trail sufficiently to gain respite for analysis of the situation, for planning.

He had the driver drop him at the trip-station. He assumed that somewhere Cat was reading his mind to learn his destination. He began chanting softly in Navajo, a section of the Blessingway. He entered the station and moved toward a booth. The place's only occupant was an old man seated on a wooden bench against the side wall to his right. The man looked up from his news printout and nodded to him.

" 'Evening," the man said.

He entered the booth and pressed the coordinates for Victoria Station.

. . . in beauty.

Now to Munich . . .

. . . all about me.

He cleaned himself in the washroom there and tripped to Rome.

. . . to the right of me.

He had a sandwich and a glass of wine.

. . . to the left of me.

He tripped to Ankara. For a time, he stood outside the terminal and watched the sun rising upon a hot, dusty day.

. . . *before me.*

He tripped to Al Hillah in Saudi Arabia, and from there to a bank of booths in the Rab al Khali National Petroleum Forest.

Yes. Here, he decided, stepping forth among the great-leafed, towering trees, their barks scaled and brown and ringing in the wind. He followed a marked footpath through their shade.

Here, amid Freeman Dyson's old dream, he thought, he might be able to feel his way to something that he needed to know, here in what had once been known as the Empty Quarter, now an enormous forest of genetically tailored trees larger than redwoods, their sap rising, their programmed metabolism synthesizing petroleum which flowed downward through a special set of vessels into roots which formed a living network of pipelines, connecting at various points to an artificial pipeline which conveyed it to the vast storage areas which constituted one of the world's great petroleum reserves, against those functions which still required the substance. They filled what had once been a wasteland, utilizing the abundant sunlight available there. Self-repairing and timeless against the blue of the sky, they were both natural and the product of the technology which informed the planet's culture, as surely as the trees of the street parks which delivered their own products, or the data net which, had he not disassociated himself from it, could at this moment deliver to him almost any information he needed.

Almost. Some things had to be worked out alone. But

here, in this combination of the old and the new, the primitive and the modern, he felt more at ease than he had since the entire business began. There were even birds singing in the branches. . . .

He walked for a long while through the forest, pausing when he came to a small cleared area containing a pair of picnic tables, a waste bin, a shed. He looked into the shed: foresters' maintenance equipment—power diggers, pickaxes, saws; chains and cables; gloves and climbing spikes. It was dusty, and spiderwebs like gossamer bridges connected each to each.

He closed the door and moved away, sniffed the air and looked around. He seated himself with his back to the bole of a middle-sized tree, some few stalks of coarse saffron and lime grass tufted about the hillock among the roots. He filled his pipe and lit it.

Cat wanted his death and had tried to convince him that he did, too. The idea seemed absurd, but he looked at it more closely. Much of the universe was one's adversary. He had learned that as a boy. One took precautions and hoped for the best. Time was flowing water, neither good nor evil and not to be grasped. One could cup one's hand and hold a little of it for a while, and that was all. It had become a torrent, though, in the past decade of his own life—which covered about thirty years of real time—and he could contain none of it. The big world had changed rapidly during that span. The dancers had exchanged masks; he could no longer identify the enemies.

Save for Cat.

But that was unfair, he saw, even to Cat. Cat he could understand. Cat was simple, monomaniacal, in his desire. The rest of the world was dangerous in changing and complicated ways, though it generally lacked malice and premeditation. It was an adversary, not an enemy. Cat was the enemy. The universe was that which ground down and rolled over one. And now . . .

The tempo had increased. He had felt it all his life, from his first school days on, intensifying, like a drumbeat. There had been lapses, true; periods when he had come to terms with the new rhythms. But now— He felt tired. The last responses were no longer appropriate, not even among his own people. Looking back, he saw that he had felt best on those occasions when he had gone away, into the timeless places among the stars, hunting. It was the return that was always the shock. Now . . . now he just wanted to rest. Or to go away again, even though the next return . . .

Dora. It had been peaceful with Dora also. But that did not help him now. Thinking of Dora now only caused him to look away from the real problems. Did he really want to die? Was Cat right?

He could almost hear singing within the unnatural tree which paralleled his backbone, vibrations humming along his nerves.

To want to run away, to want to rest and change no more . . . perhaps . . .

He bit down hard on the pipestem. He did not like all of this *bellicano* thinking, this hunting for hidden motives. But . . .

Perhaps there was something to it. His jaw muscles relaxed again.

If the hidden sources of his feelings did equal what Cat had been talking about, he had been running toward death ever since Dora's fall and—

Dora? How did she figure into this part? No, let the dead rest and not trouble the living. It would be enough to admit that all of the changes in society itself—a society into which he had not been born but of which he had tried to make himself a part—were sufficiently overwhelming to have brought him to this point. Take it from there. What next? What did he really want? And what should he do about it?

Suddenly a memory unfolded, startling him with a knowledge he had possessed all along. After the shock of the recognition he grew depressed, for he knew then that Cat's words had been true.

Each time that he had fled by means of a trip-box he had had his ultimate destination at the back of his mind. All of the jumping about he had done before heading for his goal had been as nothing. Cat had needed but to read that final destination, to go there and begin patrolling the city, hunting first his mind and then his body. This seemed more than carelessness on his part. It was as if he had intentionally given himself to Cat and kept the information hidden from his own scrutiny. How could he trust himself to do anything now?

On the other hand, doing nothing could prove equally fatal. He was surprised at his sudden willingness to admit to a hidden death wish. He was determined not to yield to it, however, not in this duel with Cat. He puffed on his pipe and listened to the birds.

Had he this destination in mind when he had departed Kenmare on the first of this latest series of jumps? It seemed that he had. . . .

All right. He rose. He had to assume that Cat was aware of it and could put in an appearance at any time. The longer he remained here, the greater the beast's chances of finding him unprepared. He dusted off his trousers and muttered "Damn!" He still needed time to plan.

He slapped the side of the tree and headed across the picnic area toward the trail. A huge crow darted past him and he halted. Thoughts of Black-god tumbled through his mind, and of the ways of the hunt.

The only trip-station in the area was the one he had used. Cat could emerge there at any moment, perhaps just as he was approaching. No, that would not do. Because he was defenseless, it was prudent to continue the flight. But the risk involved in attempting it right now seemed too high.

It came down from Utah and Colorado, and it was big and black and nasty. When it attacked, the people fled for cover and waited. It lashed and splashed and filled gullies. From Lake Powell through the Carrizos it boiled and roared. It licked Shiprock with tongues of flame. The patches of white in the high places were diminished beneath its slavering. It rolled across the land and hauled itself over the mountain peaks. Its breath was fast and sharp, snapping limbs from pine trees, twisting piñons. Arroyos became muddy snakes. There were mists, and in some places rainbows. The thunder no longer slept. Legends could no longer be told.

> *The Keeper of Clouds has unpenned his charges.*
> *The Keeper of Winds has unlocked his gates.*
> *The Keeper of Waters has opened the sky.*
> *The Keeper of Lightnings waves his lances.*
> *The Keeper of Satellites has observed,*
> *"One hundred percent of probability of precipitation."*

He emerged from the trip-box and looked about. He stood for a time as if listening. Then he dropped to all fours and entered the forest, his form altering as he advanced. He had detected the mind which he sought. It was filled again with the feelings of that chanting and all of the obscure imagery associated with it. But while this masked the underlying thoughts it in no way obscured the direction and location of the thinker. Finding the body should not be all that difficult.

His movements grew more and more graceful as the lines of his body flowed to assume the catlike form he favored. His eye sparkled like a liquid thing. His incisors overhung his lower lip by several inches. They, too, sparkled. His passage among the great petroleum trees was almost soundless. Whenever he froze and sought impressions he became almost invisible within the dappled patterns of light and shadow.

On one such occasion a leaf fell. Cat pounced upon it, a living blur. He straightened then and shook his head. He stared at the leaf. Then he started forward again.

Perhaps this should be the time. The game was not prov-
ing as complex as he had hoped. If there were no interesting
fight or flight, if nothing exciting happened this time, it
might be best to conclude things here. The hunter seemed to
have lost his edge, seemed weary, too troubled to provide the
necessary struggle.

He glared for a moment at the black bird which cried out
above his head, circling and then darting away.

Come back, dearie. Just for a moment. Come look again.

But the bird was gone.

Cat flicked his wide tail and pressed on across a low
spongy section of forest floor. It was not that much
farther. . . . He increased his pace and did not slow again until he was near to the picnic area. Then he studied and circled
and studied again.

The man was just sitting there, his back against a picnic
bench, smoking his pipe, his mind filled with that senseless
chant. It was almost too easy, but this was the way he had
read him earlier: willfully careless, ready to die. Still . . .

There was no sport in it. A few taunts, and perhaps he
will bolt.

*You see. It is as I said. When you run from me you ap-
proach me. Why was I not freed at some other time, when
you still cared to live?*

The hunter did not reply. The chant continued.

*So you have admitted the truth. You accept what I told
you. Is that your death song that you sing?*

Again there was no response.

Very well. I see no reason to prolong things, hunter.

Cat passed among the trees and entered the cleared area.

Last chance. Will you not at least draw your knife?

Billy stood and turned slowly to face him.

At last. You are awake. Are you going to run?

Billy did not move. Cat bounded forward. There followed a splintering sound.

When the ground gave way beneath the beast, the moment was frozen in Billy's mind. He had had some doubt as to the appropriate width when wielding the power shovel to dig the trench which encircled him. As its covering gave way and Cat vanished below he was pleased that his estimate had proven adequate. He moved immediately to bridge it with the picnic table.

You will not hold me here for long, hunter, Cat told him from below.

Long enough, I hope.

Billy crossed over the trench and emptied the wastebin against the trunk of a nearby tree. He struck a light and set it to the heap of papers.

What are you doing?

If one of these trees goes up, the whole area burns, he said. *They're all connected below and full of inflammables. You won't make it back to the box if you let this burn.*

Billy turned and began running.

Congratulations, Cat told him. *You have made it interesting again.*

Goodbye, Billy said.

Not quite. We've an appointment.

He ran on until the trip-box was in sight. Rushing into it, he inserted his strip, activating the control and punched coordinates at random without looking at them.

You have bought respite, Cat told him. But at another level you have betrayed yourself again.

Have I? Billy answered, as the forest blurred.

He walks in a twilight land amid jungle-shrouded cities. The cries of unseen birds come to him across the shimmering air. It is pleasantly warm, and there is a smell of dampness and decay. His path is a glistening ribbon among ruins which appear less and less ruined as he advances. He smells burning copal *and his guide gives him a strange beverage to drink. Colors flash beneath his feet and his way becomes bright red. They come at length to a pyramid atop which a blue man is held stretched across a stone by four others. Billy watches as a man in a high headdress cuts open the blue man's chest and removes the heart. He sips his drink and continues to watch as the heart is passed to another man who uses it to anoint the faces of statues. The body is then cast down the steps to where a crowd of people waits. There, another man very carefully removes the skin, its blue now streaked with red, dons it like a robe and commences dancing. The other people now fall upon the remains and begin eating, save for the hands and the feet, which are removed and set aside. His guide departs for a moment to join the crowd, returning moments later, bringing him something and indicating that he should eat. He chews mechanically, washing it down with the* balché. *He looks up, realizing suddenly that Dora is his guide. "On the fifth day of* Uayeb *my true love gave to me . . ." She is not smiling. Her face is, in fact, without expression as she turns away, beckoning for him to follow. The blood-red way leads at length to a gaping* cave-mouth. They halt before it, and he can see that within there are statues at either hand—fanged, scrolls upon their foreheads, dark circles about their eyes. As he stares, he becomes aware of people moving about slowly inside. They are placing bowls of copal, tobacco and maize upon a low altar. They are chanting softly in words which he does not understand. She leads him across the threshold, and he sees now that the place is illuminated by candlelight. He smells incense as he stands listening to the prayers. He is given to drink a beverage of corn gruel and honey at each pausing between rituals. He sits with his back against the rock, listening, tracing circles upon the poor with his fingertip. He is given another gourd of balché to drink. As he raises it to his lips he looks upward and pauses. It is not Dora who has brought him the drink but a powerful youth, clad in the old manner of the Dineh. At this person's back there stands another man—larger and even stronger-looking. He is similarly garbed, and the resemblance between the two is striking. "You seem familiar," Billy tells them. The first man smiles. "We are the slayers of the giants Seven-Macaws, Zipacna and Cabracan," he answers. "It was we," says the other, "who journeyed down the steps to Xibalba, crossing the River of Corruption and the River of Blood. We followed the Black Path to the House of the Lords of Death." The other nods. "We played strange games with them, both winning and losing," he says. And they say in unison, "We slew the Lords Hun-Came and Vucub-Came and ascended into light." Billy sips his balché. "You remind me," he says to the younger one, "of Tobadzichini, and you," to the other, "of Nayenezgani, the Warrior Twins of my people, as I always thought they must *look." The two smile. "This is true," they say, "for we get around a lot. Down here we are known as Hunahpu and Xbalanque. Rise now to your feet and look off yonder into the darker places." He gets up and looks to the rear of the grotto. He sees there a trail leading downward. Dora stands upon it, staring at him. "Follow," says Hunahpu. "Follow," says Xbalanque. She begins to move away. As he turns and follows after her, he hears the cry of a bird. . . .*

Billy stepped from the trip-box and looked about. It was dark, with a tropical brilliance to the stars. The air was cool and damp, bearing smells he had long associated with jungle foliage. The coolness seemed to indicate that the night was nearing its end.

He passed beyond the station's partitioning, where he read the sign which identified it. Yes. Things were as he had sensed them. He had come to the great archaeological park of Chichén Itzá.

He stood upon a low hill. Narrow trails led off in many directions. These paths were faintly illuminated, and here and there he saw people passing slowly along them. He could discern the massive dark forms of the ancient structures themselves, more solid and deep than the night's lesser gloom. Periodically, some portion of ruin would be brilliantly lighted for several minutes, for the benefit of night-viewers. He recalled reading somewhere that this ran through a regular cycle, its schedule available at various points along the way, along with computerized commentary and the answering of questions concerning the place.

He began walking. The ruin was big and dark and quiet

and Indian. It comforted him to pass along its ways. Cat could not find him here. This he knew. He also understood Cat's parting words. He had betrayed himself, in a sense, for his final destination had been present in his mind even as he had struck the random coordinates which had brought him here. When he finally journeyed to that last place it would be to face his enemy.

He laughed softly then. There was nothing to prevent his remaining here until Cat's time limit had run out.

Some of the more fragile ruins he passed were protected by force fields, others permitted entry, climbing, wandering. He was reminded of this as he brushed against a force screen—soft, harder, harder, impenetrable. It reminded him of Cat's cage back at the Institute. Cat's had also been electrified, however, providing shocks which increased in direct proportion to the intensity of the pressure from within. Cat had seldom brushed against it, though, because of his peculiar sensitivity to electrical currents. In fact, that was how Billy had captured him—accidentally, when Cat had collided with the electrified force screen which had surrounded one of the base camps during an attempt at backtracking and ambush. The memory suddenly gave rise to a new train of thought.

A light flashed on far to his right, and he halted and stared. He had never been here before, but he had seen pictures, had read about the place. It was the Temple of the Warriors that he beheld, a bristling of columns before it, their shadows black slashes upon its forward wall. He began to move toward it.

The light went out before he got there, but he had the location as well as the image fixed in his mind. He continued until he was very near, and when he discovered that no force field blocked his way he passed among the styli and began to climb the steep stair on its forward face.

When he reached the level area at the top he located himself to what he took to be the east and sat down, his back against the wall of the smaller structure situated at the center. He thought of Cat and of the death wish that was defeating him because he could not adapt, because he was no longer Navajo. Or was that true? He thought of his recent years of withdrawal. Now they seemed filled with ashes. But his people had many times tasted the ashes of fear and suffering, sorrow and submission, yet they had never lost their dignity nor all of their pride. Sometimes cynical, often defiant, they had survived. Something of this must still be with him, to match against his own death prayer. He dozed then and had a peculiar dream which he could not later recall in its entirety.

When he woke the sun was rising. He watched the waves of color precede it into the world. It was true that there was nothing to prevent his remaining here until Cat's time limit had run out. He knew that he would not do this. He would go on to face his *chindi*.

. . . After breakfast, he decided. After breakfast.

"I don't care!" Mercy Spender said, raising the bottle with one hand, the glass with the other. "I've got to have another drink!"

Elizabeth Brooke laid a hand upon her shoulder.

"I really don't think you should, dear. Not just now, anyhow. You're agitated and—"

"I know! That's why I want it!"

With a snapping sound, the bottom fell out of the bottle. The gin raced shards of glass to the floor. The odor of juniper berries drifted upward.

"What. . . ?"

Walter Sands smiled. "Mean of me," he said. "But we still need you. I know you'd like to go and rest in the home again. It will be harder for us if you drop out now, though. Wait a while."

Mercy stared downward. A look of anger passed and her eyes brimmed, sparkled.

"It's silly," she said then. "If he wants to die, let him."

"It's not that simple. He's not that simple," Ironbear said. "And we owe him."

"*I* don't owe him anything," she said, "and we don't even know what to do, really. I—" Then, "We all have something that hurts, I guess," she said. "Maybe . . . Okay. I'll take some tea."

"I wonder what hurts the thing that's after him?" Fisher asked.

"The data are incomplete on the ecology of the place it comes from," Mancin said.

"Then there is only one way to find out, isn't there?" asked Ironbear. "Go to the source."

"Ridiculous," Fisher said. "It's hard enough touching a human who's gone primitive. The beast seems able to do it at short ranges because they share some bond. But to go after the thing itself and then—I couldn't."

"Neither could I," said Elizabeth. "None of us could. But we might be able to."

"We? Us? Together? Again? It could be dangerous. After that last time—"

"Again."

"We don't even know where the cat-thing is."

"Walford's man can order another check on TripCo's computer network. Locate Singer again and the beast will soon be there."

"And what good would that do us?"

"We won't know till we get that information and give it a try."

"I don't like this," said Fisher. "We could get hurt. It's a damned alien place you're talking about. I touched one of the Strageans yesterday and had a headache for half an hour afterwards. Couldn't even see straight. And they're similar to us in a lot of ways."

"We can always back out if it gets too rough."

"I've got a bad feeling about this," Mercy said, "but I guess it does seem like the Christian thing to do."

"The hell with that. Is it going to do any good?"

"Maybe you're right," Mancin said. "It doesn't seem all that promising when you analyze it. Let's tell Walford how Singer did it, tell him about the beast and the deal they made. Then get the computer check to narrow the field. They can send an armed force after it."

"Send it after the thing that killed the thing an armed force couldn't stop?"

"Let's locate them," Ironbear said, "find out what we can and then decide."

"That much makes sense," Sands said. "I'll go along with it."

"So will I," said Elizabeth. Mancin glanced at Fisher. "Looks as if we're outvoted," he said, sighing. "Okay." Fisher nodded. "Call Tedders. Run it through TripCo. I'll be with you."

Billy stepped through into his hogan, leaving the transport slip in place. He switched on the guard and turned off the buzzer. He was not receiving calls just now.

His secretary unit told him that Edwin Tedders had called several times. Would he please call back? Another caller left no name, only the message, "They grew them with insulation, I learned. You knew that, didn't you?"

He turned on the coffee maker, undressed and stepped into the shower. As he was vibrated clean, he heard the rumble of thunder above the cries of the nozzles.

When he had emerged and dressed himself in warmer clothing he took his coffee out onto his porch. The sky was grey to the north and curtains of rain hung there. A fast wind fled past him. To the south and the east the sky was clear. Light clouds drifted in the west. He watched the rolling weeds and listened to the wind for a time, finished his coffee and returned to the inside.

Billy picked up the weapon and checked it over. Old-fashioned. A tazer, it was called, firing a pronged cable and delivering a strong electrical jolt at the far end. They had fancier things now which ionized a path through the air and sent their charge along it. But this would do. He had used a similar device on Cat before, once he had learned his weakness.

Then he honed a foot-long Bowie knife and threaded his belt through the slits in its sheath. He inspected an old 30.06 he had kept in perfect condition. If he could succeed in stunning Cat, it could pump sufficient rounds through that tough hide to hit vital organs, he knew. On the other hand, the weapon was fairly heavy. He finally selected a half-meter laser snub-gun, less accurate but equally lethal. He planned on using it at close range, anyway. That decided, he set to putting together a light pack with minimal gear for the trek he had in mind. When everything was assembled, he set an alarm, stretched out on his bedroll and slept for two hours.

When the buzzer roused him the rain was drumming on the roof. He donned a waterproof fleece-lined jacket, shouldered his pack, slung his weapons and found a hat. Then he crossed to his communications unit, checked a number and punched it.

Shortly the screen came to life, and Susan Yellowcloud's wide face appeared before him.

"Azaethlin!" she said. She brushed back a strand of hair and smiled. "It's been a couple of years."

"Yes," he said, and he exchanged greetings and a bit of small talk. "Raining over your way?" he finally asked.

"Looks as if it's about to."

"I need to get over to the north rim," he told her. "You're the closest person I know to the spot I have in mind. Okay if I come over?"

"Sure. Get in your box and I'll key ours.

He stepped in, pocketed his strip and punched TRANS.

He came through in the corner of a cluttered living room. Jimmy Yellowcloud arose from a chair set before a viewscreen to press palms with him. He was short, wide-shouldered, thick around the waist.

"Hosteen Singer," he said. "Have a cup of coffee with us."

"All right," Billy said.

As they drank it, Jimmy remarked, "You said you're going over to the canyon?"

"Yes."

"Not down in it, I hope."

"I'm going down in it."

"The spring flooding's started."

"I'd guessed."

"Nasty-looking gun. Could I see it?"

"Here."

"Hey, laser! You could punch another hole in Window Rock with this thing. It's old, isn't it?"

"About eighty years. I don't think they make them just like that anymore."

He passed it back.

"Hunting something?"

"Sort of."

They sat in silence for a time, then, "I'll drive you over to wherever you want on the rim," he said.

"Thanks."

Jimmy took another sip of coffee.

"Going to be down there long?" he asked.

"Hard to say."

"We don't see much of you these days."

"Been keeping to myself."

Jimmy laughed.

"You ought to marry my wife's sister and come live over here."

"She pretty?" Billy asked.

"You bet. Good cook, too."

"Do I know her?"

"I don't think so. We'll have to have a squaw dance."

A sudden drumming of rain occurred on the north side of the house.

"Here it comes," Jimmy said. "Don't suppose you'd care to wait till it stops?"

Billy chuckled.

"Could be days. You'd go broke feeding me."

"We could play cards. Not much else for a ranger to do this time of year."

Billy finished his coffee.

"You could learn to make jewelry—conchos, bracelets, rings."

"My hands just don't go for that."

Jimmy put down his cup.

"Nothing else to do. I might as well change clothes and go along with you. I've got a high-powered hunting rifle with a radar sight. Knock over an elephant."

Billy traced a design on the tabletop.

"Not this time," he said.

"All right. Guess we'd better get going then."

"Guess we should."

*　　*　　*

He let Jimmy drop him on the northward bulge of the

rim above the area containing the Antelope House ruin.
Since he had had the ride he had decided to come this much
farther eastward. Had he walked over, he would have descended at a point several miles farther to the west. Jimmy
would have taken him even farther eastward had he wished,
but that would have been less useful, starting him at a place
beyond the point where Black Rock Canyon branched off
from Canyon del Muerto proper. He wanted to pass that
point on foot and confuse the trail there. If he made things
too easy Cat would become suspicious.

Staring downward into the broad, serpentine canyon, he
saw a wide band of dully gleaming water passing down its
center, as he had suspected. It was not yet as deep as he had
seen it on occasions in the past, rushing with the seasonal
meltoff between orange, salmon and gray walls, splashing
the bases of obelisklike stands of stone, cascading over irreg-
ularities, rippling about boulders, bearing the mud and de-
tritus of its passage on toward the Chinle Wash, creating
pockets of quicksand all over the canyon floor. Several hundred of the People made their homes there during the
warmer months, but they all moved out for the winter. The
place would be deserted now.

A light rain was falling, making the wall rocks slippery.
He cast about for the safest way down. There, to the left.

He moved to the spot he had selected and studied it more
closely. Yes. It could be done. He checked his pack and commenced the descent. The way led down to the high, firm talus slope which followed the wall's base.

Partway down, he paused to adjust his pack, brush off
moisture and look sideways and back in at the petroglyph of

a life-sized antelope. There were a number of them about, along with those of other quadrupeds, turkeys, human figures, concentric circles; some of them continued onto the fourth-story level of the large ruin built against the base of the cliff. His people had done none of these. They went back to the Great Pueblo period, in the twelfth to fourteenth centuries, work of the old Anasazi. He worked his way down and around, and the going suddenly became easier. Here the slant and overhang of the wall protected him from the rainfall.

When he reached the bottom he turned to the east, the splashing waters off to the right, faded grasses and scrubby trees about him on the slope. He made no effort to conceal his passage but advanced with long, purposeful strides. Across the water at the base of the opposite cliff stood Battle Cove Ruin, a small masonry structure with white, red, yellow and green petroglyphs. It, too, went back to the Great Pueblo days. As a boy he might have feared such places, feared rousing the vengeful spirits of the Old Ones. On the other hand, he would probably have gone through them on a dare, he decided.

Jagged lightning danced somewhere in the east—*ikne'eka'a*. A slow roll of thunder followed. He felt that Cat was probably in Arizona by now, having seen the Canyon de Chelly Monument in his mind, the Canyon del Muerto branch in particular. Locating the trip-box at the Thunder-bird Lodge would be kind of esoteric, though. Doubtless Cat would have arrived by way of Chinle—which meant that he stil had a long way to come, even if he had gotten in a few hours ago.

Good. Black Rock Canyon was not that far ahead.

The track of the wind upon my fingertips,
mark of my mortality.
The track of the rain upon my hand,
mark of the waiting world.
A song that rises unbidden within me,
mark of my spirit.
The light of that half-place
where his mount danced for Crazy Horse,
mark of that other world
where powers still walk, stones talk
and nothing is what it seems to be.
We will meet in an old place.
The earth will tremble. The stones will drink.
Things forgotten are shadows.
The shadows will be as real
as wind and rain and song and light,
there in the old place.
Spider Woman atop your rock,
I would greet you,
but I am going the other way.
Only a fool would pursue a Navajo
into the Canyon of Death.
Only a fool would go there at all
when the waters are running.
I am going to an old place.
He who follows must go there, too.
Windmark, raintouch, songrise, light,
with me, on me, in me, about me.

It is good to be a fool when the time is right.
I am a son of the Sun
and Changing Woman.
I go to an old place.
Na-ya!

*　　　*　　　*

When Cat emerged from the trip-box at Chinle he wore a dark cloak, glasses and floppy-hat disguise. The station was empty now, though he could see a couple of minutes into the past in a limited fashion with his infrared vision and knew from the heat signatures that two people had recently been standing inside the doorway for a while. He moved forward and looked outside. Yes. A man and a woman were walking away. Presumably one had met the other here and they had stood talking for a time before going on their way. As he watched, they crossed the street and entered a café to his left. Their thoughts served to remind him that for many hours he had been growing hungry. Without moving, his eye also took in countless images of the nearby wall map. He was getting the idea of such things better now, and he would remember all of the markings on this one. When he saw something which corresponded to a feature, he would have his directions, though he felt he already knew them. In the meantime, he would follow his feelings and his hunger while gaining impressions.

He departed the station. Half of the sky was overcast and the clouds seemed to be moving to cover more. He felt the dampness and negative ionization in the air.

He passed along the street. Three men rounded the corner and stared at him for an unusually long while. *Stranger.*

Odd. Very odd, he read. *Something funny about that one, the way he moves* . . . Images then. Childhood fears. Old stories. Similar in ways to Billy's stream of consciousness.

More people approaching from the rear. No design to their movement in his direction. But the same curiosity flowing.

He selected. He broadcast fears and old forebodings: *Flee! Man-wolf, shapeshifter! Gnawer of corpses! I will shoot corruption into your bodies, blow the dust of corpses into your lungs. Wolf, wearer of the skin. I will track you and rend you!*

The men at his back hastily turned into an open shop. Those before him halted, then quickly crossed the street. Almost amused, he continued to broadcast the feelings for a time after they had departed. It cleared the way before him. People would begin to emerge from buildings and halt, then return within, as if suddenly recalling something undone inside, experiencing the resurgence of childhood fears. Better to give in and rationalize later than to brave them out for no reason.

But they are real, he reflected. I *am* the shapeshifter who could strike you down without effort. I could have stepped from your nightmare legends. . . .

He picked the direction of the Chinle Wash from a retreating mind, turned at the next corner and again at the following one.

Silly. No one in sight now. There will be no trouble, he decided.

Stretching and contracting, he bent forward. Soon he was loping along the street. Not far, not too far. This way was indeed north. The town thinned out, fell away. He departed the roadway, ran beside it, cut across country. Better, better. Soon now. Yes. Downhill. Trees and desiccated grasses. A faint flash of light. Much later, a soft growl from the eastern sky.

Down, down into a barrenness of sand and moist earth, detached tree limbs and half-sunken stones. Firm enough, firm enough to run and—

He halted. Ahead, a primitive sentience, wandering. Automatically he fell into a stalking mode of progress. Hunger remembered in this almost delicious spot, save for the moisture. Slow now, beyond the next bend . . .

He halted again as soon as he saw the canine, a lean, black dog, sniffing about the heaps of rubble. Parts of it might do, if he diluted them. . . .

He sprang forward. The dog did not even raise its head until his third bounding movement, and by then it was too late. It let out one short whimpering noise before the projected feelings hit it, and then Cat's left paw shattered its spine.

Cat raised his muzzle from tearing at the carcass and swiveled his head so as to cover every direction, including straight up, with his many-faceted gaze. Nothing. Nothing moving but the wind and its consequences. Yet . . . He had felt as if something were watching him. But no.

He fell to tearing the bones free, breaking them, grinding them, swallowing them along with large gulps of sand. Not as good as crunching the tube-crawlers back home, but better than the synthetic fare they had given him at the Institute. Much better. In his mind, he roamed again the dry plains, fearing nothing but—

What? Again. He shook himself and ran his gaze entirely around the horizon. There was nothing, yet he felt as if something were stalking him.

He dropped into a lower position, spitting out pieces of dog, baring his fangs, listening, watching. What could there be to fear? There was nothing on this planet that he would not face. Yet he felt menaced by something he did not understand. Even when he had met with *krel*, long ago, he had known where he stood. Now, though . . .

He sent forth a paralyzing wave of feelings and waited. Nothing. No indication that anything had felt it. Could this be like dreaming?

Time ticked nets about him. The sky flared briefly beyond his right shoulder.

Gradually the tension went out of him. Gone now. Strange. Very strange. Could it be something about this place?

He finished his meal, thinking again of the days of the hunt on the plains of his own world, where only one thing could cause such uneasiness in him. . . .

It struck.

Whatever it was, it fell upon him like a boulder out of nowhere. He bunched his legs beneath him and sprang straight up into the air when it hit, head thrown back, a sharp hissing noise passing his throat. For an instant, his vision swam and the world grew dim. But already his mind was spinning. This he could understand, after a fashion.

Among his kind the mating battles were always preceded by a psychic assault from the challenger. This was somehow similar, and he possessed the equipment to join it.

He could not tell exactly what it was doing inside his head, but he struck at it with all of his hate, with the desire to rend. And then it was gone.

He fell across the carcass of the dog, teeth still bared, slipping back into an earlier mode of existence. Where was the other? When would he strike? He ranged with all of his senses about the area, waiting. But there was nothing there.

After a long while, the tension flowed away. Nothing was coming. Whatever it had been, it was not one of his own kind, and it had not been a battle challenge that he had felt. It troubled him that there was something in the area which he did not understand. He turned toward the north and began walking.

*   *   *

Mercy Spender and Charles Fisher, who sat at either side of him, reached to catch hold of Walter Sands's shoulders as he slumped forward.

"Get him up onto the table—quick!" Elizabeth said.

"He just fainted," Fisher said. "I think we ought to lower his head."

"Listen to his chest! I was still with him. I felt his heart stop."

"Oh, my! Somebody give us a hand!"

They moved him onto the table and listened for a heartbeat, but there was none. Mercy began hammering on his chest.

"You know what you're doing?" Ironbear asked her.

"Yes. I started nursing training once," she grunted. "I remember this part. Somebody send for help."

Elizabeth crossed to the intercom.

"I didn't know he had a bad heart," Fisher said.

"I don't think he did either," Mancin replied, "or we'd probably have learned that when we gave each other a look. The shock when the thing struck back must have gotten to him. We shouldn't have let Ironbear talk us into going in."

"Not his fault," Mercy said, still working.

"And we all agreed," Fisher said. "The time seemed perfect, while it was remembering. And we did learn something . . ."

Elizabeth reached Tedders. They grew silent as they listened to her relay the information.

"Just a moment ago. Just a moment ago," Fisher said, "and he was with us."

"It seems as if he still is," Mancin said.

"We're going to have to try to reach Singer," Elizabeth said, crossing the room and taking her seat again.

"That's going to be hard—and what do we really have to tell him?" Fisher asked.

"Everything we know," Ironbear said.

"And who knows what form it would take, that strange state of mind he's in?" Mercy asked. "We might be better off simply calling for that force Mancin suggested."

"Maybe we should do both," Elizabeth said. "But if we don't try helping him ourselves, then Walter's attack was for nothing."

"I'll be with you," Mercy said, "when we do. Somebody's going to have to take over here pretty soon, though, till the medics trip through. I'm getting tired."

"I'll try," Fisher said. "Let me watch how you do it."

"I'd better learn, too," Mancin said, moving nearer. "I do still seem to feel his presence, weakly. Maybe that's a good sign."

Sounds of hammering continued downstairs, from where a shattered wall was being replaced.

*　　*　　*

He crossed the water above a small cascade, knowing things would be relatively solid at its top. Then he moved along the southern talus slope, leaving a clear trail. He entered Black Rock Canyon and continued into it for perhaps half a mile. The rain came down steadily upon him and the wind made a singing sound high overhead. He saw a cluster of rocks come loose from the northern wall far ahead, sliding and bumping to the floor of the canyon, splashing into the stream.

Keeping watch on driftwood heaps, he located a stick sufficient for his purpose. He walked near the water's edge for a time, then headed up onto a long rocky shelf where his footprints soon vanished. He immediately began to backtrack, walking in his own prints until he stood beside the water again. He entered it then, probing with the stick for quicksand pockets, and made his way back to the canyon's mouth.

Emerging, he crossed the main stream to its north bank, turned to his right and continued on along Canyon del Muerto toward Standing Cow Ruin, concealing his trail as he went, for the next half-mile. He found that he liked the feeling of being alone again in this gigantic gorge. The stream was wider here, deeper. His mind went back to the story he had heard as a boy, of the time of the fear of the flooding of the world. Who was that old singer? Up around Kayenta, back in the 1920s . . . The old man had been struck by lightning and left for dead. But he had recovered several days later, bearing a purported message from the gods, a message that the world was about to be flooded. In that normal laws and taboos no longer apply to a person who has lived through a lightning-stroke, he was paid special heed. People. believed him and fled with their flocks to Black Mountain. But the water did not come, and the cornfields of those who fled dried and died under the summer sun. A shaman with a vision that did not pay off.

Billy chuckled. What was it the Yellowclouds had called him? "Azaethlin"—"medicine man." We aren't always that reliable, he thought, given to the same passions and misapprehensions as others. Medicine man, heal thyself.

He started past a "wish pile" of rocks and juniper twigs, halted, went back and added a stone to it. Why not? It was there.

In time, he came to Standing Cow Ruin, one of the largest ruins in the canyons. It stood against the north wall beneath a huge overhang. The remains of its walls covered an area more than four hundred feet long, built partly around immense boulders. It, too, went back to the Great Pueblo days, containing three kivas and many rooms. But there were also Navajo log-and-earth storage bins and Navajo paintings along with those of the Anasazi. He went nearer, to view again the white, yellow and black renderings of people with arms upraised, the humpbacked archer, circles, circles and more circles, the animals. . . . And there, high up above a ledge to his left, was one of purely Navajo creation, and most interesting to him. Mounted, cloaked, wearing flat-brimmed hats, carrying rifles, was a procession of Spaniards, two of them firing at an Indian. It was believed to represent the soldiers of Lieutenant Anthony Narbona who fought the Navajos at Massacre Cave in 1805. And below that, at the base of the cliff, were other horsemen and a mounted U.S. cavalryman of the 1860s. As he watched, they seemed to move.

He rubbed his eyes. They really were moving. And it seemed as if he had just heard gunshots. The figures were three-dimensional, solid now, riding across a sandy waste. . . .

"Always down on us, aren't you?" he said to them and to the world at large.

He heard curses in Spanish. When he lowered his eyes to the other figure, he heard a trumpet sounding a cavalry charge. The great rock walls seemed to melt away about him and the waters grew silent. He was staring now at a totally different landscape—bleak, barren and terribly bright. He raised his eyes to a sun which blazed almost whitely from overhead. A part of him stood aside, wondering how this thing could be. But the rest of him was engaged in the vision.

He seemed to hear the sound of a drum as he watched them ride across that alien desert. It was increasing steadily in tempo. Then, when it had reached an almost frantic throbbing, the sands erupted before the leading horseman and a large, translucent, triangular shape reared suddenly before him, leaning forward to enfold both horse and rider with slick membranous wings. More of them exploded into view along the column, shrugging sands which yellowed the air, falling upon the other riders and their mounts, enveloping them, dragging them downward to settle as quivering, gleaming, rocklike lumps on the barren landscape. Even the cavalryman, now brandishing his saber, met a similar fate, to the notes of the trumpet and the drum.

Of course.

What other fate might be expected when one encountered a *krel*, let alone a whole crowd of them? He had given up quickly on any notion of bringing one back to the Institute. Two close calls, and he had decided that they were too damned dangerous. That world of Cat's had bred some very vicious creatures. . . .

Cat. Speak of the Devil . . . There was Cat crossing the plain, lithe power personified. . . .

Again, amid a shower of sand, the *krel* rose. Cat drew back, rearing, forelimbs lengthening, slashing. They came together and Cat struggled to draw away. . . .

With the sound of a single drumbeat, the scene faded. He was staring at anthropomorphic figures, horses and the large Standing Cow. He heard the sounds of the water at his back.

Peculiar, but he had known stranger things over the years, and he had always felt that a kind of power dwelled in the old places. Something about this manifestation of it seemed heartening, and so he took it as a good omen. He chanted a brief song of thanks for the vision and turned to continue along his way. The shadows had darkened perceptibly and the rock walls were even higher now, and for a time he seemed to regard them through a mist of rainbows.

Going back. A part of him still stood apart, but it seemed even smaller and farther away now. Parts of his life between childhood and now had become dreamlike, shimmering, and he had not noticed it happening. He began recalling seldom used names for things around him which he had thought long forgotten. The rain increased in intensity off to his right, though his way was still sheltered by the canyon wall. A trick of lightning seemed to show momentarily a reddish path stretching on before him.

"A *krel*, a *krel*," he chanted as he walked, not knowing why. Free a cat to kill a Stragean, find a *krel* to kill a cat . . . What then? He chuckled. No answer to the odd vision. His mind played games with the rock shapes around him. The Plains Indians had made more of a cult out of the Rock people than his people had. But now it seemed he could almost catch glimpses of the presence within the forms. Who was that *bellicano* philosopher he had liked? Spinoza. Yes. Everything alive, all of it connected, inside and out, all over. Very Indian.

"*Hah la tse kis!*" he called out, and the echo came back to him.

The zigzag lightning danced above the high cliff's edge and when its afterglow had faded he realized that night was coming on. He increased his pace. He felt it would be good to be past Many Cherry Canyon by the time full darkness fell.

The ground dropped away abruptly, and he made his way across a bog, probing before him with his stick. He cleaned his boots then before continuing. He ran a hand across the surface of a rock, feeling its moist smoothnesses and roughnesses. Then he licked his thumb and stared again into the shadowy places.

Moments came and went like dark tides among the stones as he strode along, half-glimpsed images giving rise to free association, racial and personal.

It seemed to sail toward him out of the encroaching darkness, its prow cutting a V across his line of sight. It was Shiprock in miniature, that outcrop ahead. As he swung along it grew larger and it filled his mind. . . .

Irresistibly, he was thrown back. Again the sky was blue glass above him. The wind was sharp and cold, the rocks rough, the going progressively steeper. Soon it would be time to rope up. They were approaching the near-vertical heights. . . .

He looked back at her, climbing steadily, her face flushed. She was a good climber, had done it in many places. But this was something special, a forbidden test. . . .

He gnashed his teeth and muttered, "Fool!"

They were climbing *tse bi dahi*, the rock with wings. The white men called it Shiprock. It stood 7,178 feet in height and had only been climbed once, some two hundred years earlier, and many had died attempting the ascent. It was a sacred place, and it was now forbidden to climb upon it.

And Dora had liked climbing. True, she had never suggested this, but she had gone along with him. Yes, it had been his idea, not hers.

In his mind's eye, he saw their diminutive figures upon its face, reaching, hauling themselves higher, reaching. His idea.

Tell him why. Tell Hastehogan, god of night, why—so that he may laugh and send a black wind out of the north to blow upon you.

Why?

He had wanted to show her that he did not fear the People's taboo, that he was better, wiser, more sophisticated than the People. He had wanted to show her that he was not really one of them in spirit, that he was free like her, that he was above such things, that he laughed at them. It did not occur to him until much later that such a thing did not matter to her, that he had been dancing a dance of fears for himself only, that she had never thought him inferior, that his action had been unnecessary, unwarranted, pathetic. But he had needed her. She was a new life in a new, frightening time, and—

When he heard her cry out he turned as rapidly as he could and reached out for her. Eight inches, perhaps, separated their fingertips. And then she was gone, falling.

He saw her hit, several times. Half blinded with tears, he had cursed the mountains and cursed the gods and cursed himself. It was over. He had nothing now. He was nothing. . . .

He cursed again, his eyes darting over the terrain to where, with a flick of its tail, he would have sworn a coyote had stood a moment ago, laughing, before it vanished into the shadows beyond the rise. Fragments of the chants from the old Coyoteway fire ritual came to him:

> *I will walk in the places where the black clouds*
> *come at me.*

*I will walk in the places where the rain falls
upon me.
I will walk in the places where the lightning
flashes at me.
I will walk in the places where the dark fogs
move about me.
I will walk where the rainbows drift and the
thunders roll.
Amid dew and pollen will I walk.
They are upon my feet. They are upon my
legs. . . .*

When he reached the spot where he thought he had seen
the creature, he searched quickly in the dim light and
thought that he detected a pawprint. Not important,
though. It meant something. What, he could not say.

*He is walking in the water. . . .
On the trail beyond the mountains.
The medicine is ready.
. . . It is his water,
a white coyote's water.
The medicine is ready.*

As he passed Many Cherry Canyon he was certain that
Cat was on his way. Let it be. This thing seemed destined, if
not with Cat at his back then in some other fashion. Let it be.
Things were looking different now. The world had been
twisted slightly out of focus.

Dark, dark. But his eyes adjusted with unusual clarity. He would pass the cave of the Blue Bull. He would go on. He would take his rations as he walked. He would not rest. He would create another false way at Twin Trail Canyon. After that, he would obscure his passage even further. He would go on. He would walk in the water.

Come after me, Cat. The easy part is almost over.

Weak flash. The wind and the water swallow the thunder. He is laughing and his face is wet.

The black medicine lifts me in his hand. . . .

The Third Day

When the call came through that Walter Sands was dead, having failed to respond to treatment, Mercy Spender said a prayer, Fisher looked depressed and Mancin looked out of the window. Ironbear poured a cup of coffee, and for a long while no one said anything.

Finally, "I just want to go home," Fisher said.

"But we reached Singer," Elizabeth replied.

"If you want to call it that," he replied. "He's gone around the bend. He's . . . somewhere else. His mind is running everything through a filter of primitive symbolism. I can't understand him, and I'm sure he can't understand me. He thinks he's deep under the earth, traveling along some ancient path."

"He is," Ironbear said. "He is walking the way of the shaman."

Fisher snorted. "What do you know about it?"

"Enough to understand some," he answered. "I got interested in Indian things again when my father died. I even remembered some stuff I'd forgotten for a long time. For all of his education and travels, Singer doesn't think in completely modern terms. In fact, he doesn't even think like a modern Indian. He grew up in almost the last possible period and place where someone could live in something close to a neolithic environment. So he's been to the stars. A part of him's always been back in those crazy canyons. And he was a shaman—a real one—once. He set out several days ago to go back to that part of himself, intentionally, because he thought it might help him. Now it's got hold of him, after all those years of repression, and it's coming back with a vengeance. That's what I think. I've been reading tapes on the Navajos ever since I learned about him, in all of my spare moments here. They're a lot different from other Indians, even from their neighbors. But they do have certain things in common with the rest of us—and the shaman's journey often goes underground when things are really tough."

"'Us'?" Mancin said, smiling.

"Slip of the tongue," he answered.

"So you're saying this vicious alien beast is chasing a crazy Indian," Mercy stated. "And we just learned that the authorities won't go into those canyons after them because the place is too treacherous in the weather they're having. Sounds as if there's nothing we can do. Even if we coordinate as a group mind, the beast seems able to strike back at us pretty hard—and Singer can't understand us. Maybe we *should* go home and let them work it out between themselves."

"It would be different if there were something we could do," Fisher said, moving to stand beside Ironbear. "I'm beginning to see how you feel about the guy, but what the hell. If you're dead, lie down."

"We could attack the beast," Ironbear said softly.

"Too damned alien," Mancin said. "We don't have the key to his mind. He'd just slap us away like he did last time.

Besides, this mass-mind business seems very risky. Not too much has really been done with it, and who knows how we might mess ourselves up? In any kind of cost-benefit analysis of it there's little to gain against unknown risks."

Ironbear rose to his feet and turned toward the door.

"Fuck your cost-benefit analysis," he said as he left the room.

Fisher started after him, but Elizabeth caught his eye.

"Let him go," she said. "He's too angry. You don't want a fight with a friend. There's nothing you can say to him now."

Fisher halted near the door.

"I couldn't reach him then, can't reach him now," he said. "I know he's mad, but . . . I don't know. I've got a feeling he could do something foolish."

"Like what?" Mancin asked.

"I don't know. That's just it. Maybe I'd better . . ."

"He'll brood for a while," Mancin said, "and then come back and try to talk us into something. Maybe we ought to agree to try to reach Singer and get him to head for some safe spot where he can be picked up. That might work."

"I've got a feeling it won't, but it's the best suggestion so far. How'll we know where a good spot is?"

Mancin thought for a time, then, "That friend of Singer's, the ranger," he said, "Yellowcloud. He'd know. Where's the printout with his number on it?"

"Ironbear had it," Elizabeth said.

"It's not on his chair. Not on the table either."

"You don't think. . . ?"

Ironbear, wait! Elizabeth broadcast. *We're going to help! Come back!*

But there was no response.

They headed for the stair.

He was nowhere on the premises, and they guessed that he had tripped out from one of the downstairs boxes. They obtained the number from Information, but no one answered at Yellowcloud's place. It was not until half an hour later, while they were eating, that someone noticed that a burst-gun was missing from the guard room.

PETROGRAFFITI

COYOTE STEALS VOICES FROM ALL LIVING THINGS

Nothing was capable of movement following Coyote's theft of sound from the world. Not until he was persuaded to call the Sun and Moon to life by giving a great shout and restoring noise to the land

NAYENEZGANI CONTINUES CIVIC IMPROVEMENT PLAN

At *Tse'a haildehe'*, where a piece of rock brought up from the underworld was in the habit of drawing itself apart to form a pair of cliffs and closing again whenever travelers passed between, Nayenezgani today solved the problem by the ingenious use of a piece of elk's horn

2-RABBIT, 7-WIND. HOME TEAM SUCCESSFUL.

Quetzalcoatl, arriving this morning in Tula, was heard to remark, "Every man has his own rabbit." This was taken as a good sign by the local population, who responded with tortillas, flowers, incense, butterflies and snakes

Commercial traveler,
passing through

KIT CARSON GO HOME

I KILLED THREE DEER ACROSS THE WAY

BET THEY WERE LAME

SINGERS DO IT IN COLORED SANDS

FOUR APACHES KILLED A NAVAJO NEAR HERE

THAT'S HOW MANY
IT TAKES

SPIDER WOMAN DEMONSTRATES NEW ART

"I believe I'll call it textiles," she said, when questioned
concerning

SOMEDAY VON DANIKEN WILL SAY

THIS IS AN ASTRONAUT

FORT SUMNER SUCKS

CHANGING WOMAN PUZZLED BY SONS' BEHAVIOR

"I suppose they get it from their father," she was heard
to say, when told of the latest

BILLY BLACKHORSE SINGER AND HIS *CHINDI* PASSED THIS
WAY 0-SINGER, 0-*CHINDI*, AT END OF FIRST HALF

BLACK-GOD IS WATCHING

THE YELLOW MEDICINE LIFTS ME IN HIS HAND

When Ironbear occurred within the trip-box in Yellowcloud's home, the first thing to catch and hold his attention was a shotgun in the other man's hands, pointed at his midsection from a distance of approximately six feet.

"Drop that gun you're carrying," Yellowcloud said.

"Sure. Don't be nervous," Ironbear answered, letting the weapon fall. "Why are you pointing that thing at me?"

"Are you Indian?"

"Yes "

"*Ha'át'íísh biniinaa yíníya?*"

Ironbear shook his head. "I don't understand you."

"You're not Navajo."

"Never said I was. Matter of fact, I'm Sioux. Can't talk that either, though. Except maybe a few words."

"I'll say it in English: Why'd you come here?"

"I told you on the phone. I've got to find Singer—or the thing that's after him."

"I think maybe you're what's after him. It's easy to get rid of bodies around here, especially this time of year."

Ironbear felt his brow grow moist as he read the other man's thoughts.

"Hold on," he said. "I want to help the guy. But it's a long story and I don't know how much time we've got."

Yellowcloud motioned toward a chair with the barrel of his weapon.

"Have a seat. Roll up the rug first, though, and kick it out of the way. I'd hate to mess up a Two Gray Hills."

As he complied, Ironbear probed hard, trying to penetrate beyond the stream of consciousness. When he found what he was seeking, he was not certain he could wrap his tongue around the syllables, but he tried.

"What did you say?" Yellowcloud asked, the weapon's barrel wavering slightly.

He repeated it, Yellowcloud's secret name.

"How'd you know that?" the other asked him.

"I read it in your mind. I'm a paranormal. That's how I got involved in this thing in the first place."

"Like a medicine man?"

"I suppose in the old days I would have been one. Anyway, there was a group of us and we were tracking the thing that's tracking Singer. Now the others want to quit, but I won't. That's why I want your help."

The rain continued as he talked. When the callbox buzzed, Yellowcloud switched it off. Later he got them coffee.

*   *   *

Running now, into the bowels of the earth, it seemed. Darker and darker. Soon he must slow his pace. The world had almost completely faded about him, save for the sounds—of wind, water, his drumming feet. Slow now. Yes. Now.

Ahead. Something in that stand of trees. Not moving. A light.

He advanced cautiously.

It appeared to be— But no. That was impossible. Yet. There it was. A trip-box. He was positive that it was against regulations to install one in the canyon.

He moved nearer. It certainly looked like a trip-box, there among the trees. He advanced and looked inside.

A strange one, though. No slot for the credit strip. No way to punch coordinates. He entered and studied it more closely. Just an odd red-and-white-flecked button. Without thinking, he moved his thumb forward and pushed it.

A mantle of rainbows swirled before his eyes and was gone. He looked inside. Nothing had changed. He had not been transported anywhere. Yet—

A pale light suffused the canyon now, as if a full moon hung overhead. But there was no moon.

He looked again at the box, and for the first time saw the sight on its side. SPIRIT WORLD, it said. He shrugged and walked away from it. Save for the light, nothing seemed altered.

After some twenty paces, he turned and looked back. The box was gone. The stand of trees stood silvery to his rear, empty of any unnatural presence. To his right, the water gleamed in its rippling progress. The rain which fell into it seemed to be descending in slow motion, more a full-bodied mist than a downpour. And the next flash of lightning seemed a stylized inscription on the heavens.

Plainly marked before him now was the trail he must follow. He set his foot upon it and the wind chanted a staccato song of guidance as he went.

He moved quickly, approaching a bend in the canyon; more slowly then, as his slope steepened and narrowed. He dropped to a wider shelf as his way curved, hurried again as he followed it.

As he made the turn, he saw outlined to his right, ahead, a human figure standing on the opposite bank of the stream, at the very tip of a raised spit of land which projected out

into the water. It was a man, and he seemed somehow familiar, and he had a kind of light about him which Billy found
disturbing.

He slowed as he drew nearer, for the man was staring directly at him. For a moment, he was not certain how to address him, for he could not recall the circumstances of their
acquaintance, and a meeting here struck him as peculiar.
Then suddenly he remembered, but by then the other had already greeted him.

He halted and acknowledged the call.

"You are far from home," he said then, "from where I
met you just the other day, in the mountains, herding sheep."

"Yes, I am," the other replied, "for I died that same evening."

A chill came across the back of Billy's neck.

"I did nothing to you," he said. "Why do you return to
trouble me?"

"I have not returned to trouble you. In fact, I have not returned at all. It is you who have found your way to this
place. That makes it different. I will do you no harm."

"I do not understand."

"I told you to follow a twisted way," the old singer said,
"and I see that you have. Very twisted. That is good."

"Not entirely," Billy told him. "My *chindi* is still at my
back."

"Your *chindi* turned right instead of left, following the
false trail into Black Rock Canyon. You are still safe for a
time."

"That's something, anyway," Billy said. "Maybe I can
do it again."

"Perhaps. But what is it exactly that you are doing?"

"I am following a trail."

"And it brought you here. Do you think that we have met by accident?"

"I guess not. Do you know why we met?"

"I know only that I would like to teach you an old song of power."

"That's fine. I'll take all the help I can get," said Billy, glancing back along the way. "I hope it's not a real long one, though."

"It is not," the old singer told him. "Listen carefully now, for I can only sing it three times for you. To sing it four times is to make it work."

"Yes."

"Very well. Here is the song. . . ."

The old man began chanting a song of the calling of Ikne'etso, which Billy followed, understood and had learned by the third time he heard it. When the singer was finished he thanked him, and then asked, "When should I use this song?"

"You will know," the other answered. "Follow your twisted way now."

Billy bade him goodbye and continued along the northern slope. He considered looking back, but this time he did not do it. He trekked through the sparkling canyon and images of other worlds and of his life in cities rose and mingled with those about him until it seemed as if his entire life was being melted down and stirred together here. But all of the associated feelings were also swirled together so that it was an emotional white noise which surrounded him.

He passed a crowd of standing stones and they all seemed to have faces, their mouths open, singing windsongs. They were all stationary, but at the far end of the group something came forward out of darkness. It was a man, a very familiar man, who stood leaning against the last windsinger, smiling. He was garbed according to the latest fashion, his hair was styled, his hands well manicured.

"Hello, Billy," he said in English, and the voice was his own.

He saw then that the man was himself, as he could have been had he never come back to this place.

"That's right. I am your shadow," the other said. "I am the part of yourself you chose to neglect, to thrust aside when you elected to return to the blanket because you were afraid of being me."

"Would I have liked being you?"

The other shrugged.

"I think so. Time and chance, that's all. You and Dora would eventually have moved to a city after you'd proved to your own satisfaction how free you'd become. You took a chance and failed. If you'd succeeded you would have come this route. Time and chance. Eight inches of space. Such is the stuff lives are bent by."

"You are saying that if I'd proved how free I had become I still wouldn't really have been free?"

"What's free?" said the other, a faint green light beginning to play about his head. "To travel all good paths, I suppose. And you restricted yourself. I am a way that you did not go, an important way. I might have been a part of you, a saving part, but you slighted me in your pride that you knew best."

He smiled again, and Billy saw that he had grown fangs.

"I know you," Billy said then. "You are my *chindi*, my real *chindi*, aren't you?"

"And if I am," the other said, "and if you think me evil, you see me so for all of the wrong reasons. I am your negative self. Not better, not worse, only unrealized. You summoned me a long time ago by running from a part of yourself. You cannot destroy a negation."

"Let's find out," Billy said, and he raised the laser snub-gun and triggered it.

The flash of light passed through his double with no visible effect.

"That is not the way to deal with me," said the other.

"Then the hell with you! Why should I deal with you at all?"

"Because I can destroy you."

"Then what are you waiting for?"

"I am not quite strong enough yet. So keep running, keep regressing into the primitive and I will grow in strength as you do. Then, when we meet again . . ." The other dropped suddenly to all fours and took on the semblance of Cat, single eye glistening, ". . . I will be your adversary by any name."

Billy drew the tazer and fired it. It vanished within the other's body, and the other became his double again and rose, lunging at him, the dart and cable falling to the ground and rewinding automatically.

Billy swung his left fist and it seemed to connect with something. His double fell back upon the ground. Billy turned and began running.

"Yes, flee. Give me strength," it called out after him.

When he looked back, Billy saw only a faint greenish glow near the place of the windsingers. He continued to hurry, until it vanished with another turning of the way. The voices of the windsingers faded. He slowed again.

The canyon widened once more; the stream was broader and flowed more slowly. He seemed to see distorted faces, both human and animal, within the water.

He had felt himself the object of scrutiny for some time now. But the feeling was growing stronger, and he cast about, seeking its source among fugitive forms amid shadow and water.

Cat?

No reply, which could mean anything. But no broadcast apprehensions either—unless they came on only to be lost amid the emotional turbulence.

Cat? If it is you, let's have it out. Any time now. I'm ready whenever you are.

Then he passed a sharp projection of the canyon wall and he knew that it was not Cat whose presence he had felt. For now he beheld the strange entity which regarded him, and its appearance meshed with the sensation.

It looked like a giant totem pole. His people had never made totem poles. They were a thing of the people of the Northwest. Yet this one seemed somehow appropriate to the moment if incongruous to the place. It towered, and it bore four faces—and possibly a shadowy fifth, at the very top.

There were the countenances of two women, one heavy-featured, one lean, and two men, one black and one white. And above them it seemed that a smiling masculine face hovered, smokelike. All of their eyes were fixed upon him, and he knew that he beheld no carving but a thing alive.

"Billy Blackhorse Singer," a neuter-gendered voice addressed him.

"I hear you," he replied.

"You must halt your journey here," it stated.

"Why?" he asked.

"Your mission has been accomplished. You have nothing to gain by further flight."

"Who are you?" he said.

"We are your guardian spirits. We wish to preserve you from your pursuer. Climb the wall here. Wait at the top. You will be met there after a time and borne to safety."

Billy's gaze shifted away from the spirit tower to regard the ground at his feet and the prospect before him.

"But I still see my trail out within this canyon," he said finally. "I should not depart it here."

"It is a false trail."

"No," he said. "This much I know: I must follow it to its end."

"That way lies death."

He was silent again for a time. Then, "Still must I follow it," he said. "Some things are more important than others. Even than death."

"What are these things? Why must you follow this trail?"

He took several deep breaths and continued to stare at the ground, as if considering it for the first time.

"I await myself at its ending," he said at last, "as I should be. If I do not follow this trail, it will be a different sort of death. Worse, I think," he added.

"We may not be able to help you if you go on."

"Then that is as it must be," he said. "Thank you for trying."

"We hear you," said the totem as it sank slowly into the ground, face by face sliding from view beneath stone, until only the final, shadowy one remained for an instant, smiling, it seemed, at him. "Gamble, then," it seemed to whisper, and then it, too, was gone.

He rubbed his eyes, but nothing changed. He went on.

> *. . . I walk on an invisible arch,*
> *feet ready to bear me anywhere.*

*   *   *

outcoming fra thplatz fwaters flwng awa thheadtopped tre andriving now to each where five now four apartapart horse on the mountain ghoti in thrivr selves towar bodystake like a longflwung water its several bays to go and places of ourown heads to sort sisters in the sky old men beneath the ground while coyote trail ahead blackbrid shadow overall and brotherone within the chalce of minds a partaparta-trapatrap

"My God!" Elizabeth said, sinking back into her chair.

Alex Mancin poured a glass of water and drained it.

"Yes," said Fisher, massaging his temples.

Mercy Spender commenced a coughing spell which lasted for close to half a minute.

"Now what?" Fisher said softly.

Mancin shook his head.

"I don't know."

"Ironbear was right about his thinking he's in another world," Elizabeth said. "We're not going to move him."

"The hell with that," Fisher said. "We tried, and we got through, even if he did turn us into a totem. That's not what's bothering me, and you know it."

"*He* was there," Mercy said, "in the spirit."

"Somebody call the hospital and make sure Sands is really dead," Fisher said.

"I don't see how they could be mistaken, Charles," Elizabeth said. "But Mercy is right. He was with us, somehow, and it seems as if he's still somewhere near."

"Yes," Mercy put in. "He is here."

"You don't need the spirit hypothesis for what I think happened," Mancin finally stated.

"What do you mean?" Elizabeth asked.

"Just the memory of how he died. We were all of us together, functioning as that single entity of which we understand so little. I think that the trauma of his death served to produce something like a holograph of his mind within our greater consciousness. When we are apart like this it is weakened, but we all bear fainter versions, which is why we seem to have this sense of his presence. When we recreated the larger entity just now, the recombination of the traces was sufficient to reproduce a total functioning replica of his mind as it was."

"You see him as a special kind of memory when we are in that state?" Elizabeth asked. "Will it fade eventually, do you think?"

"Who can say?"

"So what do we do now?" Fisher asked.

"Check on Singer, I suppose, at regular intervals," Mancin said, "and renew the invitation to be picked up if he'll climb to some recognizable feature."

"He'll just keep refusing. You saw how fixed that mental set of his was."

"Probably—unless something happens to change it. You never know. But I've been thinking about some of the things Ironbear said. He's owed the chance, and we seem the only ones who can give it to him."

"Okay by me. It seems harmless enough. Just don't ask me to go after that alien beast again. Once was enough."

"I'm not too anxious to touch it myself."

"What about Ironbear?"

"What about him?"

"Shouldn't we try to get in touch and let him know what we're doing?"

"What for? He's mad. He'll just shut us out. Let him call us when he's ready."

"I'd hate to see him do anything foolish."

"Like what?"

"Like go after that thing and find it."

Mancin nodded.

"Maybe you're right. I still don't think he'd listen, but—"

"He might listen to me," Fisher said, "but I'm not sure I

can reach him myself at this distance."

"Why don't we locate the nearest trip-box to that canyon and go there?" Elizabeth said. "It will probably make everything easier."

"Aren't Indian reservations dry?" Mercy asked.

"Let's tell Tedders and get our stuff together. We'll meet back here in fifteen minutes," Fisher said.

"Walter thinks it's a good idea, too," Mercy said.

* * *

There is danger where I walk,
in my moccasins, leggings, shirt
of black obsidian.
My belt is a black arrowsnake.
Black snakes coil and rear about my head.
The zigzag lightning flashes from my feet,
my knees, my speaking tongue.
I wear a disk of pollen upon my head.
The snakes eat it.
There is danger where I walk.
I am become something frightful.
I am whirlwind and gray bear.
The lightning plays about me.
There is danger where I walk.

* * *

"Idropped him back here," Yellowcloud said, jabbing at the map, and Ironbear nodded, staring down at the outline of the long, sprawled canyons.

The rain, growing sleetlike, pelted against the floatcar in which they sat, parked near the canyon's rim. Reflexively,

Ironbear raised the collar of his borrowed jacket. Pretty good fit. Lucky we're both the same size, he decided.

"I watched for a time," Yellowcloud continued, "to make sure he got down okay. He did, and I saw that he headed east then." His finger moved along the map and halted again. "Now, at this point," he went on, "he could have turned right into Black Rock Canyon or he could have kept on along Canyon del Muerto proper. What do you think?"

"Me? How should I know?"

"You're the witch-man. Can't you hold a stick over the map, or something like that, and tell?"

Ironbear studied the map more closely.

"Not exactly," he said. "I can feel him out there, down there. But a rock wall's just a rock wall to me, whether I'm seeing it through his eyes or my own. However . . ." He placed his finger on the map and moved it. "I'd guess he continued along del Muerto. He wanted lots of room, and Black Rock seems to dead-end too soon."

"Good, good. I feel he went that way, too. He chose a spot before it on purpose, I'd say. I'll bet the trail gets confused at the junction." Yellowcloud folded the map, turned off the interior light and started the engine. "Since we both agree," he said, turning the wheel, "I'll bet I can save us some time. I'll bet that if we head on up the rim, past that branch, and if we climb down into del Muerto, we'll pick up his trail along one of the walls."

"It'll be kind of dark."

"I've got goggles and dark-lights. Full spectrum, too."

"Can you figure out where he might be from where you

dropped him and how fast he might be going?"

"Bet I can make a good guess. But we don't want to come down right on top of him now."

"Why not?"

"If something's after him, he's liable to shoot at anything he sees coming."

"You've got a point there."

"So we'll go down around Many Turkey Cave, Blue Bull Cave—right before the canyon widens. Should be easier to pick up the trail where it's narrow. Then we'll ignore any false signs leading into Twin Trail Canyon and start on after him."

Winds buffeted the small car as it made its way across a nearly trailless expanse, turning regularly to avoid boulders and dips which dropped too abruptly.

". . . Then I guess we just provide him with extra fire-power."

"I'd like to try talking him out of it," Ironbear said.

Yellowcloud laughed.

"Sure. You do that," he said.

Ironbear scanned the other's thoughts, saw his impression of the man.

"Oh, well," he said. "At least I learned to shoot in the P-Patrol."

"You were P-Patrol? I almost joined that."

"Why didn't you?"

"Afraid I'd get claustrophobia in one of those beer cans in the sky. I like to be able to see a long way off."

They were silent for a time as they traveled through the blackness, dim shapes about them, snowflakes spinning in the headlight beams, changing back to rain, back to snowflakes again.

Then, "That thing that's after him," Yellowcloud said, "you say it's as smart as a man?"

"In its way, yeah. Maybe smarter."

"Billy may still have an edge, you know. He'll probably be mad to see us."

"That beast has chased him all over the world. It's built for killing, and it hates him."

"Even Kit Carson was afraid to go into these canyons after the Navajo. Had to starve us out in the dead of winter."

"Why was he scared?"

"The place was made for ambushes. Anyone who knows his way around down there could hold off a superior force, maybe slaughter it."

"This beast can read thoughts."

"So it reads that there's someone up ahead waiting to kill it. Doesn't have to be a mind reader to know that. And if it keeps following that's what could happen."

"It can change shape."

"It's still got to move in order to make progress. That makes it a target. Billy's armed now. It won't have it as easy as you seem to think."

"Then why'd you decide to come?"

"I don't like to see any outsider chasing Navajos on our land. And I couldn't let a Sioux have the first shot at the thing."

Without Yellowcloud, I wouldn't be worth much out here, Ironbear told himself. Even the little kids around here must know more than I do about getting around in this terrain, tracking, hunting, survival. I'm a damn fool for butting into this at all, physically. The only things I know about being an Indian come from Alaska, and that was a long time ago. So why am I here? I keep saying I like Singer, but why? Because he was some kind of a hero? I don't really think that's it. I think it's because he's an old-style Indian, and because my father might have been that way. At least I think of him that way. Could I be trying to pay off a debt of guilt here? It's possible, I guess. And all of my music had an Indian beat to it. . . .

The car slowed, worked its way into the shelter of a stone outcrop, came to a halt. The snow had turned back to rain, a slow, cold drizzle here.

"Are we there?" he asked.

"Almost," Yellowcloud replied. "There's an easy way down near here. Well, relatively easy. Let me get us some lights and I'll show you."

Outside, they donned small packs and slung their weapons. Yellowcloud shined his light toward the canyon.

"Follow me," he said. "There was a slide here a few years ago. Made a sort of trail. We'll be more sheltered once we reach the bottom."

Ironbear fell in behind him and they made their way to the rim of the canyon. Its floor was invisible, and the rocks immediately before him looked jagged and slippery. He said nothing, and shortly they began the descent, Yellowcloud playing his light before them.

As they climbed, the force of the rainfall lessened, until about halfway down they entered the full rainshadow of the wall and it ceased entirely. The rocks were drier and the pace of their descent increased. He listened to the wind and the noises of the rain.

Moving from rock to rock, he came, after a time, to wonder whether there was indeed a bottom. It began to seem as if they had been descending forever and that the rest of time would be a simple repetition of the grasping and lowering. Then he heard Yellowcloud call out, "Here we are!" and shortly thereafter he found himself standing on the canyon's floor, stony shapes distorted and flowing in the blacklight.

"Just stay put for a minute," Yellowcloud said. "I don't want any trails messed up." Then, "Can you use that trick of yours to tell whether there's anyone nearby?" he asked.

"There doesn't seem to be," Ironbear replied a few moments later.

"Okay. I'm going to use a normal light for a while here. Make yourself comfortable while I see what I can turn up."

Several minutes passed while Ironbear watched Yellowcloud's slowly moving light as the other man studied the ground, ranging farther and farther ahead, passing from left to right and back again. Finally Yellowcloud halted. His figure straightened. He gestured for Ironbear to come along, and then he began walking.

"Got something?" Ironbear asked, coming up beside him.

"He's been this way," he answered. "See?"

Ironbear nodded as he regarded the ground. He saw nothing, but he read the recognition of signs within the other's mind.

"How long ago was he by here?"

"I can't say for sure. Doesn't really matter, though.

Come on."

They hiked for nearly a quarter-hour in silence before Ironbear thought to inquire, "Have you seen any signs of his pursuer?"

"None. A few dog tracks here and there are the only other things. It couldn't be that size, from what you told me."

"No. It's got a lot more mass."

Yellowcloud ignored the false signs at Twin Trail Canyon and continued along the northeasterly route of the main gap.

There was a hypnotic quality to the steady trudging, the unrolling trail of rock, puddle, mud, shrub. The cold was not as bad as it might have been with the wind softened as it was, but the numbness Ironbear began to feel was more a mental thing. The waters splashed and gurgled past. His arms swung and his feet strode in a near mechanical fashion.

. . . *Yes, yes, yes, yes, yes, yes, yes* . . .

The wind seemed to be talking to him, seemed to have been talking to him for a long while, lulling words, restful within the routine of the movements.

. . . *Lull, lull, lull, lull. Yes, rest, yes, rest, yest, yest, yest* . . .

It was more than the wind and the rhythm, he suddenly knew. There was someone—

Yes. Yes.

Power. Blackness. Death. It walked at his back. The thing. The beast. It was coming.

Yes. Yes.

And there was nothing he could do about it. He could not even slow his pace, let alone deviate from his course. It had him completely in its power, and so deftly had it taken control of him that he had not even felt the insinuation of its presence. Until now, when it was far too late.

Yes. Yes, son of cities. You seem different from this other one, and both of you block my way. Keep walking. I will catch up with you soon. It will not matter then.

Ironbear tried again to turn aside, but his muscles refused to obey him. He was about to probe Yellowcloud's mind to see whether the other man had yet become aware of his condition. He held back, however. The creature somewhere to the rear was exerting a form of telepathic control over his nervous system. He could not tell whether it was also reading his thoughts. Perhaps. Perhaps not. He wanted to keep his own telepathic ability away from its awareness if he possibly could. Why, he was not certain. But he felt—

He heard a sound to the rear. A dislodged stone turning over, it seemed. He knew that if he did not break free in a few moments nothing that he felt would matter anymore. It would all be over for him. Everything. The beast Singer called Cat was almost upon him.

His feet continued their slow, steady movements. He tried to visualize Cat, but he could not. A malevolent shadow with sinuous movements . . . a large eye drifting like a moon . . . The images came and departed. None seemed adequate for the approaching beast—powerful, fearless . . .

Fearless?

An image leaped to mind, a question keeping it company: How strong a mental impression could he project?

Fisher could create solid-seeming illusions with ease. Could he manage with a fraction of that verisimilitude if he backed it with everything he had? Perhaps just enough to disconcert?

There was no real pause, though, between the idea and the effort. The speculation ran simultaneous with the attempt, habit of the reflective part of himself.

The sandy stretch across which he had just passed . . . He projected the image of its eruption, with the shining triangular form bursting upward, lunging forward, reaching to embrace his pursuer. . . .

Krel! Krel! he sent, concentrating to achieve perfection in its display. He halted, feeling the panic waves from behind him, aware of controlling his own movements once more, aware, too, that Yellowcloud had halted.

Krel! But even as he reinforced the image with every feeling of menace and terror with which he found himself freshly familiar, even as he unslung the burst-gun and fitted his hand to its grip, he realized that while his movements were now his own he was afraid to execute the necessary turn to face the thing which stood behind him.

The report of Yellowcloud's weapon shattered his paralysis. He spun about, the burst-gun at ready.

Cat, in the light of Yellowcloud's beam, was dropping to the ground from an erect posture, and that awful eye seemed fixed upon his own, burning, boring.

He triggered his weapon, moving it, and dirt and gravel blew backward from a line traced on the ground in front of the beast.

Yellowcloud fired again and Cat jerked as he plunged forward. Ironbear raised the muzzle of his own weapon and triggered another burst. It stitched a wavering line along Cat's neck and shoulder.

And then everything went silent and black as he felt the impact of Cat's body upon his own.

*　　*　　*

They sat or lay in their rooms at the Thunderbird Lodge, not far from the mouths of the canyons. It was as if they were all together in one room, however, for the walls did not impede their conversation.

Well? Elizabeth asked. *What have you learned?*

I'm going to try again, Fisher answered. *Wait a few minutes.*

You've been at it for quite a while, Mancin said.

Sometimes there are snags—unusual states of mind that are hard to pick up. You know.

Something's wrong, Mancin said. *I've been trying, too.*

Maybe we're too late, Mercy put in.

Don't be ridiculous!

I'm just trying to be realistic.

I got through to Yellowcloud's house while you were trying for contact, Elizabeth said. *His wife told me that he and Ironbear left together some time ago. They went over to the canyon, she said.*

After Singer? Mancin asked.

She wouldn't say any more about it. But why else?

Indeed.

I'm going to try again now, Fisher said.

Wait, Elizabeth told him.

Why?

You're not getting anywhere by yourself.

You mean we should get together again and try?

Why not? That is why we're here. To work together.

Do you think Sands. . . ? Mancin began.

Probably, Elizabeth said.

Yes, Mercy said. *But he wouldn't hurt us.*

Well, you're right about why we're here, Mancin said to Elizabeth.

And if we can't locate Jimmy? Fisher said. *What then?*

Try again with Singer, Elizabeth said. *Perhaps this time he'll listen.*

*　　*　　*

Now you travel your own trail, alone.

What you have become, we do not know.

What your clan is now, we do not know.

Now, now on, now, you are something not of

this world.

*　　*　　*

Walking. Through the silver and black landscape. Slow here. Confuse the way. As if for an ambush from behind those rocks. Erase the next hundred feet or so with a branch of shrubbery. Good. Go on. The way is clear. Vaguely red-and-white flecked. Walking. Skyflash mirrored in waters twisting. Faint drumbeat once again. Consistency of wind-sound within the slant of walls. Small spray glassmasking face here, eyelash prisms spectrumbreaking rainbows geometric dance of lights. Wipe. Shadows leapback. Coyotedog smile fading between the light and the dark. Cross here, splashing. Wherever trail runs follow the feet. Around. Over. Masked dancers within the shadows, silent. Far, far to the rear, a faint green light. Why look back? To turn is to embrace. Climb now. Descend again. It narrows soon, then widens again. A thing with many eyes sits upon a high ledge but does not stir. Frozen, perhaps, or only watching. Louder now the drumbeat. Moving to its rhythms. Fire within the heart of a stone. Rain *yei* bending, bridgelike, from above to below. Birdtracks behind a mooncurved wall. Thighbone of horse. Empty hogan. Half-burned log. Touch the mica that glistens like pollen. Remember the song the old man—

. . . *Singer.*

Faint, faint. The wind or its echo. Tired word of tired breath.

Billy Blackhorse . . .

Across again now, to that rocky place.

I feel you—up there, somewhere—tracker . . .

Something. Something he should remember. This journey. To follow his trail. But.

Your friends did not stop me. I am still coming, hunter.

Ghost of the echo of the wind. Words in his head. Old friends, perhaps. Someone known.

Why do you not answer me? To talk gives nothing away.

Ghost-cat, *chindi*-thing. Yes. Cat.

I am here, Cat.

And I follow you.

I know.

It is a good place you have chosen.

It chose me.

Either way. Better than cities.

Billy paused to muddle his trail, create the impression of another possible ambush point.

. . . Coming. You cannot run forever.

Only so far as I must. You are hurt . . .

Yes. But not enough to stop me. We will meet.

We will.

I feel you are stronger here than you were before.

Perhaps.

Whichever of us wins, it is better this way than any other. We are each of us the last of our kind. What else is there for us?

I do not know.

It is a strange country. I do not understand everything about it.

Nor do I.

Soon we will meet, old enemy. Are you glad that you ran?

Billy tried hard to think about it.

Yes, he finally said.

Billy thought of the song but knew that it was not the time to sing it. Thunder mumbled down the canyon.

You have changed, hunter, since last we were this close.

I know where I'm going now, Cat.

Hurry then. I may be closer than you think.

Watch the shadows. You may even be nearer than you think.

Silence. The big widening and a clear view far ahead. He halted, puzzled, suddenly able to see for a great distance. Like a ribbon, his trail led on and on and then wound upward. He did not understand, but it did not matter. He broke into his ground-eating jog. In the darkness high overhead, he heard the cry of a bird.

> *Farther yet, he returns with me, Nayenezgani,*
> *spinning his dark staff for protection.*
> *The lightnings flash behind him and before him.*
> *To the ladder's first rung,*
> *to the Emergence Place*
> *he returns with me;*
> *and the rainbow returns with me*
> *and the talking* ketahn *teaches me.*
> *We mount the ladder's twelve rungs.*
> *Small blue birds sing above me,*
> *Cornbeetle sings behind me.*
> Hashje-altye *returns with me.*
> *I will climb Emergence Mountain,*
> *Chief Mountain, Rain Mountain,*
> *Corn Mountain, Pollen Mountain. . . .*
> *Returning. Upon the pollen figure to sit.*
> *To own the home, the fire, the food,*
> *the resting place, the feet, the legs, the body,*
> *to hold the mind and the voice, the power*
> *of movement. The speech, that is blessed.*
> *Returning with me. Gathering these things,*
> *Climbing. Through the mists and clouds,*
> *the mosses and grasses,*
> *the woods and rocks, the earth,*
> *of the four colors. Returning.*
> "*Grandchild, we stand upon the rainbow.*"

*   *   *

Running. The wind and water-sounds now a part of the drumbeat. Path grown clearer and clearer. Blood-red now and dusted as with ice flakes.

The ground seemed to shake once, and something like a tower of smoke rose before him in a twisting at the side of the trail. Changing colors, the pillar braided itself as it climbed, and five shifting faces took form within it. He recognized his guardian spirits.

"Billy, we have come to ask you again," they said in a single voice. "The danger increases. You must leave the trail, leave the canyon. Quickly. You must go to a place where you will be met and taken to safety."

"I cannot leave the trail now," he answered. "It is too late to do that. My enemy approaches. My way is clear before me. Thank you again. There is no longer a choice for me in this."

"There is always a choice."

"Then I have already made it."

The smoke-being blew apart as he passed it.

He saw what appeared to be the end of the trail now, and a small atavistic fear touched him as he realized where it would take him. It was to the Mummy Cave, an old place of the dead, that it ran, high up the canyon wall.

As he advanced, it seemed to grow before him, a ruin within a high alcove. A green light played behind one of the windows for an eyeblink and a half. And then the wind was muffled, and then it rose again. And again. Again.

Now the sound came like the flapping of a giant piece of canvas high in the sky. He kept his eyes upon his goal and continued to follow his trail toward the foot of the wall. And as he ran the sound grew louder, felt nearer. Finally it seemed directly overhead, and he sensed each beat upon his body. Then a dark shape moved past, through the upper air.

When he raised his eyes he beheld an enormous bird-form dipping to settle atop the cliff wall high above the place of the Mummy Cave. He slowed as he neared the foot of the wall and encountered the talus slope. And he knew as he beheld the dark thing, settling now and staring downward, that he beheld Haasch'ééshzhiní, Black-god, master of the hunt. He looked away quickly, but not before he met the merciless stare of a yellow eye fixed upon him.

Must I end this thing beneath your gaze, Dark One? he wondered. For I am both the hunter and the hunted. Which side does that put you on?

He mounted the slope, his eyes now following the trail gone vertical up toward the recessed ruin. Yes, that did seem the easiest route. . . .

He approached the wall, took the first foothold and handhold and commenced climbing.

Climbing. Slowly over the more slippery places. A strange tingling in the palms of the hands as he mounted higher. Like the time—

No. He halted. Everything he was a part of the hunt. But it was also a part of the past. Let it go. Climb. Hunt. Position is what is important. That lesson comes with memory. Achieve it now. He drew himself higher, not looking at the dark shadow far above, not looking back. Soon.

Soon he would enter the place of death and await his pursuer. The running should be nearing its end. Hurry. Important to be up there and out of sight when Cat enters the area. Wet handhold. Grip tightly.

Glance upward. Yes. In sight now. Soon. Careful. Pull. There.

After several minutes, he drew himself up onto a ledge, moved to the left. Another hold. Up again.

Half crawling. Okay now. Rise again. Move toward the wall. Enter. No green light. Over the wall . . .

He passed along the rear of the wall, peering through gaps out over the floor of the canyon. Nothing. Nothing yet in sight. Keep going. That large opening . . .

All right. Halt. Unsling the weapon. Check it out. Rest it on the ledge. Wait.

Nothing. Still nothing. The place was damp and filled with rubble. He ran his eyes across the open spaces before him, the entire prospect palely illuminated through screens of phosphorescent mist. But waiting was a thing at which he excelled. He settled with his back against a block of stone, his eyes upon the canyon, one hand upon the weapon.

Nearly an hour passed with no changes in the scene before him.

And then a shadow, slow, inching along the wall, far to his left and ahead. Its creeping barely registered, until at some point he realized that there was nothing to cast it.

He raised the weapon—it had a simple sight—and zeroed it in on the shadow. Then he thought about the accuracy of the thing and lowered it again. Too far. If the shadow were really Cat he did not want to take a chance on missing and giving away his position.

It stopped. It flowed into the form of a rock and re-mained stationary for a long while. He could almost believe that the entire sequence had been a trick of light and shadow. Almost. He drew a bead on the rock and held it there.

You are somewhere near, Billy. I can feel you.

He did not respond.

Wherever you are, I will be there shortly.

Should he risk a shot after all? he wondered. It would take Cat a while to assume a more mobile shape. He would doubtless have several opportunities during that time. . . .

Movement again. The rock shifted, flowed, reformed farther along the wall.

Suffer, tracker. You are going to die. Your first shot will betray you and I will dodge all of the successive ones. You will see me when I am ready to be seen and you will fire it then.

The movement commenced again, drifting toward a real rock beneath a shelflike overhang. Within the amorphous form the glittering of Cat's eye became visible; his limbs began to take form.

Billy bit his lip, recalling having seen a torglind metamorph run up a near-vertical wall on the home planet. He triggered the weapon then and missed.

Cat froze for a split second as the flash occurred high overhead, then moved more slowly than Billy had anticipated, leading Billy to believe that the beast was indeed injured. Cat sprang back toward a line of stones nearer the wall. And then, realizing his mistake as he glanced upward, his legs bunched beneath him and he sprang forward again. But not in time.

A large slab of stone facing, blasted loose by the shot, slid down the wall, striking the shelf beneath which Cat crouched. Even as his feet left the ground, it descended upon him.

Hunter! I believe—you've won. . . .

Billy fired again. This time he scorched the earth ten yards off to the right of the fall. He moved the barrel slightly to the left and triggered the weapon again. This time the top of the rubble heap exploded.

It seemed that he could make out a single, massive forelimb projected near the front of the pile. But at that distance he could not be certain.

Was that a twitch?

He fired again, blasting the center of the heap.

The canyon rang with a massive cawing note. The flapping sound began again, slowly. He looked up briefly and glimpsed the shadow moving off to his right.

"It is over," he sang, head rested upon his forearm, "and my thanks rise like smoke. . . ."

His words trailed off as his eyes moved across the canyon floor. Then his brow furrowed. He raised himself. He leaned forward to peer.

"Why?" he said aloud.

But nothing answered.

The trail he had followed did not terminate at this place. Somehow he had not noticed this earlier. It ran off to his right, curving out of sight beyond the canyon wall, presumably continuing on into the farther reaches of the place.

He slung his weapon and adjusted his pack. He did not understand, but he would go on.

He returned to the place where he had climbed and began his descent.

* * *

His shoulder ached. Also, it was raining on his face and a sharp stone was poking him in the back. He was aware of these things for some time before he realized that they meant he was alive.

Ironbear opened his eyes. Yellowcloud's light lay upon the ground nearby, casting illumination along a gravel slope.

He turned his head and saw Yellowcloud. The man was seated with his back against a stone, legs straight out before him. Both of his hands were gripping his left thigh.

Ironbear raised his head, reached out a hand, levered himself upward.

"I live," he said, swinging into a sitting position. "How're you?"

"Broken leg," Yellowcloud answered. "Above the knee."

Ironbear rose, crossed to the light and picked it up, turned back toward Yellowcloud.

"Bad place for a break," he said, advancing. "Can't even hobble."

He squatted beside the other man. "I'm not sure what's the best thing to do," he said. "Got any suggestions?"

"I've already called for help. My portaphone wasn't damaged. They'll be along with a medic. Get me out of here in a sling if they have to. Don't worry. I'll be okay."

"Why are we still alive?"

"It didn't think we were worth killing, I guess. Just an annoyance, to be brushed aside."

"Makes you feel real important, doesn't it?"

"I'm not complaining. Listen, there's dry wood along the wall. Get me a couple of armloads, will you? I want a fire."

"Sure." He moved to comply. "I wonder how far along that thing has gotten?"

"Can't you tell?"

"I don't want to get near it at that level. It can hurt you just with its mind."

"You going after it?"

"If I can figure a way to follow it." Yellowcloud smiled and turned his head, gesturing with his chin.

"It went that way."

"I'm not a tracker like you."

"Hell, you don't have to be. That thing's heavy and it's running, right out in the open. Nothing fancy. It couldn't care less whether one of us knows where it went. You take the light. I'll have the fire. You'll be able to see the marks it left."

He carried over the first load of kindling, went back to look for more. By the time he returned with the second load, Yellowcloud had a fire going.

"Anything else I can do for you?" he asked.

"No. Just get moving."

He slung his weapon and picked up the light. When he played the beam up the canyon he saw the tracks readily enough.

"And take this." Yellowcloud passed him the porta-phone.

"Okay. I'll go try again."

"Maybe you ought to aim for its eye."

"Maybe I should. See you."

"Good luck."

He turned and began walking. The water was a dark, speaking thing whose language he did not understand. The way was clear. The tracks were large.

*   *   *

The wind stirs the grasses.
The snow glides across the earth.
The whirlwind walks on the mountain,
raising dust.
      The rocks are ringing
high on the mountain, behind the fog.
The sun's light is running out
like water from a cracked pitcher.
We shall live again.
The snowy earth
slides out of the whirling wind.
We shall live again.

Around the curve of the canyon wall, walking. Gusts of wind here over stream grown wider, swirling glittering particles across watersong gone wild. Other side more sheltered but the red way lies close to the wall, here, rising now. Ripples like rushing pictographs. Pawprints of the perfidious one. Ice-rimed bones beside the trail. Rabbit. Burnt hogan, green glow within. Place of death. Shift eyes. Hurry on. Shine of crystal. Snow-streaked wall, texture of feathers. Trail winding on. As far as the eye will go. What now the quarry?

Pause to drink at the crossing of tributary streamlet.

Burning cold, flavored of rock and earth. Fog bank ahead, moving toward him, masked dancers within; about a south-blue blaze. Rhythms in the earth. He is become a smoke, drifting along his way, silent and featureless, rushing to merge with that place of flux and earthdance cadence. Yes, and be lost in it.

White and soft, smothering sounds, like that place where he had hunted the garlett, so long ago . . .

Dancers to the right, dancers to the left, dancers crossing his way. Do they even see him, invisible and spiritlike, passing among them, along the stillbright, stillred way written upon the ground as with fire and blood?

One draws nearer bearing something covered by a cloth woven with an old design. He halts, for the dancer moves to bar his way, thrusting the thing before him. It is uncovered, displaying a pair of hands. He stares at them. That scar near the base of the left thumb . . . They are his hands.

At the recognition they rise to hover in front of him, as if he were holding them before his face. He feels them, glovelike, at the extremity of his spirit. He had skinned game with them, fought with them, stroked Dora's hair with them. . . .

He lets them fall to his sides. It is good to have them back again. The dancer moves away. Billy swirls like a whirlwind of snow and continues along his trail.

There is no time. A cluster of gray sticks, rising from the earth on the slope to his right, beside the trail . . . He pauses to watch as the sticks turn green, bumps appearing along their surfaces to become buds. The buds crack, leaves unwind themselves, turn, enlarge. White flowers come forth.

He passes, swinging his hands. Another dancer with another parcel approaches from his left. He halts, hovering, and with his hands he accepts the gift of his feet and restores them to their places on the ground below him. The many miles we have come together . . .

Walking, again walking, upon the trail. Feeling the heartbeat of the earth through the soles of his feet. There is no time. Snowflakes blow upward before him. The stream has reversed its direction. Blood flows back into the wounded deer lying still across his way. It springs to its hoofs, turns and is gone.

Now, like curtains, a parting of the fog. Four masked dancers advance upon him, bearing the body that is his own. When he wears it again, he thanks them, but they withdraw in silence.

He moves on along the trail. The fog is shifting. Everything is shifting but the trail.

He hears a sound which he has not heard in a great counting of years. It begins off in the distance behind him and rises in pitch as it comes on: the whistle of a train.

Then he hears the chugging. They no longer make engines of this sort. There is nothing here for it to run on. There is—

He sees the rails paralleling his trail. That ledge ahead seems a platform now. . . .

The whistle sounds again. Nearer. He feels the throb of the thing, superimposed upon the earth rhythms. A train such as he has not beheld in years is coming. Coming, impossibly, through this impossible place. He keeps walking, as the sound of it fills the world. It should be rushing up beside him at any moment.

The shriek of the whistle fills his hearing. He turns his head.

Yes, it has come. An ancient, black, smoke-puffing dragon of an engine, a number of passenger cars trailing behind. He hears the screaming of its brakes begin.

He looks back to the area of the platform, to where a single, slouched figure now stands waiting. Almost familiar . . .

With a clattering and the cries of metal friction the engine draws abreast of him, slowing, slowing, and passes to halt beside the platform. He smells smoke and grease and hot metal.

The figure on the platform moves toward the first passenger car, and he now recognizes the old dead singer who had taught him the song. Just before boarding the man turns and waves to him.

His gaze slides back along the coach's windows. Behind every one is a face. He recognizes all of them. They are all people he has known who are now dead—his mother, his grandmother, his uncles, his cousins, two sisters . . .

Dora.

Dora is the only one who is looking at him. The others stare past, talking with one another, regarding the landscape, the new passenger. . . .

Dora is looking directly at him, and her hands are working with the latches at the lower corners of the window. Almost frantically, she is pushing and lifting.

The whistle blows again. The engine surges. He finds himself running, running toward the train, the car, the window. . . .

The train jerks, rattles. The wheels turn.

Dora is still working at the latches. Suddenly the window slides upward. Her mouth is moving. She is shouting, but her words are lost among the noises of the train.

He shouts back. Her name. She is leaning forward out of the window now, right arm extended.

The train is picking up speed, but he is almost beside it. He reaches. Their hands are perhaps a meter apart. Her lips are still moving, but he cannot hear her words. For a moment his vision swims, and it is as if she were falling away from him.

He increases his pace and the distance between their hands narrows—two feet, a foot, eight inches. . . .

Their hands clasp, and she smiles. He matches the train's velocity for a moment before the tension begins. Then he realizes that he must let go.

He opens his hand and watches her rush away. He falls.

How long he lies there he does not know. When he looks again, the train is gone. There are no tracks. There is no platform. His outstretched arm lies within the icy stream. Snow is falling upon him. He rises.

The big flakes drift by. The wind has died. The water sounds are muted. He raises his hand and stares at it like a new and unfamiliar thing within the silence.

After a long while, he turns and seeks the trail again. He continues his journey along it.

Trudging. Alternating elation and depression, finally all mixed together. To have caught her and then had to let her go. To ride Smohalla's ghost-train through the snow. Another breaking apart. Would there be a putting together again?

He realized then that he was traversing an enormous

sand-painting. All of the ground about him was laid out in stylized, multicolored fashion. He walked in the footprints of the rainbow, passing between *Eth-hay-nah-ashi*—Those-who-go-together. They were the twins created in the Second World by Begochiddy. First Man and the others had come up from the Underworld along this route. The painting itself was one used in *Hozhoni*, the Blessingway. His trail followed the rainbow to the cornstalk, where it changed to the yellow of corn pollen. Upward, upward along the stalk then. The sky was illuminated by a brilliant flash as he passed alongside the female rainbow and the male lightning. Passing between the figures of Big Fly, heading north to the yellow pollen footsteps.

Emerge to take up the trail again, passing the mouth of the large canyon to the right, continuing northward. Alone, singing. There was beauty in the falling snow. Beauty all around him . . .

Admire it while you may, tracker.

Cat? You're dead! It is over between us!

Am I, now?

I touched your limb at the place where you fell. It was stiff and glassy. There was no life in you.

Have it your way.

Nor could anything have gotten out from beneath that heap of stone.

You've convinced me. I will go back and lie down.

Billy looked backward, saw nothing but snowfall within the canyon.

. . . But I'll find you first.

That shouldn't be too hard.

I am glad to hear you say that.

I like to finish what I start. Hurry.

Why don't you wait for me?

I've a trail to follow.

And that is more important than me?

You? You are nothing now.

That is not too flattering. But very well. If we must meet upon your trail again, we will meet upon your trail.

Billy checked his weapons.

You should have taken the train, he said.

I do not understand you, but it does not matter.

But it does, Billy said, rounding another rock and seeing the trail go on.

A whirlwind of snow danced across the water. He heard the thump of a single drumbeat.

. . . The blue medicine lifts me in his hand.

The pain in his shoulder had subsided to a dull throbbing. He peered into pockets of shadow as he passed them, wondering whether the beast might be waiting to spring upon him, knowing the fear to be irrational since the tracks lay clear before him—and why should it go to the trouble of doubling back to lay in wait for him when it could have taken an extra second to smash him in passing back when they had met?

Ironbear cursed, still looking. His breath emerged as plumes of steam before him. His nose was cold and his eyes watered periodically.

Yellowcloud had been right. There was no problem at all in following this trail. Simple and direct. Deep and clear cut.

Was that a movement to the left?

Yes. The wind stirring bushes.

He cursed again. Had his ancestors really led war parties? So much for genetics . . .

Jimmy. Don't shut me out!

I won't, Charles. I can use the company.

Where are you? What's happening?

I'm in the canyon, following the thing.

We're here in Arizona, at the hotel near to where the canyons start.

Why?

To help, if we can. You're following the beast? Is Yellow-cloud with you?

He was, but it broke his leg. He's sent for help.

You've met it?

Yeah. Got a sprained shoulder out of the deal. Put a few shots into the thing, though.

Were you unconscious?

Yes.

I wondered why I couldn't reach you for a while there. Have you been in touch with Singer?

No.

We have. That's one crazy Indian.

I think he knows what he's doing.

Do you know what you're doing?

Being another crazy Indian, I guess.

I'd say.

Looks like we cross the water here.

I think you ought to get out. That's two trails you're following, not one.

It's starting to snow now. God, I hope it doesn't cover the tracks. Melting when it hits, though. That's good.

Sounds as if that thing almost killed you once.

They're changing shape.

The tracks?

Yeah, and moving nearer the wall. Wonder what that means?

It means you'd better shoot at anything that moves.

Something wet and glassy here . . . Wonder what its blood looks like?

How far along are you, anyway?

Don't know. My watch is broken. Seems as if I've been walking forever.

Maybe you'd better stop and rest.

Hell, no. It's time to try jogging for a while. I've got a feeling. I think I'm near and I think it's hurt.

I don't want to be in your mind if it gets you.

Don't go yet. I'm scared.

I'll wait.

For the next quarter-hour he felt Fisher's silent presence as he ran beside the pleated wall. They did not converse again until he slowed to catch his breath near a turning place.

It's going slow here, sneaking. But there's only a little of that glassy stuff, he observed.

You go slow.

I am. I'll just switch to the blacklight and put on the goggles. I'll get down low and look around the corner.

There was a long silence.

Well?

224

I don't see anything.

He turned the light toward the ground.

The trail's changing again. I'm going to follow it.

Wait. Why don't you probe?

I'm afraid to touch its mind.

I'd be a lot more afraid of the rest of it. Why not just take it very slow and easy? Just scan for its presence. Sneak up mentally. I'll help.

You're right, but I'll do it myself.

He reached out into the pocket canyon before him. Gingerly at first. Then with increased effort.

Not there. Nothing there, he said. *I see the trail, but I don't feel the beast. Singer either, for that matter. They must have gone on.*

It would seem . . .

He neared the corner, walking slowly, observing the markings on the ground. The markings were altered beyond the turning, forming a troughlike line. They narrowed, widened, halted in the form of circular depressions.

He paused when he saw where they led, rushed forward when he saw something other than rock.

Singer's prints marked the ground before the rough cairn, near to the protruding limb. It was a longer while before he could bring himself to move a few stones and then only after probing thoroughly. He kept at it for several minutes, until he was sweating and breathing heavily. But at last he beheld the eye, dull now, in the sleek, unmoving head.

He got it, Fisher said. *He nailed the thing.*

Ironbear did not respond.

It's over, Fisher told him. *Singer won.*

He's beautiful, Ironbear said. *That neck . . . the eye, like a jewel . . .*

Dead, Fisher said. *Wait while I check. I'll tell you where to climb out. We'll have someone pick you up.*

But where's Singer?

I guess he knows how to take care of himself. He's safe now. He'll turn up when he's ready. Hang on.

I'm going after him.

What? What for?

I don't know. Call it a feeling. Say I just want to see the man after all this.

How'll you find him?

I'm starting to get the hang of this tracking business. I don't think it will be too hard.

It's all over—and that's a dangerous place.

His trail has run through safe spots so far. Besides, I've got a phone here.

Don't you flip out, too!

Don't worry about it.

Ironbear turned away, pushed up his goggles, shifted to normal spectrum, began following Singer's tracks.

I'm going to leave you for a time, Fisher said. *I'm going to tell the others. Also, I've got to rest.*

Go ahead.

Ironbear headed north. For a moment it seemed that he heard a train whistle, and he thought of his father. Fat snowflakes filled the air. He wrapped his muffler around his nose and mouth and kept going.

*   *   *

Mercy Spender

when she heard the news,
opened the bottle of gin she had brought along
& poured herself a stiff one,
humming "Rock of Ages" all the while;
feeling responsibility dissolve,
giving thanks,
deciding which books to read
& what to knit
during her convalescence;
offered a word or two
for the soul of Walter Sands,
whom she saw before her
in the glass,
suddenly,
shaking his head;
"Rest in peace," she said
& chugged it,
& when she went to pour another
the glass broke somehow
& she was very sleepy
& decided to turn in
& save the serious part

for tomorrow;
& her sleep was troubled.

*   *   *

Alex Mancin

tripped home when he heard the news,

the game being over,
his side having won
again;
& after he'd said goodbye to the others
& gone through,
he visited the kennels
& played with the dogs for a time,
lithe, yipping & licking—
he could read their affection for him
& it warmed him—
& then visited his console,
a glass of warm milk at his right hand,
taking action on the multitude of messages
which had come in,
as always;
too keyed up to sleep,
thoughts of the recent enterprise
dashing into and out of his mind
like puppies;
& the smile of Walter Sands
seemed to flash for a moment
on the screen
as he read a list of stock quotations
& toyed with a pair of souvenir dice
he'd found in the bottom drawer
of the dresser in the back room.

*   *   *

Elizabeth Brooke

wanted to get laid,

was surprised
at the intensity of the feeling,
but realized that the previous days'
pace & tensions, suddenly relaxed,
called for some physical release, too;
& so she bade the others farewell
& tripped back to England
to call her friend to join her
for tea,
to talk of her recent experiences,
listen to some chamber music
& lay the ghost of Walter Sands
which had been troubling her
more than a little.

*　　　*　　　*

Charles Dickens Fisher

in his room at the Thunderbird Lodge
with a pot of coffee,
looked out of the window at the snow,
thinking about his brother-in-law
& the Indians
in western movies he had seen
& wilderness survival
& the great dead beast
whose image he caused to appear
before him on the lawn
(frightening a couple across the way
who happened to look out
at that moment),

recalled from a video picture
he had summoned earlier,
eye blazing like Waterford crystal,
fangs like stalactites;
& then he banished it
& produced a full-sized
image of Walter Sands,
sitting in the armchair
looking back at him,
& when he asked him,
"How do you like being dead?"
Sands shrugged
& replied,
"It has its benefits,
it has its drawbacks."

Going. Along the western rim of the canyon now, heading into the northeast. Turning, taking an even more northerly route. Away from the canyon, across the snows, toward the trees. His way had brought him over the water and up the wall nearly an hour before. Up here where the wind was strong, though the snowfall had lessened to an occasional racing flake.

He bore on. A coyote howled somewhere in the trees or beyond them, ahead. A woodland smell came to him as he advanced, and the sounds of rattling branches.

He looked back once before he entered the wood. It seemed that there was a greenish glow rising just above the rim of the canyon. He lost sight of it in a snowswirl a moment later, and then there were trees all around him and a diminishment of the wind. Ice fell with crisp and glassy sounds when he brushed against boughs. It was like another place, a place of perpetual twilight and cold, where he had hunted what he came to call the ice bears, the sun a tiny, pale thing creeping along the horizon. At any moment the high-pitched whistle of the bears might come to him, and then he would have only moments in which to throw up the barrier and lay down a paralytic fire before the pack swirled in toward him. Move the barrier then to preserve the fallen before their fellows devoured them. Call for the shuttle ship. . . .

He glanced overhead, half expecting to see it descending now. But there was only a pearl-gray folding of clouds in every direction. This hunt was different. The thing he sought would not be taken so simply, nor borne away for enclosure. All the more interesting.

He crossed an ice-edged streamlet and his way swerved abruptly, following its course through an arroyo where something with green eyes regarded him from within a small cave. The ground rose as he advanced, and when he emerged the trees had thinned.

His way took him to the left then, continuing uphill. He mounted higher and higher until he came at last to stand atop a ridge commanding a large view of the countryside. There he halted, staring into the black north, into which his trail ran on and on for as far as he could see in the odd half-light which had accompanied him on this journey. Opening his pouch, he cast pollen before him onto it. Turning then to the blue south, way to the earth-opening from which he had emerged, he cast more pollen, noticing for the first time that there was no trail behind him, that his way to this place had been vanishing even as he walked it. He felt that he would be unable to take a step in that direction if he were to try. There was to be no return along the way that he followed.

He faced the yellow west, place where the day was folded and closed. Casting pollen, he thought about endings, about the closing of cycles. Then to the east, thinking of all the mornings he had known and of the next one which would come out of it. Seeing for a great distance into the east with unusual clarity, he thought of the land over which his vision moved, adding features from the internal landscape of memory, wondering why he had ever wished to deny this Dinetah which was so much a part of him.

For how long he looked into the east he could not tell. Suddenly the air about his head was filled with spinning motes of light accompanied by a soft buzzing sound. It was like a swarm of fireflies dancing before him. Abruptly they darted off to his right. He realized then that it was a warning of some sort.

He looked to the right. There was a green glow moving among the trees in the distance. He looked away, placing his gaze upon his trail once again, and then he moved off along it.

Shortly he was running, ice particles stinging his face, driven by gusts of wind which raised them in occasional brief clouds. The snow did not obscure the trail, however. It was visible through everything with perfect clarity. Continuing to follow it into the distance with his eyes, he saw that it ran into an arroyo twisting off to the left. It seemed to narrow as it entered that place. Following, he saw that the narrowing continued until it appeared the thinness of a Christmas ribbon toward the center of the declivity. Strangely, however, the portion he was traversing appeared no narrower, though he knew that he had already reached and passed beyond the place where the thinning had begun. Instead, he detected a new phenomenon.

At first it was only that the arroyo had seemed somewhat deeper and longer than his initial impression had indicated. As he moved more deeply into it, however, the place itself seemed larger, a huge canyon with high walls. And the farther he progressed, the steeper the walls became, the greater the distance from wall to wall. It also was now strewn with massive boulders which had not been apparent at first. Yet the red way he followed remained undiminished. There were no signs of the contraction he had noticed earlier.

An enormous white wheel flew past him, sculpted and brilliant, five-limbed like a starfish. Immediately another moved slowly overhead, descending. He realized that it was a snowflake.

The place was larger than Canyon del Muerto, much larger. In moments, its walls had receded into the distance, vanished. He increased his pace, running, leaping, among the huge rocks.

He topped a rise to discover a massive glassy mountain looming before him, its prismatic surfaces retailing rainbows at peculiar angles.

Then he was descending toward it, and he could see where his trail ran into a large opening in its side, a jagged slash-mark through stone and sheen, like a black lightning bolt running from about a third of its height downward to the earth.

A gust of wind blew him over and he regained his footing and ran on. A snowflake crashed to the earth like a falling building. He raced across the top of a small pond which vibrated beneath him.

The mountain towered higher, nearer. Finally he was close enough to see into the great opening, and he saw that it shone within as well as without, the walls sparkling almost moistly, rising in a pitched-tentlike fashion to some unseen point of convergence high overhead.

He rushed within and halted almost immediately. His hand went to his knife before he realized that the men who surrounded him were multiple images of himself reflected in the gleaming walls. And his trail running off in all directions . . . Twisted images.

He bumped into a wall, ran his hands down its surface. His trail seemed to go straight ahead here, but he saw now where the real only seemed to join the illusory. It slid to the right, he could tell now.

Three paces and he bumped into another wall. This could not be. There was nothing else for the trail to do. It proceeded directly ahead here, with no deviations, reflected or otherwise.

He reached forward, felt the wall, searched it. His reflection mimicked his movements.

Abruptly, there was nothing. His hand moved forward as he realized that only the upper portion of his way was blocked. He dropped to all fours and continued onward.

As he crawled, the reflections shifted in the shadows

around him. For a moment, from the corner of his eye, to the right, it seemed that he was a slow, lumbering bear, pacing himself. He glanced quickly to the left. A deer, a six-pointer, dark eyes alert, nostrils quivering. Multiple reflections caused them all to merge then, into something that was bear and deer and man, something primeval, working its way, like First Man, through narrow, dark tunnels upward to the new world.

The reflections ahead showed him that the overhead space was growing larger again, turning into a high, narrow, Gothic arch. He rose to his feet as soon as he noticed this, and the animal images slipped away, leaving nothing but the infinity of himself on all sides. All colors, in various intensities, lay ahead. He went on, and when he saw that he was heading toward a way out, he began to run.

The area of light seemed to grow slightly smaller as he advanced upon it. The reflections which ran beside him now varied through prisms and shadows. And he noted that they were all differently garbed. One bounded along in a pressurized suit, another in a tuxedo; another wore only a loincloth. One ran nude. Another wore a parka. One had on a blue velveteen shirt he had long forgotten, a sandcast concho belt binding it above the hips. In the distance, he saw himself as a boy, running furiously, arms pumping.

Smiling, he ran out through the opening, along the red way. The canyon walls appeared and closed in on him, diminishing in height as he advanced.

He halted and looked back.

There was no shining mountain. He retraced his steps a dozen paces and stooped to pick up a piece of stone containing a cracked quartz crystal which lay on the ground. He held it up to his eyes. A rainbow danced within it. He dropped it into his pocket, feeling as if it held half of time and space.

He ran for nearly an hour then, and ice crystals scratched like the claws of cats at rocks and tree limbs, at his face. The frozen earth made noises like crinkling cellophane beneath his feet. Streaks of snow lay like crooked fingers on the hillsides. A patch of sky lightened and thunder rumbled nearby. His way led into the mountains, and soon he began to climb.

> *When I call,*
> *they come to me*
> *out of Darkness Mountain.*
> *Pipelines cross it,*
> *satellites pass above it,*
> *but I hold the land before me,*
> *and all things that hunt*
> *and are hunted within it.*
> *I have followed the People*
> *across the eons,*
> *giving the proper hunter his prey*
> *in the proper time.*
> *Those who hunt themselves,*
> *however, fall into a special category.*
> *Certain sophistications were unknown*
> *in ancient times.*
> *But you are never too old to learn,*
> *which is what makes this business interesting*
> *and keeps me black-winged. Na-ya!*

Out of Darkness Mountain, then:
Send an ending.

*   *   *

And climbing, Everything strange. He had lost track of time and space. Sometimes the countryside seemed to roll by him, other times it seemed that he had moved for ages to cover a small distance. The trail took him among more mountains. He was no longer certain as to precisely where he was, though he was sure that he was still heading north. The snow turned into rain. The rain came and went. The trail led upward once again and moved through rocky passages. In places, streamlets rushed by him, and he passed through narrow necks with his back pressed against stone, fingertips and heels his only purchase. The clouds were occasionally delineated by a bright scribbling, to be wiped away by the grayness moments later.

He passed through an opening so narrow that he had to strip off his pack and jacket and go sideways. It cut sharply to the left, and he knew that he could have missed it even in full daylight without the guiding trail that led him on. Glowing forms seemed to writhe in crevasses he passed before the way widened again, like the mating movements of the tall, spindly anklavars on the world called Bayou.

When he turned and stretched his cramped muscles, he halted. What was this place? There was a ruin built into the cliff face to the right. Farther ahead there was another, to the left and higher, at a place where the canyon continued its widening. Stone and rotted adobe, they were ruins with which he was not familiar, though he had once thought that he was aware of almost all of them. He was tempted to pause for a quick investigation, but the drumbeat commenced again, slowly, and his trail ran on to greater heights.

The canyon turned to the right, its floor rising even farther, its walls spread wider. He climbed, and there were more ruins about. The name "Lukachukai" passed through his mind as he remembered the story of a lost Anasazi ruin. The wind grew still and the pulse of the drum quickened. Shadowy shapes darted behind broken walls. He stared at the high, level place before him. He saw the end of his trail. A chill passed over his entire body, and he felt the hairs rise on the nape of his neck.

He took a step forward, then another. He moved cautiously, slowly, as if the ground might give way beneath him at any point. It was right, though, wasn't it? Of course. All trails end the same way. Why should this one be any different? If you tracked anything through its entire life, from its first faltering step until its final faltering step, the end was always the same.

Back beside a rock, beneath an overhang, his trail ended before the vacant gaze of an age-browned human skull. Beyond that, he could not see the way.

The rhythm of the drumbeat changed. *Mah-ih*, the Trickster, Coyote, He-who-wanders-about, peered at him from beyond the corner of a nearby ruin. A white rainbow *yei* formed an arc from the top of one canyon wall to the other. He heard the shaking of rattles now, accompanying the drumbeat. A green stem poked through the ground, rose upward, put forth leaves and then a red flower.

He walked on. As he advanced, the skull seemed to jerk slightly forward. A flickering occurred within it, and then a pale green light grew behind all of its apertures which faced him. Far off to the right, Coyote made a sudden, low, growling sound.

As he neared the end of the trail the skull tipped backward and turned slightly to the right, keeping the eyesockets fixed directly upon him.

A rasping voice emerged from the skull:

"Behold your *chindi*."

Billy halted.

"I used to play soccer," he said, smiling and drawing back his foot. "Those two rocks up by the ruin can be the goal posts."

The ground erupted before him. The skull shot upward to a position perhaps a foot higher than his head. It rode upon the shoulders of a massive, nude, male body which had grown up like the flower before him. The green light danced all around it.

"Shadow-thing!" Billy said, unslinging his weapon.

"Yes. Your shadow. Shoot if you will. It will not save you."

Billy continued the movement which brought the snub-gun forward, reversing it in his hands, driving its butt hard upward against the skull. With a brief crunching noise the skull shattered, and its pieces fell to the ground. The trunk beneath dropped to one knee and the arms shot forward. A massive hand caught hold of the weapon and tore it from Billy's grasp. It cast it backward over its shoulder, to fall with a clatter among rocks far up the canyon and to vanish there.

The left hand caught his right wrist and held it with a grip like a steel band. He chopped at the other's biceps with the edge of his left hand. It had no apparent effect, and so he drew his hunting knife, cross-body, and plunged it into the headless one, in the soft area below the left shoulder joint.

Suddenly his wrist was free and the thing before him was falling backward, knees folding up toward the chest, arms clasping them.

Billy watched as the other rolled away, darkening, losing features, growing compact, making crunching noises in passing over gravel and sand. It had become a big, round boulder, slowing now. . . .

It came to a halt perhaps fifteen meters distant, and then, slowly, it began to unfold into a new form. It unwound limbs and shaped a head, a tail . . .

An eye.

Cat stood facing him across the canyon of the lost city. *We shall continue where we left off before the interruption,* he said.

Mercy Spender was jerked out of a deep, dreamless sleep. She began to scream, but the cry died within her. There was a twisted familiarity to what was happening. She drew herself into a fetal position and pulled the blankets up over her head.

Alex Mancin was spinning figures across his video console when it hit. When his vision wavered and dimmed, he thought that he was having a stroke. And then he realized what was happening and did not resist it, for his curiosity was stronger than his fear.

Elizabeth Brooke twisted from side to side. It was getting better every second. In just a few more moments . . . Her mind began to twist also, and she shrieked.

Fisher was in communication with Ironbear when the mental storm broke and they were sucked into another state of awareness.

What the hell is it? he asked.

We're being pulled back together again, Ironbear replied.

Who's doing it?

Sands. Can't you feel him? Like a broken lodestone, reassembling itself—

Nice image. But I still don't under— Ah!

Plosion ex. Im noisolp.

ashes falling back into bonfire, fireflame along the

across the night arcing east drawn tgthr brainbow four containing ffth reassembling spring pushing upward beneath erth snows clds sorting moisture bright spikes fllng waters flwng hllw-eyd ruins facing knifemanhanded and rockdreamt beast lost within this place of old ones weeee! frthgo endlessly unwrapping thoughtveiling countereal ity downow bhind substances tessences and above fireflame waterfiow and blow weI flsh the toilet of the world and let the spiral remain powr now the pwr ander seav nightebbing kraft tofil manshadow in shdworld he travel and wI the fireflame Iwe like blude tofil circulate and recur along the mariform outreach hmsel

fireflame along the

plosion

He stands, crouching, blade in his left hand. He moves the weapon slowly, turning it, raising it, lowering it, hoping for a glint or two to catch the vision behind the eye. The beast takes a step forward. The green light is trapped within the facets of that eye. Whether the blade holds any fascination for it he cannot tell.

The beast takes another step.

A gentle rain is falling. He is uncertain when it commenced again. It increases slightly in intensity.

Another step. . .

His right hand moves to his belt buckle and catches hold of it. He turns to extend his left shoulder, continuing the movements of the blade.

Another step . . .

The beast's tongue darts once, in and out. Something is not right. Size? Pattern of movement? The cold absence of projected feelings when it had communicated?

Another step.

Still a little too far to spring yet, he decides. He turns his body a little more. He releases the belt buckle and slides his hand farther to his left, the movement masked by the flap of his jacket, by the angle at which he now stands. Is it reading his mind at this moment? He begins the Blessingway chant again, mentally, to fill his thoughts. Something inside him seems to take it up. It runs effortlessly within his breast, the accompanying feelings flowing without exertion.

Another . . .

Soon. Soon the rush. His right hand comes upon the butt of the tazer. His fingers wrap about it.

Almost . . .

Two more steps, he decides.

One . . .

Now is the time of the cutting of the throat . . .

Two.

He draws the weapon and fires it. It strikes home and the beast halts, stiffens.

He drops the tazer, snatches the knife into his right hand and lunges forward.

He halts several paces before the creature, for it begins melting and turning to steam. In moments, the form has dissolved and the vapors have collected into a small cloud about three meters above the ground. Lowering the knife, he raises his eyes.

Smokelike, it now drifts, passing to the left toward a huge pile of rubble from some ancient landslide. He follows, watching, waiting.

Neat trick, that.

I am not the beast you slew. I am that which you cannot destroy. I am all of your fears and failings. And I am stronger now because you fled me.

I did not flee you. I followed a trail.

What trail? I saw no trail save your own.

It is the reason I am in this place, and I presume I am the reason you are here.

The smoke ceases its movement, to hover above the rock heap.

Of course. I am the part of yourself which will destroy you. You have denied me for too long.

The smoke begins to contour itself into a new form.

I no longer deny you. I have faced the past and am at peace with it.

Too late. *I have become autonomous under the conditions you created.*

De-autonomize, then. Go back where you came from.

The form grows manlike.

I cannot, for you are at peace with the past. Like Cat, I have only one function now.

Cat is dead.

. . . And I lack a sense of humor.

The form continues its coalescence. Billy regards an exact double of himself, similarly garbed, holding a knife the exact counterpart of his own, looking back at him. It is smiling.

Then how can you be amused?

I enjoy my one function.

Billy raises the point of his blade.

Then what are you waiting for? Come down and be about it.

The double turns and leaps to his left, landing on the farther side of the heap. Billy rushes around it, but by the time he reaches him the other has regained his footing. He wipes his brow with his free hand, for the rain still descends. Then he drops into a crouch, both hands extended, low, knees bent. The other does the same.

Billy backs away as the other advances, then shuffles to his right, feinting, beginning the circle. He studies the ground quickly, hoping to steer the other into a slippery place. As his eyes move, his double lunges. He blocks with his left forearm and thrusts for the body. The point of the other's blade pierces his jacket sleeve and enters his arm. He is certain his own blade has bitten deeply into his adversary's left side, but the double gives no sign of it and Billy sees no blood.

"I am beginning to believe you," he says aloud, feeling his own blood dampen his arm. "Perhaps I cannot kill you."

"True. But I can kill you," the other replies. "I will kill you."

Billy parries the blade, slashes the other's cheek. No wound opens. No blood appears.

"So why do you not give up?" the other says.

"Supposing I were to throw down my knife and say to hell with it?" he asks.

"I would kill you."

"You say you will kill me whether I fight or do not fight?"

"Yes."

"Then I might as well fight," Billy says, thrusting again, parrying again, slashing low, moving back, thrusting high, circling.

"Why?"

"Warrior tradition. Why not? It's the best fight around."

As he backs away from a fresh attack, Billy almost stumbles when his right foot strikes an apple-sized stone. But he recovers and brushes it backward as if it were an annoyance. He slashes and thrusts furiously then, halting the other. Then he takes a big step back, positioning his foot just so. . . .

He kicks the stone as hard as he can, directly toward his double. It flies as from a catapult, striking the other's right kneecap with a satisfying *thunk*.

The figure bends forward, blade lowering. His head falls into a tempting position and Billy swings his left fist as hard as he can against the right side of his adversary's jaw.

The double falls back onto his left side, and Billy kicks again, toward the knife hand. His boot makes contact and the blade goes clattering across rocks into the distance. He flings himself upon the fallen form, his own blade upraised.

As he drives the blade downward toward the other's throat, his adversary's left hand flies up and the fingers wrap around his wrist. His arm stops as if it has encountered a wall. The pressure on his wrist is enormous. Then the right hand rises and he knows somehow that it is about to go for his throat.

He drives another left against the other's jaw. The head rolls to the side and the grip on his wrist slackens slightly. He strikes again and again. Then he feels a powerful movement beneath him.

His adversary bunches his legs, leans forward and begins to rise, bearing Billy along with him. He strikes again, but it seems to make no difference. The other's movement carries them both to their feet and that right hand is coming forward again. Billy seizes the extending wrist and barely manages to halt it. He pushes as hard as he can but he is unable to advance his knife hand.

Then, gradually, his left hand is forced back. His right wrist feels as if it is about to snap.

"You *chindis* are strong sons of bitches," he says. The other snarls and flexes his fingers. Billy drives his knee into his groin. The double grunts and bends forward. Billy's knife advances slightly.

But as the other bends forward, Billy sees over him, beyond him. And he begins singing the song the old man taught him, the calling of Ikne'etso, the Big Thunder, recalling now when he had transferred power from the sandpainting to his own hand.

Sees . . .

First, to where the totem stands—the same four figures below; but now, crowning the spirit pole, the shadowy fifth form has grown more distinct and is shining with an unearthly glow. It seems to be smiling at him.

You have, I see, gambled. Good, it seems to say, and then the pole begins to elongate, stretching toward the now brightened heavens. . . .

To where, second, the rainbow now arches in full spectrum.

And his gaze continues to mount, to the rainbow's crest. There he sees the Warrior Twins regarding him as on that occasion so long ago. A dark form circles above them.

Nayenezgani strings his great bow. He puts an arrow to it, draws it partway back and begins to raise it. The dark form descends, and Black-god comes to sit upon Nayenezgani's shoulder.

The double tightens his grip and twists, and the knife falls from Billy's hand. He can feel the blood running up his left arm as the strength begins to ebb and the other draws him nearer. He continues to utter the words of the song, calling. . . .

The pole stands to an enormous height now, and the figure atop it—now a man from the waist up—is raising his right hand and lowering his left, pointing at him. He is reaching, reaching. . . .

The drumbeat grows louder, comes faster. The rattling sounds like a hailstorm.

Despite a final effort to thrust him back, the double stands his ground and draws Billy into a crushing embrace. But Billy continues to choke out the words.

Nayenezgani draws his bowstring all the way back, releases the arrow with a forward snapping motion of his left arm.

The world explodes in a flash more brilliant than sunlight. In that moment he knows that he has entered his double and his double has entered him, that he has fused with the divided one, that the pieces of himself, scattered, have come home, have reassembled, that he has won. . . .

And that is all that he knows.

The Fourth Day

DISK IV

BANK OF NOVA SCOTIA COMPUTER PLEADS
NOLO CONTENDERE

STRAGEAN TRADE AGREEMENT NEARER REALITY

DOLPHINS SETTLE OUT OF COURT

ILI REPORTS MISSING METAMORPH

*   *   *

Now you travel your own trail, alone.
What you have become, we do not know.
What your clan is now, we do not know.
Now, now on, now, you are something not of
this world.

*   *   *

NEW YORK PHILHARMONIC TO
PREMIERE "LEVIATHAN" SYMPHONY

Charlie, an aged humpback whale who makes his home in Scammon Lagoon, will hear the first instrumental performance of his composition via a satellite hookup to full fidelity underwater speakers. Although he has refused to comment on the rehearsals, Charlie seemed

TAXTONIES DO IT AGAIN

When their leader's clone's bullet-riddled body was found in the East River, a potential riot situation was only temporarily averted

SMUDGE POTS IN VOLCANO CRATER CAUSE PANIC
ALIENS REPRIMANDED

A pair of tourists from Jetax-5, whose culture is noted for its eccentric sense of humor, admitted to

GENERAL ACCEPTS NOBEL PEACE PRIZE

*   *   *

crawling, he made it into a sheltered place. He leaned his back against a wall and dipped his finger into the blood. Reaching out

*   *   *

WHOOPING CRANE FLOCKS TO BE PRUNED

Hunting permits will be issued to deal with the overpopulation problem in flocks of the once rare crane which has now become a nuisance.

"Who can sleep with all that whooping?" complained residents

BERSERK FACTORY DESTROYS OUTPUT
HOLDS OFF NATIONAL GUARD FOR 8 HOURS
HOSTAGES RELEASED UNHARMED

There was an old bugger from Ghent
Spilled his drink in the sexbot's vent.

He screamed and he howled
As if disemboweled.
Instead of coming, he went.

COMPUTER THERAPIST CHARGED WITH MALPRACTICE

BLACK HOLE TO BE AUCTIONED

At Sotheby Park Bernet next Wednesday

A WET SPRING FOR MUCH OF THE NATION

t otempl fling across beside the waters andown theating of thearth after fireflow fromigh wright but rong oh sands the merger each with sands sands sands sands ourglass runneth over days roulette struck fire andown thever narrowing tunnels of being we go fireflow part a part freverdreaming newslvs dreams tove touched the shaman mind beneath the bead fireflow across the windrawn days andown conditions of being focused through fireflood lens anew the hunted self achieved rainwet snowblow windcut daythrust knifeslash fireflown are the hunted and hunting selves the landscape dreamspoken nder earth of mind through heart of stars toth still the running the burgeoning the everrun foreverrun one frevermore as lps that kss the lightning creationheat everflow firetotem apart a part one frever and run

Mercy Spender, awakening with a taste for tea and the desire to attend a dog race—strange thought—called Fisher and asked him to join her in the dining room. Then she showered, dressed, combed her hair and thought about makeup for the first time since her early singing days.

Fisher rummaged through his thoughts, wondering whether his illusions could use a touch more class. How long since he had been to an art gallery? Studied himself in the mirror. Perhaps he ought to let his hair grow longer.

Out the window, new day clearing, snow melting, water dripping. He hummed a tune—Ironbear's, now he thought of it. Not bad, that beat.

Alex Mancin decided to undertake a retreat at a monastery he had heard of in Kentucky. The money market could take care of itself, and the dogs would be fed and groomed by the kennel keeper, poor bastard. They were such stupid little things.

Ironbear turned and sidled, passing through the narrow, rockfallen place between sheer rises. As he had progressed, his ability to read the trail signs had grown better and better, exceeding perhaps what it had been in those long-forgotten days in the Gateway to the Arctic. Now, as he entered the canyon, he felt that he was nearing the trail's end.

He did not pause to study the ruins about him but moved directly to the area amid charred brush and grasses where the ground indicated that a struggle had occurred. He squatted and remained unmoving for a long while when he reached it, studying the earth. Chips of turquoise, dried blood . . . Whatever had gone on here had been very violent.

Finally he rose and turned toward the ruin to his left. Something had crawled or been dragged in that direction.

He opened his mind and probed carefully but could detect nothing.

Vague images passed through his awareness as he approached the ruin. He had been present as part of the being which the Sands construct had formed here under highly symbolic circumstances, had felt the telekinetic power reaching, felt the blast. But after that event, nothing. He was swept away at that very point, to continue his tracking.

. . . And then he saw him, propped against a wall near a corner of the ruin. At first Ironbear could not tell whether he was breathing, though his eyes were open and directed to his right.

Moving nearer, he saw the pictograph Singer himself had drawn on the wall with his own blood. It was a large circle, containing a pair of dots, side by side, about a third of the way down its diameter. Lower, beneath these, was an upward-curving arc.

Inhaling the moment, Ironbear shook his head at what was rare, at what was powerful. Like the buffalo, it probably would not last. A life's gamble. But just now, just this instant, before he advanced and broke the feeling's spell, there was something. Like the buffalo.

> High on the mountain of fire
> in the lost place of the Old Ones,
> fire falling to the right of me,
> to the left of me,
> before, behind, above, below,
> I met my self's chindi,
> chindi's self.

Shall I name me a name now,
to have eaten him?

I walk the rainbow trail.
In a time of ice and fire
in the lost place of the Old Ones
I met my self's chindi,
became my chindi's self.
I have traveled through the worlds.
I am a hunter in all places.
My heart was divided into four parts
and eaten by the winds.
I have recovered them.
I sit at the center of the entire world
sending forth my song.
I am everywhere at home,
and all things have been given back to me.
I have followed the trail of my life
and met myself at its end.
There is beauty all around me.

Nayenezgani came for me
into the Darkness House,
putting aside with his staff
the twisted things, the things reversed.
The Dark Hunter remembers me,
Coyote remembers me,
the Sky People remember me,
this land remembers me,
the Old Ones remember me,

I have remembered myself
coming up into the world.

I sit on the great sand-pattern
of Dinetah, here at its center.
Its power remembers me.

Coyote call across the darkness bar . . .
I have eaten myself and grown strong.
There is beauty all around me.
Before me, behind me, to the right
and to the left of me,
corn pollen and rainbow.
The white medicine lifts me in his hand.

The dancer at the heart of all things
turns like a dust-devil before me.
My lightning-bead is shattered.
I have spoken my own laws.
My only enemy, my self, reborn,
is also the dancer.
My trail, my mind, is filled with stars
in the great wheel of their turning
toward springtime. Stars.
I come like the rain with the wind
and all growing things.
The white medicine lifts me in his hand.
Here at lost Lukachakai I say this:
The hunting never ends.
The way is beauty.

The medicine is strong.
The ghost train doesn't stop here

anymore. I am the hunter
in the eye of the hunted. If I call
they will come to me
out of Darkness Mountain.

ISLE OF THE DEAD

To Banks Mebane.

I

Life is a thing—if you'll excuse a quick dab of philosophy before you know what kind of picture I'm painting—that reminds me quite a bit of the beaches around Tokyo Bay.

Now, it's been centuries since I've seen that Bay and those beaches, so I could be off a bit. But I'm told that it hasn't changed much, except for the condoms, from the way that I remember it.

I remember a terrible expanse of dirty water, brighter and perhaps cleaner way off in the distance, but smelling and slopping and chill close at hand, like Time when it wears away objects, delivers them, removes them. Tokyo Bay, on any given day, is likely to wash anything ashore. You name it, and it spits it up some time or other: a dead man, a shell that might be alabaster, rose and pumpkin bright, with a sinistral whorling, rising inevitably to the tip of a horn as innocent as the unicorn's, a bottle with or without a note which you may or may not be able to read, a human foetus, a piece of very smooth wood with a nail hole in it—maybe a piece of the True Cross, I don't know—and white pebbles and dark pebbles, fishes, empty dories, yards of cable, coral, seaweed, and those are pearls that were his eyes. Like that. You leave the thing alone, and after awhile it takes it away again. That's how it operates. Oh yeah—it also used to be lousy with condoms, limp, almost transparent testimonies to the instinct to continue the species but not tonight, and sometimes they were painted with snappy designs or sayings and sometimes had a feather on the end. These are almost gone now, I hear, the way of the Edsel, the klepsydra and the button hook, shot down and punctured by the safety pill, which makes for larger mammaries, too, so who complains? Sometimes, as I'd walk along the beach in the sun-spanked morning, the chill breezes helping me to recover from the effects of rest and recuperation leave from a small and neatly contained war in Asia that had cost me a kid brother, sometimes then I would hear the shrieking of birds when there were no birds in sight. This added the element of mystery that made the comparison inevitable: life is a thing that reminds me quite a bit of the beaches around Tokyo Bay. Anything goes. Strange and unique things are being washed up all the time. I'm one of them and so are you. We spend some time on the beach, maybe side by side, and then that slopping, smelling, chilly thing rakes it with the liquid fingers of a crumbling hand and some of the things are gone again. The mysterious bird-cries are the open end of the human condition. The voices of the gods? Maybe. Finally, to nail all corners of the comparison to the wall before we leave the room, there are two things that caused me to put it there in the first place: sometimes, I suppose, things that are taken away might, by some capricious current, be returned to the beach. I'd never seen it happen before, but maybe I hadn't waited around long enough. Also, you know, somebody could come along and pick up something he'd found there and take it away from the Bay. When I learned that the first of these two things might actually have happened, the first thing I did was puke. I'd been drinking and sniffing the fumes of an exotic plant for about three days. The next thing I did was expel all my house guests. Shock is a wonderful soberer, and I already knew that the second of the two things was possible—the taking away of a thing from the Bay—because it had happened to me, but I'd never figured on the first coming true. So I took a pill guaranteed to make me a whole man in three hours, followed it with a sauna bath and then stretched out on the big bed while the servants, mechanical and otherwise, took care of the cleaning up. Then I began to shake all over. I was scared.

I am a coward.

Now, there are a lot of things that scare me, and they are all of them things over which I have little or no control, like the Big Tree.

I propped myself up on my elbow, fetched the package from the bedside table and regarded its contents once more.

There could be no mistake, especially when a thing like that was addressed to me.

I had accepted the special delivery, stuffed it into my jacket pocket, opened it at my leisure.

Then I saw that it was the sixth, and I'd gotten sick and called things to a halt.

It was a tri-dee picture of Kathy, all in white, and it was dated as developed a month ago.

Kathy had been my first wife, maybe the only woman I'd ever loved, and she'd been dead for over five hundred years. I'll explain that last part by and by.

I studied the thing closely. The sixth such thing I'd received in as many months. Of different people, all of them dead. For ages.

Rocks and blue sky behind her, that's all.

It could have been taken anywhere where there were rocks and a blue sky. It could easily have been a fake, for there are people around who can fake almost anything these days.

But who was there around, now, who'd know enough to send it to me, and why? There was no note, just that picture, the same as with all the others—my friends, my enemies.

And the whole thing made me think of the beaches around Tokyo Bay, and maybe the Book of Revelations, too.

I drew a blanket over myself and lay there in the artificial twilight I had turned on at midday. I had been comfortable, so comfortable, all these years. Now something I had thought scabbed over, flaked away, scarred smoothly and forgotten had broken, and I bled.

If there was only the barest chance that I held a truth in my shaking hand . . .

I put it aside. After a time, I dozed, and I forget what thing out of sleep's mad rooms came to make me sweat so. Better forgotten, I'm sure.

I showered when I awoke, put on fresh clothing, ate quickly and took a carafe of coffee with me into my study. I used to call it an office when I worked, but around thirty-five years ago the habit wore off. I went through the past month's pruned and pre-sorted correspondence and found the items I was looking for amid the requests for money from some oddball charities and some oddball individuals who hinted at bombs if I didn't come across, four invitations to lecture, one to under take what once might have been an interesting job, a load of periodicals, a letter from a long-lost descendant of an obnoxious in-law from my third marriage suggesting a visit, by him, with me, here, three solicitations from artists wanting a patron, thirty-one notices that lawsuits had been commenced against me and letters from various of my attorneys stating that thirty-one actions against me had been quashed.

The first of the important ones was a letter from Marling of Megapei. It said, roughly:

"Earth-son, I greet you by the twenty-seven Names that still remain, praying the while that you have cast more jewels into the darkness and given them to glow with the colors of life.

"I fear that the time of the life for the most ancient and dark green body I am privileged to wear moves now toward an ending early next year. It has been long since these yellow and failing eyes have seen my stranger son. Let it be before the ending of the fifth season that he comes to me, for all my cares will be with me then and his hand upon my shoulder would lighten their burden. Respects."

The next missive was from the Deep Shaft Mining and Processing Company, which everyone knows to be a front organization for Earth's Central Intelligence Department, asking me if I might be interested in purchasing some used-but-in-good-condition off-world mining equipment located at sites from which the cost of transport would be prohibitive to the present owners.

What it really said, in a code I'd been taught years before when I'd done a contract job for the federal government of Earth, was, *sans* officialese and roughly:

"What's the matter? Aren't you loyal to the home planet? We've been asking you for nearly twenty years to come to Earth and consult with us on a matter vital to planetary security. You have consistently ignored these requests. This is an urgent request and it requires your immediate cooperation on a matter of the gravest importance. We trust, and etc."

The third one said, in English:

"I do not want it to seem as if I am trying to presume on something long gone by, but I am in serious trouble and you are the only person I can think of who might be able to help me. If you can possibly make it in the near future, please come see me on Aldebaran V. I'm still at the old address, although the place has changed quite a bit. Sincerely, Ruth."

Three appeals to the humanity of Francis Sandow. Which, if any of them, had anything to do with the pictures in my pocket?

The orgy I had called short had been a sort of going-away party. By now, all of my guests were on their ways off my world. When I had started it as an efficient means of getting them loaded and shipped away, I had known where I was going. The arrival of Kathy's picture, though, was making me think.

All three parties involved in the correspondence knew who Kathy had been. Ruth might once have had access to a picture of her, from which some talented person might work. Marling could have created the thing. Central Intelligence could have dug up old documents and had it forged in their labs. Or none of these. It was strange that there was no accompanying message, if somebody wanted something.

I had to honor Marling's request, or I'd never be able to live with myself. That had been first on my agenda, but now—I had through the fifth season, northern hemisphere, Megapei—which was still over a year away. So I could afford some other stops in between.

Which ones would they be?

Central Intelligence had no real claim on my services and Earth no dominion over me. While I was willing to help Earth if I could, the issue couldn't be so terribly vital if it had been around for the full twenty years they'd been pestering me. After all, the planet was still in existence, and according to the best information I had on the matter, was functioning as normally and poorly as usual. And for that matter, if I was as important to them as they made out in all their letters, they could have come and seen me.

But Ruth—

Ruth was another matter. We had lived together for almost a year before we'd realized we were cutting each other to ribbons and it just wasn't going to work out. We parted as friends, remained friends. She meant something to me. I was surprised she was still alive after all this time. But if she needed my help, it was hers.

So that was it. I'd go see Ruth, quickly, and try to bail her out of whatever jam she was in. Then I'd go to Megapei. And somewhere along the line, I might pick up a lead as to who, what, when, where, why and how I had received the pictures. If not, then I'd go to Earth and try Intelligence. Maybe a favor for a favor would be in order.

I drank my coffee and smoked. Then, for the first time in almost five years, I called my port and ordered the readying of *Model T*, my jump-buggy, for the distance-hopping. It would take the rest of the day, much of the night, and be ready around sunrise, I figured.

Then I checked my automatic Secretary and Files to see who owned the *T* currently. S & F told me it was Lawrence J. Conner of Lochear—the "J" for "John." So I ordered the necessary identification papers, and they fell from the tube and into my padded in-basket about fifteen seconds later. I studied Conner's description, then called for my barber on wheels to turn my hair from dark brown to blond, lighten my suntan, toss on a few freckles, haze my eyes three shades darker and lay on some new fingerprints.

I have a whole roster of fictitious people, backgrounds complete and verifiable when you're away from their homes, people who have purchased the *T* from one another over the years, and others who will do so in the future. They are all of them around five feet, ten inches in height and weigh in at about one-sixty. They are all individuals I am capable of becoming with a bit of cosmetic and the memorization of a few facts. When I travel, I don't like the idea of doing it in a vessel registered in the name of Francis Sandow of Homefree or, as some refer to it, Sandow's World. While I'm quite willing to make the sacrifice and live with it, this is one of the drawbacks involved in being one of the hundred wealthiest men in the galaxy (I think I'm 87th, as of the last balance-sheet, but I could be 88th or 86th): somebody always wants something from you, and it's always blood or money, neither of which I am willing to spend too freely. I'm lazy and I scare easily and I just want to hang onto what I've got of both. If I had any sense of competition at all, I suppose I'd be busy trying to be 87th, 86th, or 85th, whichever. I don't care, though. I never did much, really, except maybe a little at first, and then the novelty quickly wore off. Anything over your first billion becomes metaphysical. I used to think of all the vicious things I was probably financing without realizing it. Then I came up with my Big Tree philosophy and decided the hell with the whole bit.

There is a Big Tree as old as human society, because that's what it is, and the sum total of its leaves, attached to all its branches and twigs, represents the amount of money that exists. There are names written on these leaves, and some fall off and new ones grow on, so that in a few seasons all the names have been changed. But the Tree stays pretty much the same: bigger, yes; and carrying on the same life functions as always, in pretty much the same way, too. I once went through a time when I tried to cut out all the rot I could find in the Tree. I found that as soon as I cut out a section in one place, it would occur somewhere else, and I had to sleep sometime. Hell, you can't even give money away properly these days; and the Tree is too big to bend like a *bonsai* in a bucket and so alter its growth. So I just let it grow on its merry way now, my name on all those leaves, some of them withered and sere and some bright with the first-green, and I try to enjoy myself, swinging around those branches and wearing a name that I don't see written all around me. So much for me and the Big Tree. The story of how I came to own so much greenery might provoke an even funnier, more elaborate and less botanical metaphor. If so, let's make it later. Too many, and look what happened to poor Johnny Donne: he started thinking he wasn't an Islande, and he's out there at the bottom of Tokyo Bay now and it doesn't diminish me one bit.

I began briefing S & F on everything my staff should do and not do in my absence. After many playbacks and much mindracking, I think I covered everything. I reviewed my last will and testament, saw nothing I wanted changed. I shifted certain papers to destructboxes and left orders that they be activated if this or that happened. I sent an alert to one of my representatives on Aldebaran V, to let him know that if a man named Lawrence J-for-John Conner happened to pass that way and needed anything, it was his, and an emergency i.d. code, in case I had to be identified as me. Then I noticed that close to four hours had passed and I was hungry.

"How long to sunset, rounded to the nearest minute?" I asked S & F.

"Forty-three minutes," came its neuter-voiced reply through the hidden speaker.

"I will dine on the East Terrace in precisely thirty-three minutes," I said, checking my chronometer. "I will have a lobster with french fried potatoes and cole slaw, a basket of mixed rolls, a half-bottle of our own champagne, a pot of coffee, a lemon sherbet, the oldest Cognac in the cellar and two cigars. Ask Martin Bremen if he would do me the honor of serving it."

"Yes," said S & F. "No salad?"

"No salad."

Then I strolled back to my suite, threw a few things into a suitcase, and began changing clothes. I activated my bedroom hookup to S & F, and amidst a certain stomach-wringing, neck-chilling feeling, gave the order I had been putting off and could properly put off no longer:

"In exactly two hours and 11 minutes," I said, checking my chronometer, "ring Lisa and ask her if she would care to have a drink with me on the West Terrace—in half an hour's time. Prepare for her now two checks, each in the amount of fifty thousand dollars. Also, prepare for her a copy of Reference A. Deliver these items to this station, in separate, unsealed envelopes."

"Yes," came the reply, and while I was adjusting my cuff-links these items slid down the chute and came to rest in the basket on my dresser.

I checked the contents of the three envelopes, sealed them, placed them in an inside pocket of my jacket and made my way to the hallway that led to the East Terrace.

Outside, the sun, an amber giant now, was ambushed by a wispy strand which gave up in less than a minute and swam away. Hordes of overhead clouds wore gold, yellow and touches of deepening pink as the sun descended the merciless blue road that lay between Urim and Thumim, the twin peaks I had set just there to draw him and quarter him at each day's ending. His rainbow blood would splash their misty slopes during the final minutes.

I seated myself at my table beneath the elm tree. The overhead force-projector came on at the weight of my body upon the chair, keeping leaves, insects, bird droppings and dust from descending upon me from above. After a few moments,

Martin Bremen approached, pushing a covered cart before him.

"Good efening, sir."

"Good evening, Martin. How go things with you?"

"Chust fine, Mister Sandow. And yourself?"

"I'm going away," I said.

"Ah?"

He laid the setting before me, uncovered the cart and began to serve the meal.

"Yes," I said, "maybe for quite some time."

I sampled my champagne and nodded approval.

". . . So I wanted to say something you're probably already aware of before I go. That is, you prepare the best meals I've ever eaten—"

"Thank you, Mister Sandow." His naturally ruddy face deepened a shade or two, and he fought the corners of his mouth into a straight line as he dropped his dark eyes. "I'fe enchoyed our association."

". . . So, if you'd care to take a year's vacation—full salary and all expenses, of course, plus a slush fund for buying any recipes you might be interested in trying—I'll call the Bursar's Office before I go and set things up."

"Venn vill you be leafing, sir?"

"Early tomorrow morning."

"I see, sir. Yes. Thank you. That sounds wery pleasant."

". . . And find some more recipes for yourself while you're at it."

"I'll keep vun eye open, sir."

"It must be a funny feeling, preparing meals the taste of which you can't even guess at."

"Oh no, sir," he protested. "The tasters are completely reliable, and vile I'll admit I'fe often speculated as to the taste of some of your meals, the closest situation iss, I suppose, that of being a chemist who does not really vish to taste all of his experiments, if you know vatt I mean, sir."

He held the basket of rolls in one hand, the pot of coffee in his other hand, the dish of cole slaw in his other hand, and his other hand rested on the cart's handle. He was a Rigelian, whose name was something like Mmmrt'n Brrm'n. He'd learned his English from a German cook, who'd helped him pick an English equivalent for Mmmrt'n Brrm'n. A Rigelian chef, with a good taster or two from the subject race, prepares the greatest meals in the galaxy. They're quite dispassionate about it, too. We'd been through the just-finished discussion before, many times, and he knew I was always kidding him when I talked that way, trying to get him to admit that human food reminded him of garbage, manure or industrial wastes. Apparently, there is a professional ethic against acknowledging any such thing. His normal counter is to be painfully formal. On occasion, however, when he's had a bit too much of lemon juice, orange juice or grapefruit juice, he's as much as admitted that cooking for *homo sapiens* is considered the lowest level to which a Rigelian chef can stoop. I try to make up to him for it as much as I can, because I like him as well as his meals, and it's very hard to get Rigelian chefs, no matter how much you can afford to spend.

"Martin," I said, "if anything should happen to me this time out, I'd like you to know that I've made provision for you in my will."

"I—I don't know vatt to say, sir."

"So don't," I told him. "To be completely selfish about it, I hope you don't collect. I plan on coming back."

He was one of the few persons to whom, with impunity yet, I could mention such a thing. He had been with me for thirty-two years and was well past the point which would entitle him to a good lifetime pension anyway. Preparing meals was his dispassionate passion, though, and for some unknown reason he seemed to like me. He'd make out quite a bit better if I dropped dead that minute, but not enough to really make it worth his while to lace my cole slaw with Murtanian butterfly-venom.

"Look at that sunset, will you!" I decided.

He watched for a minute or two, then said, "You certainly do them up brown, sir."

"Thank you. You may leave the Cognac and cigars now and retire. I'll be here awhile."

He placed them on the table, drew himself up to his full eight feet of height, bowed, and said, "Best of luck on your churney, sir, and good efening."

"Sleep well," I said.

"Thank you," and he slithered away into the twilight.

When the cool night breezes slipped about me and the toadingales in their distant wallows began a Bach cantata, my orange moon Florida came up where the sun had gone down. The night-blooming danderoses spilled their perfumes upon the indigo air, the stars came on like aluminum confetti, the ruby-shrouded candle sputtered on my table, the lobster was warm and buttery in my mouth and the champagne cold as the heart of an iceberg. I felt a certain sadness and the desire to say "I will be back" to this moment of time.

So I finished the lobster, the champagne, the sherbet, and I lit a cigar before I poured a snifter of Cognac, which, I have been told, is a barbaric practice. I toasted everything in sight to make up for it, and then poured a cup of coffee.

When I had finished, I rose and took a walk around that big, complex building, my home. I moved up to the bar on the West Terrace and sat there with a Cognac in front of me. After a time, I lit my second cigar. Then she appeared in the archway, automatically falling into a perfume-ad pose.

Lisa wore a soft, silky blue thing that foamed about her in the light of the terrace, all sparkles and haze. She had on white gloves and a diamond choker; she was ash-blonde, the angles and curves of her pale-pink lips drawn up so that there was a circle between them, and she tilted her head far to one side, one eye closed, the other squinting.

"Well-met by moonlight," she said, and the circle broke into a smile, sudden and dewy, and I had timed it so that the second moon, pure white, was rising then in the west. Her voice reminded me of a recording stuck on a passage at middle C. They don't record things on discs that stick that way any more, but even if no one else remembers, I do.

"Hello," I said. "What are you drinking?"

"Scotch and soda," she said, as always. "Lovely night!"

I looked into her two too blue eyes and smiled. "Yes," as I punched out her order and the drink was made and delivered, "it is."

"You've changed. You're lighter."

"Yes."

"You're up to no good, I hope."

"Probably." I passed it to her. "It's been what? —Five months now?"

"A bit more."

"Your contract was for a year."

"That's right."

I passed her an envelope, and, "This cancels it," I said.

"What do you mean?" she asked, the smile freezing, diminishing, gone.

"Whatever I say, always," I said.

"You mean I'm dismissed?"

"I'm afraid so," I told her, "and here's a similar amount, to prove to you it isn't what you think." I passed her the second envelope.

"What is it, then?" she asked.

"I've got to go away. No sense to your wilting here in the meantime. I might be gone quite awhile."

"I'll wait."

"No."

"Then I'll go with you."

"Even if it means you might die along with me, if things go bad?"

I hoped she'd say yes. But after all this time I think I know something about people. That's why Reference A was handy.

"It's possible, this time around," I said. "Sometimes a guy like me has to take a few risks."

"Will you give me a reference?" she said.

"I have it here."

She sipped her drink.

"All right," she said.

I passed it to her.

"Do you hate me?" she asked.

"No."

"Why not?"

"Why?"

"Because I'm weak, and I value my life."

"So do I, though I can't guarantee it."

"That's why I'll accept the referral."

"That's why I have it ready."

"You think you know everything, don't you?"

"No."

"What will we do tonight?" she asked, finishing her drink.

"I don't know everything."

"Well, I know something. You've treated me all right."

"Thanks."

"I'd like to hang onto you."

"But I just scared you?"

"Yes."

"Too much?"

"Too much."

I finished my Cognac, puffed on the cigar, studied Florida and my white moon Cue Ball.

"Tonight," she said, taking my hand, "you'll at least forget to hate me."

She didn't open her envelopes. She sipped her second drink and regarded Florida and Cue Ball also.

"When will you leave?"

"Ere dawn," I said.

"God, you're poetical."

"No, I'm just what I am."

"That's what I said."

"I don't think so, but it's been good knowing you."

She finished her drink and put it down.

"It's getting chilly out here."

"Yes."

"Let us repair within."

"I'd like to repair."

I put down my cigar and we stood and she kissed me. So I put my arm around her trim and sparkling, blue-kept waist and we moved away from the bar, toward the archway, through the archway and beyond, into the house we were leaving.

Let's make it a triple-asterisk break:

*   *   *

Perhaps the wealth I acquired along the way to becoming who I am is one of the things that made me one of the things that I am; *i.e.*, a bit of a paranoid. No.

It's too pat.

I could justify the qualms I feel each time I leave Homefree by saying that this is their source. Then I could turn around and justify that, by saying that it isn't really paranoia if there really are people out to get you. And there are, which is one of the reasons things are arranged to such an extent that I could stand all alone on Homefree and defy any man or government that wanted me to come and take me. They'd have to kill me, which would be a fairly expensive proposition, as it would entail destroying the entire planet. And even then, I think I've got an out that might work, though I've never had to test it under field conditions.

No, the real reason for my qualms is the very ordinary fear of death and non-being that all men know, intensified many times, though once I had a glimpse of a light that I can't explain . . . Forget that. There's me and maybe a few Sequoia trees that came onto the scene in the twentieth century and have managed to make it up until now, the thirty-second. Lacking the passivity of the plant kingdom, I learned after a time that the longer one exists the more strongly one becomes infected with a sense of mortality. Corollary to this, survival—once a thing I thought of primarily in Darwinian terms, as a pastime of the lower classes and phyla—threatens to become a preoccupation. It is a much subtler jungle now than it was in the days of my youth, with something like fifteen hundred inhabited worlds, each with its own ways of killing men, ways readily exportable when you can travel between the worlds in no time at all; seventeen other intelligent races, four of whom I consider smarter than men and seven or eight who are just as stupid, each with its own ways of killing men; multitudes of machines to serve us, numerous and ordinary as the automobile was when I was a kid, each with its own ways of killing men; new diseases, new weapons, new poisons and new mean animals, new objects of hatred, greed, lust and addiction, each with its own ways of killing men; and many, many, many new places to die. I've seen and met a lot of these things, and because of my somewhat unusual occupation there may be only twenty-six people in the galaxy who know more about them than I do.

So I'm scared, even though no one's shooting at me just now, the way they were a couple weeks before I got sent to Japan for rest and recuperation and found Tokyo Bay, say twelve hundred years ago. That's close. That's life.

*   *   *

I left in the dead of pre-dawn night without purposely saying goodbye to anybody, because that's the way I figure I have to be. I did wave back at a shadowy figure in the Operations Building who had waved at me after I'd parked my buggy and had begun walking across the field. But then, I was a shadowy figure, too. I reached the dock where the *Model T* sat squat, boarded her, stowed my gear, spent half an hour checking systems. Then I went outside to inspect the phase-projectors. I lit a cigarette.

In the east, the sky was yellow. A rumble of thunder came out of the dark mountains to the west. There were some clouds above me and the stars still clung to sky's faded cloak, less like confetti than dewdrops now.

For once, it wasn't going to happen, I decided.

Some birds sang, and a gray cat came and rubbed against my leg, then moved off in the direction of the birdsongs.

The breeze shifted so that it came up from the south, filtered through the forest that began at the far end of the field. It bore the morningdamp smells of life and growth.

The sky was pink as I took my last puff, and the mountains seemed to shiver within their shimmering as I turned and crushed it out. A large, blue bird floated toward me and landed on my shoulder. I stroked its plumage and sent it on its way.

I took a step toward the vehicle . . .

My toe struck a projecting bolt in a dock-plate and I stumbled. I caught hold of a strut and saved myself from a complete fall. I landed on one knee, and before I could get up a small, black bear was licking my face. I scratched his ears and patted his head, then slapped him on the rump as I rose. He turned and moved off toward the wood.

I tried to take another step, then realized that my sleeve was caught in the place where the strut I had grabbed crossed over another one.

By the time I'd disentangled myself, there was another bird upon my shoulder and a dark cloud of them flapping across the field from the direction of the forest. Above the noise of their cries, I heard more thunder.

It was happening.

I made a dash for the ship, almost stumbling over a green rabbit who sat on her haunches before the hatch, nose twitching, pink, myopic eyes staring in my direction. A big glass snake slithered toward me across the dock, transparent and gleaming.

I forgot to duck my head, banged it on the upper hatchplate and reeled back. My ankle was seized by a blond monkey, who winked a blue eye at me.

So I patted her head and pulled free. She was stronger than she looked.

I passed through the hatch, and it jammed when I tried to close it.

By the time I'd worked it free, the purple parrots were calling my name and the snake was trying to come aboard.

I found a power-pull and used it.

"All right! Goddamn it!" I cried. "I'm going! Goodbye! I'll be back!"

The lightnings flashed and the thunders rolled and a storm began in the mountains and raced toward me. I worked the hatch free.

"Clear the field!" I yelled, and slammed it.

I dogged it shut, moved to the control seat and activated all systems.

On the screen, I saw the animals departing. Wisps of fog drifted by, and I heard the first drops of rain spattering on the hull.

I raised the ship, and the storm broke about me.

I got above it, left the atmosphere, accelerated, achieved orbit and set my course.

It's always like that when I try to leave Homefree, which is why I always try to sneak away without telling the place goodbye. It never works, though.

Anyway, it's nice to know that somewhere you are wanted.

*   *   *

At the proper moment, I broke orbit and raced away from the Homefree System. For several hours I was queasy and my hands tended to shake. I smoked too many cigarettes and my throat began to feel dry. Back at Homefree, I had been in charge of everything. Now, though, I was entering the big arena once again. For a moment, I actually contemplated turning back.

Then I thought of Kathy and Marling and Ruth and Nick the long-dead dwarf and my brother Chuck, and I continued on to phase-point, hating myself.

It happened suddenly, just after I had entered phase and the ship was piloting itself.

I began laughing, and a feeling of recklessness came over me, just like in the old days.

What did it matter if I died? What was I living for that was so damned important? Eating fancy meals? Spending my nights with contract courtesans? Nuts! Sooner or later Tokyo Bay gets us all, and it would get me one day, too, I knew, despite everything. Better to be swept away in the pursuit of something halfway noble than to vegetate until someone finally figured a way to kill me in bed.

. . . And this, too, was a phase.

I began to chant a litany in a language older than mankind. It was the first time in many years that I had done so, for it was the first time in many years that I had felt fit to.

The light in the cabin seemed to grow dim, though I was sure it burnt as brightly as ever. The little dials on the console before me receded, became sparks, became the glowing eyes of animals peering at me from out a dark wood. My voice now sounded like the voice of another, coming by some acoustical trick from a point far before me. Within myself, I followed it forward.

Then other voices joined in. Soon my own ceased, but the others continued, faint, high-pitched, fading and swelling as though borne by some unfelt wind; they touched lightly at my ears, not really beckoning. I couldn't make out any words, but they were singing. The eyes were all around me, neither advancing nor receding, and in the distance there was a very pale glow, as of sunset on a day filled with milk-clouds. I realized then that I was asleep and dreaming, and that I could awaken if I wished. I didn't, though. I moved on into the west.

At length, beneath a dream-pale sky, I came to the edge of a cliff and could go no farther. There was water, water that I could not cross over, pale and sparkling, wraiths of mist folding and unfolding, slowly, above it; and out, far out from where I stood, one arm half-extended, crag piled upon terrace upon cold terrace, rocky buttresses all about, fog-dimmed pinnacles indicating a sky that I could not see, the whole stark as a sandblasted iceberg of ebony, I beheld the source of the singing, and a chillness clutched at my neck and perhaps the hair rose upon it.

I saw the shades of the dead, drifting like the mists or standing, half-hid, by the dark rocks of that place. And I knew that they were the dead, for among them I saw Nick the dwarf, gesturing obscenely, and I saw the telepath Mike Shandon, who had almost toppled an empire, *my* empire, the man I had slain with my own hands, and there was my old enemy Dango the Knife, and Courtcour Bodgis, the man with the computer mind, and Lady Karle of Algol, whom I had loved and hated.

Then I called upon that which I hoped I could still call upon.

There came a rumble of thunder and the sky grew as bright and blue as a pool of azure mercury. I saw her standing there for a moment, out across those waters in that dark place, Kathy, all in white, and our eyes met and her mouth opened and I heard my name spoken but nothing more, for the next clap of thunder brought with it total darkness and laid it upon that isle and the one who had stood upon the cliff, one arm half-extended. Me, I guess.

*   *   *

When I awoke, I had a rough idea of what it had meant. A rough idea only. And I couldn't understand it worth a damn, though I tried to analyze it.

I had once created Boecklin's Isle of the Dead to satisfy the whim of a board of unseen clients, strains of Rachmaninoff dancing like phantom sugar plums through my head. It had been a rough piece of work. Especially, since I am a creature who thinks in a mostly pictorial format. Whenever I think of death, which is often, there are two pictures that take turns filling my mind. One is the Valley of Shadows, a big, dark valley beginning between two massive prows of gray stone, with a greensward that starts out twilit and just gets darker and darker as you stare farther and farther into it, until finally you are staring into the blackness of interstellar space itself, *sans* stars, comets, meteors, anything; and the other is that mad painting by Boecklin, *The Isle of the Dead*, of the place I had just viewed in the land of dream. Of the two places, the Isle of the Dead is far more sinister. The Valley seems to hold a certain promise of peace. This, however, may be because I never designed and built a Valley of Shadows, sweating over every nuance and overtone of that emotion-wringing landscape. But in the midst of an otherwise Eden, I had raised up an Isle of the Dead one time, and it had burnt itself into my consciousness to such an extent that not only could I never wholly forget it, but I had become a part of it as surely as it was a part of me. Now, this part of myself had just addressed me in the only way that it could, in response to a sort of prayer. It was warning me, I felt, and it was also giving me a clue, a clue that might make sense as time went on. Symbols, by their very nature, conceal as well as indicate, damn them!

Kathy *had* seen me, within the fabric of my vision, which meant that there might be a chance . . .

I turned on the screen and regarded the spirals of light, moving in both clockwise and counterclockwise directions about a point directly before me. These were the stars, visible only in this fashion, there, on the underside of space. As I hung there and the universe moved about me, I felt the decades' layers of fat that padded my soul's midsection catch fire and begin to burn. The man I had worked so hard at becoming died then, I hope, and I felt that Shimbo of Darktree Tower, Shrugger of Thunders, still lived.

I watched the spinning stars, grateful, sad and proud, as only a man who has outlived his destiny and realized he might yet forge himself another, can be.

After a time, the whirlpool in the sky sucked me down to sleep's dark center, dreamless and cool, soft and still, like the Valley of Shadows perhaps.

*   *   *

It was as two weeks' time before Lawrence Conner brought his *Model T* to berth on Aldebaran V, which is called Driscoll, after its discoverer. It was as two weeks inside the *Model T*, though no time at all passed during phase. Don't ask me why, please. I don't have time to write a book. But had Lawrence Conner decided to turn around and head back for Homefree, he could have enjoyed another two weeks of calisthenics, introspection and reading and quite possibly have made it back on the afternoon of the same day

Francis Shadow had departed, doubtless pleasing the wild-life no end. He didn't, though. Instead, he helped Sandow nail down a piece of the briar business, which he didn't really want, just to keep up appearances while he examined the puzzle-pieces he'd found. Maybe they were pieces from several different puzzles, all mixed together. There was no way of telling.

I wore a light tropical suit and sunglasses, for the yellow sky had in it only a few orange-colored clouds and the sun beat waves of heat about me, and they broke upon the pastel pavements where they splashed and rose in a warm, reality-distorting spray. I drove my rented vehicle, a slip-sled, into the art colony of a city called Midi, a place too sharp and fragile and necessarily beside the sea for my likingw—ith nearly all its towers, spires, cubes and ovoids that people call home, office, studio, or shop built out of that stuff called glacyllin, which may be made transparent in a colorless or tinted fashion and opaqued at any color, by means of a simple, molecule-disturbing control—and I sought out Nuage, a street down by the waterfront, driving through a town that constantly changed color about me, reminding me of molded jello—raspberry, strawberry, cherry, orange, lemon and lime—with lots of fruits inside.

I found the place, at the old address, and Ruth had been right.

It had changed, quite a bit. It had been one of the few strongholds against the creeping jello that ate the city, back when we had lived there together. Now it, too, had succumbed. Where once there had been a high, stucco wall enclosing a cobbled courtyard, a black iron gate set within its archway, a hacienda within, sprawled about a small pool where the waters splashed sun-ghosts on the rough walls and the tiles, now there was a castle of Jell-O with four high towers. Raspberry, yet.

I parked, crossed a rainbow bridge, touched the announcement-plate on the door.

"This home is vacant," reported a mechanical voice through a concealed speaker.

"When will Miss Laris be back?" I asked.

"This home is vacant," it repeated. "If you are interested in purchasing it, you may contact Paul Glidden at Sunspray Realty, Incorporated, 178 Avenue of the Seven Sighs."

"Did Miss Laris leave a forwarding address?"

"No."

"Did she leave any messages?"

"No."

I returned to the slip-sled, raised it onto an eight-inch cushion of air and sought out the Avenue of the Seven Sighs, which had once been called Main Street.

He was fat and lacking in hair, except for a pair of gray eyebrows about two inches apart, each thin enough to have been drawn on with a single pencil-stroke, high up there over eyes slate-gray and serious, higher still above the pink catenary mouth that probably even smiled when he slept, there, under the small, upturned thing he breathed through, which looked even smaller and more turned-up because of the dollops of dough his cheeks that threatened to rise even further and engulf it completely, along with all the rest of his features, leaving him a smooth, suffocating lump (save for the tiny, pierced ears with the sapphires in them), turning as ruddy as the wide-sleeved shirt that covered his northern hemisphere, Mister Glidden, behind his desk at Sunspray, lowering the moist hand I had just shaken, his Masonic ring clicking against the ceramic sunburst of his ashtray as he picked up his cigar, in order to study me, fish-like, from the lake of smoke into which he submerged.

"Have a seat, Mister Conner," he chewed. "What have I got that you want?"

"You're handling Ruth Laris's place, over on Nuage, aren't you?"

"That's right. Think you might want to buy it?"

"I'm looking for Ruth Laris," I said. "Do you know where she's moved?"

A certain luster went out of his eye.

"No," he said. "I've never met Ruth Laris."

"She must want you to send the money someplace."

"That's right."

"Mind telling me where?"

"Why should I?"

"Why not? I'm trying to locate her."

"I'm to deposit in her account at a bank."

"Here in town?"

"That is correct. Artists Trust."

"But she didn't make the arrangements with you?"

"No. Her attorney did."

"Mind telling me who he is?"

He shrugged, down there in his pool. "Why not?" he said. "Andre DuBois, at Benson, Carling and Wu. Eight blocks north of here."

"Thanks."

"You're not interested in the property then, I take it?"

"On the contrary," I said. "I'll buy the place, if I can take possession this afternoon—and if I can discuss the deal with her attorney. How does fifty-two thousand sound?"

Suddenly he was out of his pool.

"Where may I call you, Mister Conner?"

"I'll be staying at the Spectrum."

"After five?"

"After five is fine."

So what to do?

First, I checked in at the Spectrum. Second, using the proper code, I contacted my man on Driscoll to arrange for the necessary quantity of cash to be available to Lawrence Conner for the purchase. Third, I drove down to the religious district, parked the sled, got out, began walking.

I walked past shrines and temples dedicated to Everybody, from Zoroaster to Jesus Christ. I slowed when I came to the Pei'an section.

After a time, I found it. All there was above the ground was an entranceway, a green place about the size of a one-car garage.

I passed within and descended a narrow stairway.

I reached a small, candle-lit foyer and moved on through a low arch.

I entered a dark shrine containing a central altar decked out in a deep green, tiers of pews all about it.

There were hundreds of stained glassite plates on all five walls, depicting the Pei'an deities. Maybe I shouldn't have gone there that day. It had been so long . . .

There were six Pei'ans and eight humans present, and

four of the Pei'ans were women. They all wore prayer-straps.

Pei'ans are about seven feet tall and green as grass. Their heads look like funnels, flat on top, their necks like the necks of funnels. Their eyes are enormous and liquid green or yellow. Their noses are flat upon their faces—wrinkles parenthesizing nostrils the size of quarters. They have no hair whatsoever. Their mouths are wide and they don't really have any teeth in them, per se. Like, I guess the best example is an elasmobranch. They are constantly swallowing their skins. They lack lips, but their dermis bunches and hardens once it goes internal and gives them horny ridges with which to chew. After that, they digest it, as it moves on and is replaced by fresh matter. However this may sound to someone who has never met a Pei'an, they are lovely to look at, more graceful than cats, older than mankind, and wise, very. Other than this, they are bilaterally symmetrical and possess two arms and two legs, five digits per. Both sexes wear jackets and skirts and sandals, generally dark in color. The women are shorter, thinner, larger about the hips and chests than the men—although the women have no breasts, for their young do not nurse, but digest great layers of fat for the first several weeks of their lives, and then begin to digest their skins. After a time, they eat food, pulpy mashes and seastuff mainly. That's Pei'ans.

Their language is difficult. I speak it. Their philosophies are complex. I know some of them. Many of them are telepaths, and some have other unusual abilities. Me, too.

I seated myself in a pew and relaxed. I draw a certain psychic strength from Pei'an shrines, because of my conditioning in Megapei. The Pei'ans are exceedingly polytheistic. Their religion reminds me a bit of Hinduism, because they've never discarded anything—and it seems they spent their entire history accumulating deities, rituals, traditions. Strantri is what the religion is called, and over the years it has spread considerably. It stands a good chance of becoming a universal religion one day because there's something in it to satisfy just about anybody, from animists and pantheists through agnostics and people who just like rituals. Native Pei'ans only constitute around ten percent of the Strantrians now, and theirs will probably be the first large-scale religion to outlive its founding race. There are fewer Pei'ans every year. As individuals, they have godawful long lifespans, but they're not very fertile. Since their greatest scholars have already written the last chapter in the immense *History of Pei'an Culture*, in 14,926 volumes, they may have decided that there's no reason to continue things any further. They have an awful lot of respect for their scholars. They're funny that way.

They had a galactic empire back when men were still living in caves. Then they fought an ages-long war with a race which no longer exists, the Bahulians—which sapped their energies, racked their industries and decimated their number. Then they gave up their outposts and gradually withdrew to the small system of worlds they inhabit today. Their home world—also called Megapei—had been destroyed by the Bahulians, who by all accounts were ugly, ruthless, vicious, fierce and depraved. Of course, all these accounts were written by the Pei'ans, so I guess we'll never know what the Bahulians were really like. They weren't Strantrians, though, because I read somewhere that they were idolators.

On the side of the shrine opposite the archway, one of the men began chanting a litany that I recognized better than any of the others, and I looked up suddenly to see if it had happened.

It had.

The glassite plate depicting Shimbo of Darktree, Shrugger of Thunders, was glowing now, green and yellow.

Some of their deities are Pei'apomorphic, to coin a term, while others, like the Egyptians', look like crosses between Pei'ans and things you might find in a zoo. Still others are just weird-looking. And somewhere along the line, I'm sure they must have visited the Earth, because Shimbo is a man. Why any intelligent race would care to make a god of a savage is beyond me, but there he stands, naked, with a slight greenish cast to his complexion, his face partly hidden by his upraised left arm, which holds a thunder cloud in the midst of a yellow sky. He bears a great bow in his right hand and a quiver of thunderbolts hangs at his hip. Soon all six Pei'ans and the eight humans were chanting the same litany. More began to file in through the door. The place began to fill up.

A great feeling of light and power began in my middle section and expanded to fill my entire body.

I don't understand what makes it happen, but whenever I enter a Pei'an shrine, Shimbo begins to glow like that, and the power and the ecstasy is always there. When I completed my thirty-year course of training and my twenty-year apprenticeship in the trade that made me my fortune, I was the only Earthman in the business. The other worldscapers are all Pei'ans. Each of us bears a Name—one of the Pei'an deities'—and this aids us in our work, in a complex and unique fashion. I chose Shimbo—or he chose me—because he seemed to be a man. For so long as I live, it is believed that he will be manifest in the physical universe. When I die, he returns to the happy nothing, until another may bear the Name. Whenever a Name-bearer enters a Pei'an shrine, that deity is illuminated in his place—in every shrine in the galaxy. I do not understand the bond. Even the Pei'ans don't, really.

I had thought that Shimbo had long since forsaken me, because of what I had done with the Power and with my life. I had come to this shrine, I guess, to see if it was true.

I rose and made my way to the archway. As I passed through it, I felt an uncontrollable desire to raise my left hand. Then I clenched my fist and drew it back down to shoulder level. As I did, there came a peal of thunder from almost directly overhead.

Shimbo still shone upon the wall and the chanting filled my head as I walked up the stairway and out into the world where a light rain had begun to fall.

II

Glidden and I met in DuBois' office at 6:30 and concluded the deal, for fifty-six thousand. DuBois was a short man with a weatherbeaten face and a long shock of white hair. He'd opened his office at that hour because of my insistence on dealing that afternoon. I paid the money, the papers were signed, the keys were in my pocket, hands were shaken all around and the three of us departed. As we walked across the damp pavement toward our respective vehicles, I said, "Damn! I left my pen on your desk, DuBois!"

"I'll have it sent to you. You're staying at the Spectrum?"

"I'm afraid I'll be checking out very shortly."

"I can send it to the place on Nuage."

I shook my head. "I'll be needing it tonight"

"Here. Take this one." He offered me his own.

By then Glidden had entered his vehicle and was out of earshot. I waved to him, then said, "That was for his benefit. I want to speak with you in private."

The squint that suddenly surrounded his dark eyes removed their look of incipient disgust and replaced it with one of curiosity.

"All right," he said, and we re-entered the building and he unlocked his office door again.

"What is it?" he asked, reassuming the padded chair behind his desk.

"I'm looking for Ruth Laris," I said.

He lit a cigarette, which is always a good way to buy a little thinking time.

"Why?" he asked.

"She's an old friend. Do you know where she is?"

"No," he said.

"Isn't it a trifle—unusual—to conserve assets in this quantity for a person whose whereabouts you don't even know?"

"Yes," he said, "I'd say so. But that is what I've been retained to do."

"By Ruth Laris?"

"What do you mean by that?"

"Did she retain you personally, or did somebody else do it on her behalf?"

"I don't see that this is any business of yours, Mister Conner. I believe I am going to call this conversation to a close."

I thought a second, made a quick decision.

"Before you do," I said, "I want you to know that I bought her house only to search it for clues as to her whereabouts. After that, I'm going to indulge a whim and convert it into a hacienda, because I don't like the architecture in this city. What does that indicate to you?"

"That you're something of a nut," he observed.

I nodded and added, "A nut who can afford to indulge his whims. Therefore a crackpot who can cause a lot of trouble. What's *this* building worth? A couple million?"

"I don't know." He looked a little uneasy.

"What if someone bought it for an apartment building

and you had to go looking for another office?"

"My lease would not be that easy to cancel, Mister Conner."

I chuckled. ". . . And then," I said, "you were suddenly to find yourself the subject of an inquiry by the local Bar Association?"

He sprang to his feet.

"You *are* a madman."

"Are you sure? I don't know what the charges would be," I said, "yet. But you know that even an inquiry would give you some trouble—and then if you started running into difficulties finding another place . . ." I didn't like doing things this way, but I was in a hurry. So, "Are you sure? Are you very sure that I'm a madman?" I finished.

Then, "No," he said, "I'm not."

"Then, if you've nothing to hide, why not tell me how the arrangements were made? I'm not interested in the substance of any privileged communications, simply the circumstances surrounding the house's being put up for sale. It puzzles me that Ruth didn't leave a message of any sort."

He leaned his head against the back of his chair and studied me through smoke.

"The arrangements were made by phone—"

"She could have been drugged, threatened . . ."

"That is ridiculous," he said. "What is your interest in this, anyway?"

"Like I said, she's an old friend."

His eyes widened and then narrowed. A few people still knew who one of Ruth's old friends had been.

". . . Also," I continued, "I received a message from her recently, asking me to come see her on a matter of some urgency. She is not here and there is no message, no forwarding address. It smells funny. I am going to find her, Mister DuBois."

He was not blind to the cut and therefore the cost of my suit, and maybe my voice has a somewhat authoritarian edge from years of giving orders. At any rate, he didn't switch on the phone and call for the cops.

"All the arrangements were made over the phone and through the mails," he said. "I honestly do not know where she is presently. She simply said that she was leaving town and wanted me to dispose of the place and everything in it, the money to be deposited in her account at Artists Trust. So I agreed to handle the matter and turned it over to Sunspray." He looked away, looked back. "Now, she did leave a message with me, to be delivered to someone other than yourself should he call here for it. If not, I am to transmit it to that individual after thirty days have elapsed from the time I received it."

"May I inquire as to the identity of that individual?"

"That, sir, *is* privileged."

"Switch on the phone," I said, "and call 73737373 in Glencoe, reversing the charges. Make it person-to-person to Domenic Malisti, the director of Our Thing Enterprises on this planet. Identify yourself, say to him, 'Baa baa blacksheep' and ask him to identify Lawrence John Conner for you."

DuBois did this, and when he hung up he rose to his feet, crossed the office, opened a small wall safe, removed an envelope and handed it to me. It was sealed, and across the face of it lay the name "Francis Sandow," typewritten.

"Thank you," I said and tore it open.

I fought down my feelings as I regarded the three items the envelope contained. There was another picture of Kathy, different pose, slightly different background, a picture of Ruth, older and a bit heavier but still attractive, and a note.

The note was written in Pei'an. Its salutation named me and was followed by a small sign which is used in holy texts to designate Shimbo, Shrugger of Thunders. It was signed "Green Green," and followed by the ideogram for Belion, who was not one of the twenty-seven Names which lived.

I was perplexed. Very few know the identities of the Name-bearers, and Belion is the traditional enemy of Shimbo. He is the fire god who lives under the earth. He and Shimbo take turns hacking one another up between resurrections.

I read the note. It said, *If you want your women, seek there on the Isle of the Dead. Bodgis, Dango, Shandon and the dwarf are also waiting.*

Back on Homefree there were tri-dees of Bodgis, Dango, Shandon, Nick, Lady Karle (who might qualify as one of my women) and Kathy. Those were the six pictures I'd received. Now he'd taken Ruth.

Who?

I did not know Green Green from anywhere that I could recall, but of course I knew the Isle of the Dead.

"Thank you," I said again.

"Is something wrong, Mister Sandow?"

"Yes," I said, "but I'll set it right. Don't worry, you're not involved. Forget my name."

"Yes, Mister Conner."

"Good evening."

"Good evening."

*   *   *

I entered the place on Nuage. I walked through the foyer, the various living rooms. I found her bedroom and searched it. She had left the place completely furnished. She'd also left several closets and dressers full of clothing, and all sorts of little personal items that you just don't leave behind when you move. It was a funny feeling, walking through that place which had replaced the other place and every now and then seeing something familiar—an antique clock, a painted screen, an inlaid- cigarette box—reminding me how life redistributes what once was meaningful amidst the always to be foreign, killing its personal magic, save in a memory you carry of the time and the place where once it stood, until you meet it again, it troubles you briefly, surrealistically, and then that magic, too, dies away as, punctured by the encounter, emotions you had forgotten are drained from the pictures inside your head. At least, it happened to me that way, as I searched for clues as to what might have occurred. As the hours passed and, one by one, each item in the place was passed through the sieve of my scrutiny, the realization which had come upon me in DuBois's office, the thing that had ridden with me from Homefree since the day the first picture had arrived, completed its circuit: brain to intestines to brain.

I seated myself and lit a cigarette. This was the room where the photo of Ruth had been taken; hers hadn't been the rocks-and-blue-sky setting of the others. I had searched though and found nothing: no evidence of violence, no clue as to the identity of my enemy. I said the words aloud, "My enemy," the first words I had spoken since "Good evening" to the suddenly cooperative, white-haired attorney, and the words sounded strange in that big fishbowl of a place. My enemy.

It was out in the open now. I was wanted, for what I wasn't sure. Offhand, I'd say death. It would have been helpful if I could have known which of my many enemies was behind it. I searched my mind. I considered my enemy's odd choice of rendezvous-point, battlefield. I thought back upon my dream of the place.

It was a foolish place for anyone to lure me if he wished to harm me, unless he knew nothing whatsoever concerning my power once I set foot upon any world I've made. Everything would be my ally if I went back to Illyria, the world I'd put where it was, many centuries ago, the world which held the Isle of the Dead, *my* Isle of the Dead.

. . . And I would go back. I knew that. Ruth, and the possibility of Kathy . . . These required my return to that strange Eden I'd once laid out. Ruth and Kathy . . . Two images which I did not like to juxtapose, but had to. They had never existed simultaneously for me, and I did not like the feeling now. I'd go, and whoever had baited the trap in this fashion would be sorry for a brief time only, and then he would dwell upon the Isle of the Dead forever.

I crushed out my cigarette, locked the ruddy castle gate and drove back to the Spectrum. I was suddenly hungry.

I dressed for dinner and descended to the lobby. I'd noticed a decent-looking little restaurant off to the left. Unfortunately, it had just closed a few minutes before. So I inquired at the desk after a good eating place that was still open.

"Bartol Towers, on the Bay," said the night clerk, smothering a yawn. "They'll be open for several hours yet."

So I took his directions on how to get there, and went out and nailed down a piece of the briar business. Ridiculous is a better word than strange, but then everybody lives in the shade of the Big Tree, remember?

I drove over, and I left the slip-sled to be parked by a uniform which I see wherever I go, smiling face above it, opening before me doors which I can open for myself, handing me a towel I don't want, snatching at a briefcase I don't care to check, right hand held at waist-level and ready to turn palm up at the first glint of metal or the crinkling of the proper type paper, large pockets to hold these items. It has followed me for over a thousand years, and it's not really the uniform that I resent. It's that damned smile, which is turned on by one thing only. My car went from here to there and was dropped between a pair of painted lines. Because we are all tourists.

At one time, tips were given only for things you logically would want to have done efficiently and promptly, and they served to supplement a lower payscale for certain classes of employment. This was understood, accepted. It was tourism, back in the century of my birth, cluing in the underdeveloped countries to the fact that all tourists are marks, that set the precedent, which then spread to all countries, even back to the tourists' own, of the benefits which might be gained by those who wear uniforms and render the undesired and the unrequested with a smile. This is the army that conquered the world. After their quiet revolution in the twentieth century, we all became tourists the minute we set foot outside our front doors, second-class citizens, to be ruthlessly exploited by the smiling legions who had taken over, slyly, completely.

Now, in every city into which I venture, uniforms rush upon me, dust dandruff from my collar, press a brochure into my hand, recite the latest weather report, pray for my soul, throw walkshields over nearby puddles, wipe off my windshield, hold an umbrella over my head on sunny or rainy days, or shine an ultra-infra flashlight before me on cloudy ones, pick lint from my belly-button, scrub my back, shave my neck, zip up my fly, shine my shoes and smile—all before I can protest—right hand held at waist-level. What a goddamn happy place the universe would be if everyone wore uniforms that glinted and crinkled. Then we'd all have to smile at each other.

I took the elevator up to the sixtieth floor, where the big place was. Then I realized that I should have called ahead from the hotel for a reservation. It was crowded. I'd forgotten that the following day was a holiday on Driscoll. The hostess took my name and told me fifteen or twenty minutes, so I went into one of a pair of bars and ordered a beer.

I looked about me as I sipped, and across the little foyer in the matching bar on the other side, hovering in the gloom, I saw a fat face that looked somewhat familiar. I slipped on a pair of special glasses which act like telescopes, and I studied the face, now in profile. The nose and the ears were the same. The hair was the wrong color and the complexion darker, but that's easily done.

I got up and started to walk that way when a waiter stopped me and told me that I couldn't carry a drink out of the place. When I told him I was going to the other bar, he offered to carry the drink for me, smiling, right hand at waist-level. I figured it would be cheaper to buy another one, so I told him he could drink it for me, too.

He was alone, a tiny glass of something bright before him. I folded my glasses and tucked them away as I approached his table, and in a fake falsetto said, "May I join you, Mister Bayner?"

He jumped, just slightly, within his skin, and the fat only quivered for an instant. He photographed me with his magpie eyes in the following second, and I knew that the machine that lay behind them was already spinning its wheels like a demon on an exercise bike.

"You must be mistaken—" he began, and smiled then, and followed that with a frown. "No, *I* am," he corrected himself, "but then it's been a long time, Frank, and we've both changed."

". . . Into our traveling clothes, yes," I said in my normal voice, seating myself across from him.

He caught the attention of a waiter as easily as if he'd had a lariat, and he asked me, "What are you drinking?"

"Beer," I said, "any brand."

The waiter overheard me, nodded, departed.

"Have you eaten?"

"No, I was waiting for a table, across the way there, when I spotted you."

"I've already eaten," he said. "If I hadn't indulged a sudden desire for an after-dinner drink on my way out, I might have missed you."

"Strange," I said, then, "Green Green."

"What?"

"Verde Verde. Grün Grün."

"I'm afraid I don't follow you. Is that some kind of code-phrase I'm supposed to recognize?"

I shrugged.

"Call it a prayer for the confoundment of my enemies. What's new?"

"Now that you're here," he said, "I've got to talk with you, of course. May I join you?"

"Surely. "

So, when they called for Larry Conner, we moved to a table in one of the countless dining rooms that filled that floor of the tower. We'd have had a pleasant view of the bay on a clear night, but the sky was overcast and an occasional buoy-light and an unpleasantly rapid searchlight were all that shone above the dark swells of the ocean. Bayner decided that he had a bit of an appetite left and ordered a full meal. He shoveled away a mound of spaghetti and a mess of bloody looking sausages before I'd half-finished my steak, and he moved on to shortcake, cheesecake and coffee.

"Ah, that was good!" he said, and he immediately inserted a toothpick into the upper portion of the first smile I'd seen him smile in, say, forty years.

"Cigar?" I offered.

"Thank you, I believe I will."

The toothpick went away, the cigars were lit, the check arrived. I always do that in crowded places when they're slow to bring me the check. A lit stogie, a quick blue haze and they're right beside me with the tab.

"This is on me," he announced as I accepted the bill.

"Nonsense. You're my guest."

"Well . . . All right."

After all, Bill Bayner is the forty-fifth wealthiest man in the galaxy. It isn't every day I get a chance to dine with successful people.

As we left, he said, "I've got a place where we can talk. I'll drive."

So we took his car, leaving a uniform and a frown behind us, and spent about twenty minutes driving around the city, shaking off hypothetical tails, and we finally arrived at an apartment building about eight blocks from Bartol Towers. As we entered the lobby, he nodded to the doorman, who nodded back to him.

"Think it'll rain tomorrow?" he asked.

"Clear," said the doorman.

Then we rode up to the sixth floor. The wainscotting in the hallway was full of artificial gems, some of which had to be eyes. We stopped and he knocked at an ordinary-looking door: three, pause, two, pause, two. He'd change it tomorrow, I knew. A dour-faced young man in a dark suit answered the door, nodded, and departed when Bayner gestured over his shoulder with a thumb. Inside, he secured the door, but not before I'd noticed from its edge that a metal plate was sandwiched between its inner and outer veneers of fake wood. For the next five or ten minutes, he tested the room with an amazing variety of bug-detection equipment, after giving me a keep-quiet sign, and then set several bug-scramblers into operation as an added precaution, sighed, removed his jacket and hung it on the back of a chair, turned to me and said, "It's okay to talk now. Can I fix you a drink?"

"Are you sure it'll be safe?"

He thought about it for a moment, then said, "Yes."

"Then I'll have bourbon and water if you've got it."

He withdrew into the next room and returned after about a minute with two glasses. His was probably filled with tea if he was planning on talking any kind of business with me. I couldn't have cared less.

"So what's up?" I asked him.

"Damn it, the stories they tell about you are true, aren't they? How'd you find out?"

I shrugged.

"But you're not going to move in on me on this one, not the way you did on those Vegan mining franchises."

"I don't know what you're talking about," I said.

"Six years ago."

I laughed.

"Listen," I told him, "I don't pay much attention to what my money does, so long as it's there when I want it. I trust various people to handle it for me. If I got a good deal in the Vegan system six years ago, it's because some good man in my employ lined it up. I don't run around shepherding money the way you do. I've delegated all that."

"Sure, sure, Frank," he said. "So you're incognito on Driscoll and you arrange to run into me the night before I deal. Who'd you buy on my staff?"

"Nobody, believe me."

He looked hurt.

"I'd tell *you*," he said. "I won't hurt him. I'll just transfer him somewhere where he won't do any more harm."

"I'm really not here on business," I said, "and I ran into you by pure chance."

"Well, you're not going to grab the whole thing this time, whatever you've got up your sleeve," he said.

"I'm not even in the running. Honest."

"Damn it!" he said. "Everything was going so smoothly!" and his right fist smashed against his left palm.

"I haven't even seen the product," I said.

He got up and stalked out of the room, came back and handed me a pipe.

"Nice pipe," I said.

"Five thousand," he told me. "Cheap."

"I'm really not much of a pipe-smoker."

"I won't cut you in for more than ten percent," he said. "I've been handling this thing personally, and you're not going to queer it."

And then I got mad. All that bastard thought about, besides eating, was stacking up his wealth. He automatically assumed I spent my time the same way, just because a lot of leaves on the Big Tree say "Sandow." So, "I want a third, or I make my own deal," I said.

"A third?"

He leaped to his feet and began screaming. It was a good thing that the room was soundproof and debugged. It had been a long time since I'd heard some of those expressions. He grew red in the face and he paced. Greedy, money-grubbing, unethical me sat there thinking about pipes while he ranted.

A guy with a memory like mine has many odd facts in his head. Back in my youth, on Earth, the best pipes were made either of meerschaum or briar. Clay pipes draw awfully hot and wooden ones crack or burn out quickly. Corncobs are dangerous. In the latter part of the twentieth century, possibly because of a generation growing up in the shadow of a Surgeon General's Report on respiratory diseases, pipe smoking had undergone something of a renaissance. By the turn of the century, the world's supply of briar and meerschaum was largely exhausted. Meerschaum, or hydrous magnesium silicate, is a sedimentary rock which occurred in strata composed in part of seashells that had fused together over the ages, and when it was all gone, that was it. Briar pipes were made from the root of the White Heath, or *Erica arborea*, which grew only in a few areas about the Mediterranean and had to be around a hundred years old before it was of any use. The White Heath had been subjected to wanton harvesting, with anything like a reforestation plan far from mind. Consequently, substances like pyrolitic carbon now do for the bulk of pipe smokers, but meerschaum and briar linger in memories and collections. Small deposits of meerschaum have been discovered upon various worlds and turned into fortunes overnight. Nowhere but on Earth, however, has *Erica arborea* or a suitable substitute ever turned up. And pipe smoking is the mainliner's way of smoking these days, DuBois and me being mavericks. The pipe Bayner had shown me was a pretty, flame-grained briar. Therefore . . .

". . . Fifteen percent," he was saying, "which barely allows me a small profit—"

"Nuts! Those briars are worth ten times their weight in platinum!"

"You cut my heart out if you ask for more than eighteen percent!"

"Thirty."

"Be reasonable, Frank."

"Then let's talk business, not nonsense."

"Twenty percent is all I can let you in for, and it will cost you five millions—"

I laughed.

So for the next hour I haggled, out of pure cussedness, resenting the estimation he'd placed on me and refused to disbelieve. I lived up to it, too. Like twenty-five and a half percent for four million, which required a phone call to Malisti to swing the financing. I really hated to wake him.

And that's how I nailed down a piece of the briar business on Driscoll. Ridiculous is a better word than strange, but then everyone lives in the shade of the Big Tree, remember?

After it was all over, he slapped me on the shoulder and told me I was a cool dealer and that he'd rather have me with him than against him, made us another round of drinks, sounded me out on getting Martin Bremen away from me, as he'd never been able to hire a Rigelian chef, and asked me once, again who had tipped me off.

He dropped me at Bartol Towers, the uniform moved my car a few feet and held the door for me, got its money,, turned off its smile and went away. I drove back to the Spectrum, wishing I'd eaten there and gotten to bed early instead of spending my evening autographing leaves.

The radio in the sled played a Dixieland number I hadn't heard in ages. That, and the rain that came a moment later, made me feel lonely and more than a little sad. Traffic was light. I hurried.

*   *   *

The following morning, I sent a courier-gram to Marling of Megapei, telling him to rest easy in the knowledge that Shimbo would be with him before the fifth season, and asking him if he knew a Pei'an named Green Green, or some equivalent thereof, who might in any way be associated with the Name Belion. I asked him to reply by courier-gram, reverse-charge, and send his answer to Lawrence J. Conner, c/o Homefree, and I didn't sign it. I planned on leaving Driscoll for Homefree that same day. A couriergram is about the fastest and one of the most expensive ways there is of sending an interstellar message; and even so, I knew there would be a lapse of a couple of weeks before I received a reply.

It was true that I was running a small risk of blowing my cover on Driscoll by sending a message of that class with a Homefree return on it, but I was leaving that day and I wanted to expedite things.

I checked out of the hotel and drove to the place on Nuage, to give it a final once-over, stopping for a late breakfast on the way.

I found only one thing new at the Raspberry Palace. There was something in the message-slot. It was a wide envelope, bearing no return address.

The envelope was for "Francis Sandow, c/o Ruth Laris." I took it inside with me and did not open it until I'd satisfied myself that there were no lurkers. Then I repocketed a tiny tube, capable of producing instant, silent and natural-seeming death, seated myself and opened my mail.

Yes.

Another picture.

It was Nick, my old friend Nick, Nick the dwarf, dead Nick, snarling through his beard and ready to leap at the photographer, standing there on a rocky ledge.

"Come visit Illyria. All your friends live there," said a note, in English.

I lit my first cigarette of the day.

Malisti, Bayner and DuBois knew who Lawrence John Conner was.

Malisti was my man on Driscoll, and I paid him enough so that he was, I thought, above bribery. Admitted, other pressures can be brought to bear on a man—but he himself had only learned my true identity the day before, when *Baa-baa blacksheep* had provided the key for the decoding of a special instruction. Not much time had passed in which to apply pressure.

Bayner had nothing, really, to gain by bugging me. We were partners in a joint venture which represented one of those drops in those buckets people talk about. That was all. Our fortunes were such that, even if our interests did conflict on occasion, it was a very impersonal thing. He was out.

DuBois didn't impress me as the sort to give away my name either, not after the way I'd spoken in his office concerning my willingness to resort to extreme means to obtain what I wanted.

Nobody at Homefree had known where I was going, except for S & F, whose memory of the fact I'd erased prior to my departure.

I considered an alternative.

If Ruth had been kidnapped, forced to write the note she had written, then whoever had taken her could safely assume I'd receive this latest if I responded, and if not, no harm done.

This seemed possible, probable.

So it meant there was somebody on Driscoll whose name I'd like to know.

Was it worth sticking around for? With Malisti on the job, I might be able to ferret out the sender of the latest picture.

But if there was a man behind the man and he was smart, his subordinate would know very little, might even be a totally innocent party. I resolved to put Malisti on the trail and have him send his findings to Homefree. I'd use a phone other than the one at my right hand, however.

In just a few hours, it wouldn't matter who knew that Conner was Sandow. I'd be on my way, and I'd never be Conner again.

*　　*　　*

"Everything that's miserable in the world," Nick the dwarf once said to me, "is because of beauty."

"Not truth or goodness?" I'd asked.

"Oh, they help. But beauty is the culprit, the real principle of evil."

"Not wealth?"

"Money is beautiful."

"So is anything else you don't have enough of—food, water, screwing. . ."

"Exactly!" he announced, slamming his beer mug down so heavily on the tabletop that a dozen heads were turned in our direction. "Beauty, goddamn it!"

"What about a good-looking guy?"

"They're either bastards because they know they've got it made, or they're self-conscious because they know other guys hate their guts. Bastards are always hurting other people, and the self-conscious guys screw themselves up. Usually they go queer or something, all because of that goddamn beauty!"

"What about beautiful objects?"

"They make people steal, or feel bad because they can't get at them. Damn—!"

"Wait a minute," I said. "It's not an object's fault that it's beautiful, or the pretty people's fault that they're pretty. It just happens that way."

He shrugged.

"Fault? Who said anything about fault?"

"You were talking about evil. That implies guilt somewhere along the line."

"Then beauty is guilty," he said. "Goddamn it!"

"Beauty, as an abstract principle?"

"Yes."

"And in individual objects?"

"Yes."

"That's ridiculous! Guilt requires responsibility, some kind of intent—"

"Beauty's responsible!"

"Have another beer."

He did, and belched again.

"Take a look at that good-looking guy over at the bar," he said, "that guy trying to pick up the broad in the green dress. Somebody's going to bust him one in the nose sometime. It wouldn't have to happen if he was ugly."

Nick later proved his point by busting the guy one in the nose, because he'd called him Shorty. So maybe there was something to what he said. Nick was around four feet tall. He had the shoulders and arms of a powerful athlete. He could beat anybody I knew at wrist-wrestling. He had a normal-sized head, too, full of blond hair and beard, with a couple blue eyes above a busted nose that turned off to the right and a mean smile that usually revealed only half a dozen of his yellow-stained teeth. He was all gnarled below the waist. He'd come from a family lousy with professional soldiers. His father'd been a general, and all of his brothers and sisters except for one were officers in something or other. Nick had grown up in an environment alive with the martial arts. Any weapon you cared to name, he could operate it. He could fence, shoot, ride, set explosive charges, break boards and necks with his hands, live off the land, and fail any physical examination in the galaxy because he was a dwarf. I'd hired him as a game hunter, to kill off my experiments that went bad. He hated beautiful things and things that were bigger than he was.

"What I think is beautiful and what you think is beautiful," I said, "might disgust a Rigelian, and vice-versa. Therefore, beauty is a relative thing. So you can't condemn it as an abstract principle if—"

"Crap!" he said. "So they hurt, rape, steal and screw themselves up over different things. It's still because beauty sits there demanding violation."

"Then how can you blame an individual object—"

"We do business with Rigelians, don't we?"

"Yes."

"Then it can be translated. Enough said."

Then the good-looking guy at the bar who'd been trying to pick up the broad in the green dress passed by on his way to the men's room and called Nick "Shorty" when he asked him to move his chair out of the way. That ended our evening in that bar.

Nick swore he'd die with his boots on, on some exotic safari, but he found his Kilimanjaro in a hospital on Earth, where they'd cured everything that was bothering him, except for the galloping pneumonia he'd picked up in the hospital.

That had been, roughly, two hundred and fifty years ago. I'd been a pallbearer.

*   *   *

I mashed out my cigarette and made my way back to the slip-sled. Whatever was rotten in Midi, I'd find it out later. It was time to go.

The dead are too much with us.

*   *   *

For two weeks, I puzzled over what I'd found and I kept myself fit. When I entered the Homefree system, my life was further complicated by the fact that Homefree had picked up an additional satellite. Not a natural one, either.

WHAT THE HELL! I sent ahead in code.

VISITOR, came the reply. LANDING PERMISSION REQUESTED. DENIED. STILL CIRCLING. SAYS HE'S AN EARTH INTELLIGENCE MAN.

LET HIM LAND, I said, HALF A HOUR AFTER I'M DOWN.

There came the acknowledgment, and I swung into a tight orbit and pushed the *Model T* down and around and down.

After a frolic with the beasts, I repaired to my home for a shower, shucked my Conner face, then dressed for dinner.

It would appear that something finally meant enough to the wealthiest government in existence for someone to at last authorize a trip on the part of some underpaid civil servant in one of the cheapest interstellar vehicles available.

I vowed to at least feed him well.

III

Lewis Briggs and I regarded one another across the remains of dinner and the wide table they occupied. His identification papers informed me that he was an agent of Earth's Central Intelligence Department. He looked like a shaved monkey. He was a wizened little guy with a perpetually inquisitive stare, and it seemed as if he must be pushing retirement age. He'd stuttered just a bit when he'd introduced himself, but the dinner appeared to have relaxed him and the falter had halted.

"It was a very pleasant meal, Mister Sandow," he acknowledged. "Now, if I may, I'd like to discuss the business that brought me here."

"Then let's adjourn to the upstairs, where we can get some fresh air while we talk."

We arose, taking our drinks with us, and I led him to the elevator.

Five seconds later, it admitted us to the roof garden, and I gestured toward a couple lounging chairs set beneath a chestnut tree. "How about there?" I asked. He nodded and seated himself. A cool breeze came out of the twilight and we breathed it in and gave it back.

"It's quite impressive," he said, looking around the garden shadows, "the way you satisfy your every whim."

"This particular whim in which we're relaxing," I said,

"is landscaped to make this place virtually undetectable by means of aerial reconnaissance."

"Oh, the thought hadn't occurred to me."

I offered him a cigar, which he declined. So I lit it for myself and asked him, "So what is it you want of me?"

"Will you consent to accompany me back to Earth and talk to my chief?" he asked.

"No," I said. "I've answered that question a dozen times, in as many letters. Earth grates on my nerves, it gives me a big pain these days. That's why I live out here. Earth is overcrowded, bureaucratic, unhealthy, and suffering from too many mass-psychoses to bother classifying. Whatever your chief wants to say, you can say for him; and I'll answer you, and you can take it back to him."

"Normally," he said, "these matters are handled at the Division level."

"Sorry about that," I replied, "but I'll foot the bill for a coded courier-gram from here, if it comes to that."

"The reply would cost the Department too much," he said. "Our budget, you know."

"For Chrissake, I'll pay it both ways then! Anything to stop cluttering my incoming basket with what is still strangely referred to as surface-carrier mail."

"God! No!" A tone of panic clung to his words. "It's never been done before, and the man-hours involved in determining how to bill you would be prohibitive!"

Inwardly, I wept for thee, Mother Earth, and the prodigies that had been wrought upon thee. A government is born, it flourishes, strong is its nationalism and great its frontiers, then comes a time of solidification, division of labor unto specialization, and the layers of management and chains of command, yes, and Max Weber spoke of this. He saw bureaucracy in the necessary evolution of all institutions, and he saw that it was good. He saw that it was necessary and good. While it may be necessary, put a comma after that word and after the last one add "God" and an exclamation point. For there comes a time in the history of all bureaucracies when they must inevitably parody their own functions. Look what the breakup of the big Austro-Hungarian machine did to poor Kafka, or the Russian one to Gogol. It drove them out of their cotton-picking minds, poor bastards, and now I was looking at a man who had survived an infinitely more inscrutable one until the end of his days was in sight. This indicated to me that he was slightly below average intelligence, emotionally handicapped, insecure, or morally suspect; or else he was an iron-willed masochist. For these neuter machines, combining as they do the worst of both father-image and mother-image—*i.e.*, the security of the womb and the authority of an omniscient leade—always manage to attract the nebbish. And this is why, Mother Earth, I wept inwardly for thee at that moment of the immense parade called Time: the clowns were passing, and everybody knows that inside, somewhere, their hearts are broken.

"Then tell me what you would like of me and I'll answer you now," I said.

He reached into his inside pocket and withdrew a sealed envelope bearing various security stamps, which I didn't bother examining too closely, even when he handed it to me.

"Should you not consent to accompany me back to Earth, I was instructed to deliver this to you."

"If I had agreed to go along, what would you have done with it?"

"Returned it to my chief," he said.

"So that he could hand it to me?"

"Probably," he said.

I tore it open and withdrew a single sheet of paper.

I held it close and squinted through the dim light. It was a list of six names. I kept my face under control as I read them.

They were all names of people I had loved or hated, and they were each of them, somewhere, the subject of a moldering obituary.

Also, they had all figured prominently in some recent photography I had been called upon to witness.

I puffed smoke, refolded the list, replaced it in the envelope and dropped it on the table between us.

"What does it signify?" I asked, after a time.

"They are all potentially alive," he said. "I request that you destroy the list at your earliest convenience."

"Okay," I said, and, "Why are they potentially alive?"

"Because their Recall Tapes were stolen."

"How?"

"We don't know."

"Why?"

"We don't know that either."

"And you came to me. . . ?"

"Because you are the only link we could find. You knew all of them—well."

My first reaction was disbelief, but I concealed it and said nothing. Recall Tapes are the one thing in the universe which I had always considered inviolate, unreachable, for the thirty days of their existence—and then they were gone forever. I tried to get hold of one once and failed. Their guardians were incorruptible, their vaults impenetrable.

And this was part of another reason why I don't visit Earth much any more. I don't like the idea of wearing a Recall Plate, even temporarily. Persons born there have them implanted at birth and they are required by law to wear them for as long as they remain on Earth. Persons moving to Earth for purposes of residing there are required to have them installed. Even a visitor must bear one for the duration of his stay.

What they do is monitor the electromagnetic matrix of the nervous system. They record the shifting patterns of a man's being, and each is as unique as a fingerprint. Their one function is to transmit that final pattern, at the moment of death. Death is the trigger, the shot is the psyche, the target's a machine. It's an enormous machine, and it records that transmission on a strip of tape you can hold in the palm of your hand-all that a man ever was or hoped to be-weighing less than an ounce. After thirty days, the tape is destroyed. That's it.

In a small and classified number of cases over the past several centuries, however, that wasn't it. The purpose for the whole strange and costly setup is this: there are some individuals who, dying suddenly, on the planet Earth, at crucial points in significant lives, depart this lachrymose valley with information vital to the economy/technology/national interest of Earth. The whole Recall System is there for the purpose of retrieving such data. Even the mighty machine is not sufficiently sophisticated to draw this information from the recorded matrix, however. That is why every wearer of the Plate has a frozen tissue culture, somewhere. This culture is associated with the tape and held for thirty days subsequent to death, and both are normally destroyed together. Should Recall be necessary, an entire new body is grown from the culture, in an AGT (that's an accelerated growth tank), and this body duplicates the original in all things, save that its brain is a tabula rasa. On this clean plate, then, is superimposed the recorded matrix, so that the recalled individual possesses every thought and memory which existed in the original up until the moment of death. He is then in a position to supply the information which the entire World Congress has deemed to be of sufficient value to warrant Recall. An iron-clad security setup guards the entire system, which is housed in a quarter-mile square fortress in Dallas.

"Do you think I stole the tapes?" I asked.

He crossed and uncrossed his legs, looked away.

"You'll admit there's a pattern, and that it seems somehow related to you?"

"Yes. But I didn't do it "

"You'll admit that you were investigated and charged at one time for attempting to bribe a government official in order to obtain the tape for your first wife, Katherine?"

"It is a matter of public record, so I can't deny it. But the charges were dismissed," I said.

"True—because you could afford a lot of bad publicity and good lawyers, and you hadn't succeeded in obtaining the tape, anyway. It was later stolen, though, and it was years before we discovered that it hadn't been destroyed on the scheduled date. There was no way of linking it to you, or of obtaining jurisdiction in the place you were then residing. There was no other way of reaching you, either."

I smiled at his accent on the word "reaching." I, too, have a security network.

"And what do you think I would have done with the tape, had I obtained it?"

"You're a wealthy man, Mister Sandow—one of the few who could afford to duplicate the machinery necessary for Recall. And your training—"

"I'll admit I once had that in mind. Unfortunately, I didn't obtain the tape, so the attempt was never made."

"Then how do you explain the others? The subsequent thefts which occurred over several centuries, always involving friends or enemies of yours."

"I don't have to explain," I said, "because I don't owe you an explanation for anything I do. But I will tell you this: I didn't do it. I don't have the tapes, never had them. I had no idea up until now that they were missing."

But, Good Lordl *They* were the six!

"Then accepting that as true, for the moment," he said, "can you supply us with any sort of lead as to who might have had sufficient interest in these people to go to such extremes?"

"I cannot," I said, seeing the Isle of the Dead in my mind's eye, and knowing that I would have to find out.

"I feel I should point out," said Briggs, "that this case will never be closed on our books until we have been satisfied as to the disposition of the tapes."

"I see," I said. "Would you mind telling me how many unclosed cases you're carrying on your books at the present time?"

"The number is unimportant," he said. "It's the principle involved. We never give up."

"It's just that I heard there were quite a few," I said, "and that some of them are getting pretty moldy."

"I take it you won't cooperate?"

"Not 'won't.' Can't. I don't have anything to give you."

"And you won't return to Earth with me?"

"To hear your chief repeat everything you've just said to me? No thanks. Tell him I'm sorry. Tell him I'd help if I could, but I don't see any way I can."

"All right. I guess I'll be leaving then. Thanks for the dinner."

He rose.

"You might as well stay overnight," I said, "and get a decent night's sleep in a comfortable bed before you shove off."

He shook his head.

"Thanks, but I can't. I'm on per diem, and I have to account for all the time I spend on a job."

"How do they calculate per diem when you're in subspace?"

"It's complicated," he said.

* * *

So I waited for the mailman. He's a big fac-machine who picks up messages beamed to Homefree and turns them into letters and gives them to S & F, who sorts them and drops them into my basket. While I waited, I made my preparations for the visit to Illyria. I'd followed Briggs every step of the way. I'd seen him to his vessel and monitored its departure from my system. I supposed I might see him again one day, or his chief, if I found out what had really happened and made it back home. It was obvious that whoever wanted me on Illyria had not set the thing up for purposes of throwing a party on my behalf. That's why my preparations mainly involved the selection of weapons. As I picked and chose from among the smaller of the deadlies in my arsenal, I thought some thoughts of Recall.

Briggs had been right, of course. Only a wealthy man could afford to duplicate the expensive Recall equipment housed in Dallas. Some research would be involved, too, for a few of the techniques were still classified. I sought candidates from among my competitors. Douglas? No. He hated me, but he wouldn't go to such elaborate ends to nail me if he ever decided it was worthwhile. Krellson? He'd do it, if he could; but I kept him under such close surveillance that I was certain he hadn't had the opportunity for anything of this magnitude. The Lady Quoil of Rigel? Virtually senile by now. Her daughters ran her empire and wouldn't humor such an expensive request for revenge, I was sure. Who then?

I checked my records, and they didn't show recent transactions. So I sent a courier-gram to the Central Registration Unit for that stellar district. Before the answer came back, however, I received Marling's reply to my message from Driscoll.

"Come to Megapei immediately," it said, and that was all. None of the formal flourishes characteristic of Pei'an writing style were present. Only that single, bald statement. It was the keynote of urgency. Either Marling was worse off than he'd suspected or my query had struck something big.

I arranged for CRU's message to be forwarded to me in Megapei, Megapei, Megapei, and then I was gone.

IV

Megapei. If you're going to pick a place to die, you might as well pick a comfortable one. The Pei'ans did, and I consider them wise. It had been a pretty desolate place, I'm told, when they found it. But they refurbished it before they moved in and settled down to the business of dying.

Megapei's around seven thousand miles through the middle, with two big continents in the northern hemisphere and three small ones to the south. The larger of the northern ones looks like a tall teapot tilted to pour (the handle broken at the top), and the other resembles an ivy leaf from which some hungry caterpillar took a big, northwestern bite. These two are about eight hundred miles apart, and the bottom of the ivy leaf dips about five degrees into the tropic zone. The teapot is around the size of Europe. The three continents in the southern hemisphere look like continents; that is to say, irregular chunks of green and gray surrounded by a cobalt sea, and they don't remind me of anything else. Then there's lots of little islands and a few fairly large ones scattered all about the globe. The icecaps are small and keep pretty much to themselves. The temperature is pleasant, as the ecliptic and the equator are fairly close. The continents all possess bright beaches and peaceful mountains, and any pleasant habitation you care to imagine somewhere in between. The Pei'ans had wanted it that way.

There are no large cities, and the city of Megapei on the continent of Megapei, there on Megapei, is therefore not a large city. (Megapei the continent is the chomped ivy leaf. Megapei the city lies on the sea in the middle of the chomp.) No two habitations within the city are nearer than a mile from one another.

I orbited twice, because I wanted to look down and admire that handiwork. I still couldn't spot a single feature which I'd have cared to change. They were my masters when it came to the old art, always would be.

Memories poured back, of the gone happy days before I'd become rich and famous and hated. The population of the entire world was less than a million. I could probably lose myself down there, as once I had, and dwell on Megapei for the rest of my days. I knew I wouldn't. Not yet, anyhow. But sometimes it's pleasant to daydream.

On my second pass, I entered the atmosphere, and after a time the winds sang about me, and the sky changed from indigo to violet to a deep, pure azure, with little wisps of cirrus hovering there between being and nothingness.

The stretch on which I landed was practically Marling's back yard. I secured the ship and walked toward his tower, carrying a small suitcase. It was about a mile's distance.

As I walked the familiar trail, shaded by broad-leafed trees, I whistled once, lightly, and a bird-call mimicked my note. I could smell the sea, though I could not yet view it. All was as it had been, years before, in the days when I had set myself the impossible task and gone forth to wrestle the gods, hoping only for forgetfulness, finding something far different.

Memories, like stained slides, suddenly became illuminated as I encountered, successively, an enormous, mossed-over boulder, a giant *parton* tree, a *crybbl* (an almost-lavender greyhound-like creature the size of a small horse, with long lashes and a crown of rosy quills), which quickly bounded away, a yellow sail—when the sea came into view—then Marling's pier, down in the cove, and finally the tower itself, entire, mauve, serene, severe and high, above the splashing, below the sunrich skies, clean as a tooth and far, far older than I.

I ran the last hundred yards and banged upon the grillwork that covered the arched way into the small courtyard.

After perhaps two minutes, a strange young Pei'an came and stood and regarded me from the other side. I spoke to him in Pei'an. I said: "My name is Francis Sandow, and I have come to see *Dra* Marling." At this, the Pei'an unlatched the gate and held it open. Not until I had entered (for such is their custom) did he answer: "You are welcome, *Dra* Sandow. *Dra* Marling will see you after the tidal bell has rung. Let me show you to a place of rest and bring you refreshment." I thanked him and followed him up the winding stair.

I ate a light meal in the chamber to which he had conducted me. I still had more than an hour until the turning of the tide, so I lit a cigarette and stared out over the ocean through that wide, low window beside the bed, my elbows upon the sill that was harder than intermetallide plastic, and gray.

Strange to live like this, you say? A race capable of damn near anything, a man named Marling capable of building worlds? Maybe. Marling could have been wealthier than Bayner and I put together and multiplied by ten, had he chosen. But he'd picked a tower on a cliff overlooking the sea, a forest at his back, and he decided to live there till he died, and was doing it. I will trace no morals, such as a drawing away from the overcivilized races who were flooding the galaxy, such as repugnance for any society at all, even that of one's fellows. Anything would be an oversimplification. He was there because he wanted to be there, and I cannot go behind the fact. Still, we are kindred spirits, Marling and I, despite the differences in our fortresses. He saw that before I did, though how he could tell that the power might dwell in the broken alien who'd turned up on his doorstep one day, centuries before, is something that I do not understand.7

Sick of wandering, frightened by Time, I had gone to seek counsel of what was said to be the oldest race around. How frightened I had become, I find it hard to describe. To see everything die—I don't think you know what it's like. But that's why I went to Megapei. Shall I tell you a little of myself? Why not? I told me again, as I waited for the bell.

I was born on the planet Earth, into the middle of the twentieth century, that period in the history of the race when man succeeded in casting off many of the inhibitions and taboos laid upon him by tradition, reveled for a brief time, and then discovered that it didn't make a bloody bit of difference that he had. He was still just as dead when he died, and he still was faced with every life-death problem that had confronted him before, compounded by the fact that Malthus was right. I left my indefinite college major at the end of my sophomore year to enlist in the Army, along with my younger brother who was just out of high school. That's how I found Tokyo Bay. Afterwards, I returned to school for a degree in engineering, decided that was a mistake, returned again to pick up the requirements for medical school. Somewhere along the line, I got sidetracked by the life sciences, went on for a master's in Biology, kept pursuing a growing interest in ecology. I was twenty-six years old and the year was 1991. My father had died and my mother had remarried. I had fallen for a girl, proposed to her, been rebuffed, volunteered for one of the first attempts to reach another star system. My mixed academic background got me passage, and I was frozen for a century's voyage. We made it to Burton, began setting up a colony. Before a year's time, however, I was stricken by a local disease for which we lacked a cure, not to mention a name. I was then refrozen in my cold bunker, to await some eventual therapy. Twenty-two years later, I came around. There had been eight more shiploads of colonists and a new world lay about me. Four more shiploads arrived that same year, and only two would remain. The other two were going on to a more distant system, to join an even newer colony. I got passage by trading places with a colonist who'd chickened out on the second leg of the flight. It was a once-in-a-lifetime opportunity, or so I thought, and since I could no longer recall the face—let alone the name—of the girl who had caused me to make the initial move, my desire to go on was predicated, I am certain, solely upon curiosity and the fact that the environment in which I then found myself had already been somewhat tamed, and I had had no part in its taming. It took a century and a quarter of cold sleep to reach the world we then sought, and I didn't like the place at all. That's why I signed up for a long haul, after only eight months-a two hundred seventy-six year journey out to Bifrost, which was to be man's farthest outpost, if we could make a go of it. Bifrost was bleak and bitter and scared me, and convinced me that maybe I wasn't meant to be a colonist. I made one more trip to get away, and it was already too late. People were suddenly all over the place, intelligent aliens were contacted, interstellar trips were matters of weeks and months, not centuries. Funny? I thought so. I thought it was a great joke. Then it was pointed out to me that I was possibly the oldest man alive, doubtless the only survivor of the twentieth century. They told me about the Earth. They showed me pictures. Then I didn't laugh any more, because Earth had become a different world. I was suddenly very alone. Everything I had learned in school seemed medieval. So what did I do? I went back to see for myself. I returned to school, discovered I could still learn. I was scared, though, all the time. I felt out of place. Then I heard of the one thing that might give me a wedge in the times, the one thing that might save me the feeling of being the last survivor of Atlantis walking down Broadway, the one thing that might make me superior to the strange world in which I found myself. I heard of the Pei'ans, a then recently discovered race to whom all the marvels of the twenty-seventh century on Earth—including the treatments which had added a couple centuries to my life-expectancy—would seem like ancient history. So I came to Megapei, Megapei, Megapei, half out of my mind, picked a tower at random, called out at the gate till someone responded, then said, "Teach me, please."

I had gone to the tower of Marling, all unknowing at the time—Marling, of the twenty-six Names that lived.

When the tidal bell rang, the young Pei'an came for me and he conducted me up the winding stair to the top. He stepped into the room, and I heard Marling's voice greet him.

"*Dra* Sandow is here to see you," he replied.

"Then bid him enter."

The young Pei'an returned through the door and said, "He bids you enter."

"Thank you."

I went in.

Marling was seated with his back to me, facing out the window toward the sea, as I knew he would be. The three large walls of his fanshaped chamber were a pale green, resembling jade, and his bed was long, low and narrow. One wall was an enormous console, somewhat dusty. And the small, bedside table, which might not have been moved in centuries, still held the orange figurine resembling a horned dolphin leaping.

"*Dra*, good afternoon," I said.

"Come over here where I can see you."

I rounded his chair and stood before him. He was thinner and his skin was darker.

"You came quickly," he said, his eyes moving across my face.

I nodded.

"You said 'immediately.'"

He made a hissed, rattling sound, which is a Pei'an chuckle, then, "How have you been treating life?"

"With respect, deference and fear."

"What of your work?"

"I'm between jobs just now."

"Sit down."

He indicated a bench alongside the window, and I crossed to it.

"Tell me what has happened."

"Pictures," I said. "I've been receiving pictures of people I used to know—people who have been dead for some time now. All of them died on Earth, and I recently learned that their Recall Tapes were stolen. So it's possible that they *are* alive, somewhere. Then I received this."

I handed him the letter signed "Green Green." He held it close and read it slowly.

"Do you know where the Isle of the Dead is?" he asked.

"Yes; it's on a world I made."

"You are going?"

"Yes. I must."

"Green Green is, I believe, Gringrin-tharl of the city Dilpei. He hates you."

"Why? I don't even know him."

"That is unimportant. Your existence offends him, so naturally he wishes to be avenged for this affront. It is sad."

"I'd say so. Especially if he succeeds. But how has my existence served to offend him?"

"You are the only alien to be a Name-bearer. At one time it was thought that none but a Pei'an could master the art you have learned—and not too many Pei'ans are capable, of course. Gringrin undertook the study and he completed it. He was to have been the twenty-seventh. He failed the final test, however."

"The *final* test? I'd thought that one pretty much a matter of form."

"No. It may have seemed so to you, but it is not. So, after half a century of study with Delgren of Dilpei, he was not confirmed in the trade. He was somewhat exercised. He spoke often of the fact that the last man to be admitted was not even Pei'an. Then he departed Megapei. With his training, of course, he soon grew wealthy."

"How long ago was that?"

"Several hundred years. Perhaps six."

"And you feel he's been hating me all this time, and planning revenge?"

"Yes. There was no great hurry, and a good piece of revenge requires elaborate preparation."

It is always strange to hear a Pei'an speak so. Eminently civilized, they nevertheless have made revenge a way of life. It is doubtless another of the reasons why there are so few Pei'ans. Some of them actually keep vengeance books—long, elaborate lists of those who require a comeuppance—in order to keep track of everyone they intend to punish, complete with progress reports on the status of each vengeance scheme. A piece of vengeance isn't worth much to a Pei'an unless it's complicated, carefully planned and put into motion, and occurs with fiendish precision many years after the affront which stimulated it. It was explained to me that the fun of it is really in the planning and the anticipation. The actual death, madness, disfigurement or humiliation which results is quite secondary to this. Marling once confided in me that he had had three going which had lasted over a thousand years apiece, and that's no record. It's a way of life, really. It comforts one, providing a cheering object of contemplation when all other things are going poorly; it renders a certain satisfaction as the factors line themselves up, one by one—little triumphs, as it were—leading up to the time of fulfillment; and there is an esthetic pleasure to be had—some even say a mystical experience—when the situation occurs and the carefully wrought boom is lowered. Children are taught the system at an early age, for full familiarity with it is necessary for attaining advanced old age. I had had to learn it in a hurry, and was still weak on some of the finer points.

"Have you any suggestions?" I asked.

"Since it is useless to flee the vengeance of a Pei'an," he told me, "I would recommend your locating him immediately and challenging him to a walk through the night of the soul. I will provide you with some fresh *glitten* roots before you leave."

"Thank you. I'm not real up on that, you know."

"It is easy, and one of you will die, thus solving your problems. So if he accepts, you will have nothing to worry about. Should you die, you will be avenged by my estate."

"Thank you, *Dra.*"

"It is nothing."

"What of Belion, with respect to Gringrin?"

"He is there."

"How so?"

"They have made their own terms, those two."

"And. . . ?"

"That is all I know."

"Will he see fit to walk with me, do you think?"

"I do not know."

Then, "Let us regard the waters in their rising," he said, and I turned and did so until he spoke again, perhaps half an hour later.

"This is all," he said.

"There is no more?"

"No."

The sky darkened until there were no sails. I could hear the sea, smell it, and there was its black, rolling, star-flecked bulk in the distance. I knew that soon an unseen bird would shriek, and one did. For a long while, I stood in a pertinent corner of my mind, examining things I had left there a long time ago and forgotten, and some things which I had never fully understood. My Big Tree toppled, the Valley of Shadows faded and the Isle of the Dead was only a hunk of rock dropped into the middle of the Bay and sinking without a ripple. I was alone, I was absolutely alone. I knew what the next words that I would hear would be; and then, sometime later, I heard them.

"Journey with me this night," he said.

"*Dra . . .*"

Nothing.

Then, "Must it be *this* night?" I said.

Nothing.

"Where then will dwell Lorimel of the Many Hands?"

"In the happy nothing, to come again, as always."

"What of your debts, your enemies?"

"All of them paid."

"You had spoken of next year, in the fifth season."

"That, now, is changed."

"I see."

"We will spend the night in converse, Earthson, that I may give you my final secrets before sunrise. Sit down," and I did, at his feet, as in days far away through the smoke of memory seen and younger, younger by far. He began to speak and I closed my eyes, listened.

He knew what he was doing, knew what he wanted. This didn't keep me from being frightened as well as saddened, however. He had chosen me to be his guide, the last living thing that he would see. It was the highest honor he could pay a man, and I was not worthy of it. I hadn't used what he had given me as well as I might have. I'd screwed up a lot of things I shouldn't have. I knew he knew it, too. But it didn't matter. I was the one. Which made him the only person in the whole galaxy able to remind me of my own father, dead these thousand-plus years. He had forgiven me my trespasses.

The fear and the sadness . . .

Why now? Why had he chosen this time?

Because there might not be any other.

In Marling's estimation, I was obviously off on a venture from which I would probably not be returning. This, therefore, would have to be our final encounter. "Everyman, I will go with thee and be thy guide, in thy most need to go by thy side." —A good line for Fear, though Knowledge spoke it. They've a lot in common, when you stop to consider it.

And so the fear.

We did not speak of the sadness either. It would not have

been proper. We spoke for a time of the worlds we had made, of the places we had built and seen populated, of all the sciences that are involved in the feat of transforming rubble into a habitation and, ultimately, we spoke of the art. The ecology game is more complicated than any chess game, goes beyond the best formulations of any computer. This is because, finally, the problems are esthetic rather than scientific ones. All the thinking power within the seven-doored chamber of the skull is required, true; yet a dash of something still best described as inspiration is really the determining factor. We dwelled upon these inspirations, many of which now existed, and the night sea-wind rose up so shrill and cold that I had to secure the windows against it and kindle a small fire, which blazed then like a holy thing in that oxygen-rich place. I can remember none of the words that were spoken that night. Only there, preserved within me, are the soundless pictures we shared, memory now, glaced over with distance and time. "This is all," as he'd said, and after awhile there was dawn.

He fetched me the *glitten* roots when the faint false-dawn occurred, sat for a time and then we made the final preparations.

About three hours later, I summoned the servants and ordered them to hire mourners and to send a party ahead into the mountains to open the family burial crypt. Using Marling's equipment, I sent formal messages to the other twenty-five Names Which Lived, and to those he'd specified among friends, acquaintances and relatives that he wished to be present. Then I prepared the ancient and dark green body he had worn, found my way down to the kitchen for breakfast, lit a cigar and walked by the bright seaside where purple and yellow sails once more cut the horizon, found me a small tidal pool, sat down beside it, smoked.

I was numb. That's the easiest way to put it. I had been there before—the place from which I had just returned—and, as before, I came away with a certain indecipherable scribbling upon my soul. I wished now for the sadness or the fear again—anything. But I felt nothing, not even anger. This would come later, though, I knew; but for the moment, I was too young or too old.

Why did the day bloom so bright and the sea sparkle so before me? Why did the air burn salt and pleasant within me, and the life-cries of the wood come like music into my ears? Nature is not so sympathetic as the poets would have you believe. Only other people sometimes care when you close your doors and do not open them again. I would stay in Megapei Megapei Megapei and listen to the litany of Lorimel of the Many Hands while the thousand-year-old flutes covered it like a sheet a statue. Then Shimbo would walk into the mountains once again, in procession with the others, and I, Francis Sandow, would see the opening of the cavern and gray, charcoal, black, the closing of the crypt. I would stay a few days more, to help order my master's affairs, and then depart upon my own journey. If it ended the same way—well, that's life.

So much for nightthoughts at mid-morning. I rose up and returned to the tower to wait.

In the days that followed, Shimbo walked again. I remember the thunder, as in a dream. There was thunder and flutes and the fiery hieroglyphs of lightnings above the mountains, beneath the clouds. This time Nature wept, for Shimbo dragged the bell-pull. I recall the green and gray procession, winding its way through the forest to the place where the timber broke and the dirt gave way to stone. As I walked, behind the creaking cart, the headgear of a Name-bearer upon me, the singed shawl of mourning about my shoulders, I bore in my hands the mask of Lorimel, a strip of dark cloth across the eyes. No more would his light burn in the shrines, unless another was given the Name. I understand that it did burn for a moment, though, at the time of his passing, in every shrine in the universe. Then the last door was closed, gray, charcoal, black. A strange dream, is it not?

After it was all over, I sat in the tower for a week, as was expected of me. I fasted, and my thoughts were my own. During that week, a message came in from the Central Registration Unit, via Homefree. I didn't read it until Weeksend, and when I did, I learned that Illyria was now owned by the Green Development Company.

Before the day was over, I was able to ascertain locally that the Green Development Company was Gringrin-tharl, formerly of Dilpei, ex-student of Delgren of Dilpei who bore the Name Clice, Out of Whose Mouth Proceedeth Rainbows. I called Delgren and made arrangements to see him the following afternoon. Then I broke my fast and I slept, for a long, long time. There were no dreams that I can recall.

*　　　*　　　*

Malisti had uncovered no one, nothing, on Driscoll. Delgren of Dilpei was of very little assistance, as he had not seen his former pupil for centuries. He hinted that he might be planning a surprise for Gringrin should he ever return to Megapei. I wondered if the feeling and the plans were mutual.

Whatever, these things no longer mattered. My time on Megapei had come to an end.

I boosted the *Model T* into the sky and kept going until space and time ended for a space and a time. I continued.

*   *   *

I anesthetized and cut open the middle finger of my left hand, implanted a laser crystal and some piezoelectric webbing, closed the incision and kept the hand in a healant unit for four hours. There was no scar. It would sting like hell and cost me some skin if I used it, but if I were to extend that finger, clench the others and turn my palm upward, the beam it emitted would cut through a two-foot slab of granite. I packed rations, medical supplies, food, *glitten* root in a light knapsack, which I cached near the port. I would not need a compass or maps, of course, but some firesticks, a sheet of flimsy, a hand torch and some night-specs seemed advisable. I laid out everything I could think of, including my plans.

I decided not to descend in the *Model T*, but to orbit and ride in on a non-metallic drift-sled. I'd give myself an Illyrian week on the surface. I would instruct the *T* to descend at the end of that time and hover above the strongest power-pull nexus—and then return once every day after that.

I slept, I ate. I waited, I hated.

Then one day there came a humming sound, rising to a whine. Then silence. The stars fell like fiery sleet, then froze all about me. Ahead, there hung one bright one.

I ascertained Illyria's position and moved toward a rendezvous.

A. couple lifetimes or days later, I regarded it: a little green opal of a world, with flashing seas and countless bays, inlets, lakes, fjords; lush vegetation on the three tropical continents, cool woodlands and numerous lakes on the four temperate ones; no really high mountains, but lots of hills; nine small deserts, for variety's sake; one humpbacked river, half again the length of the Mississippi; a system of oceanic currents I was really proud of; and a five hundred mile land bridge/mountain range I had raised between two continents, just because geologists hate them as much as anthropologists love them. I watched a storm-system develop near the equator, move northward, disperse its wet burden over the ocean. One by one, as I drew nearer, the three moons—Flopsus, Mopsus and Kattontallus—partly eclipsed the world.

I set the *Model T* into an enormous, elliptical orbit, beyond the farthest moon; and, hopefully, also beyond the range of any detection devices. Then I set to work figuring the problem of the descents—my initial one, and those later ones, by the vessel itself.

Then I checked my current position, set an alarm and took a nap.

When I awoke, I visited the latrine, checked the driftsled, went over my gear. I took an ultrasonic shower and dressed myself in black shirt and trousers, of a water-repellent synthetic the name of which I can never remember, even though I own the company. I put on what I call combat boots, but what everyone else calls hiking boots these days, and bloused the trousers up inside. Then I clasped on a soft leather belt with a dark, two-piece buckle which could become the handles for the strangling-wire that tore loose through the center seam. I hung a pistol-belt over that, to hold a laser handgun at my right hip, and I hooked a row of small grenades along the back. I wore a pendant around my neck, with a spit-bomb inside, and on my right wrist I strapped a chrono set for Illyria and gimmicked to spray para-gas from nine o'clock when the stem was pulled. A handkerchief, a comb and the remains of a thousand-year-old rabbit's foot went into my pockets. I was ready.

I had to wait, though. I wanted to descend at night, drifting down like thistledown but black, onto the continent Splendida, going to ground no closer than a hundred, no farther than three hundred miles from my destination.

I wriggled into the knapsack, smoked a cigarette and worked my way back to the sled-chamber. I sealed it off and boarded the sled. I pulled shut the half-bubble, locked it about me, felt a tiny jet of air just above my head, a small wave of warmth just about my feet. I pushed the button that raised the hatch.

The wall opened, and I stared down at the crescent moon my world had become. The *T* would launch me at the proper moment; the sled would brake itself at the right time. I had only to control the drift, once I'd entered the atmosphere. The sled and I together would weigh only a few pounds, because of the anti-grav elements in the hull. It had rudders, ailerons, stabilizers; also, sails and chutes. It's less like a glider than one assumes on first hearing of it. It's more like a sailboat for use on a three-dimensional ocean. And I waited in it and looked down at the wave of night washing day from Illyria. Mopsus moved into view; Kattontallus moved out of it. My right ankle began to itch.

As I was scratching it, a blue light came on above my head. As I fastened my belts, it went out and the red one came on.

As I relaxed, the buzzer sounded and the red light went out and a mule kicked me in the backside and there were stars all about, dark Illyria before me, and no hatch to frame them.

Then drifting, not down, but ahead. Not falling, just moving, and even that undetectable when I closed my eyes. The world was a pit, a dark hole. Slowly, it grew. The warmth had filled the capsule, and the only sounds were my heart, my breath, the air jet.

When I turned my head, I could not see the *Model T.* Good.

It had been years since I'd used a drift-sled for purposes other than recreation. And each time I had, like now, my mind skipped back to a pre-dawn sky and the rocking of the sea and the smell of sweat and the bitter after-taste of Dramamine in my throat and the first *thud* of artillery-fire as the landing vehicle neared the beach. Then, as now, I'd wiped my palms on my knees, reached into my left sidepocket and touched the dead bunnysfoot there. Funny. My brother had had one, too. He would have enjoyed the drift-sled. He'd liked airplanes and gliders and boats. He'd liked water-skiing and skindiving and acrobatics and aerobatics—that's why he'd gone Airborne, which is probably why he Got It, too. You can only expect so much from one lousy rabbit's foot.

The stars blazed like the love of God, cold and distant, as soon as I dropped the blackspot on the bubble and blocked out the light of the sun. Mopsus caught the light, though, and cast it down into the pit. She held the middle orbit. Flopsus was nearest the planet, but was on the other side just then. The three made for generally tranquil seas, and once in a score or so of years they'd put on a magnificent tidal display when all of them were in conjunction. Isles of coral would appear in sudden deserts of purple and orange, as the waters rolled back, humped up, became a green mountain, moved round the world; and stones and bones and fishes and driftwood would lie like the footprints of Proteus, and the winds would follow, and the temperature-shifts, the inversions, the fields in the clouds, the cathedrals in the sky; and then the rains would come, and the wet mountains would break themselves upon the land, as the fairy cities shattered and the magic isles returned to the depths and Proteus, God knows where, would laugh like thunder, as with each bright flash Neptune's whitehot trident dipped, sizzled, dipped, sizzled Afterwards, you'd rub your eyes.

Now Illyria was moonbeams over cheesecloth. Somewhere, in her sleep, a cat-like creature would stir soon. She would awaken, stretch, rise and begin to prowl. After a time, she would stare at the sky for a moment, at the moon, beyond the moon. Then a murmur would run through the valleys, and the leaves would move upon the trees. They would feel it. Born of my nervous system, fractioned from my own DNA, shaped in the initial cell by the unassisted power of my mind, they would feel it, all of them. Anticipation. —*Yes, my children, I am coming. For Belion has dared to walk among you*. . . .

Drifting.

If only it had been a man, there on Illyria, waiting for me, it would have been easy. As it was, I felt that my armaments were mainly trappings. If it had only been a man, though, I wouldn't even have bothered with them. But Green Green was not a man; he was not even a Pei'an—which, in itself, is a frightening thing to be. Rather, he was something more than either.

He bore a Name, albeit improperly; and Name-bearers can influence living things, even the elements about them, when they raise up and merge with the shadow that lies behind the Name. I am not getting theological. I've heard some scientific-sounding explanations for everything involved, if you'll buy voluntary schizophrenia along with a god-complex and extrasensory faculties. Take them one at a time, and bear in mind the number of years' training a worldscaper undergoes, and the number of candidates who complete it.

I had the edge on Green Green, I felt, because it was my world he'd chosen for the encounter. How long he'd had to fool around with it, of course, was a thing I didn't know and a thing that worried me. What changes had he effected? He'd chosen the perfect bait. How perfect was the trap? How much of an edge did he think he had? Whatever, he couldn't be sure of anything, not against another Name. Nor, of course, could I.

Did you ever witness the combat of *Betta splendens*, the Siamese Fighting Fish? It's not like a cock fight or a dog fight or a cobra-mongoose match, or anything else in the world but itself. You place two males in the same bowl. They move together quickly, unfurling their brilliant fins, like red, blue, green shadows, expanding their branchial membranes. This gives the illusion of their suddenly blooming into something larger than they had been. Then they approach one another slowly, remain side by side for perhaps a quarter of a minute, drifting. Then they move, so fast that the eye can't even follow what is happening. Then, slow and peaceful again, they drift. Then suddenly, the colored whirlagig. Then drifting. Then movement. This pattern continues. The colored-shadow fins. And even this may be misleading. After a time, a reddish haze will surround them. Another flurry. They slow. Their jaws are locked. A minute passes, perhaps two. One opens his jaws and swims away. The other drifts.

This is how I saw what was to come.

I passed the moon, the dark bulk of the world grew before me, occluding stars. As I neared it, my descent slowed. Devices beneath the cockpit were activated, and when I finally entered the upper atmosphere I was already drifting, slowly. The impression of moonlight on a hundred lakes: coins at a dark pool's bottom.

I monitored for artificial light, detected none. Flopsus appeared upon the horizon, adding her light to her sister's. After perhaps half an hour, I could make out the more prominent features of the continent. I combined these with memory and feeling and began to steer the sled.

Like the falling of a leaf on a still day, tacking, sideslipping, I headed for the ground. The lake called Acheron, with its Isle of the Dead, lay, I calculated, some six hundred miles to the northwest.

Far below me, clouds appeared. I drifted on and they were gone. I lost very little altitude during the next half-hour and gained perhaps forty miles on my goal. I wondered what detection devices might be functioning below me.

The high-altitude winds caught me, and I fought them for a time; finally, though, I had to descend several thousand feet to escape the worst of them.

For the next several hours I made my way, steadily, north and west. At a height of some fifty thousand feet, I was still over four hundred miles from my goal.

Within the next hour, though, I descended twenty thousand feet and gained about seventy miles. Things seemed to be breaking nicely.

Finally, a false dawn began in the east, and I dropped a mile to get beneath it. My speed increased as I did so. It was like descending into an ocean, light water to dark.

But the light followed me. After a time, I ran again. I plowed through a cloudbank, estimated my position, continued to descend. How many miles to Acheron?

Two hundred, perhaps.

The light caught me, passed me, went away.

I dropped to fifteen thousand feet, picked up forty miles. I deactivated several more plates.

I was cruising at three thousand feet when the real dawn began to occur.

I continued for ten minutes, dropping, found a clear place and went to ground.

The sun cracked open the east, and I was a hundred miles from Acheron, give or take around ten. I opened the bubble, pulled the destruct-cord, leapt to the ground and ran.

A minute later, the sled collapsed upon itself and began to smolder. I slowed to a walk, took my bearings, headed across the field toward the place where the trees began.

V

During the first five minutes Illyria returned to me, and it was as if I had never been gone. Filtered through the forest's mists, the sunlight came rose and amber; dewdrops glistened on the leaves and the grasses; the air was cool, smelled of damp earth and decomposing vegetation, which is sweet. A small yellow bird circled my head, lighted on my shoulder, perched there for a dozen paces, was gone. I stopped to cut myself a walking stick, and the smell of the white wood took me back to Ohio and the creek where I'd cut willows to fashion whistles, soaking the wands overnight, tapping the bark with. the handle of my knife to loosen it, near the place where the strawberries grew. And I found some wild berries, huge and purple, crushed them between my fingers and licked the juice, which was tart. A crested lizard, bright as a tomato, stirred sluggishly atop his rock and moved to sit on the toe of my boot as I was doing this. I touched his crown, then pushed him away and moved on. When I looked back, his salt-and-pepper eyes met my own. I walked beneath forty- and fifty-foot trees, and moisture occasionally dripped down upon me. Birds began to awaken, and insects. A big-bellied green whistler began his ten-minute song of deflation on a limb above me. Somewhere to my left, a friend or relative joined in. Six purple *cobra de capella* flowers exploded from the ground and emitted hisses as they swayed upon their stalks, their petals rippling like flags, their heavy perfumes released with bomb-like efficiency. But I wasn't startled, for it was as if I had never gone away.

I walked on and the grasses diminished. The trees were larger now, ranging from fifty to seventy feet, with numerous boulders lying among them. A good place for an ambush; likewise, a good place to take cover from one.

The shadows were deep, and para-monkeys chanted overhead while a legion of clouds advanced from the west. The low sun tickled their quarters with flame, shot shafts of light through the leaves. Vines that clung to some of the giants held blossoms like silver candelabra, and the air about them hinted of temples and incense. I forded a pearly stream and crested water snakes swam beside me, hooting like owls. They were quite poisonous, but very friendly.

From the other bank, the ground began to slope upward, gently at first; and, as I advanced, some subtle change seemed to come over the world. There was nothing objective to which I could relate it, only a feeling that the decks of order had been slightly riffled.

The coolness of morning and the wood did not depart as the day advanced. Rather, it seemed to deepen. There was a definite chill in the air; and later it became an almost clammy feeling. Still, the sky was more than half-filled with clouds by then, and the ionization that precedes a storm often gives rise to such feelings.

When I stopped to eat, sitting with my back against the bole of an ancient mark-tree, I frightened a pandrilla who had been digging among its roots. As soon as he began to flee, I knew that something was wrong.

I filled my mind with the desire that he return, and laid it upon him.

He halted then in his flight and turned and regarded me. Slowly, he approached. I fed him a cracker and tried to see through his eyes as he ate it.

Fear, recognition, fear . . . There had been a moment of misplaced panic.

It didn't belong.

I released him and he remained, content to eat my crackers. His initial response had been too unusual to dismiss, however. I feared what it indicated.

I was entering enemy territory.

I finished eating and moved on. I descended into a foggy vale, and when I left it the mists were still with me. The sky was almost completely overcast. Small animals fled before me, and I made no effort to change their minds. I walked on, and my breath was white, moist wings now. I avoided two powerpulls. If I were to use one, it could betray my position to another sensitive.

What is a power-pull? Well, it's a part of the makeup of everything with an electromagnetic field. Every world has numerous, shifting points in its gravitational matrix. There, certain machines or specially talented people can plug in and act as switchboards, batteries, condensors. Power-pull is a handy term for such a nexus of energy, a term used by people who can employ it in such a fashion. I didn't want to use one until I was certain as to the nature of the enemy, however, for all Namebearers normally possess this capability.

So I let the fog dampen my garments and take the sheen from my boottops, when I could have dried out. I walked with my staff in my left hand, my right one free to draw and fire.

Nothing attacked me, though, as I advanced. In fact, after a time no living thing crossed my path.

I hiked until evening, making perhaps twenty miles that day. The dampness was all-pervasive, but there was no rain. I located a small cave in the foothills I was then negotiating, cast my flimsy—a ten by ten sheet of tough plastic material, three molecules in thickness—for insulation against the dirt and some of the dampness, ate a dry meal and slept, my gun near my hand.

* * *

The morning was as bleak as the night and the day before, and the fog had thickened. I suspected an intent behind it, and I moved cautiously. It struck me as just a bit too melodramatic. If he thought he was going to shake me up with shadow, mist, chill and the alienation of a few of my creatures, he was wrong. Discomfort just irritates me, makes me angry and fixes my determination to get at its source and deal with it as quickly as possible.

I slopped my way through much of the second day, topped the hills and began my downward trek. It was along about evening that I picked up a companion.

A light appeared off to my left and moved parallel to my own course. It hovered anywhere from two to eight feet above the ground, and its color varied from pale yellow through orange to white. It could have been anywhere from twenty to a hundred feet away at any given time. Occasionally, it disappeared; always, it returned. A will-o'-the-wisp, sent to lure me into some crevasse or marshy bog? Probably. Still, I was curious, I admired its persistence—and it was nice to have company.

"Good evening," I said. "I'm coming to kill whoever sent you, you know.

"But then you might just be marsh gas," I added. "In which case, you may dismiss my last remark.

"Either way," I went on, "I'm not in the mood to be led astray just now. You can take a coffee break if you'd like."

Then I began whistling *It's a Long Way to Tipperary*. The thing continued to pace me. I stopped and sheltered beneath a tree, to light a cigarette. I stood there and smoked it. The light hovered about fifty feet away, as if waiting. I tried to touch it with my mind, but it was as if there was nothing there. I drew my gun and thought better of it, reholstered it. I finished my cigarette, crushed it out, moved ahead.

Again, the light moved with me.

About an hour later, I made camp in a small clearing. I wrapped myself in my flimsy, my back against a rock. I built a small fire and heated some soup I'd brought along. The light wouldn't carry far on a night like this.

The will-o'-the-wisp hovered just outside the circle of firelight. "Care for a cup of coffee?" I asked it. There was no reply, which was a good thing. I had only one cup with me.

After I'd finished eating, I lit a cigar and let the fire go down to embers. I puffed my cigar and wished for stars. The night was soundless about me, and the chill was reaching for my backbone. It had already seized my toes and was gnawing on them. I wished I'd thought to bring a flask of brandy.

My fellow traveler stood vigil, unmoving, and I stared back at him. If it wasn't a natural phenomenon, it was there to spy on me. Dared I sleep? I dared.

When I awoke, my chrono showed me that an hour and a quarter had passed. Nothing had changed. Not forty minutes later, either, nor two hours and ten minutes after that, when I awoke again.

I slept out the rest of the night and found it waiting in the morning.

This day was like the previous one, cold and blank. I broke camp and moved on, reckoning that I was about a third of the way to my destination.

Suddenly, there was a new development. My companion moved from my left and drifted slowly ahead. It turned right then and hovered, about sixty feet before me. By the time I reached that spot, it had moved on, anticipating my path.

That was a thing I didn't like. It was as though the guiding intelligence were mocking me, saying, "Look here, old boy, I know where you're headed and how you intend getting there. Why don't you let me make the way a bit easier?" It was a successful mock, too, for it made me feel like a complete fool. There were several things I could do about it, but I didn't feel like doing them yet.

So I followed. I followed till lunchtime, when it politely halted until I was quite finished; till dinnertime, when it did the same.

Shortly thereafter, however, the light again changed its behavior. It drifted off to the left and vanished. I stopped and stood still for a moment, for I'd grown used to it. Was I supposed to have become so conditioned to following it all day that fatigue and habit would combine to lead me after it now, off my intended path? Perhaps.

I wondered how far it would lead me if I gave it the opportunity.

I decided that twenty minutes of walking after it would be quite enough. I loosened my pistol in its holster and waited for it to come again.

It did. When it repeated its previous performances, I turned and followed. It hurried ahead, waited for me to catch up, hurried on.

After about five minutes, a light rain began to fall. Though the darkness deepened, I could see without using my hand torch. Soon I was soaked all the way through. I cursed and sloughed along, shivering.

Approximately half a mile further along, wetter, colder, darker the day, stronger still the feeling of alienation, I was left alone. The light went out. I waited, but it did not return.

Carefully, I made my way to the place where I had last seen it, circling in from the right, gun in hand, searching with my eyes and my mind.

I brushed against a dry tree-limb and heard it snap.

"Stop! For the love of God! Don't!"

I threw myself to the ground and rolled.

The cry had come from right beside me. I covered that area from a distance of twelve feet.

Cry? Had it been a truly physical sound, or something within my mind? I wasn't certain.

I waited.

Then, so softly that I wasn't certain how I was hearing it, there came to me a sound of sobbing. Soft sounds are difficult to pinpoint, and this was no exception. I turned my head slowly, from right to left, saw no one.

"Who is it?" I asked in a shrill whisper, for these, too, are without direction.

No answer. But the sobbing continued. Reaching out with my mind, I felt pain and confusion, nothing more.

"Who is it?" I repeated.

There was silence, then, "Frank?" said the voice.

This time I decided to wait. I let a minute go by, then said my name.

"Help me," came the reply.

"Who are you? Where are you?"

"Here. . . ."

And the answers came into my mind, and the nape of my neck crawled and my hand tightened on the pistol.

"Dango! The Capel Knife!"

I knew then what had happened, but I didn't have guts enough to turn on my torch and take a good look. I didn't need to, though.

My will-o'-the-wisp chose that moment to return.

It drifted past me, rose high, higher, brightness increasing in intensity to a level far beyond anything it had exhibited earlier. It hovered at a height of fifteen or twenty feet and blazed like a flare. Below it stood Dango. He had no choice but to stand.

He was rooted to the spot.

His lean, triangular face bore a long, black beard and flowing hair that twined away among his limbs, his leaves. His eyes were dark and sunken and wretched. The bark that was a part of him bore insect holes, bird-droppings and char-marks of numerous small fires about the base. I saw then that blood dripped from the limb I had broken as I'd passed him by.

I rose, slowly.

"Dango. . ." I said.

"They're gnawing at my feet!" he told me.

". . . I'm sorry." I lowered the gun, almost dropped it.

"Why didn't he let me stay dead?"

"Because once you were my friend, and then you were my enemy," I said. "You knew me, well."

"Because of you?" The tree swayed, as if reaching after me. He began to curse me, and I stood there and listened as the rain mingled with his blood and soaked into the ground. We had been partners in a joint venture one time, and he'd tried to cheat me. I'd brought charges, he was acquitted and tried to kill me afterwards. I put him in the hospital, back on Earth, and he'd died in an auto accident a week after his discharge. He would have killed me if he'd gotten the chance—with a knife, I know. But I never gave him the chance. You might sort of say I helped his bad luck along when it came to the accident. I knew he'd never rest until he'd nailed me or was dead, and I didn't feel like getting nailed.

The raking light made his features look ghastly. He had the complexion of a mushroom and the eyes of an evil cat. His teeth were broken and there was a festering sore on his left cheek. The back of his head was joined with the tree, his shoulders merged with it and there were two branches which might contain his arms. From the waist down he was tree.

"Who did it?" I asked.

"The big green bastard. Pei'an. . . ." he said. "Suddenly, I was here. I don't understand. There was an accident. . ."

"I'll get him," I said. "I'm going after him now. I'm going to kill him. Then I'll get you out—"

"No! Don't go!"

"It's the only way, Dango."

"You don't understand what it's like," he said. "I can't wait. . . . Please."

"It may only take a few days, Dango."

". . . And he may get you instead. Then it'll be never. Christ! How it hurts! I'm sorry about that deal, Frank. Believe me. . . . Please!"

I looked down at the ground and up at the light.

I raised the gun and lowered it.

"I can't kill you any more," I said.

He bit his lip and the blood ran down his chin and into his beard and the tears came out of his eyes. I looked away from his eyes.

I stumbled backwards and began mumbling in Pei'an. Only then did I realize I was near a power-pull. I could feel it suddenly. And I grew taller and taller, and Frank Sandow grew smaller and smaller, and when I shrugged the thunders rumbled. When I raised my left hand they roared. When I drew it down to my shoulder the flash that followed blinded me and the shock raised my hair upon my head.

. . . I was alone with the smells of ozone and smoke, there, before the charred and splintered thing that had been Dango the Knife. Even the will-o'-the- wisp was gone now. The rain came down in torrents and laid the smells to rest.

I staggered back in the direction from which I had come, my boots making sucking sounds in the mud, my clothes trying to crawl under my skin.

Somehow, somewhere—I don't remember exactly—I slept.

*　　*　　*

Of all the things a man may do, sleep probably contributes most to keeping him sane. It puts brackets about each day. If you do something foolish or painful today, you get irritated if somebody mentions it, today. If it happened yesterday, though, you can nod or chuckle, as the case may be. You've crossed through nothingness or dream to another island in Time. How many memories can be summoned up in a single instant? Many, it would seem. Actually, though, they're only a small fraction of those which exist, somewhere. And the longer you've been around, the more of them you have. So, once I have slept, there are many things which come to aid me when I wish to anesthetize a particular occurrence. This may sound callous. It is not. I do not mean that I live without pain for things gone by, without guilt. I mean that over the centuries I have developed a mental reflex. When I have been swamped emotionally, I sleep. When I awaken, thoughts of other days come forth, fill my head. After a time, memory the vulture circles closer and closer, then descends upon the thing of pain. It dismembers it, gorges itself upon it, digests it with the past standing to witness. I suppose it is a thing called perspective. I have seen many persons die. In many fashions. I have never been unmoved. But sleep gives memory a chance to rev its engine and hand me back my head each day. For I have also seen people live, and I have looked upon the colors of joy, sorrow, love, hate, satiation, peace.

I found her in the mountains one morning, miles from

anywhere, and her lips were blue and her fingers were frost-bitten. She was wearing a tiger-striped pair of leotards and she was curled into a ball beside a scrubby little bush. I put my jacket around her and left my mineral bag and my tools on a rock, and I never did recover them. She was delirious, and it seemed I heard her say the name "Noel" several times while I was carrying her back to my vehicle. She had some bad bruises and a lot of minor cuts and abrasions. I took her to a clinic where they treated her and kept her overnight. The following morning I went to see her and learned that she'd refused to supply her identity. Also, she seemed unable to supply any money. So I paid her bill and asked her what she was going to do, and she didn't know that either. I offered to put her up at the cottage I was renting and she accepted. For the first week, it was like living in a haunted house. She never talked unless I asked her a question. She prepared meals for me and kept the place clean and spent the rest of the time in her room, with the door closed. The second week she heard me picking at an old mandolin—the first time I'd touched the thing in months—and she came out and sat across the living room from me and listened. So I kept playing, for hours longer than I'd intended, just to keep her there, be-cause it was the only thing in over a week that had evoked any sort of response. When I laid it aside, she asked me if she could try it, and I nodded. She crossed the room, picked it up, bent over and began to play. She was far from a virtuoso, but then so was I. I listened and brought her a cup of coffee, said "Good night" and that was it. The next day, though, she was a different person. She'd combed the tangles out of her dark hair and trimmed it. Much of the puffiness was gone from beneath her pale eyes. She talked to me at breakfast, about everything from the weather, the news reports, my mineral collection, music, antiques to exotic fishes. Everything excepting herself. I took her places after that: restaurants, shows, the beach—everywhere but the mountains. About four months went by like this. Then one day I realized I was beginning to fall in love with her. Of course, I didn't mention it, though she must have seen it. Hell, I didn't really know anything about her, and I felt awkward. She might have a husband and six kids somewhere. She asked me to take her dancing. I did, and we danced on a terrace under the stars until-they closed the place down, around four in the morning. The next day, when I rose at the crack of noon, I was alone. On the kitchen table there was a note that said: *Thank you. Please do not look for me. I have to go back now. I love you.* It was, of course, unsigned. And that's all I know about the girl without a name.

When I was around fifteen years old, I found a baby starling beneath a tree while I was mowing the lawn in our back yard. Both its legs were broken. At least, I surmised this, because they stuck out at funny angles from its body and it sat on its backside with its tail feathers bent way up. When I crossed its field of vision, it threw its head back and opened its beak. I bent down and saw that there were ants all over it, so I picked it up and brushed them off. Then I looked for a place to put it. I decided on a bushel basket lined with freshly cut grass. I set the thing on our picnic table on the patio under the maple trees. I tried an eyedropper to get some milk down its throat, but it just seemed to choke on it. I went back to mowing the lawn. Later that day, I looked in on it and there were five or six big black beetles down in the grass with it. Disgusted, I threw them out. The next morning, when I went out with milk and an eyedropper, there were more beetles. I cleaned house once again. Later that day, I saw a huge dark bird perched on the edge of the basket. She went down inside, and after a moment flew away. I kept watching, and she returned three times within the half hour. Then I went out and looked into the basket and saw more beetles. I realized that she'd been hunting them, bringing them to it, trying to feed it. It wasn't able to eat, however, so she just left them there in the basket. That night a cat found it. There were only a few feathers and some blood among the beetles when I went out with my eyedropper and some milk the next morning.

There is a place. It is a place where broken rocks ring a red sun. Several centuries ago, we discovered a race of arthropod-like creatures called *Whilles*, with whom we could not deal. They rejected friendly overtures on the parts of every known intelligent race. Also, they slew our emissaries and sent their remains back to us, missing a few pieces here and there. When first we contacted them, they possessed vehicles for travel within their own solar system. Shortly thereafter, they developed interstellar travel. Wherever they went, they killed and they stole and then beat it back home. Perhaps they didn't realize the size of the interstellar community at that time, or perhaps they didn't care. They guessed right if they thought it would take an awfully long time to reach an accord when it came to declaring war on them. There is actually very little precedent for interstellar war. The Pei'ans are about the only ones who remember any. So the attacks failed, what remained of our forces were withdrawn, and we began to bombard the planet. The *Whilles* were, however, further along technologically than we'd initially thought. They had a near-perfect defense system against missiles. So we withdrew and tried to contain them. They didn't stop their raids, though. Then the Names were contacted, and three worldscapers, Sang-ring of Greldei, Karth'ting of Mordei and I, were chosen by lot to use our abilities in reverse. Later, within the system of the *Whilles*, beyond the orbit of their home world, a belt of asteroids began to collapse upon itself, forming a planetoid. Rock by rock, it grew, and slowly it altered its course. We sat, with our machinery, beyond the orbit of the farthest planet, directing the new world's growth and its slow spiral inward. When the *Whilles* realized what was happening, they tried to destroy it. But it was too late.

They never asked for mercy, and none of them tried to flee. They waited, and the day came. The orbits of the two worlds intersected, and now it is a place where broken rocks ring a red sun. I stayed drunk for a week after that.

Once I collapsed in a desert, while trying to walk from my damaged vehicle to a small outpost of civilization. I had been walking for four days, without water for two, and my throat felt like sandpaper and my feet were a million miles away. I passed out. How long I lay there, I do not know. Perhaps an entire day. Then, what I thought to be a product of delirium came and crouched beside me. It was purplish in color, with a ruff around its neck and three horny knobs on its lizard-like face. It was about four feet in length and scaly. It had a short tail and there were claws on each of its digits.

Its eyes were dark ellipses with nictitating membranes. It carried a long, hollow reed and a small pouch. I still don't know what it was. It regarded me for a few moments, then dashed away. I rolled onto my side and watched it. It poked the reed into the ground and held its mouth over the end, then withdrew the reed, moved on and repeated the activity. About the eleventh time it did it, its cheeks began to bulge like balloons. Then it ran to my side, leaving the reed in place, and it touched my mouth with its forelimb. I guessed what it was trying to indicate and I opened my mouth. Leaning close, slowly, carefully, so as not to waste a drop, it trickled the hot, dirty water from its mouth into my own. Six times it returned to the reed and brought back water, giving it to me in this fashion. Then I passed out again. When I awakened, it was evening and the creature brought me more water. In the morning, I was able to walk to the tube, crouch beside it and draw my fill of liquid. The creature awakened slowly, sluggish in the pre-dawn cold. When it had come around, I took off my chrono and my hunting knife and I emptied my pockets of money and placed these things before it. It studied the items. I pushed them toward it and pointed at the pouch it bore. It pushed them back toward me and made a clicking sound with its tongue. So I touched its forelimb and said thanks in every language that I knew, picked up my stuff and started walking again. I made it into the settlement the following afternoon.

A girl, a bird, a world, a drink of water, and Dango the Knife riven from head to foot.

The cycles of recollection place pain beside thought, sight, sentiment and the always who-what- why? Sleep, the conductor of memory, keeps me sane. More than this I do not know, really. But I did not think I was callous by arising the following morning more intent upon what lay before me than behind.

*　　　*　　　*

What it was, was fifty to sixty miles of progressively difficult terrain. The ground was rockier, drier. Leaves possessed sharp, serrate edges.

The trees were different, the animals were different, from what I had left behind. They were parodies of the things in which I had taken such pride. My Midnight Warblers here emitted harsh croaking sounds, the insects all had stings and the flowers stank. There were no straight, tall trees. They were all of them twisted or squat. My, gazelle-like leogahs were cripples. Smaller animals snarled at me and ran. Some of the larger ones had to be stared down.

My ears cracked with the increasing altitude and the fog was still with me, but I pushed on, steadily, and I made perhaps twenty-five miles that day.

Two more days, I figured. Perhaps less. And one to do the job.

That night I was awakened by one of the most godawful explosions I'd heard in years. I sat up and listened to the echoes—or perhaps it was only the ringing in my ears. I sat there with my gun in my hand and waited, beneath a large, old tree.

In the northwest, despite the fog, I could see a light. It was a sort of generalized orange glow. It began to spread.

The second explosion was not so loud as the first. Neither was the third or the fourth. By then, however, I had other things to think about.

The ground was trembling beneath me.

I stayed where I was and waited. The shocks increased in intensity.

Judging from the sky, a quarter of the world was on fire.

Since there wasn't much I could do about it at the moment, I reholstered my pistol, sat with my back against the tree and lit a cigarette. Something seemed out of whack. Green Green was sure as hell going to a lot of trouble to impress me when he should have known I wasn't that impressionable. That kind of activity could not be natural in this region, and he was the only one other than myself who was on the scene and able to do it. Why? Was he just saying, "Look, I'm tearing up your world, Sandow. What are you going to do about it?" Was he demonstrating the power of Belion with hopes of frightening me?

I toyed for a moment with the notion of seeking out a power-pull and unleashing the worst electrical storm he'd ever seen, over the entire area, just to show him how impressed I was. But I shelved the idea quickly. I did not want to fight him from a distance. I wanted to meet him face to face and tell him what I thought of him. I wanted to confront him and show myself to him and ask him why he was being such a bloody fool—why my being a homo sap had aroused such a hatred that he'd gone to such lengths to hurt me.

He obviously knew I had already arrived, was there on the world somewhere—else there would have been no will-o'-the-wisp to take me to Dango. So I betrayed nothing by what I did next.

I closed my eyes and bowed my head and summoned up the power. I tried to picture him somewhere near the Isle of the Dead, a gloating Pei'an, watching his volcano rise, watching the ashes spew forth like black leaves, watching the lava glow and boil, watching the snakes of sulfur crawl through the heavens—and with the full power of my hatred behind it, I sent forth the message:

"Patience, Green Green. Patience, Gringrin-tharl. Patience. In but a few days, I will be with you for a short time. A short time only."

There was no reply, but then I hadn't expected one.

In the morning, the going was rougher. A black snowfall of ashes descended through the mist. There was still an occasional temblor, and animals fled past me, heading in the opposite direction. They ignored me completely, and I tried to ignore them.

The entire north seemed to be on fire. If it were not that I possess a sense of absolute direction on all my worlds, I would have thought that I was heading into a sunrise. I found it quite disillusioning.

Here was a Pei'an, almost a Name, a member of the most subtle race of avengers who had ever lived; and here he was acting like a clown before the abominable Earthman. Okay, he hated me and he wanted to get me. That was no reason to be sloppy about it and to forget the fine old traditions of his race. The volcano was a childish display of the power I fully expected to meet, eventually. I felt a bit ashamed for him, for such a crude exhibition at this point in the game. Even I, in my brief apprenticeship, had learned sufficient of the fine points of vengeanceship to know better than that. I was beginning to see why he'd flunked his test.

I chewed some chocolate as I walked, putting off lunch-break until later in the afternoon. I wanted to cover sufficient ground so that I'd only have a few hours' hike in the morning. I maintained a steady pace, and the light grew and grew before me, the ashes came more densely down, the ground gave a good shake about once every hour.

Around midday, a wart-bear attacked me. I tried to control it, but I couldn't. I killed it and cursed the man who had made it into what it was.

The fog had let up a good deal by then, but the drifting ash more than compensated. It was a constant twilight through which I walked, coughing. I didn't make good time because of the rearrangements of the terrain, and I added another day to my hiking schedule.

By the time I turned in that night I'd covered a lot of ground, though. I knew I'd reach Acheron before noon of the following day.

I found a dry spot for a campsite, on a small rise with half-buried boulders jutting at odd angles about its crown. I cleaned my equipment, pitched the flimsy, kindled a fire, ate some rations. Then I smoked one of my last cigars, to do my bit for air pollution, and crawled into the sack.

I was dreaming when it happened. The dream eludes me now, save for the impression that it was pleasant at first, then became a nightmare. I remember tossing about on my bed of rushes, then realizing I was awake. I kept my eyes closed and shifted my weight as though moving in my sleep. My hand touched my pistol. I lay there and listened for the sounds of danger. I opened my mind to impressions.

I tasted the smoke and cold ashes that had filled the air. I felt the damp chill in the ground beneath me. I got the impression of someone, something, nearby. Listening, I heard the tiny click of a dislodged stone, somewhere off to my right. Then silence.

My finger traced the trigger's curve. I shifted the muzzle in that direction.

Then, as delicately as a hummingbird invades a flower, came the touch of the tamperer in the dark house where I live, my head.

You are asleep, something seemed to say, *and you will not awaken yet. Not until I permit it. You sleep and you hear me now. This is as it should be. There is no reason to awaken. Sleep deeply and soundly as I address you. It is very important that you do so . . .*

I let it continue, for I was fully awake. I suppressed my reactions and feigned slumber while I listened for another telltale sound.

After a minute of being reassured that I was asleep, I heard a sound of movement from the same direction as before.

I opened my eyes then, and without moving my head I began to trace the limits of the shadows.

Beside one of the rocks, perhaps thirty feet distant, was a form which had not been present when I had retired. I studied it until I detected an occasional movement. When I was certain as to its position, I flipped off the safety catch, aimed very carefully and pulled the trigger, tracing a line of fire on the ground about five feet before it. Because of the angle, a shower of dust, dirt and gravel was kicked backwards.

If you so much as take a deep breath, I'll cut you in half, I advised.

Then I stood and faced him, holding the pistol steady. When I spoke, I spoke in Pei'an, for I had seen in the light of the burning beam that it was a Pei'an who stood beside the rock.

"Green Green," I said, "you are the clumsiest Pei'an I've ever met."

"I have made a few mistakes," he acknowledged, from back in the shadows.

I chuckled.

"I'd say so."

"There were extenuating circumstances involved."

"Excuses. You did not properly learn the lesson of the rock. It appears to rest, but it does move, imperceptibly." I shook my head. "How will your ancestors rest after a bungled piece of vengeance like this?"

"Poorly, I fear, if this be the end."

"Why shouldn't it be? Do you deny that you assured my presence here solely for purposes of obtaining my death?"

"Why should I deny the obvious?"

"Why should I fail to do the logical thing?"

"Think, Francis Sandow, *Dra* Sandow. How logical would it be? Why should I approach you in this fashion, when I might have allowed you to come to me where I held a position of power?"

"Perhaps I rattled your nerves last evening."

"Do not judge me that unstable. I came to place you under my control."

"And failed."

". . . And failed."

"Why did you come?"

"I require your services."

"To what end?"

"We must leave here quickly. You possess a means of departure?"

"Naturally. What are you afraid of?"

"Over the years, you have collected some friends and many enemies, Francis Sandow."

"Call me Frank. I feel as if I've known you a long time, dead man."

"You should not have sent that message, Frank. Now your presence here is known. Unless you help me to escape, you will face a vengeance greater than mine."

A shifting of the breeze brought me the sweet, musty smell of that which passes for blood in a Pei'an. I flicked on my hand torch and aimed it at him.

"You're hurt."

"Yes. "

I dropped the torch, sidled over to my knapsack, opened it with my left hand. I fished out the first aid pouch and tossed it to him.

"Cover your cuts," I said, picking up the light once more. "They smell bad."

He unrolled a bandage and wrapped it about his gashed right shoulder and forearm. He ignored a series of smaller wounds on his chest.

"You look as if you've been in a fight."

"I have."

"What shape is the other guy in?"

"I hurt him. I was lucky. I almost killed him, in fact. Now it is too late."

I saw that he wasn't carrying a weapon, so I holstered my own. I advanced and stood before him.

"Delgren of Dilpei sends his greetings," I said. "I think you've managed to make his fecal roster."

He snorted, chuckled.

"He was to be next," he said, "after yourself."

"You still haven't given me a good reason for keeping you alive."

"But I've aroused your curiosity, which is keeping me alive. Getting me bandaged, even."

"My patience departs, like sand through a sieve."

"Then you have not learned the lesson of the rock."

I lit a cigarette. "I'm in a position to choose my proverbs as I go along. You are not," I said.

He finished bandaging himself, then, "I wish to propose a bargain."

"Name it."

"You have a vessel hidden somewhere. Take me to it. Take me with you, away from this world."

"In return for what?"

"Your life."

"You're hardly in a position to threaten me."

"I am not making a threat. I am offering to save your life for the moment, if you will do the same for me."

"Save me from what?"

"You know that I can restore certain persons to life."

"Yeah, you stole some Recall Tapes. How did you do it, by the way?"

"Teleportation. It is my talent. I can transfer small objects from one place to another. Many years ago, when I first began studying you and plotting my vengeance, I made visits to Earth—each time one of your friends or enemies died there, in fact. I waited then until I had accumulated sufficient funds to purchase this world, which I thought to be a fitting place for what I had in mind. It is not difficult for a worldscaper to learn to employ the tapes."

"My friends, my enemies—you restored them here?"

"That is correct."

"Why?"

"For you to see your loved ones suffer once again, before you died yourself; and for your enemies to watch you in your pain."

"Why did you do what you did to the one called Dango?"

"The man annoyed me. By setting him up as an example and warning for you, I also removed him from my presence and provided him with a maximum of pain. In this fashion, he served three useful purposes."

"What was the third?"

"My amusement, of course."

"I see. But why here? Why Illyria?"

"Second to Homefree, which is inaccessible, is this world not your favorite creation?"

"Yes."

"What better place then?"

I dropped my cigarette, ground it out with my heel.

"You are stronger than I thought, Frank," he said after a moment, "because you killed him once, and he has beaten me, taken away from me a thing without price. . . .

Suddenly I was back on Homefree, in my roof garden, puffing a cigar, seated next to a shaved monkey named Lewis Briggs. I had just opened an envelope, and I was running my eyes down a list of names.

So it wasn't telepathy. It was just memory and apprehension.

"Mike Shandon," I said softly.

"Yes. I did not know him for what he was, or I would not have recalled him."

It should have hit me sooner. The fact that he had recalled all of them, I mean. It should have, but it didn't. I'd been too busy thinking about Kathy and blood.

"You stupid son of a bitch," I said. "You stupid son of a bitch. . . ."

*   *   *

Back in the century into which I had been born, like number twenty, the art or craft—as the case may be—of espionage enjoyed a better public image than either the U.S. Marine Corps or the AMA. It was, I suppose, partly a romantic escape mechanism with respect to international tensions. It got out of hand, though, as anything must if it is to leave a mark upon its times. In the long history of popular heroes, from Renaissance princes through poor boys who live clean, work hard and marry the bosses' daughters, the man with the cyanide capsule for a tooth, the lovely traitoress for a mistress and the impossible mission where sex and violence are shorthand for love and death, this man came into his own in the seventh decade of the twentieth century and is indeed remembered with a certain measure of nostalgia—like Christmas in Medieval England. He was, of course, abstracted from the real thing. And spies are an even duller lot today than they were then. They collect every bit of trivia they can lay their hands on and get it back to someone who feeds it to a data-processing machine, along with thousands of other items, a minor fact is thereby obtained, someone writes an obscure memo concerning it and the memo is filed and forgotten. As I mentioned earlier, there is very little precedent for interstellar warfare, and classical spying deals, basically, with military matters. When this extension of politics becomes well-nigh impossible because of logistic problems, the importance of such matters diminishes. The only real talented, important spies today are the industrial spies. The man who delivered into the hands of General Motors the microfilmed blueprints of Ford's latest brainchild or the gal with Dior's new line sketched inside her bra, *these* spies received very little notice in the twentieth century. Now, however, they are the only genuine items around. The tensions involved in interstellar commerce are enormous. Anything that will give you an edge—a new manufacturing process, a classified shipping schedule—may become as important as the Manhattan Project once was. If somebody has something like this and you want it, a real spy is worth his weight in meerschaum.

Mike Shandon was a real spy, the best one I'd ever employed. I can never think of him without a certain twitch of envy. He was everything I once wished I could be.

He was around two inches taller than me and perhaps twenty-five pounds heavier. His eyes were the color of just-polished mahogany and his hair was black as ink. He was damnably graceful, had a sickeningly beautiful voice and was always dressed to perfection. A farm boy from the breadbasket world Wava, he'd had an itchy heel and expensive tastes. He'd educated himself while being rehabilitated after some antisocial acts. In my youth, you would have said he'd spent his free hours in the prison library while doing time for grand larceny. You don't say it that way any more, but it amounts to the same thing. His rehabilitation was successful, if you judge it by the fact that it was a long time before he got caught again. Of course, he had a lot going for him. So much, in fact, that I was surprised he'd *ever* been tripped up—though he often said he was born to come in second. He was a telepath, and he had a damn near photographic memory. He was strong and tough and smart and he could hold his liquor and women fell all over him. So I think my certain twitch is not without foundation.

He'd worked for me for several years before I'd actually met him. One of my recruiters had turned him up and sent him through Sandow Enterprises' Special Executive Training Group (Spy School). A year later he emerged second in his class. Subsequent to that, he distinguished himself when it came to product research, as we call it. His name kept cropping up in classified reports, so one day I decided to have dinner with him.

Sincerity and good manners, that's all I remembered afterwards. He was a born con man.

There are not too many human telepaths around, and telepathically obtained information is not admissible in court. Nevertheless, the ability is obviously valuable.

Valuable as he might have been, however, Shandon was something of a problem. Whatever his earnings, he spent more.

It was not until years after his death that I learned of his blackmail activities. The thing that tripped him up, actually, was his moonlighting.

We knew there was a major security leak at SE. We didn't know how or where, and it took close to five years to find out. By then, Sandow Enterprises was beginning to totter.

We nailed him. It wasn't easy, and it involved four other telepaths. But we cornered him and brought him to trial. I testified at great length, and he was convicted, sentenced and shipped off for more rehabilitation. I undertook three worldscaping jobs then, to keep SE functioning smoothly. We weathered the vicissitudes that followed, but not without a lot of trouble.

. . . One item of which was Shandon's escape from rehabilitative custody. This was several years later, but word of it spread fast. His trial had been somewhat sensational.

So his name was added to the wanted lists. But the universe is a big place. . . .

It was near Coos Bay, Oregon, that I'd taken a seaside place for my stay on Earth. Two to three months had seemed in order, as I was there to watch over our merger with a couple North American companies.

Dwelling beside a body of water is tonic for the weary psyche. Sea smells, sea birds, seawrack, sands—alternately cool, warm, moist and dry—a taste of brine and the presence of the rocking, slopping bluegraygreen spit-flecked waters, has the effect of rinsing the emotions, bathing the outlook, bleaching the conscience. I walked beside it every morning before breakfast, and again in the evening before retiring. My name was Carlos Palermo, if anybody cared. After six weeks, the place had gotten me to feeling clean and healthy; and what with the mergers, my financial empire was finally coming back into balance.

The place where I stayed was set in a small cove. The house, a white, stucco building with red-tiled roof and an enclosed courtyard behind it, was right by the water. Set in the seaside wall was a black, metal gate, and beyond this lay the beach. To the south, a high escarpment of gray shale; a tangled mass of bushes and trees ended the beach to the north. It was peaceful, I was peaceful.

The night was cool—you could almost say chill. A big, three-quarter moon was working its way down into the west and dripping light onto the water. The stars seemed exceptionally bright. Far out over the heaving bulk of the ocean, a cluster of eight sea-mine derricks blocked starlight. A floating island occasionally reflected moonbeams from off its slick surfaces.

I didn't hear him coming. Apparently he had worked his way down through the brush to the north, waited till I was as near as I was going to be, approached as close as he could and rushed me when I became aware of his presence.

It is easier than you might think for one telepath to conceal himself from another, while remaining aware of the other's position and general activities. It is a matter of "blocking"—imagining a shield around yourself and remaining as emotionally inert as possible.

Admitted, this is rather difficult to do when you hate a man's guts and are stalking him for purposes of killing him. This, probably, is what saved my life.

I cannot really say that I realized there was a vicious presence at my back. It was just that as I took the night air and strolled along the line of the surf, I suddenly became apprehensive. Those nameless thoughts that sometimes run through the back of your head when you awaken for no apparent reason in the middle of a still, warm summer night, lie there awhile wondering what the hell woke you up, and then hear an unusual sound in the next room, magnified by the quiet, electrified by your inexplicable resurrection into a sense of emergency and stomach-squeezing tension—those thoughts raced in an instant, and my toes and fingertips (old anthropoid reflex!) tingled, and the night seemed a shade darker and the sea a home for possible terrors whose sucking tentacles mingled with the wave even then heading toward me; overhead, a line of brightness signified an upper-atmosphere transport which could any moment cease to function and descend like a meteor upon me.

So, when I heard the first, quick crunch of sand behind me, the adrenalin was already there.

I turned quickly, dropping into a crouch. My right foot skidded out behind me as I moved, and I fell to one knee.

A blow to the side of my face sent me sprawling to my right. He was upon me then, and we grappled in the sand, rolling, wrestling for position. Crying out would have been a waste of breath, for there was nobody else around. I tried to scuff sand into his eyes, I tried to knee him in the groin and jab him in any of a dozen painful places. He had been well trained, however, and he outweighed me and seemed faster, too.

Strange as it sounds, we fought for close to five minutes before I realized who he was. We were in the wet sand then, with the surf breaking about us, and he had already broken my nose with a forward smash of his head and snapped two of my fingers when I'd tried for a lock about his throat. The moonlight touched his moist face and I saw that it was Shandon and knew that I would have to kill him to stop him. A knockout would not be good enough. A prison or a hospital would only postpone another encounter. He had to die if I was to live. I imagine his reasoning was the same.

Moments later, something hard and sharp jabbed me in the back, and I wriggled to the left. If a man decides he wants to kill me, I don't much care how I do it to him. Being first is the only thing that matters.

As the surf splashed about my ears and Shandon pushed my head backwards into the water, I groped with my right hand and found the rock.

The first blow glanced off the forearm he had raised in defense. Telepaths have a certain advantage in a fight, because they often know what the other fellow is planning to do next. But it is a terrible thing to know and not be able to do a thing about it. My second blow smashed into his left eyesocket, and he must have seen his death coming because he howled then, like a dog, right before I pulped his temple. I hit him twice again for good measure, pushed him off and rolled away, the rock slipping from my fingers and splashing beside me.

I lay there for a long while, blinking back at the stars, while the surf washed me and the body of my enemy rocked gently, a few feet away.

When I recovered, I searched him, and among other things I found a pistol. It carried a full charge and was in perfect operating condition.

In other words, he'd wanted to kill me with his hands. He had estimated he was able to, and he had preferred risking injury in order to do it that way. He could have nailed me from the shadows, but he had had guts enough to follow the dictates of his hate. He could have been the most dangerous man I had ever faced, if he had used his brains. For this, I respected him. If it had been the other way around, I would have done it the easy way. If the reasons for any violence in which I may indulge are emotional ones, I never let those feelings dictate the means.

I reported the attack, and Shandon lay dead on Earth. Somewhere in Dallas, he had become a strip of tape you could hold in the palm of your hand—all that he ever was or hoped to be—weighing less than an ounce. After thirty days, that too, would be gone.

Weeks later, on the eve of my departure, I stood on the same spot, there on the other side of the Big Pond from Tokyo Bay, and I knew that once you go down in it you do not come again. The reflected stars buckled and twisted, like in warp-drive, and though I did not know it at the time, somewhere a green man was laughing. He had gone fishing in the Bay.

*   *   *

"You stupid son of a bitch," I said.

VI

To have it all to do over again annoyed me. But more than annoyance, there was a certain fear. Shandon had slipped up, selling himself to his emotions once. He would not be likely to make the same mistake again. He was a tough, dangerous man, and now he apparently had a piece of something which made him even more dangerous. Also, he had to be aware of my presence on Illyria, after my sending to Green Green earlier in the evening.

"You have complicated my problem," I said, "so you are going to help me resolve it."

"I do not understand," Green Green said.

"You baited a trap for me and it has grown more teeth," I told him, "but the bait is just as much an inducement now as it was before. I'm going after it, and you're coming along."

He laughed.

"I am sorry, but my path leads in the opposite direction. I will not go back willingly, and I would be of no use to you as a prisoner. In fact, I would represent a distinct impediment."

"I have three choices," I said. "I can kill you now, let you go your way, or allow you to accompany me. You may dismiss the first for the time being, as you are of no use to me dead. If you go your way, I will proceed as I began, on my own. If I obtain what I wish, l will return to Megapei. There,

I will tell how you failed in your centuries-long plan of vengeance on an Earthman. I will tell how you dropped your plan and fled, because another man of that same race had scared the hell out of you. If you wish then to take wives, you must seek them from among your people on other worlds—and even there, the word may reach them eventually. None would call you *Dra*, despite your wealth. Megapei would refuse your bones when you die. You will never again hear the ringing of the tidal bells and know that they ring for you."

"May the blind things at the bottom of the great sea, whose bellies are circles of light," he said, "recall with pleasure the flavor of your marrow."

I blew a smoke ring. ". . . And if I should proceed as I began, on my own," I said, "and be slain myself in the coming encounter, do you think that you will escape from harm? Did you not look into the mind of Mike Shandon as you fought him? Did you not say that you hurt him? Do you not know that he is a man who will not forget such a thing? He is not so subtle as a Pei'an. He does not consider it necessary to proceed with finesse. He will simply turn and seek you, and when he finds you he will cut you down. So whether I win or lose, your end will be disgrace or death."

"If I elect to accompany you and assist you, what then?" he asked.

"I will forget the vengeance which you sought upon me," I said. "I will show you that there was no *pai'badra,* no instrument of affront, so that you may take leave of this vengeance with honor. I will not seek recompense, and we may go our ways thereafter, each freed of the hooks of the other."

"No," he said. "There was *pai'badra* in your elevation

to a Name. I do not accept what you propose."

I shrugged. "Very well," I said, "then how does this sound? Since your feelings and intentions are known to me, it would be useless for either of us to plot vengeance along classical lines. That fine, final moment, where the enemy realizes the instrument, the mover and the *pai'badra* and knows then that his entire life has been but a preface to this irony—that moment would be diminished, if not destroyed.

"So let me offer you satisfaction rather than forgiveness," I went on. "Assist me, and I will give you a fair opportunity to destroy me afterwards. I, of course, will require an equal chance to destroy you. What do you say to that?"

"What means did you have in mind?"

"None, at the moment. Anything that is mutually agreeable will do."

"What assurance may I have of this?"

"I swear it by the Name that I bear."

He turned away and was silent for a time, then, "I agree to your terms," he said. "I will accompany you and assist you."

"Then let us move back to my campsite and become more comfortable," I said. "There are things you have hinted at which I must know more fully."

I turned my back upon him then and walked away. I knocked down the tent and spread the flimsy then for us to sit upon. I rekindled the campfire.

The ground shook very slightly before we seated ourselves upon it.

"Did you do that?" I asked him, gesturing toward the northwest.

"Partly," he replied.

"Why? Trying to frighten me?"

"Not you."

"And Shandon wasn't scared either?"

"Far from it."

"Supposing you tell me precisely what has happened."

"First, concerning our agreement," he said, "a counter-proposal has just occurred to me—one in which you will be interested."

"What is it?"

"You are going there to rescue your friends." He gestured. "Supposing it were possible to recover them without peril? Supposing Mike Shandon could be avoided completely? Would you not prefer to do it that way? —Or do you require his blood immediately?"

I sat there and thought about it. If I let him live, he would come after me again sooner or later. On the other hand, if I could get what I wanted now without having to face him, I could find a thousand safe ways of taking him out of the game, afterwards. Still, I'd come to Illyria ready to face a deadly man. What difference did it make if the names and faces were changed? Still . . .

"Let's hear your proposal."

"The people you seek," he said, "are there only because I recalled them. You know how I did it. I used the tapes. These tapes are intact, and only I know where they are located. I told you how I obtained them. That which I did before I can do now. I can transport the tapes here immediately, if you so bid me. Then we can depart this place, and you can recall your people as you would. Once we are aloft in your vessel, I can show you where to burn or bomb to destroy Mike Shandon without danger to ourselves. Is this not simpler and safer? We can settle our own differences later, by agreement."

"There are two holes in it," I said. "One, there will be no tape for Ruth Laris. Two, I would be abandoning the others. Whether I can recall them again is unimportant, if I leave them behind me now."

"The analogues you recall will have no memory of this."

"That is not the point. They exist right now. They're as real as you or I. It does not matter that they can be duplicated. —They're on the Isle of the Dead, aren't they?"

"Yes."

"Then if I were to destroy it to get Shandon, I'd get everybody, wouldn't I?"

"That would necessarily follow. But—"

"I veto your proposal."

"That is your privilege."

"Have you any other suggestions?"

"No."

"Good. Now that you've exhausted everything you have to change the subject, tell me what happened between you and Shandon back there."

"He bears a Name."

"What?"

"The shadow of Belion stands behind him."

"That's impossible. It doesn't work that way. He's no worldscaper—"

"Bide a moment, Frank, for I know it requires explanation. Apparently there are some things *Dra* Marling never saw fit to tell you. He was a revisionist, however, so it is understandable.

"You know," he continued, "that being a Name-bearer is not essential for the design and construction of worlds—"

"Of course it is. It is a necessary psychological device to release unconscious potentials which are required to perform certain phases of the work. One has to be able to feel like a god to act like one."

"Then why can I do the work?"

"I never heard of you before you became my enemy. I've never seen any of your work, save that which stands about me here, grafted onto my own. If it is representative, then I would say that you can't do the work. You're a lousy craftsman."

"As you would have it," he said. "Nevertheless, it is obvious that I can manipulate the necessary processes."

"Anybody can learn to do that. You were talking about creative design, of which I see no indication on your part."

"I was talking about the pantheon of Strantri. It existed before there were worldscapers, you know."

"I know. What of it?"

"Revisionists, like *Dra* Marling and his predecessors, used the old religion in their trade. They did not take it for its own sake, but, as you say, as a psychological device. Your confirmation as the Shrugger of Thunders was merely a means of coordinating your subconscious. To a fundamentalist, this is blasphemous."

"You are a fundamentalist?"

"Yes."

"Then why did you apprentice yourself to what you consider a sinful trade?"

"In order to be confirmed with a Name."

"I'm afraid you've lost me."

"It was the Name that I wanted, not the trade. My reasons were religious, not economic."

"But if it is only a psychological device—"

"That is the point! It is not. It is an authentic ceremony, and its results—personal contact with the god—are genuine. It is the ordination rite for the high priests of Strantri."

"Then why didn't you take holy orders, rather than world engineering?"

"Because only a Name may administer the rite, and the twenty-seven Names who live are all revisionists. They would not administer the rite for the old reasons."

"Twenty-six," I said.

"Twenty-six?"

"*Dra* Marling is under the mountain, and Lorimel of the Many Hands dwells in the happy nothing."

He lowered his head and was silent for a time. Then, "One less," he said. "I can remember when there were forty-three."

"It is sad."

"Yes."

"Why did you want a Name?"

"In order to be a priest, not a worldscaper. But the revisionists would not have one like me among them. They let me finish the training, then rejected me. Then, to insult me further, the next man they confirmed was an alien."

"I see. That is why you marked me for vengeance?"

"Yes."

"I was hardly responsible, you know. In fact, this is the first time I've heard the story. I had always thought that denominational differences meant very little within Strantri."

"Now you know better. You also must understand that I bear you no personal malice. By avenging myself on you, I strike back at those who blaspheme."

"Why do you indulge in what worldscaping you do, if you consider it immoral?"

"Worldscaping is not immoral. It is the subjugation of the true religion to this end that I find objectionable. I do not bear a Name in the orthodox sense of the term, and the work pays me well. So why should I not do it?"

"No reason I can think of," I told him, "if someone's willing to pay you to try. But what then is your connection with Belion, and Belion with Mike Shandon?"

"Sin and retribution, I suppose. I undertook the confirmation rite myself one night, in the temple at Prilbei. You know how it is, when the sacrifice is made and the words are spoken and you move along the outer wall of the temple, paying homage to each of the gods—how one tablet lights up before you and you feel the power come into you, and that is the Name you will bear?"

"Yes."

"It happened to me at the Station of Belion."

"So you confirmed yourself."

"He confirmed me, in his own Name. I did not want it to be him, for he is a destroyer, not a creator. I had hoped that Kirwar of the Four Faces, Father of Flowers, would come to me."

"Each must abide by his disposition."

"That is true, but I had gotten mine wrongly. Belion would move me even when I did not summon him. I do not know but that he may even have moved me in my ven-

geance-design for you, because you bear the Name of his ancient enemy. I can feel my thinking changing, even now as I
speak of these things. Yes, it may be possible. Since he left
me, things have been so different. . ."

"How could he leave you? The disposition is for life."

"But the nature of my confirmation may not have bound
him to me. He is gone now."

"Shandon. . . ."

"Yes. He is one of the rare ones among your people who
can communicate without words, such as yourself."

"I was not always so. The power grew in me slowly, as I
studied with Marling."

"When I recalled him to life, the first thing that I saw in
his mind was the anguish of his passing by your hand. But
then, quickly, very quickly, he cast this off and became ori-
ented. His mental processes intrigued me and I favored him
above the others, some of whom had to be maintained as
prisoners. I talked with him often and taught him many
things. He came to assist me in the preparations for your
visit."

"How long has he been around?"

"About a *splanth*," he said. (A *splanth* is around eight
and a half Earth-months.) "I called them all back at approximately the same time."

"Why did you kidnap Ruth Laris?"

"I thought that perhaps you did not believe your dead
had been recalled. There followed no massive search on your
part after I began sending the pictures. It would have been
enjoyable had you searched for a long while to find that this
was the place. Since you did not respond, I decided to be-

come more obvious. I kidnapped one of various people who meant something to you. Had you not responded after that, when I even took the trouble of leaving you a message, then I would have taken another, and another—until you saw fit to come looking."

"So Shandon became your protégé. You trusted him."

"Of course. He was a very willing pupil and assistant. He is intelligent and possesses a pleasing manner. It was pleasant having him about."

"Until recently."

"Yes. It is unfortunate that I misread his interest and co-operativeness. Quite naturally, he shared my desire for vengeance upon you. So, of course, did your other enemies, but they were not so clever and none of them telepaths. I enjoyed having someone here with whom I could communicate directly."

"What then caused the falling-out between two such fine friends?"

"When it happened yesterday, it seemed that it was the matter of the vengeance. Actually, though, it was the power. He was more devious than I had allowed for. He tricked me."

"In what fashion?"

"He said that he wanted more than your death as we had planned it. He said that he wanted *personal* vengeance, that he wanted to kill you himself. We argued over this. Finally, he refused to follow my orders and I threatened to discipline him."

He was silent for a moment, then continued: "He struck me then. He hit me with his hands. As I defended myself, the fury grew in me and I decided to hurt him badly before I destroyed him. I called upon the Name that I had taken and Belion heard and came to me. I reached a power-pull, and standing in the shadow of Belion, I burst the ground at our feet and called up the vapors and flames that dwell at the heart of the world. This was how I almost slew him, for he tottered a moment on the brink of the abyss. I scalded him badly then, but he recovered his balance. He had achieved his intention; he had forced me to summon Belion."

"What end did this serve?"

"He knew my story, even as I have told it to you. He knew how I had obtained the Name, and he had a plan concerning it which he had been able to conceal from me. Had I known of it, however, I would have been amused. Nothing more. When I saw what he was attempting, I laughed. I, too, believed that such things could not be. But I was mistaken. He made a pact with Belion.

"He had aroused me to anger and placed my life in jeopardy, knowing I would summon Belion if these things occurred and I was given sufficient time. He fought poorly, to give me that time. Then, when the shadow came over me and I stood as one apart, he reached out with his mind and there was communion. In this fashion did he gamble with his life for power. He said, had he spoken with words, 'Look upon me. Am I not a superior vessel to he whom You have chosen? Come number the ways of my mind and the powers of my body. When You have done this thing, You may choose to forsake the Pei'an and walk with me all the days of my life. I invite You. I am better suited than any man alive to serve Your ends, which I take to be fire and destruction. This one who stands before me is weak and would have consorted with the Father of Flowers had he been given a choice. Come over to me, and we both shall profit by the association.'"

Here he paused again.

"And?" I said.

"Suddenly I was alone."

Somewhere a bird croaked. The night manufactured moisture and began to paint the world with it. Soon a light would begin in the east, fade away, come again. I stared into the fire and saw no faces.

"Seems to shoot hell out of the autonomous complex theory," I said. "But I have heard of transferred psychoses among telepaths. It could be something like that."

"No. Belion and I were bound by confirmation. He found a better agent and he left me."

"I am not convinced that he is an entity in his own right."

"You—a Name-bearer—do not believe. . . ? You give me cause to dislike you."

"Don't go looking for new *pai'badra*, huh? Look where your last one got you. I only said that I'm not wholly convinced. I don't know. —What happened after Shandon made his pact with Belion?"

"He turned slowly from the fissure which had opened between us. He turned his back on me, as if I no longer existed. I reached out with my mind to touch him, and Belion was there. He raised his arms and the entire isle began to tremble. I turned and fled then. I took the boat from its mooring and headed for the shore. After a time, the waters boiled about me. Then the eruptions began. I made it across to the shore, and when I looked back the volcano was already rising from the lake. I could see Shandon on the isle, his arms still upraised, the smoke and the sparks coloring the air about him. I went then in search of you. After a time, I received your message."

"Was he able to use the power-pulls before this thing happened?"

"No, he could not even detect their presence."

"What of the others who have been recalled?"

"They are all of them on the isle. Several of them are drugged, to keep them tranquil."

"I see."

"Perhaps you will now change your mind and do as I suggested?"

"No. "

We sat there until light came into the world about fifteen minutes later. The fog was beginning to lift, but the sky was still overcast. The sun set clouds on fire. The wind came cool. I thought of my ex-spy, playing with his volcano and communing with Belion. Now was the time to hit him, while he was still intoxicated with his new strengths. I'd have liked to draw him away from the isle, into some section of Illyria Green Green had not corrupted, where everything that lived would be my ally. He would not respond to anything that obvious, though. I wanted to get him away from the others, if possible, but I could not figure a way to accomplish it.

"How long did it take you to crap this place up?" I asked.

"I began altering this section about thirty years ago," he said.

I shook my head, stood and kicked dirt into the fire until I'd smothered it.

"Come on. We'd better get moving."

*   *   *

Ginnunga-gap, according to the Norsemen, existed in the center of all space in the morning of time, shrouded with perpetual twilight. Its northern rim was ice and its southern was flame. Over the ages, these forces fought and the rivers flowed and life stirred within the abyss. Sumerian myth has it that En-ki did battle with and subdue Tiamat, the dragon of the sea, thus separating the earth and the waters. En-ki himself, though, was sort of like fire. The Aztecs held that the first men were made of stone, and that a fiery sky portended a new age. And there are many stories of how a world may end: Judgment Day, Götterdämmerung, the fusion of atoms. For me, I have seen worlds and people begin and end, actually and metaphorically, and it will always be the same. It's always fire and water.

No matter what your scientific background, emotionally you're an alchemist. You live in a world of liquids, solids, gases and heat-transfer effects that accompany their changes of state. These are the things you perceive, the things you feel. Whatever you know about their true natures is grafted on top of that. So, when it comes to the day-to-day sensations of living, from mixing a cup of coffee to flying a kite, you treat with the four ideal elements of the old philosophers: earth, air, fire, water.

Let's face it, air isn't very glamorous, no matter how you look at it. I mean, I'd hate to be without it, but it's invisible and so long as it behaves itself it can be taken for granted and pretty much ignored. Earth? The trouble with earth is that it endures. Solid objects tend to persist with a monotonous regularity.

Not so fire and water, however. They're formless, colorful, and they're always doing something. While suggesting you repent, prophets very seldom predict the wrath of the gods in terms of landslides and hurricanes. No. Floods and fires are what you get for the rottenness of your ways. Primitive man was really on his way when he learned to kindle the one and had enough of the other nearby to put it out. Is it coincidence that we've filled hells with fires and oceans with monsters? I don't think so. Both principles are mobile, which is generally a sign of life. Both are mysterious and possess the power to hurt or kill. It is no wonder that intelligent creatures the universe over have reacted to them in a similar fashion. It is the alchemical response.

Kathy and I had been that way. It had been a stormy, mobile, mysterious thing, full of the power to hurt, to give birth and to give death. She had been my secretary for almost two years before our marriage, a small, dark girl with pretty hands, who looked well in bright colors and liked to feed crumbs to the birds. I had hired her through an agency on the world Mael. In my youth, people were happy to hire an intelligent girl who could type, file and take shorthand. What with the progressive debasement of the academic machine and the upward-creep of paper-requirements in an expanding, competitive labor market, however, I'd hired her on advice of my personnel office on learning she held a doctorate in Secretarial Science from the Institute of Mael. God! that first year was bad! She automated everything, screwed up my personal filing system and set me six months behind on correspondence. After I had a twentieth-century typewriter reconstructed, at considerable expense, and she learned to operate it, I taught her shorthand and she became as good as a twentieth-century high school graduate with a business major. Business returned to normal, and I think we were the only two people around who could read Gregg scribbles—which was nice for confidential matters, and gave us something in common. Her a bright little flame and me a wet blanket, I'd reduced her to tears many times that first year. Then she became indispensable, and I realized it was not just because she was a good secretary. We were married and there were six happy years—six and a half, actually. She died in the fire, in the Miami Stardock disaster, on her way to meet me for a conference. We'd had two sons, and one of them is still living. On and off, before and since, the fires have stalked me through the years. Water has been my friend.

While I feel closer to the water than the fire, my worlds are born of both. Cocytus, New Indiana, St. Martin, Buningrad, Mercy, Illyria and all the others came into being through a process of burning, washing, steaming and cooling. Now I walked through the woods of Illyria—a world I'd built as a park, a resort—I walked through the woods of an Illyria purchased by the enemy who walked by my side, emptied of the people for whom I had created it: the happy ones, the vacationers, the resters, the people who still believed in trees and lakes and mountains with pathways among them. They were gone, and the trees among which I walked were twisted, the lake toward which I headed was polluted, the land had been wounded and the fire her blood spurted from the mountain that loomed before, waiting, as the fire always is, waiting for me. Overhead hung the clouds, and between their matted whiteness and my dirty blackness flew the soot the fire sent, an infinite migration of funeral notices. Kathy would have liked Illyria, had she seen it in another time and another place. The thought of her in this time and this place, with Shandon running the show, sickened me. I cursed softly as I walked along, and those are my thoughts on alchemy.

*　　*　　*

We walked for about an hour and Green Green began complaining about his shoulder and fatigue in general. I told him he could have my sympathy so long as he kept walking. This must have satisfied him because it shut him up. An hour after that, I did let him take a break while I climbed a tree to check out the forward terrain. We were getting close, and it was about to become a steady downhill hike the rest of the way in. The day had lightened as much as it was going to and the fog had vanished almost entirely. It was already warmer than it had been at any time since my landing. The perspiration rolled down my sides as I climbed and the flaky bark bit into my hands, which had grown soft in recent years. With each branch that I disturbed a fresh cloud of dust and ashes appeared. I sneezed several times, and my eyes burned and watered.

I could see the top of the isle above the fringe of distant trees. To the left of it and somewhat back, I could see the smoldering top of a fresh-grown cone of volcanic rock. I cursed again, because I felt like it, and climbed back down.

It took us about two more hours to reach the shore of Acheron.

Reflected in the oily surface of my lake were the fires and nothing more. Lava and hot rocks spit and hissed as they struck the water. I felt dirty and sticky and hot as I looked out across what remained of my handiwork. Small waves left lines of scum and black crud upon the shore. The water was spotted with clouds of such stuff heading in toward the beach. Fishes rocked belly up in the shallows, and the air smelled like rotten eggs. I sat upon a rock and regarded it, smoking a cigarette the while.

A mile out stood my Isle of the Dead, still unchanged—stark, and ominous as a shadow with nothing to cast it. I leaned forward and tested the water with my finger. The lake was hot, quite hot. Far out and to the east, there was a second light. It seemed as if a smaller cone were growing there.

"I came to shore about a quarter mile to the west of here," said Green Green.

I nodded and continued to stare. It was still morning and I felt like contemplating the prospect. The southern face of the isle—the one I looked upon—had a narrow strip of beach following the curve of a cove perhaps two hundred feet across. From there, a natural-seeming trail zigzagged upwards, reaching various levels and, ultimately, the high, horned peaks.

"Where do you think he is?" I asked.

"About two-thirds of the way up, on this side," said Green Green, "in the chalet. That is where I had my laboratory. I expanded many of the caves behind it."

A frontal approach was almost mandatory, as the other faces of the isle possessed no beaches and rose sharply from the water.

Almost, but not quite.

I doubted that Green Green, Shandon or anybody else was aware that the northern face could be climbed. I had designed it to look unscalable, but it was not all that bad. I had done it just because I like everything to have a back door as well as a front door. If I were to employ that route, it would require my ascending all the way and coming down toward the chalet from above.

I decided I would do it that way. I also decided that I would keep it to myself until the last minute. After all, Green Green was a telepath, and for all I knew, the story he'd given me could be a line of *rouke* manure. He and Shandon could be working together, and for that matter there might not even be a Shandon. I wouldn't have trusted him worth a plugged nickel, back when they still had nickels to plug.

"Come on," I said, rising and flipping my cigarette into the cesspool my lake. "Show me where you left the boat."

So we made our way to the left, along the shoreline, to the place where he remembered beaching the thing. Only it was not there.

"Are you sure this is the place?"

"Yes."

"Well, where is it?"

"Perhaps it was loosened by one of the shocks and drifted away."

"Could you swim as far as the isle, bad shoulder and all?"

"I am a Pei'an," he replied, which meant he could damn well swim the English Channel with two bum shoulders, then turn around and go back again. I'd only said it to irritate him.

". . . But we won't be able to swim to the isle," he added.

"Why not?"

"There are hot currents from the volcano. They are worse farther out."

"Then we are going to build a raft," I said. "I'll cut the wood with my pistol while you locate something suitable for binding it together."

"Such as?" he inquired.

"You're the one who screwed up this forest," I told him, "so you know it better than I do now. I've seen some tough-looking vines, though."

"They are somewhat abrasive," he said. "I will need your knife."

I hesitated a moment.

"All right. Here."

"Waters can come over the edges of a raft. They may be very warm."

"Then the waters must be cooled."

"How?"

"Soon it will begin to rain."

"The volcanos—"

"There won't be that much water."

He shrugged, nodded and went off to cut vines. I felled and stripped trees, perhaps six inches in diameter, ten feet in length, paying as much attention as possible to my back.

Soon it began to rain.

For the next several hours, a steady, cold drizzle descended from the heavens, drenching us to the skin, poking holes in Acheron, washing some of the filth from the shrubbery. I shaped two broad paddles and cut us a pair of long poles while I waited for Green Green to harvest sufficient cordage to bind things. While I was still waiting, the ground heaved violently and a terrific eruption split the near side of the cone halfway up. A river the color of sunsets poured from the gap. My ears rang for minutes after the explosion. Then the surface of the lake picked itself up and rushed toward me—a baby tidal wave. I ran like hell and climbed the highest tree in sight.

The water reached the base of the tree, but did not get much higher than a foot. There were three such waves in twenty minutes; then the waters began to recede, trading me a lot of mud for the timber I'd cut, plus both oars.

I grew angry. I knew my rain could not put out his bloody volcano, might even exacerbate things a bit . . . But I was mad as hell, seeing all that work washed away.

I began to speak the words.

From somewhere, I heard the Pei'an calling. I ignored him.

After all, I wasn't exactly Francis Sandow at that point.

I dropped to the ground and felt the tug of a powerpull from several hundred yards to my left. I moved in that direction, climbing a small rise to reach its nexus. From that point, I had a clear line of vision across the bothered waters out to the isle itself. Perhaps my visual acuity had increased. I saw the chalet quite clearly. I fancied that I also detected a movement of sorts at the place where the rail guarded the end of the courtyard that overlooked the waters. Human eyes are not as acute as a Pei'an's. Green Green had said he'd seen Shandon clearly after crossing over the waters.

I felt her pulse as I stood there above one of Illyria's larger veins or smaller arteries, and the power came into me and I sent it upward.

Soon the drizzle became a heavy downpour, and when I lowered my upraised hand the lightning flashed and the thunders skated round and round in the tin drum of the sky. A wind, sudden as a springing cat and cold as the Arctic's halations, struck me in the back and shaved my cheeks as it passed.

Green Green cried out again. From somewhere off to my right, I think.

Then the heavens began to sizzle, and they sent down rains so heavily that the chalet vanished from sight and the isle itself faded to a gray outline. The volcano was the faintest of sparks above the water. Soon the wind raced by like a freight train and its howling joined with the thunders to create a perpetual din. The shores of Acheron lengthened and the waters were buffeted until they moved, in waves like the ones we had received, back in that direction from which they had come. If Green Green called out again, I could not hear him.

The water ran in rivers through my hair, down my face and neck. But I did not need my eyes to see. The power enfolded me and the temperature plummeted; the rain came in sheets that cracked like whips now; the day grew dark as night. I laughed, and the waters rose up in spouts and swayed like genies, and the lightnings ran their gauntlets again and again, but the machine never said "Tilt."

Stop it, Frank! He will know you are here! came the thoughts, addressed to that part of me which Green Green wished to address.

He does already, doesn't he? I might have replied. *Take cover till this is over. Wait!*

And as the waters came down and the winds went forth,

the ground began to rock beneath me once again. The spark that hovered before me grew and glowed like a buried sun. Then the lightnings walked about it; they tickled the top of the isle; they wrote names upon the chaos, and one of them was mine.

I was thrown to my knees by another shock, but I stood again and raised both arms.

. . . And then I stood in a place that was neither solid, liquid nor gaseous. There was no light, nor was there darkness. It was neither hot nor cold. Perhaps it lay within my own mind, and perhaps not.

We stared at one another, and in my pale green hands I held a thunderbolt at port arms.

He was built like a wide, gray pillar, was covered with scales. He'd a snout like a crocodile, and his eyes were fiery. His three pairs of arms assumed various attitudes as we spoke. Otherwise he, also, did not move from where he stood.

Old enemy, old comrade . . . he addressed me.

Yes, Belion. I am here.

. . . *Your cycle has ended. Save yourself the ignomy of ruin at my hands. Withdraw now, Shinbo, and preserve a world you made.*

I doubt the world shall be lost, Belion.

Silence.

Then, *Then there must be a confrontation.*

. . . *Unless you yourself choose to withdraw.*

I will not.

Then there will be a confrontation.

He sighed a flame.

So be it.

And he was gone.

. . . And I stood atop the small hill and lowered my arms slowly, for the power had gone out of me.

It was a strange experience, unlike anything I had known before. A waking dream, if you would. A fantasy born of tension and anger, if you wouldn't.

The rain was still descending, though not with its previous force. The winds had lost something of their intensity. The lightnings had ceased, as had the trembling of the ground. The fiery activity had diminished, shrinking the orange nest atop the cone, stopping the wound in its side.

I stared at all this, feeling once again the wetness and. the coldness and the firmness of the ground beneath my feet. Our long-distance battle had been cut short, our powers canceled. This was fine with me, though; the waters looked cooler and the slick, gray isle less forbidding.

Ha!

In fact, as I watched, the sun broke through the clouds for a moment and a rainbow unrolled itself amidst sparkling droplets, arcing through the air now clean and framing Acheron, the isle, the smoldering cone like a picture within a gleaming paperweight, miniature, contained and more than slightly unreal.

I departed the hillock and returned to the place I had left. There was a raft that needed building.

VII

As I lamented my missing cowardice—it had been such a lifesaving virtue in the past—it responded by rushing back and leaving me scared as hell once again.

I'd lived far too long, and with every day that passed the odds kept growing against my lasting much longer. Although they didn't put it quite that way when giving the sales pitch, my insurance company's attitude is reflected in the size of the premiums involved. Their computer classified me along with terminal xenopath cases, according to their rates and my spies. Comforting. Probably right, too. This was the first piece of dangerous business I had been out on in a long while. I felt out of practice, though I was not sorry I had skimped. If Green Green noticed that my hands were shaking, he made no comment. They held his life, and he felt badly enough about this as it was. He was in a position now to kill me any time he wanted, if you stop to think about it very carefully. He knew it. I knew it. And he knew I knew it. And . . .

The only thing that was holding him back was the fact that he needed me to get him off of Illyria—which, logically, meant that his ship was on the isle. Which, by extension, meant that if Shandon had a ship at his disposal, he could come looking for us by air, despite our hallucinatory companions' feelings with respect to a confrontation. Which meant that we would be better off working under the trees than on the beach, and that our voyage required the cover of night. Accordingly, I moved our project inland. Green Green thought this a very good idea.

The cloud cover cracked that afternoon as we assembled the raft, but it did not break completely. The rain continued, the day grew a bit brighter, and two white, white moons passed overhead—Kattontallus and Flopsus—lacking only grins and eye-sockets.

Later in the day a silver insect, three times the size of the *Model T* and ugly as a grub, left the isle and circled the lake six times, spiraling outward, then inward. We were under a lot of foliage, burrowed our ways beneath more, stayed there until it returned to the isle. I clutched my ancient artifact the while. The bunny did not sell me out.

We finished the raft a couple hours before sundown and spent the balance of the day with our backs against the boles of adjacent trees.

"A penny for your thoughts," I said.

"What is a penny?"

"An ancient monetary unit, once common on my home planet. On second thought, don't take me up on it. They're valuable now."

"It is strange to offer to buy a thought. Was this a common practice among your people, in the old days?"

"It had to do with the rise of the merchant classes," I said. "Everything has a price, and all that."

"That is a very interesting concept, and I can see how one such as yourself could well believe in it. Would you buy a *pai'badra?*"

"That would be barratry. A *pai'badra* is a cause for an action."

"But would you pay a person to abandon his vengeance against you?"

"No."

"Why not?"

"You would take my money and still seek the vengeance, hoping to lull me into a sense of false security."

"I was not speaking of myself. You know that I am wealthy, and that a Pei'an does not abandon his vengeance for any reason. —No. I was thinking of Mike Shandon. He is of your race, and may also believe that everything has a price. As I recall it, he incurred your disfavor in the first place because he needed money and did things that offended you in order to obtain it. Now he hates you because you sent him to prison and then killed him. But since he is of your race, which places a monetary value upon all things, perhaps you might pay him sufficient money for his *pai'badra* so that he will be satisfied and go away."

Buy our way out? The thought hadn't occurred to me. I had come to Illyria ready to fight with a Pei'an menace. Now I held him in my hand and he was no longer a menace. An Earthman had replaced him as my number one enemy of the moment, and there was a possibility that this assessment was correct. We are a venal lot, not necessarily more so than all of the other races—but certainly more than some. It had been Shandon's expensive tastes that had gotten him into a bind in the first place. Things had happened quickly since my arrival on Illyria, and strangely enough—for me and my

Tree—it had not occurred to me that my money might be my salvation.

On the other hand, considering Shandon's record as a spender—a thing brought out at the first trial and at the appellate level—he went through money like a *betta splendens* through that most liquid of all alchemical elements. Say I gave him a half million in universal credit drafts. Anybody else could invest it and live on the dividends. He would go through it in a couple years. Then I would have problems again. He would have hit me this once, and he would figure he could do it again. And of course I could come through again. I could come through any time. So maybe he would not want to kill his golden goose. But then again, I'd never know for sure. I could not live with that.

Still, if he were agreeable, I could buy him off now. Then I could arrange for a team of professional assassins to take him out of the game as soon as possible.

But if they should fail . . .

Then he would be on my tail immediately, and it would be him or me again.

I turned it over, looked at it from every possible angle. Ultimately, it boiled down to one thing.

He'd had a gun with him, but he'd tried to kill me with his hands.

"It won't work with Shandon," I said. "He's not a member of the merchant class."

"Oh. I meant no offense. I still do not quite understand how these things work with Earthmen."

"You're not alone in that."

I watched the day fade away and the clouds zip themselves together once again. Soon it would be time to carry the raft to the shore and make our ways across the now temperate waters. There would be no moonlight to assist us.

"Green Green," I said, "in you I see myself, as perhaps I have become more Pei'an than Earthman. I do not think this is the real reason, however, for everything that I am now is but an extension of something that was already within me. I, too, can kill as you would kill and hold with my *pai'badra* come hell or high water."

"I know that," he said, "and I respect you for it."

"What I am trying to say is that when this thing is over, if we should both live through it, I might welcome you as a friend. I might intercede for you with the other Names, that you have another chance at confirmation. I might like to see a high priest of Strantri, in the Name of Kirwar of the Four Faces, Father of Flowers, should He be willing."

"You are trying to find my price now, Earthman."

"No, I am making a legitimate offer. Take it as you would. As yet, you have given me no *pai'badra*."

"By trying to kill you?"

"Under false *pai'badra*. This does not bother me."

"You know that I may slay you whenever I wish?"

"I know that you think so."

"I had thought this thing better shielded."

"It is a matter of deduction, not telepathy."

"You *are* much like a Pei'an," he said, after a moment. "I promise you that I will withhold my vengeance until after we have dealt with Shandon."

"Soon," I said. "Soon we shall depart."

And we sat there and waited for the night to fall. After a time, it did.

"Now," I said.

"Now," and we stood and raised the raft between us. We carried it down to the water's edge, waded out into the warm shallows, set it a-drifting.

"Got your paddle?"

"Yes."

"Let's go."

We climbed aboard, stabilized the thing, began paddling, then poling.

"If he was above bribery," he said, "why did he sell your secrets?"

"He would have sold the others out," I said, "had my people paid him more."

"Then why is he above bribery?"

"Because he is of my race and he hates me. Nothing more. There is no buying that kind of *pai'badra*."

I thought then that I was right.

"There are always dark areas within the minds of Earthmen," he observed. "One day I would like to know what is there."

"Me too."

A moon came up then, because a generalized blob of light appeared behind the clouds. It drifted slowly towards midheaven.

The water splashed gently beside us, and little wavelets of it struck against our knees, our boots. A cool breeze followed us from the shore.

"The volcano is at rest," he said. "What did you discuss

with Belion?"

"You don't miss a trick, do you?"

"I tried to contact you several times, and I know what I found."

"Belion and Shimbo are waiting," I said. "There will be quick movements, and one of them will be satisfied." The water was black as ink and warm as blood; the isle was a mountain of coal against the pearl and starless night. We poled until we lost the bottom, then commenced paddling, silently, twisting the oars. Green Green had a Pei'an's love of the water in him. I could feel it in the way that he moved, in the ragtails of emotion that I picked up as we proceeded.

To cross over the dark waters . . . It was an eerie feeling, because of what the place meant to me, because of the chord it had struck within me while I was building it. The feeling of the Valley of Shadows, the sense of the serene passing, this was absent. This place was the butcher's block at the end of the run. I hated it and I feared it. I knew that I lacked the spiritual stamina to ever duplicate it. It was one of those once in a lifetime creations that made me wish I hadn't. To cross over the dark waters meant to me a confrontation with something within myself that I did not understand or accept. I was cruising along on Tokyo Bay, and suddenly this was the answer, looming, the heaped remains of everything that goes down and does not come again to shore, life's giant kitchen-midden, the rubbish heap that remains after all things pass, the place that stands in testament to the futility of all ideals and intentions, good or bad, the rock that smashes values, there, signalizing the ultimate uselessness of life itself, which must one day be broken upon it, not to rise, never, no, not ever, again. The warm waters splashed about my knees, but a chill shook me and I broke rhythm. Green Green touched my shoulder, and we matched our paddling once again. —"Why did you make it, if you hate it so?" he asked me. —"They paid me well," I replied, and, "Bear to the left. We're going in the back way." Our course altered, shifting westward as he strengthened his strokes and I lightened mine. —"The back way?" he repeated. —"Yes," I said, and I did not elaborate.

As we neared the isle, I ceased my reflections and became a mechanical thing, as I always do when there are too many thoughts to think. I paddled and we slipped through the night, and soon the isle lay to starboard, mysterious lights flecking its face. From ahead, the light that glowed atop the cone crossed our path, dappling the waters, casting a faint red glow upon the cliffs.

We passed the isle then and moved toward it from the north. Through the night, I saw the northern face as in daylight. Memory mapped its scars and ridges, and my fingertips tingled with the texture of its stone.

We drew near, and I touched the sheer, black face with my oar. We held that position while I stared upward, then said, "East."

Several hundred yards later, we came to the place where I had hidden the "trail." A cleft slanted within the rock—forty feet of chimney—where the pressure of back and feet allowed ascent to a narrow ledge, along which a man might edge his way for sixty feet, to encounter a series of hand- and foot-holds leading up.

I told this to Green Green, and he stabilized the raft

while I went on ahead. Then he followed, uncomplaining, though his shoulder must have been bothering him.

When I reached the top of the chimney, I looked down and was unable to spot the raft. I mentioned this, and Green Green grunted. I waited until he made it to the top, and helped him out of the cleft. Then we began inching our way along the cleft, eastward.

It took us about fifteen minutes to reach the upward trail. Again, I went first, after explaining that we had a five-hundred-foot climb before we reached another ledge. The Pei'an grunted again and followed me.

Soon my arms were sore, and when we made the ledge I sprawled and lit a cigarette. After ten minutes, we moved again. By midnight, we had made it to the top without mishap.

We walked, for about ten minutes. Then we saw him.

He was a wandering figure, doubtless narcotized up to the ears. Maybe not, though. You can never be too sure.

So I approached him, placed my hand upon his shoulder, stood before him, said, "Courtcour, how have you been?"

He looked up at me through heavy-lidded eyes. He weighed about three hundred fifty pounds, wore white garments (Green Green's idea, I guess), was blue-eyed, light-complexioned and soft-spoken. He lisped a bit when he answered me.

"I think I have all the data," he said.

"Good," I answered. "You know that I came here to meet this man—Green Green—in a combat of sorts. We have become allies recently, against Mike Shandon. . . ?"

"Give me a moment," he replied.

Then, "Yes," he said. "You lose."

"What do you mean?"

"Shandon kills you in three hours and ten minutes."

"No," I said. "He can't."

"If he does not," he replied, "it will be because you have slain him. Then Mister Green will kill you about five hours and twenty minutes from now."

"What makes you so sure?"

"Green is the worldscaper who did Korrlyn?"

"Are you?" I asked.

"Yes."

"Then he will kill you."

"How?"

"Probably by means of a blunt instrument," he said. "If you can avoid that, you might be able to take him with your hands. You've always proven just a bit stronger` than you look, and it fools people. I do not think it will help you this time, though."

"Thanks," I said. "Don't lose any sleep."

". . . Unless you are both carrying secret weapons," he said, "and it is possible that you are."

"Where is Shandon?"

"In the chalet."

"I want his head. How do I get it?"

"You are a kind of demon factor. You have that ability which I cannot fully measure."

"Yes. I know."

"Do not use it."

"Why?"

"He has one, too."

"I know that also."

"If you can kill him at all, you kill him without it."

"Okay."

"You do not trust me."

"I don't trust anybody."

"Do you remember the night you hired me?"

"Faintly."

"It was the best meal I ever had in my life. Pork chops. Lots of them."

"It comes back to me."

"You told me of Shimbo then. Invoke him and Shandon will invoke the other one. Too many variables. It may be fatal."

"Maybe Shandon has gotten to you."

"No. I am just measuring probabilities."

"Could Yarl the Omnipotent create a stone he could not lift?" Green Green asked him.

"No," said Courtcour.

"Why not?"

"He would not."

"That is no answer."

"Yes it is. Think about it. Would *you*?"

"I do not trust him," said Green Green. "He was normal when I brought him back, but I believe that perhaps Shandon has reached him."

"No," said Courtcour. "I am trying to help you."

"By telling Sandow he is going to die?"

"Well, he is."

Green raised his hand, and suddenly he was holding my gun, which he must have teleported from my belt, in the same fashion as he had obtained the tapes. He fired twice and handed it back to me.

"Why did you do that?"

"He was lying to you, trying to confuse you. Trying to destroy your confidence."

"He was once a close associate of mine. He had trained himself to think like a computer. I think he was trying to be objective."

"Get the tape and you can resurrect him."

"Come on. I've got two hours and fifty-eight minutes."

We walked away.

"Should I not have done that?" he asked me, after a time.

"No."

"I am sorry."

"Great. Don't kill anybody else unless I ask you to, huh?"

"All right. —You have killed many people, have you not, Frank?"

"Yes."

"Why?"

"Them or me, and I'd rather it was them."

"So?"

"You didn't have to kill Bodgis."

"I thought—"

"Shut up. Just shut up."

We walked on, passing through a cleft of rock. Tendrils of mist snaked by, touched our garments. Another shadowy figure stood off to the side, at the place where we emerged upon a downward-sloping trail.

". . . Coming to die," she said, and I stopped and looked at her.

"Lady Karle."

"Pass on, pass on," she said. "Hasten to your doom. You could not know what it means to me."

"I loved you once," I said, which was not the right thing to say at all.

She shook her head.

"The only thing you ever loved—besides yourself—was money. You got it. You killed more people than I know of to keep your empire, Frank. Now there has finally come a man who can take you. I am proud to be present at your doom."

I turned on the torch and shone it upon her. Her hair was so red and her features so white. . . . Her face was heart-shaped and her eyes were green, as I remembered them. For a moment, I ached for her.

"What if I take *him*?" I asked.

"Then I'm probably going to be yours again for awhile," she replied, "but I hope not. You are evil and I want you to die. I'd find a way myself, if you were to have me again."

"Stop," said Green Green. "I brought you back from the dead. I brought this man here to kill him. I was usurped by a human being who, fortunately or unfortunately, is possessed of a similar intention with respect to Sandow. But Frank and I have our fates cast together now. Consider me. I restored you and I will preserve you. Help us to get at our enemy and I will reward you."

She moved out of the circle of light and her laughter came down upon us.

"No," she called out. "No, thank you."

"I once loved you," I said.

There was silence, then, "Could you do it again?"

"I don't really know, but you mean something to me—something important."

"Pass on," she said. "All debts be canceled. Go to Shandon and die."

"Please," I said. "Once upon a time, when I held you it meant much to me. Lady Karle, I have never stopped caring for you, even after you left. And it was not I who broke the Ten of Algol, though this is often said."

"It was you."

"I think I could convince you that it was not."

"Don't bother trying. Pass on."

"All right," I said. "I won't stop, though."

"What? Stop what?"

"Caring for you, some," I said.

"Pass on. Please pass on!"

And we did.

All that time we had been speaking her language—Dralmin—and I hadn't even realized that I had switched from English. Funny.

"You have loved many women, haven't you, Frank?" asked Green Green.

"Yes."

"Were you lying to her—about caring for her?"

"No."

We followed the trail until I could see the lights of the chalet before/below me. We continued in that direction, and a final figure appeared, drew near.

"Nick!"

"That's right, mister."

"It's me—Frank!"

"By God, I think it is. Come closer, huh?"

"Sure. Here's a light." I spilled it all over myself so that he could see.

"Jesus! It's really you!" he said. "That guy down there is a nut, you know, and he's after you."

"Yeah, I know."

"He wanted me to help get you, and I told him to go indulge in auto-eroticism. He was mad. We had a fight. I busted his nose and got the hell out. He didn't come after me, though. He's tough."

"I know."

"I'm going to help you get him."

"Okay."

"But I don't like that guy you're with."

Nick, all out of the past and storming. . . . It was great.

"What do you mean?"

"He's the one responsible for the whole thing. He brought me back, and the others. He's a sneaky son of a bitch. If I were you, I'd take him out of the picture real quick."

"We're allies now, he and I."

Nick spat.

"I'm going to get you, mister," he said to Green Green. "When this whole thing is over, you're mine. Remember those days when you questioned me? It wasn't fun. —And now, my turn will come."

"All right."

"No, it isn't! It's not all right at all. You called me 'Shorty,' or the Pei'an equivalent thereof, you dumb vegetable! When I get my turn, I'll roast you! I'm glad I'm alive again, and I guess I owe that to you. But I'll croak you, bastard! You've got it coming, and you'd better believe it. I'll take you with anything available."

"I doubt it, little man," Green Green said.

"Let's wait and see," I said.

So Nick joined us, walking on the other side of me from Green Green.

"Is he down there now?" I asked.

"Yes. Do you have a bomb?"

"Yes."

"That would probably be the best way. Make sure he's inside and lob it in through the window."

"Is he alone?"

"Well—No. But it wouldn't exactly be murder. Once you get the tapes you can bring back the girl."

"Who is she?"

"Her name is Kathy. I don't know her."

"She was my wife," I said.

"Oh. Well, I guess that idea is out. We have to go in."

"Perhaps," I said. "If we have to, I'll take care of Shandon and you get Kathy out of the way."

"He wouldn't hurt her."

"Oh?"

"It's been several months since we woke up, Frank. We didn't know where we were or why. And this green guy said he didn't know any more about it than we did. For all we knew we were really dead. We only found out about you when he and Mike had the argument. Green dropped his guard one day and Mike picked his brains, I guess. Anyhow, Mike and the girl—Kathy, yes—sort of have a thing going between them. I guess they're in love."

"Green, why didn't you tell me this?"

"I did not deem it important. Is it?"

I didn't answer because I didn't know. I thought quickly. I leaned my back against a rock and pushed the gas pedal of my mind to the floor. I had set out to find and kill an enemy. Now he stood by my side while I sought a different enemy in his stead. Now to find out that he was shacking up with the resurrected wife I'd come to rescue . . . This did change things. How, I was not sure. If Kathy was in love with him, I was not about to burst in and shoot him down in front of her. Even if he were just using her, even if he didn't care anything for her, I could not do that—not with him meaning something to her. It seemed that Green Green's earlier suggestion was the only thing left—to contact him and try to buy him off. He had a new power and a pretty girl. Add to that a wad of money, and he might be persuaded to lay off. It still troubled me, though, that he had tried to kill me with his hands.

I could just turn around and go back. I could climb aboard the *Model T* and in less than a day be scooting toward Homefree. If she wanted Shandon, let her have him. I could settle my score with Green Green and return to my fortress.

"Yes, it is important," I said.

"Does it alter your plans?" Green Green asked me.

"Yes."

"Just because of the girl?"

"Just because of the girl," I said.

"You are a strange man, Frank, to come all this way and then change your mind because of a girl who is only an ancient memory to you."

"I have a very good memory."

I did not like the idea of leaving my Name's enemy running around in the body of a capable and clever man who would not mind seeing me dead. It was a combination that could keep me awake nights, even on Homefree. On the other hand, what good is a dead golden goose—or pigeon, as the case would be? It's funny how, if you live long enough, friends, enemies, lovers, haters move around you as at a big, masked ball, and every now and then there is some mask-switching.

"What are you going to do?" Nick asked.

"I'm going to talk to him. Make a deal if I can."

"You said he would not sell his *pai'badra*," said Green Green.

"I thought so when I said it. But this thing with Kathy now makes it necessary that I try to buy it."

"I do not understand."

"Don't try. Maybe the two of you had better wait here, in case he starts shooting."

"If he kills you, what are we to do?" asked Green Green.

"That'll be your problem then. —See you in a little while, Nick."

"Check, Frank."

I moved on down the trail, maintaining my mental shield. I used the rocks for cover, crawling among them as I neared. Finally, I lay flat on my stomach about a hundred fifty feet above the place. Two huge boulders shielded me and cast heavy shadows. I rested the pistol on my forearm and covered the back door.

"Mike!" I called out. "This is Frank Sandow!" and I waited.

Perhaps half a minute passed while he decided, then, "Yes?"

"I want to talk."

"Go ahead."

Suddenly the lights went out below me.

"Is it true what I've heard about you and Kathy?"

He hesitated, then, "I guess so."

"Is she with you now?"

"Maybe. Why?"

"I want to hear her say it."

Then, after everything, her voice:

"I guess it's true, Frank. We didn't know where we were, or anything—and I remembered that fire. . . . I don't know how to—"

I bit my lip.

"Don't apologize," I said. "That was a long time ago. I'll live."

Mike chuckled.

"You seem confident of that."

"I am. I've decided to do it the easy way."

"What do you mean?"

"How much do you want?"

"Money? You scared of me, Frank?"

"I came here to kill you, but I won't do it if Kathy loves

you. She says she does. Okay. If you've got to go on living, then I want you off my back. How much will it take for you to pick up your marbles and go away?"

"What are marbles?"

"Forget it. How much?"

"I hadn't thought you would offer, so I never thought about it. A lot, though. I'd want a guaranteed income for life, a large one. Then some really large purchases in my name—I'd have to make a list. —You really do mean it? This isn't a trick?"

"We're both telepaths. I propose we drop our screens. In fact, I'd insist on it as a condition."

"Kathy has been asking me not to kill you," he said, "and she would probably hold it against me if I did. Okay. She means more to me. I'll take your money and your wife and go away."

"Thanks a lot."

He laughed.

"My luck is finally good. How do you want to handle this?"

"If you'd like, I can give you a lump sum and then have my attorneys set up a trust."

"I like. I want everything to be legal. I want a million, plus a hundred thousand a year."

"That's a lot."

"Not to you."

"Just commenting. —Okay, I agree." I wondered how Kathy was taking all this. She could not have changed so much in a few months but that this would not sound a bit sickening to her. "Two things," I added. "The Pei'an,

Gringrin-tharl—he's mine now. We have a score to settle."

"You can have him. Who needs him? —What's the other thing?"

"Nick, the dwarf, comes away with me, in one piece."

"That little—" Then he laughed. "Sure. In fact, I kind of like him. —That's all?"

"That's all."

The sun's first rays tickled the belly of the sky and the volcanos flamed like Titan torches out over the water.

"Now what?"

"Wait till I pass a message to the others," I said. —*Green Green, he'll deal. I have his* pai'badra. *Tell Nick. We depart in a few hours. My ship will come for me later today.*

—*I hear you, Frank. We will be with you shortly.*

Now only the Pei'an remained to be dealt with. It was almost too easy. I was still on the lookout for a trick. It would have to be an awfully elaborate one, though. I was inclined to doubt the possibility of collusion between Green Green and Mike. Anyhow, I would know in a few moments, when Mike and I dropped our screens. But after all my preparations, to settle the whole thing like a couple of businessmen . . .

I could not tell whether I had chuckled or snorted. It was something that felt somewhere in between.

Then I felt that it was wrong. It? Something, I do not know what. It was a feeling that probably goes back to the caves or the trees. Hell, maybe even the oceans. Flopsus shone through the ash and the smoke and the mist, and she was the color of blood.

A quietness seemed to settle over everything as the

breezes grew still. Then that old gut-grabbing fear was back with me again, and I fought it. A big hand was about to come down out of the sky and squash me, but I lay still. I had conquered the Isle of the Dead, and Tokyo Bay burnt all about me. Now, though, I looked down the slope into the Valley of Shadow. It is so easy for me to find things to be morbid about, and all things came to remind me of this. I shuddered and stilled my shaking. It would not do for Shandon to find fear in my heart.

Finally, after I could wait no longer, "Shandon," I said, "I'm dropping my shield. You do the same."

"All right."

. . . And our minds met, moved about inside one another.

—*You mean it*. . . .

—*So do you*. . . .

—*Then it's a bargain*.

—*Yes*.

And the "No!" that slammed back from the subterranean recesses of the world and echoed down from the towers of the sky clashed like cymbals within our minds. A flash of red heat passed through my body. Then, slowly, I stood, and my limbs were as firm as the mountains. Through lines of red and green, I saw everything as clearly as by daylight. I saw where, down below me, Mike Shandon emerged from the chalet and slowly turned his head to rake the heights. Finally, our eyes met, and I knew then that what had been spoken or written in that place where I had stood with a thunderbolt in my hands had been true: —*Then there must be a confrontation*. Flames . . . —*So be it*. Darkness. There had been a patterning of events from the time I had departed

Homefree up until this moment, which overrode, defeated the agreements of men. Ours had been a series of subsidiary conflicts, their resolution unimportant to those who controlled us now.

Controlled. Yes.

I had always assumed Shimbo to be an artificial creation, conditioned into me by the Pei'ans, an alternate personality I assumed when designing worlds. There had never been a clash of wills either. He had come only when summoned, delivered and departed.

He had never taken over spontaneously, forced any sort of control upon me. Perhaps deep down inside I wanted him to be a god, because I wanted there to be a God/god/gods somewhere and perhaps this desire was the animating force, and my paranormal powers the means for what was happening. I don't know. I don't know. . . . Once there was a burst of light when he came, so bright that I cried, not knowing why. Hell, that's no answer. I just don't know.

So we stood there regarding one another, two enemies who had been manipulated by two older enemies. I imagined Mike's surprise at this turn of events. I tried to contact him, but my faculty was completely blocked. I imagined that he was remembering that strange, earlier confrontation himself, however.

Then I saw that the clouds were massing overhead, and I knew what that meant. The ground beneath my feet gave a gentle shudder, and I knew what that meant, too.

One of us was going to die, though neither of us wished this.

—*Shimbo, Shimbo,* I said within me, *Lord of Darktree Tower, must this thing be?*

. . . And even as I said it I knew that there would be no reply, not even for me—save for what followed.

The thunders rolled, soft and long, like a distant drumbeat.

The lights out over the water grew brighter.

We stood as at the ends of a dueling field in hell, waves of light washing about us, clotted with mist, dotted with ash; and Flopsus hid her face, edging the clouds with blood.

It takes the powers a time to move, after they've been built to the proper point. I felt them pass through me from the nearest power-pull, then move away in great waves. I stood, unable to move a muscle or to close my eyes against the stare of the other. In the twisted light through which I saw, he occasionally flickered, and I glimpsed the outline of the one I had come to know as Belion.

I was diminishing and expanding, simultaneously; and long moments passed before I realized that it was I, Sandow, who was becoming more and more inert, passive, smaller. Yet, at the same time I felt the lightnings take root in my fingertips, their swaying tops high above me in the sky, waiting to be turned and prodded and drawn crashing to the ground: I, Shimbo of Darktree, Shrugger of Thunders.

The gray cone to my left was slashed down the side like an arm and its orange blood spilled forth into Acheron, to sizzle and steam in the now glowing waters; its fingers flexed high and ruddy in the night. Then I split the sky with my lines of chaos and sent them down below me in a deluge of light, as the cannons of heaven saluted and the winds of the sky rose again, and the rains came.

He was a shadow, a nothingness, a shadow, then he stood there again when the light died, my enemy. The chalet was burning behind him and something cried, "Kathy!"

"Frank! Come away!" cried the green man, and the dwarf tugged at my arm, but I brushed them both aside and took the first step toward my enemy.

A consciousness touched my own, then Belion's—for I could feel the reflex that shrugged off the latter. Then the green one cried out and drew the dwarf away.

My enemy took his first step and the ground shuddered beneath it, slipped in places, collapsed upon itself.

The winds beat at him as he took his second step, and he fell to the ground, causing fissures to open about him. I fell with my second step as the ground gave way beneath me.

As we lay there, the isle gave a shaking, shrugging twist to our shoulder of rock, and it slid and settled and smoke came up from the cracks within it.

When we rose and took our third step, we stood in a nearly level place. I shattered the rocks about him as I took my fourth step; and with his, he toppled rocks toward me from above. Five was the wind and six was the rain, and his were the fire and the earth.

The volcanos lit up the lower sky and fought with my lightnings for the upper. The winds lashed the waters below us, and we continued to sink toward them with each jogging of the isle. I heard their splashing, within the wind, the thunder, the explosions, the constant *plit-plit* of the rain. At my enemy's back, the partly crumbled chalet still burned.

With my twelfth step, the cyclones arose; and with his

the entire isle began to sway and creak, the fumes coming heavier and more noxious now.

Then something touched me in a way that I should not be touched, and I looked for the cause.

The green man stood on a crag of rock, holding a weapon in his hands. A moment earlier, it had hung at my side, not to be used for the gaining of cycles such as this.

He pointed it first at me. Then his hand wavered and, before I could strike him, jerked to his right.

A line of light leaped forward and my enemy fell.

But the movement of the isle saved him. For the green man fell as it shuddered, and the weapon fell away. Then my enemy rose again, leaving his right hand on the ground beside him. He held the wrist in his left and stepped toward me.

Chasms began to open about us, and it was then that I saw the girl.

She had emerged from the burning building and edged around to the right of us, in the direction of the trail I had descended. Then she had been frozen for a time, watching our slow advance, one upon the other. Now she caught my attention as the chasm opened before her; and something cried out within my breast, for I knew that I could not reach her to save her.

. . . Then it broke, and I shuddered and ran toward her, for Shimbo was gone.

"Kathy!" I screamed, once, as she swayed and fell forward.

. . . And from somewhere Nick leaped up to the edge and seized her outflung wrist. For a moment, I thought he would be able to hold her.

For a moment. . . .

It was not a matter of his lacking the necessary strength. He had plenty of that. It was a question of weight and momentum, of balance.

I heard him curse as they fell.

Then I raised up my head and turned upon Shandon, with the death-fury lighting up my backbone. I reached for my gun and recalled, as in a dream, what had become of it.

Then the falling stones caught me and pinned me as he took another step, and I felt my right leg break beneath me as I fell. I must have blacked out for an instant, but the pain brought me back to consciousness. By then he had taken another step, which brought him very near, and the world was going to hell all around me. I looked up at the stump of his hand, at those manic-depressive eyes, at the mouth opened to finally speak or laugh; and I raised my left hand, supported it with my right and performed the necessary gesture. I screamed as my fingertip flared and his head fell from his shoulders, bounced once and rolled past me—those eyes still open and staring—and followed my wife and my best friend into the chasm below. What remained thudded to the ground before me, and I stared at it for a long while before the darkness sucked me down.

VIII

When I awoke it was dawn and I was still being rained on. My right leg throbbed, about eight inches above the knee, which is bad—the place and the pain. The rain was only rain, though. The storm was over. The ground had stopped its shaking. When I was able to raise myself, however, I forgot my pain in a moment of shock.

Most of the isle was gone, sunken into Acheron, and what remained was unrecognizable as my handiwork. I lay perhaps twenty feet above the waterline, on a wide shelf of rock. The chalet was gone and a mutilated corpse lay before me. I turned away from it and considered my own predicament.

Then, as the torches of last night's dinner of blood still sputtered and blazed, befouling the morning sky, I reached out slowly and began removing the rocks that lay upon me, one by bloody one.

*　　　*　　　*

Pain and monotonous repetition of an action numb the mind, free it to wander.

Even if they had been real gods, what did it matter? What was it to me? Here I was still, right where I was born a thousand or so years before, in the middle of the human condition—namely, rubbish and pain. If the gods were real, their only relationship with us was to use us to play their games.

Screw them all. "That includes you, too, Shimbo," I said. "Don't ever come to me again." Why the hell should I look for order where there wasn't any? Or if there was, it was an order that did not include me. I washed my hands in a puddle that had formed nearby. It felt good on my burnt finger. The water was real. So were earth, air and fire. And that was all I cared to believe in. Let it go with basics. Don't get cute and sophisticated. Basics are things you can feel and buy. If I could beat the Bay long enough I could corner the market on these commodities, and no matter how many Names were involved they would find all the property registered in my name. Then let them howl and bitch. I would own the Big Tree, the Tree of the Knowledge of Good and Evil. I rolled away the final stone and stretched out for a moment. I was free.

Now I had nothing to do but find a power-pull and rest until afternoon, when the *Model T* would come gliding in from the west. I opened my mind and felt one, pulsing somewhere to the left of me. When I felt stronger, I sat up and straightened my leg with both hands. When the throbbing subsided, I cut away the trouser-leg and saw that the flesh was not broken. I bound it as best I could without a splint—which wasn't very—above and below the fracture, and turned slowly, slowly, onto my stomach and hands and began crawling, just as slowly, in the direction of the pull, leaving what was left of Shandon behind me in the rain.

The going was not too bad, so long as it remained level. But when I had to pull myself up a ten-foot, forty-five degree slope, I was too beat even to curse for several minutes afterwards. The damned thing had been slippery as well as steep.

I looked back at Shandon and shook my head. It was not

as if he had not known he was born to come in second. His whole life was testimony to that, poor bastard. I felt a moment's pity. He had come close to having it made. But he had come into the wrong game at the wrong time and the wrong place, like my brother, and I wondered where his head and hand lay now.

I crawled on. The power-pull was only a few hundred yards away, but I took a longer route that looked easier. One time, as I rested, I thought I heard a soft, sobbing sound. But it was gone too quickly for me to be sure.

Another time, and I heard it again, louder, coming from behind me.

I paused and waited till it came again. Then I headed toward it.

Ten minutes, and I lay before a huge boulder. It was situated at the base of a high wall of rock, and there was lots of other rubble strewn about. The muffled weeping was somewhere near. A cave seemed indicated and I did not want to waste my time exploring. So I called out:

"Hello. What's the trouble?"

Silence.

"Hello?"

Then, "Frank?"

It was the voice of the Lady Karle.

"Ho, bitch," I said. "Last night you told me to pass on to my doom. What's yours like?"

"I'm trapped in a cave, Frank. There's a rock that I can't move."

"It's a honey of a rock, honey. I'm looking at it from the other side."

"Can you get me out of here?"

"How did you get in?"

"I hid in here when the trouble started. I've tried to dig my way out, but all my nails are broken and my fingers are bleeding—and I can't seem to find any way around this stone. . . ."

"There doesn't seem to be a way."

"What happened?"

"Everybody's dead but you and me, and there is only a little piece of the isle left. It's raining on it now. It was quite a fight we had."

"Can you get me out of here?"

"I'll be lucky to get myself out of here—the condition I'm in."

"Are you in another cavern?"

"No, I'm on the outside."

"Then what do you mean by 'out of here'?"

"Off this damn hunk of rock and back to Homefree is what I mean."

"Then there is help coming?"

"For me," I said. "The *Model T* will be on its way down this afternoon. I've got it programmed."

"The equipment aboard . . . Could you blast the rock, or the ground beneath it?"

"Lady Karle," I said, "I've got a busted leg, a paralyzed hand and so many sprains, strains, abrasions and contusions that I haven't even bothered counting them. I'll be lucky to get the thing going before I pass out and sleep for a week. I gave you a chance last night to be my friend again. Do you remember what you said to me?"

"Yes. . . ."

"Well now it's your turn."

I moved myself back on my elbows and began to crawl away.

"Frank!"

I did not reply.

"Frank! Wait! Do not go! Please!"

"Why not?" I cried.

"Do you remember what you said to me then, last night. . . ?"

"Yes, and I remember your reply. All of that was last night, anyhow, when I was somebody else. —You had your chance and you blew it. If I had the strength, I would scratch your name and the date on the stone. So long, it's been good to know you."

"Frank!"

I didn't even look back.

—*Your changes of character continue to amaze me, Frank.*

—*So you made it, too, Green. I suppose you're in some other damn cave and want to be dug out.*

—*No. In fact I am only a few hundred feet from you, in the direction in which you were heading. I am near the power-pull, though it can't help me now. I will call out when I hear you approaching.*

—*Why?*

—*The time is near. I will go to the land of death, and there my strength shall fail. I was hurt badly last night.*

—*What do you want me to do about it? I've got problems of my own.*

—*I want the last rite. You told me that you gave it to Dra*

Marling, so I know that you know the way. Also, you said that you had glitten—

—*I don't believe in that any more. Never did. I only did it for Marling because—*

—*You are a high priest. You bear the Name Shimbo of Darktree Tower, Shrugger of Thunders. You cannot refuse me.*

—*I have renounced the Name, and I do refuse you.*

—*You said once that if I helped you, you would intercede for me on Megapei. I did* help *you.*

—*I know that, but now that you are dying it is too late.*

—*Then give me this thing instead.*

—*I will come to you and give you what aid and comfort I can, save for the last rite. I am finished with such things, after last night.*

—*Come to me, then.*

So I did. By the time I reached him, the rain had just about let up. Too bad. It had been doing a fair job of washing away his body fluids. He had propped himself back against a rock, and the whiteness of bone shone through flesh in four places that I could see.

"The vitality of a Pei'an is a fantastic thing," I said. "You got all that in that fall last night?"

He nodded, then —*It hurts to speak, so I must continue in this fashion. I knew you still lived, so I kept myself alive until I could reach you.*

I managed to get what was left of my pack off my back. Then I opened it.

"Here, take this. It is for pain. It works for five races. Yours is one."

He brushed it aside.

—I do not wish to dull my mentality at this point.

"Green, I am not going to give you the rite. I will give you the *glitten* root and you can take it yourself if you wish. But that's all."

—Even if f I can give you that which you most desire in return?

"What?"

—All of them, back again, with no memory of what has happened here.

"The tapes!"

—Yes.

"Where are they?"

—A favor for a favor, Dra Sandow.

"Give them to me."

—The rite . . .

. . . A new Kathy, a Kathy who had never met Mike Shandon, my Kathy—and Nick, the breaker of noses.

"You drive a hard bargain, Pei'an."

—I have no choice—and please hurry.

"All right. I'll go through with it, this one last time. —Where are the tapes?"

—After the rite has begun and may not be stopped, then I will tell you.

I chuckled.

"Okay. I don't blame you for not trusting me."

—You were shielding. You must have been planning to trick me.

"Probably. I'm not really sure."

I unwrapped the *glitten*, broke off the proper proportions.

"Now we will walk together," I began, "and only one of

us two will return to this place . . ."

*   *   *

After a cold, gray time and a black, warm one, we walked in a twilit place without wind or stars. There was only bright green grass, high hills and a faint aurora borealis that licked at the grayblueblack sky, following the entire circle of the broken horizon. It was as if the stars had all fallen, been powdered, were strewn upon the hilltops.

We walked effortlessly—almost strolling, though with a purpose—our bodies whole once more. Green was at my left hand, among the hills of the *glitten-* dream—or was it a dream? It seemed true and substantial, while our broken, tired carcasses lying on rocks in the rain now seemed a dream remembered, out of times long gone by. We had always been walking here, so, Green and I—or so it seemed—and a feeling of well-being and amity lay upon us. It was almost the same as the last time I had come to this place. Perhaps I had always really been here.

We sang an old Pei'an song for a time, then Green said, "I give you the *pai'badra* I held against you, *Dra*. I hold it no more."

"This is good, *Dra* tharl."

"I promised, too, to tell you something. It was of the tapes, yes. —They lie beneath the empty green body I was privileged to wear for a time."

"I see."

"They are useless. I called them to me there with my mind, from a vault where I had kept them. They had been damaged by the forces let loose upon the isle; and so, also, were the tissue cultures. Thus do I keep my word, but poorly.

You gave me no choice, though. I could not come this way alone."

I felt that I should be upset, and knew that for a time I could not be.

"You did what you had to," I felt myself saying. "Do not be troubled. Perhaps it is better that I cannot recall them. So much has gone by since their times. Perhaps they would have felt as I once felt, lost in a strange place. They might not have gone on as I did, to embrace it. I do not know. Let it be as it is. The thing is done."

"Now I must tell you of Ruth Laris," he said. "She lies in the Asylum of Fallon in Cobacho, on Driscoll, where she is registered as Rita Lawrence. Her face has been altered, and her mind. You must remove her and hire doctors."

"Why is she there?"

"It was easier than bringing her to Illyria."

"All this pain which you caused meant nothing to you, did it?"

"No. Perhaps I had worked with the stuff of life too long . . ."

". . . And poorly. I am inclined to think it was Belion within you."

"I did not wish to say it, because I did not want to offer excuses, but I feel this way also. This is why I tried to kill Shimbo. It was this part of me that you faced, and I wished to strike at it, too. After he left me for Shandon, I felt remorse for many of the things I had done. He had to be sent away, which is why Shimbo of Darktree came. Belion could not be permitted to create more worlds of cruelty and ugliness. Shimbo, who cast them like jewels into the darkness, sparkling with the colors of life, had to confront him once again. Now that he has won, there will be more such as these."

"No," I said. "We can't operate without each other, and I've resigned."

"You are bitter over all that has happened, and perhaps justly so. But one does not easily abandon a calling such as yours, Dra. Perhaps with the passage of time . . ."

I did not answer him, for my thoughts had turned inward again.

The way that we walked was the way of death. However pleasant it seemed, this was a *glitten* experience; and while ordinary people may become addicted to *glitten* because of the euphoria and the brain-bending, telepaths use *glitten* in special ways.

Used by a single individual, it serves to heighten his powers.

Used by two persons, a common dream will be dreamed. It, also, is always a very pleasant dream—and among Strantrians it is always the same dream, because this form of religious training conditions the subconscious to produce it by reflex. It is a tradition.

. . . And two dream it and only one awakens.

It is, therefore, used in the death rite, so that one need not go alone to the place I've spent over a thousand years avoiding.

Also, it is used for dueling purposes. For, unless agreed upon and bound by ritual, it is only the stronger who comes back. It is the nature of the drug that some sleeping parts of the two minds are set in conflict, though the conscious portions be all unaware of this.

Green Green had been so bound, so I did not fear a last-ditch trick for the gaining of Pei'an vengeance. Also, even if it were a dueling situation, I did not feel that I had anything to fear, considering his condition.

But as we walked along, I considered that I was probably hastening his death by several hours, under guise of a pleasant, near-mystical ritual.

Telepathic euthanasia.

Mental murder.

I was glad to be able to help a fellow creature shuffle off in such a decent way, on the condition that he wanted it. It made me think of my own passing, which I am certain will not be a pleasant one.

I have heard people say that no matter how much you love living, now, this minute, and think that you would like to live forever, someday you will *want* to die, someday you will pray for death. They had pain in mind when they spoke. They meant they would like to go pretty, like this, to escape.

I do not expect to go pretty, gentle or resigned into this good night myself, thank you. Like the man says, I intend to rage against the dying of the light, fighting and howling every damn step of the way. The disease that was responsible for my making it this far involved quite a bit of pain, you might even say agony, and for a long while, before they froze me. I thought about it a lot then, and I decided I would never opt for the easy way out. I wanted to live, pain and all. There's a book and a man I respect: André Gide and his *Fruits of the Earth*. On his deathbed he knew he had only a few days left and he wrote like blue blazes. He finished it in about three days and died. In it, he recounts every beautiful thing about the permutations of earth, air, fire and water that surrounded him, things that he loved, and you could tell that he was saying goodbye and did not want to go, despite everything. That is how I feel about it. So, in spite of my involvement, I could not sympathize with Green's choice. I would rather have lain there, broken-boned and all, feeling the rain come down upon me and wondering at it, regretting, resenting a bit and wanting a lot. Maybe it was this, this hunger, that allowed me to learn worldscaping in the first place—so that I could do it all myself, so that I could make more of it. Hell.

We mounted a hill and paused on its summit. Even before we reached it, I knew what would be there when we looked down the far slope.

. . . Beginning between two massive prows of gray stone, with a greensward that started out as bright as that beneath our feet and grew darker and darker as I swept my eyes ahead, there was the place. It was the big, dark valley. And suddenly I was staring into a blackness so black that it was nothing, nothing at all.

"Another hundred steps will I go with you," I said.

"Thank you, *Dra*."

And we descended the hillside, moved toward the place.

"What will they say of me on Megapei when they hear that I am gone?"

"I do not know."

"Tell them, if they ask you, that I was a foolish man who regretted his folly before he came to this place."

"I will."

"And . . ."

"That, too," I said. "I will ask that your bones be taken into the mountains of the place that was your home."

He bowed his head.

"That is all. You will watch me walk on?"

"Yes. "

"It is said that there is a light at the end."

"So is it said."

"I must seek it now."

"Walk well, *Dra* Gringrin-tharl."

"You have won your battles and you will depart this place. Will you cast the worlds I never could?"

"Maybe," and I stared into that blackness, *sans* stars, comets, meteors, anything.

But suddenly there was something there.

New Indiana hung in the void. It seemed a million miles away, all its features distinct, cameo-cut, glowing. It moved slowly to the right, until the rock blocked it from my view. By then, however, Cocytus had come into sight. It crossed, was followed by all the others: St. Martin, Buningrad, Dismal, M-2, Honkeytonk, Mercy, Summit, Tangia, Illyria, Roden's Folly, Homefree, Castor, Pollux, Centralia, Dandy, and so on.

For some stupid reason my eyes filled with tears at this passage. Every world I had designed and built moved by me. I had forgotten the glory.

The feeling that had filled me with the creation of each of them came over me then. I had hurled something into the pit. Where there had been darkness, I had hung my worlds. They were my answer. When I finally walked that Valley, they would remain after me. Whatever the Bay claimed, I had made some replacements, to thumb my nose at it. I had done something, and I knew how to do more.

"There *is* a light!" said Green, and I did not realize that he had been clutching my arm, staring at the pageant.

I clasped his shoulder, said, "May you dwell with Kirwar of the Four Faces, Father of Flowers," and I did not quite catch his reply as he drew away from me, passed between the stones, walked the Valley, was gone.

I turned then and faced what had to be the east and began the long walk home.

Coming back. . . .

Brass gongs and polliwogs.

I was stuck to a rough ceiling. No. I was lying there, face up on nothing, trying to support the world with my shoulders. It was heavy and the rocks poked, gouged. Below me lay the Bay, with its condoms, its driftwood, its ropes of seaweed, empty dories, bottles and scum. I could hear its distant splashing, and it splashed so high that it kept striking my face. There it was, life, slopping, smelling, chilly. I had had a real wild romp through its waters, and now as I looked down upon it I felt myself falling once more, falling back toward its shallows. Maybe I heard bird-cries. I had walked to the Valley and now I was returning. With luck I would evade the icy fingers of the crumbling hand once more. I fell, and the world twisted about me, resolved itself into what it had been when I left it.

The sky was bleak as slate and streaked with soot. It oozed moisture. The rocks dug into my back. Acheron was pocked and wrinkled. There was no warmth in the air.

I sat up, shaking my head to clear it, shivered, regarded the body of the green man that lay beside me. I said the final words, completing the rite, and my voice shook as I said them.

I rolled Green's body into a more comfortable-looking position and covered it with my flimsy. I picked up the tapes and their bio-cylinders which he had been concealing beneath him. He had been right. They were ruined. I placed them in my knapsack. At least Earth Intelligence would be happy with this state of affairs. Then I crawled on to the power-pull and waited there, raising a screen of forces to attract the *T*, and watching the sky.

I saw her walking, walking away, her neat hips sheathed in white and swaying slightly, her sandals slapping the patio. I had wanted to go after her, to explain my part in what had happened. But I knew it would do no good, so why lose face? When a fairy tale blows up and the dream dust settles and you find yourself standing there, knowing that the last line will never be written, why not omit any exercises in futility? There had been giants and dwarves, toads and mushrooms, caves full of jewels and not one, but ten wizards. . . .

I felt the *Model T* before I saw it, when it locked with the power-pull.

Ten wizards, financial ones, the merchant barons of Algol . . .

All of them her uncles.

I had thought that the alliance would hold, sealed as it was with a kiss. I had not been planning a doublecross, but when it came from the other side something had to be done. It was not all my doing either. There was a whole combine involved. I could not have stopped them if I had wanted to.

I could feel the *T* homing in now. I rubbed my leg above the break, hurt it, and stopped.

Business arrangement to fairy tale to vendetta. . . . It was too late to recall the second phase of that cycle, and I had just won the final one. I should have felt great.

The *T* came into view, descended quickly and hung like a world overhead as I manipulated it through the pull.

I have been a coward, a god and a son of a bitch in my time, among other things. That is one of the things about living for a very long time. You go through phases. Right now I was just tired and troubled and had only one thing on my mind.

I brought the *T* down to rest on a level space, cracked the hatch, began crawling toward it.

It did not matter now, not really, all these things I had thought when the fire was high. Any way you looked at it, it did not matter.

I made it to the ship. I crawled inside.

I fiddled with the controls and brought it to a more sensitive life.

My leg hurt like hell.

We drifted.

Then I answered us, picked up the necessary equipment, crawled outside once more.

Forgive me my trespasses, baby.

I positioned myself carefully, took aim, dissolved one big rock.

"Frank? Is that you?"

"No, just us chickens."

Lady Karle rushed out, dirty, wild-eyed. "You came back for me!"

"I never left."

"You're hurt."

"I told you about it."

"You said you were going away, leaving me."

"You've got to learn to know when I'm being serious."

She kissed me then and helped me to stand on my one good leg, drawing my arm about her shoulders.

"Kind of like playing hopscotch," I said, as we headed for the *T*.

"What is that?"

"An old game. When I can walk again, maybe I'll teach it to you."

"Where now?"

"Homefree, where you may stay or go as you choose."

"I should have known you would not leave me, but when you said those things . . . Lords! It's a miserable day! What happened?"

"The Isle of the Dead is sinking slowly into Acheron. It's raining on it."

I looked at the blood on her hands, the dirt, then her messed hair.

"I did not mean everything that I said, you know."

"I know."

I looked all around me. Someday, I would fix it all up, I knew.

"Lords! It's a miserable day!" she said.

"Upstairs, the sun is shining. I think we can make it, if you help."

"Lean on me."

I did.